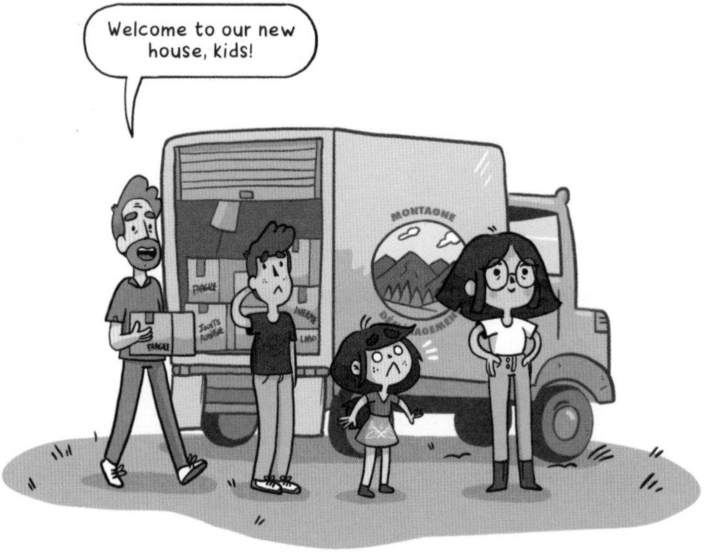
Welcome to our new house, kids!

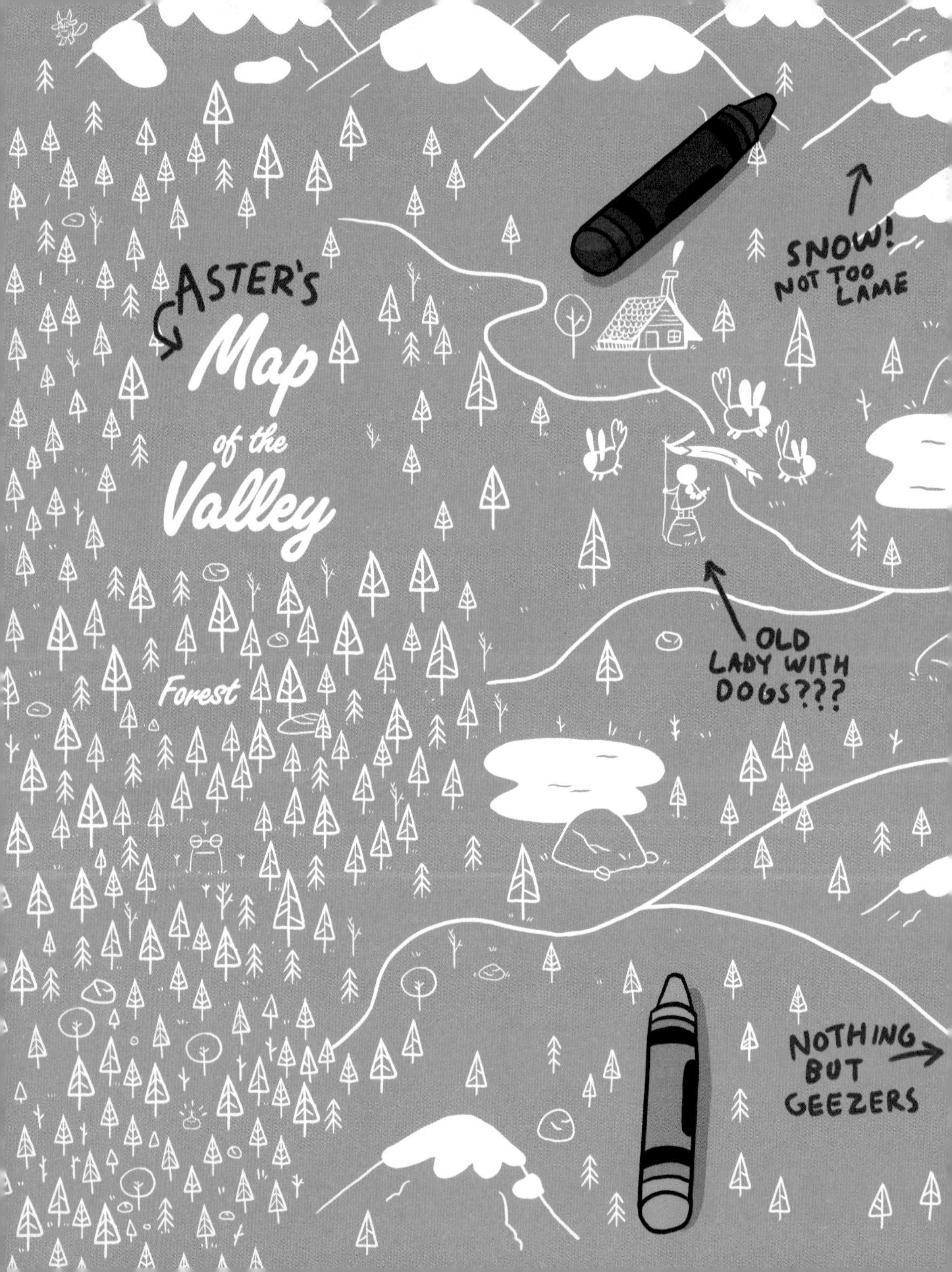
ASTER'S
Map of the Valley
SNOW! NOT TOO LAME
OLD LADY WITH DOGS???
Forest
NOTHING BUT GEEZERS

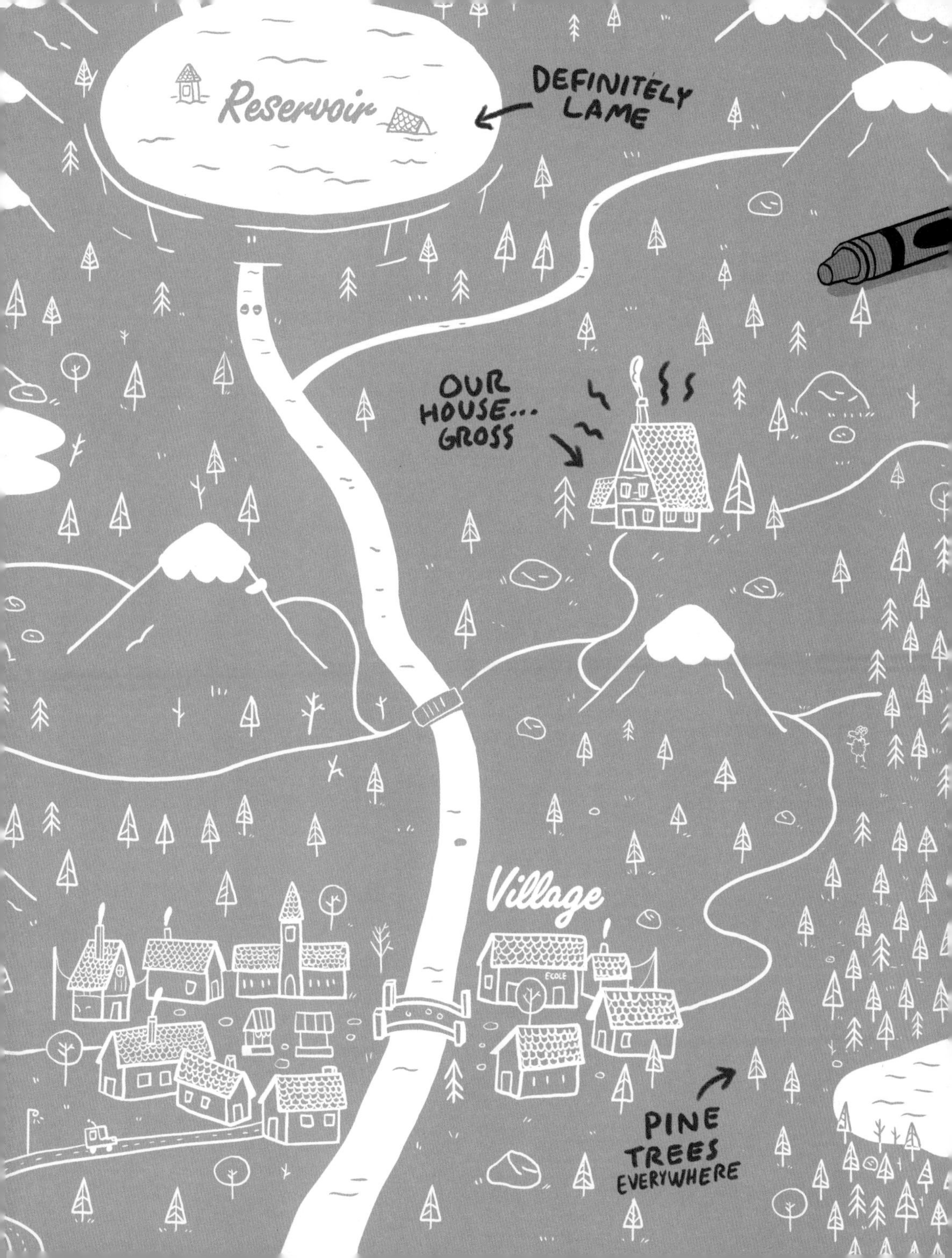

Reservoir
DEFINITELY LAME
OUR HOUSE... GROSS
Village
ECOLE
PINE TREES EVERYWHERE

Translation copyright © 2020 by Dupuis
Cover art and interior illustrations copyright © 2018, 2020 by Dupuis

Published in the United States by RH Graphic, an imprint of Random House Children's Books, a division of Penguin Random House LLC, New York. The titles in this work were originally published in two separate volumes in the French language in Belgium as *Aubépine 1: Le génie saligaud*, copyright © 2018 Dupuis by Thom Pico & Karensac, and *Aubépine 2: Le renard furax*, copyright © 2018 Dupuis by Thom Pico & Karensac, by Éditions Dupuis S.A., Marcinelle, in 2018. All rights reserved.

RH Graphic with the book design is a trademark of Penguin Random House LLC.

Visit us on the Web! RHKidsGraphic.com • @RHKidsGraphic

Educators and librarians, for a variety of teaching tools, visit us at RHTeachersLibrarians.com

Library of Congress Cataloging-in-Publication Data
Names: Pico, Thom, author. | Karensac, illustrator. | Smith, Owen (Owen M.), translator. | Smith, Anne Collins, translator. | Pico, Thom. Génie saligaud. English. | Pico, Thom. Renard furax. English.
Title: Aster and the accidental magic / Thom Pico and Karensac ; translated by Anne and Owen Smith.
Description: First Random House Graphic edition. | New York : Random House Graphic, an imprint of Random House Children's Books, a division of Penguin Random House LLC, 2020. | "Originally published in two volumes, Aubépine 1: Le génie saligaud, and Aubépine 2: Le renard furax, in France by Dupuis in 2018." | Summary: Aster is bored at her new home in the mountains in the middle of nowhere—until she meets an odd old shepherdess and her woolly dogs, a sneaky trickster, and an angry fox.
Identifiers: LCCN 2019014042 (print) | LCCN 2019017516 (ebook) | ISBN 978-0-593-11886-3 (ebook) | ISBN 978-0-593-12417-8 (hardcover) | ISBN 978-0-593-11884-9 (trade) | ISBN 978-0-593-11885-6 (lib. bdg.)
Subjects: LCSH: Graphic novels. | CYAC: Graphic novels. | Country life—Fiction. | Dogs—Fiction. | Foxes—Fiction. | Genies—Fiction. | Magic—Fiction.
Classification: LCC PZ7.7.P523 (ebook) | LCC PZ7.7.P523 As 2020 (print) | DDC 741.5/944—dc23

Designed by Patrick Crotty
Translated by Anne and Owen Smith
Thanks to Gina and Anton

MANUFACTURED IN CHINA
10 9 8 7 6 5 4 3 2 1
First American Edition

A comic on every bookshelf.

ASTER

AND THE

ACCIDENTAL MAGIC

Story and Script
THOM PICO

Story and Art
KARENSAC

To Julien, Guillaume, Bola, Élisa,
Laurence, Stéphane, and Jonathan

Aster

MAKES SOME
POORLY THOUGHT-THROUGH WISHES

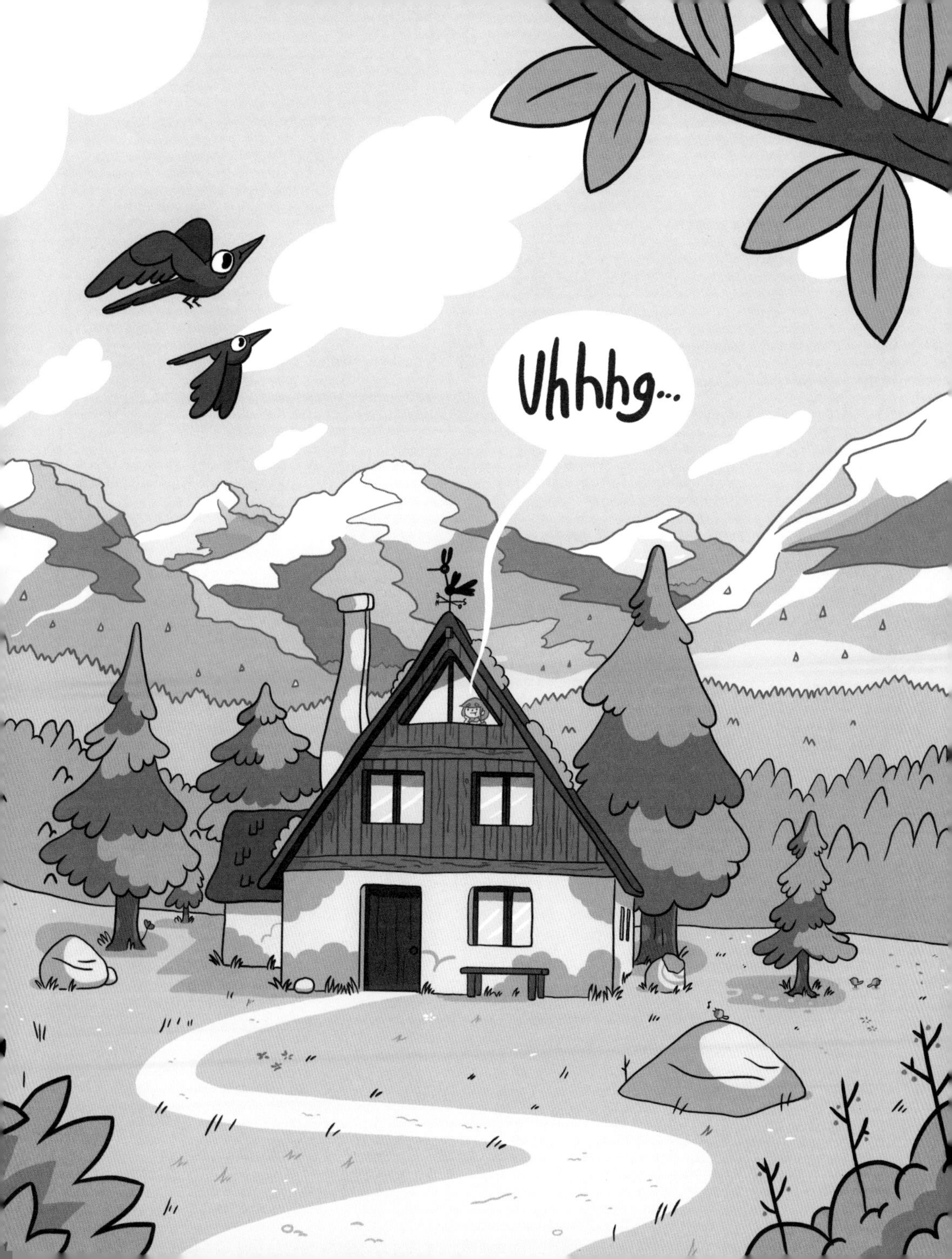
Uhhhg...

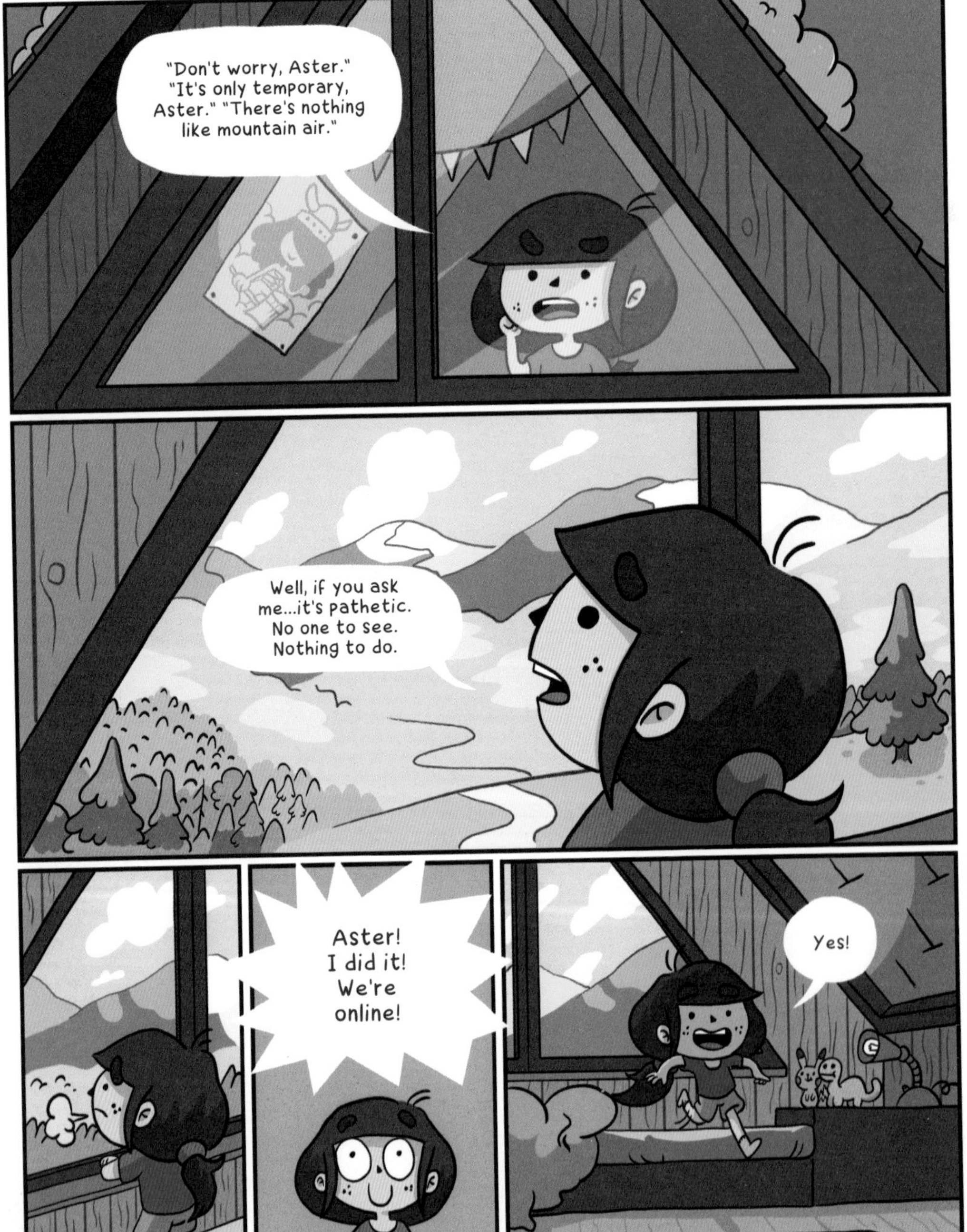
"Don't worry, Aster." "It's only temporary, Aster." "There's nothing like mountain air."
Well, if you ask me...it's pathetic. No one to see. Nothing to do.
Aster! I did it! We're online!
Yes!

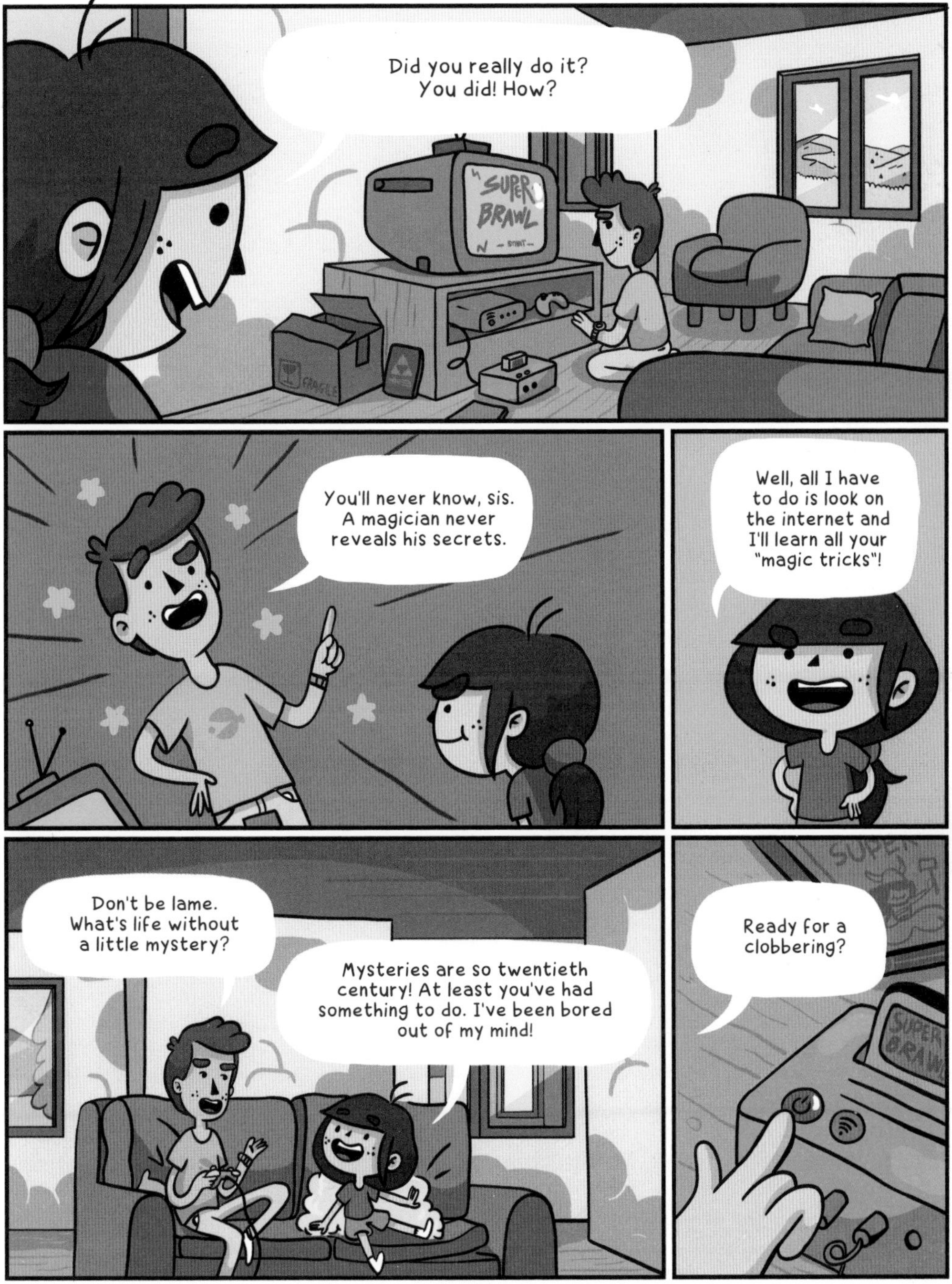
Did you really do it? You did! How?
SUPER BRAWL
You'll never know, sis. A magician never reveals his secrets.
Well, all I have to do is look on the internet and I'll learn all your "magic tricks"!
Don't be lame. What's life without a little mystery?
Mysteries are so twentieth century! At least you've had something to do. I've been bored out of my mind!
Ready for a clobbering?
SUPER BRAWL

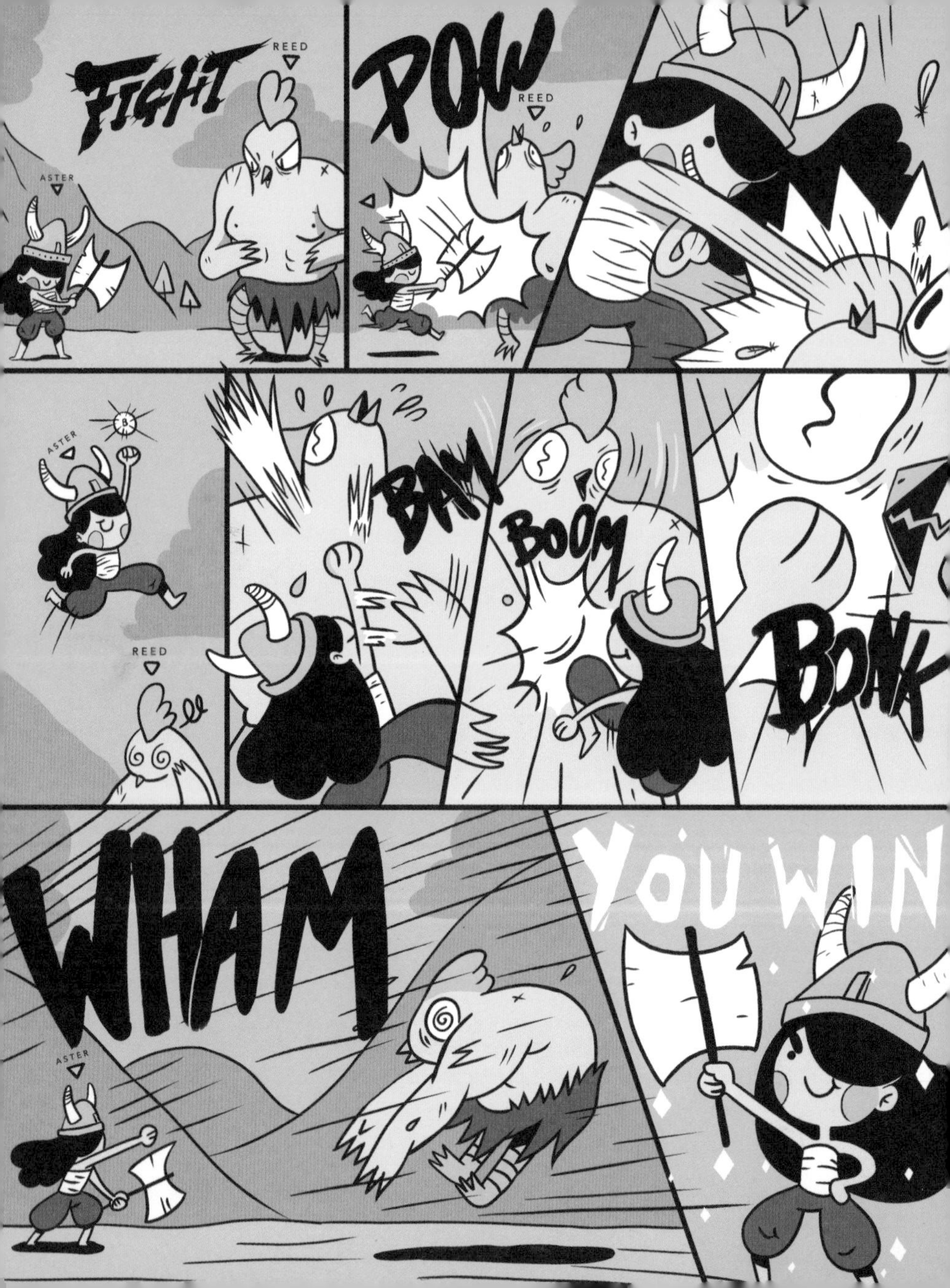
FIGHT
REED
ASTER
POW
REED
ASTER
REED
BAM
BOOM
BONK
WHAM
ASTER
YOU WIN

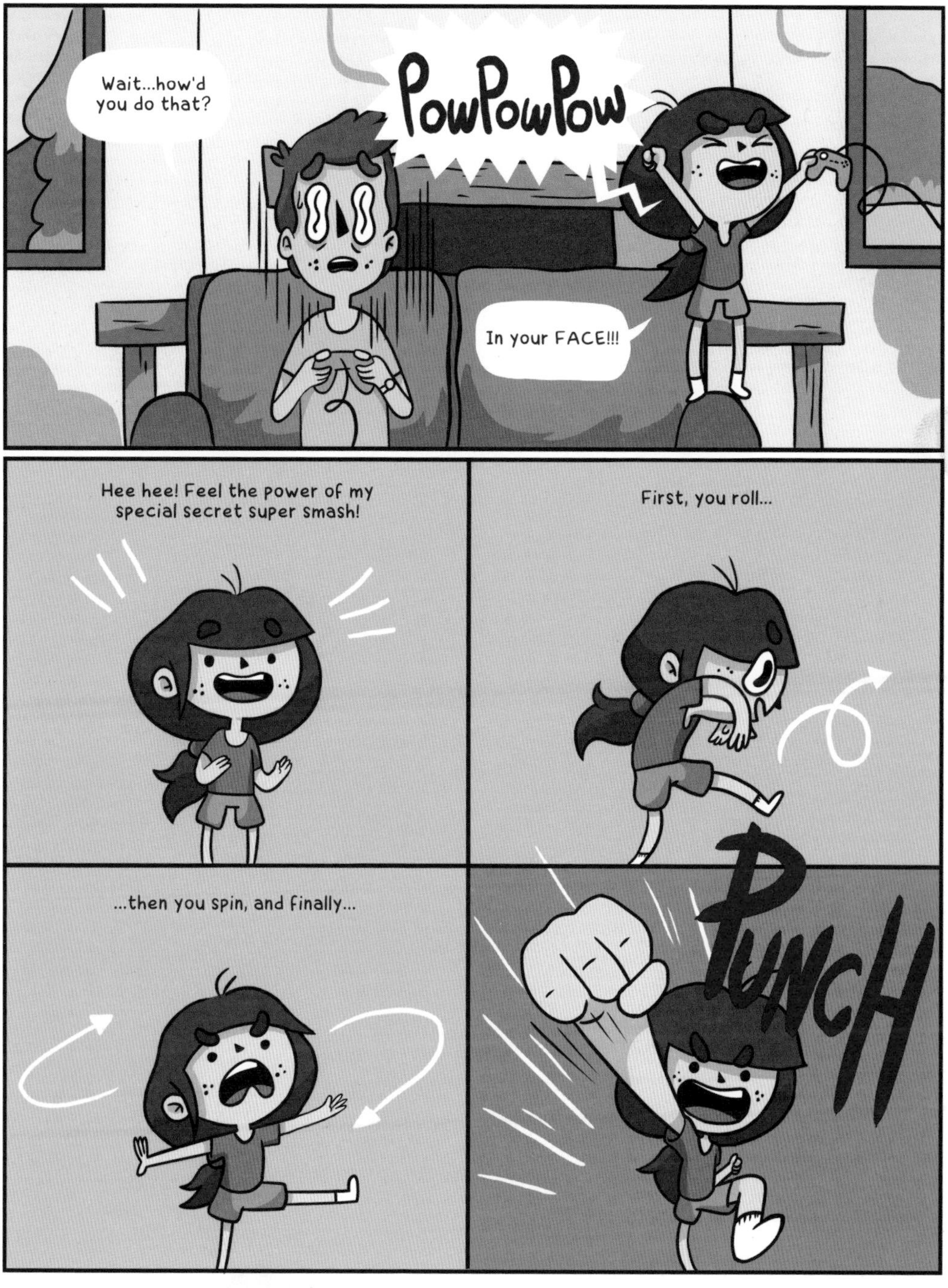

Wait...how'd you do that?
PowPowPow
In your FACE!!!
Hee hee! Feel the power of my special secret super smash!
First, you roll...
...then you spin, and finally...
PUNCH

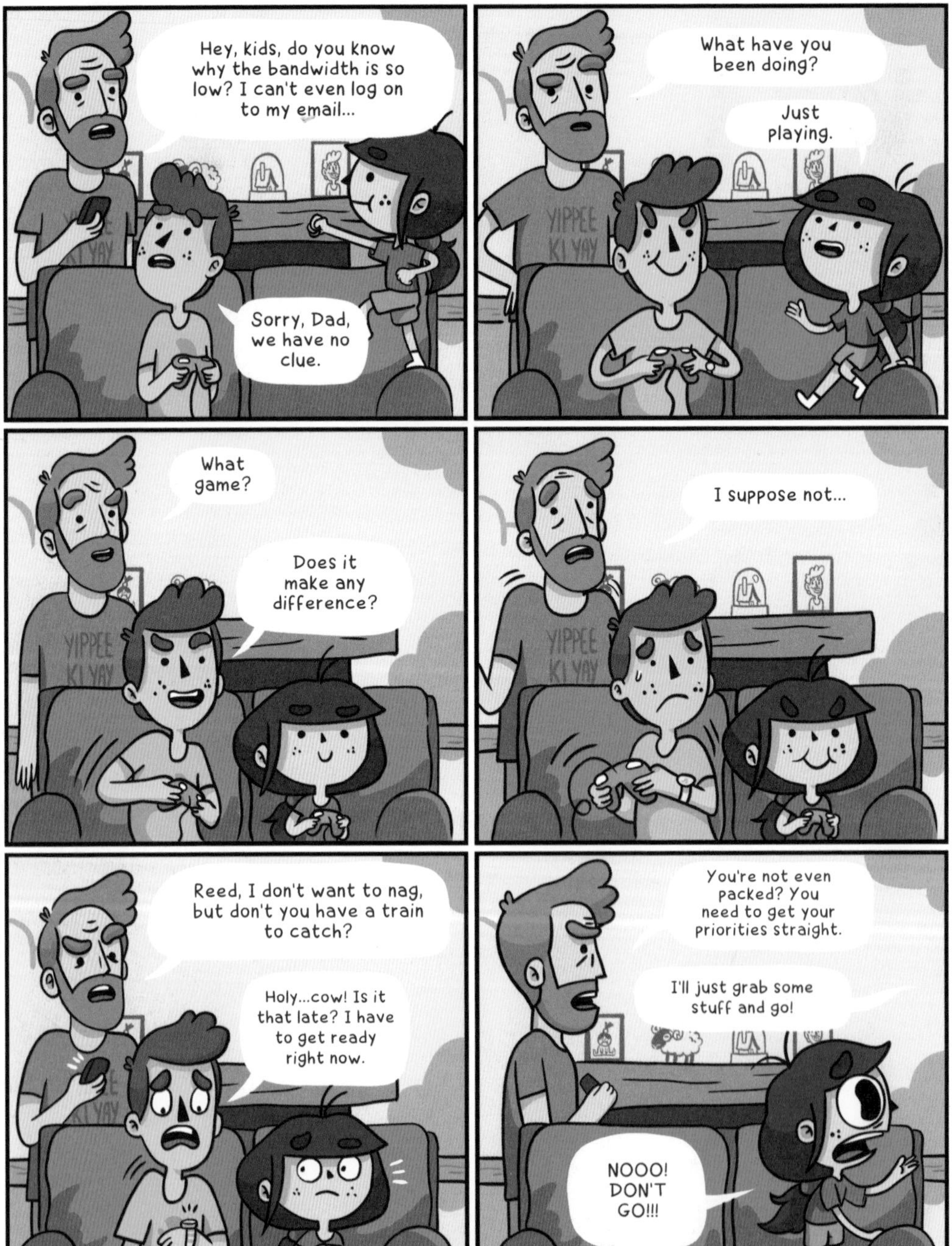
Hey, kids, do you know why the bandwidth is so low? I can't even log on to my email...
Sorry, Dad, we have no clue.
What have you been doing?
Just playing.
What game?
Does it make any difference?
I suppose not...
Reed, I don't want to nag, but don't you have a train to catch?
Holy...cow! Is it that late? I have to get ready right now.
You're not even packed? You need to get your priorities straight.
I'll just grab some stuff and go!
NOOO! DON'T GO!!!

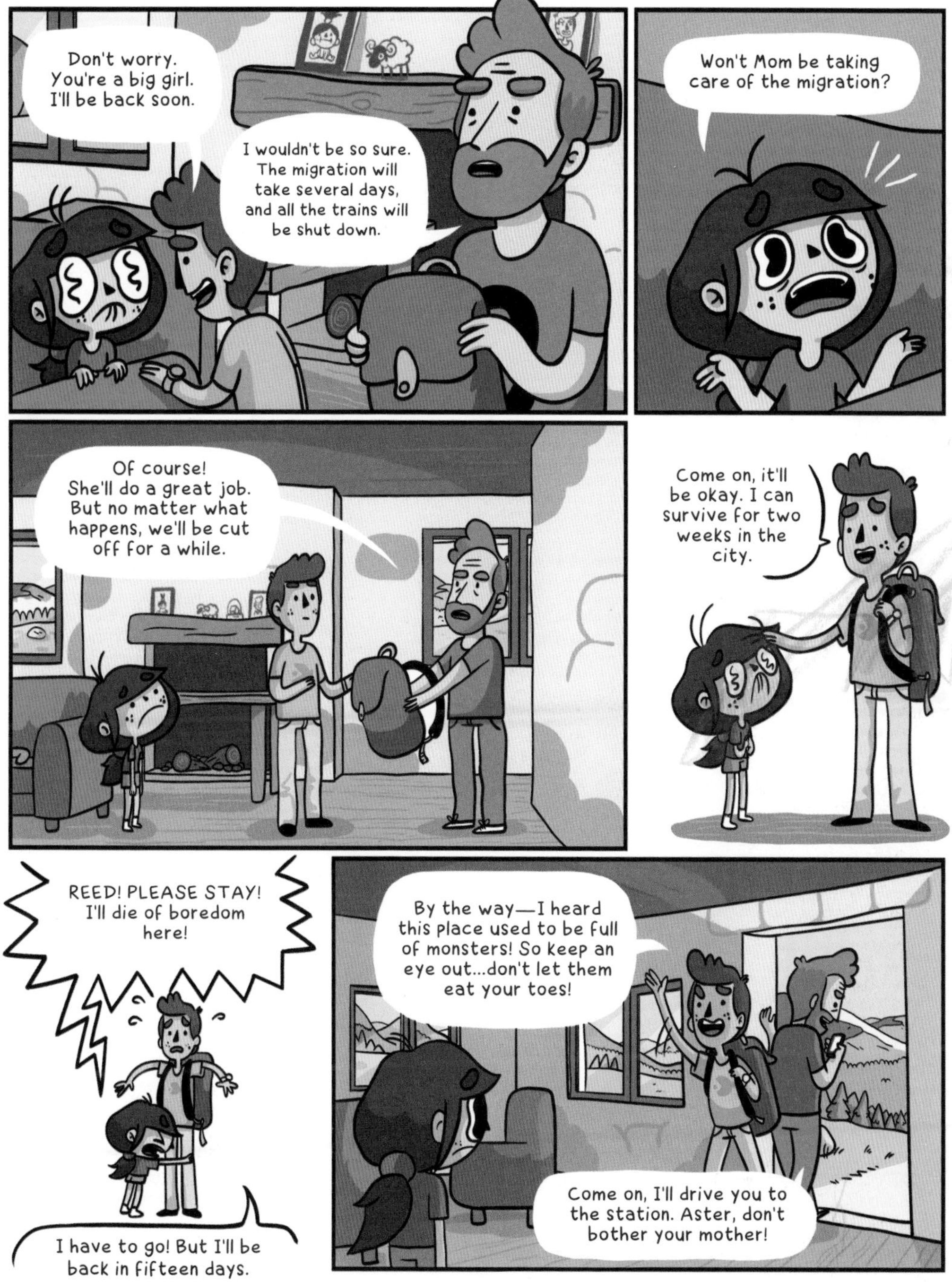
Don't worry. You're a big girl. I'll be back soon.
I wouldn't be so sure. The migration will take several days, and all the trains will be shut down.
Won't Mom be taking care of the migration?
Of course! She'll do a great job. But no matter what happens, we'll be cut off for a while.
Come on, it'll be okay. I can survive for two weeks in the city.
REED! PLEASE STAY! I'll die of boredom here!
I have to go! But I'll be back in fifteen days.
By the way—I heard this place used to be full of monsters! So keep an eye out...don't let them eat your toes!
Come on, I'll drive you to the station. Aster, don't bother your mother!

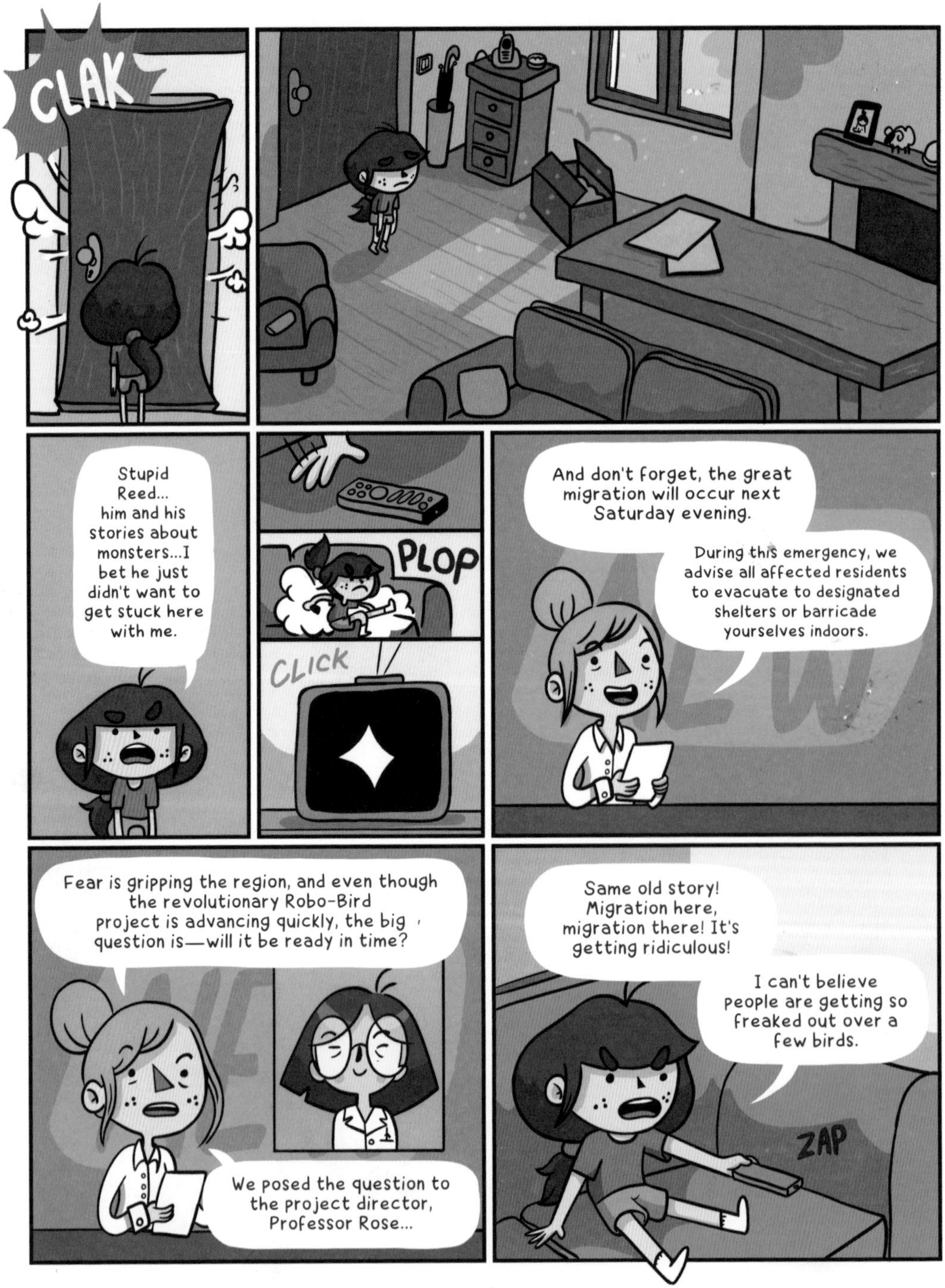
CLAK
Stupid Reed... him and his stories about monsters...I bet he just didn't want to get stuck here with me.
PLOP
CLICK
And don't forget, the great migration will occur next Saturday evening.
During this emergency, we advise all affected residents to evacuate to designated shelters or barricade yourselves indoors.
Fear is gripping the region, and even though the revolutionary Robo-Bird project is advancing quickly, the big question is—will it be ready in time?
We posed the question to the project director, Professor Rose...
Same old story! Migration here, migration there! It's getting ridiculous!
I can't believe people are getting so freaked out over a few birds.
ZAP

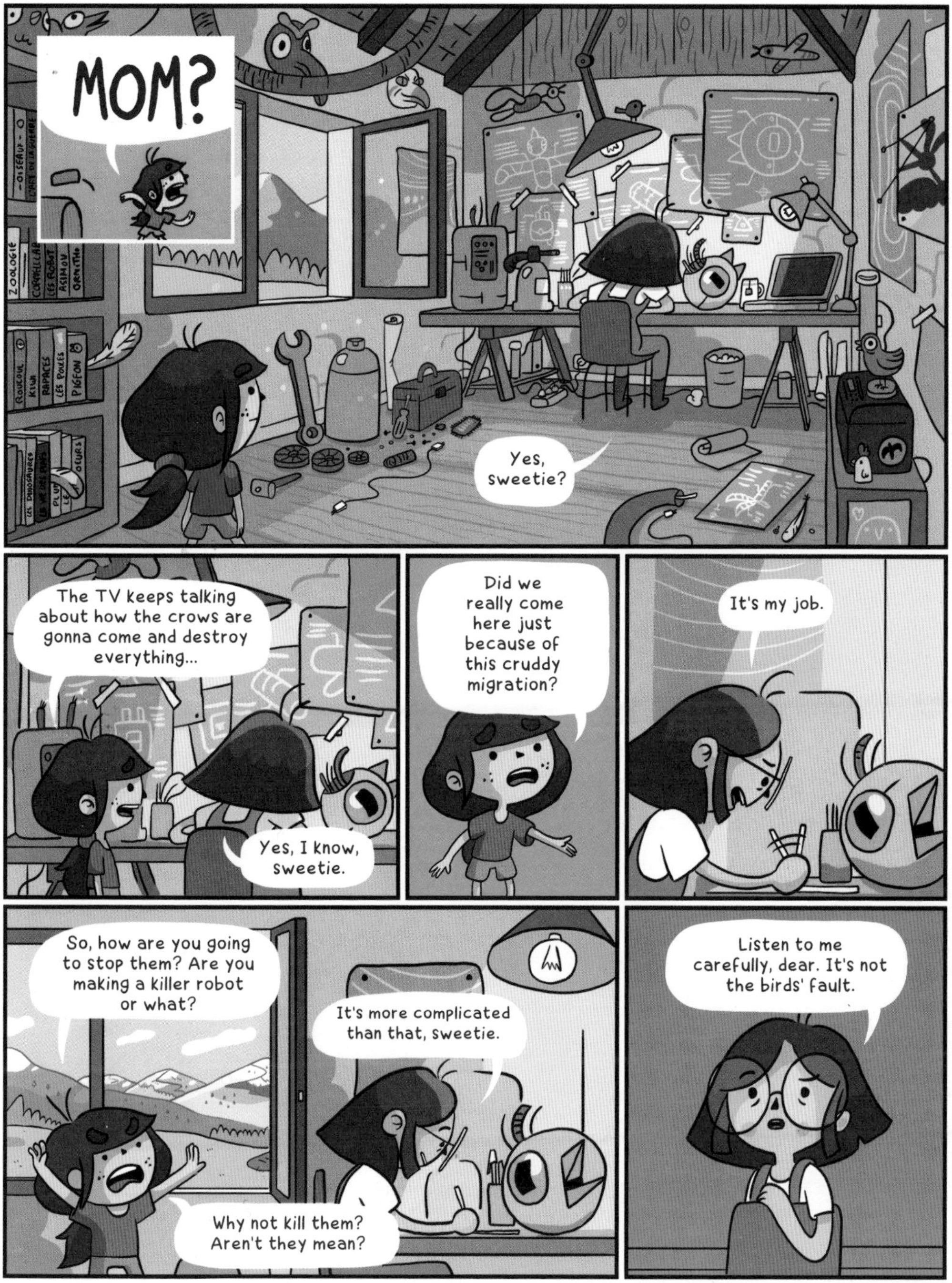
MOM?
Yes, sweetie?
The TV keeps talking about how the crows are gonna come and destroy everything...
Yes, I know, sweetie.
Did we really come here just because of this cruddy migration?
It's my job.
So, how are you going to stop them? Are you making a killer robot or what?
It's more complicated than that, sweetie.
Why not kill them? Aren't they mean?
Listen to me carefully, dear. It's not the birds' fault.

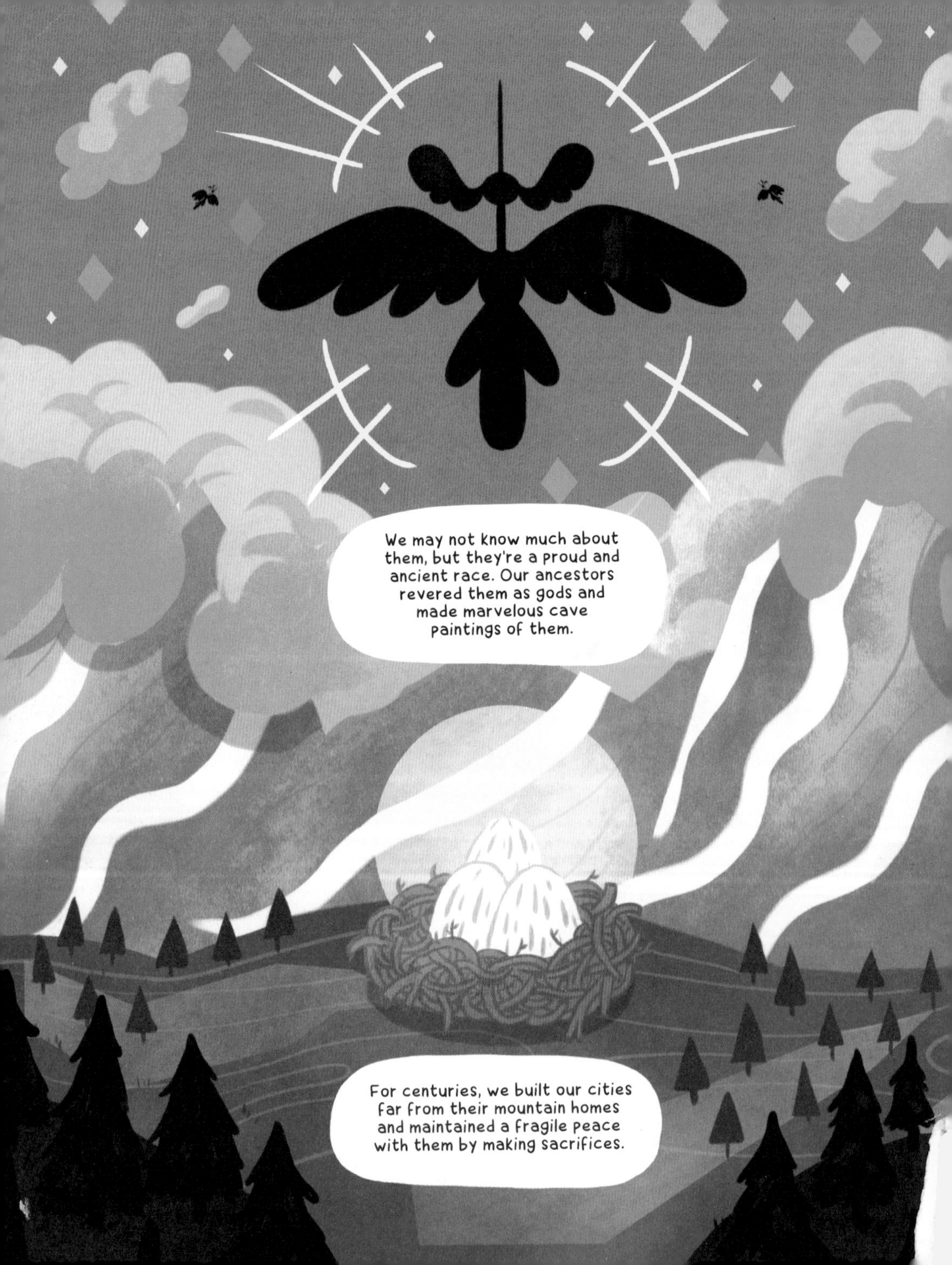
We may not know much about them, but they're a proud and ancient race. Our ancestors revered them as gods and made marvelous cave paintings of them.
For centuries, we built our cities far from their mountain homes and maintained a fragile peace with them by making sacrifices.

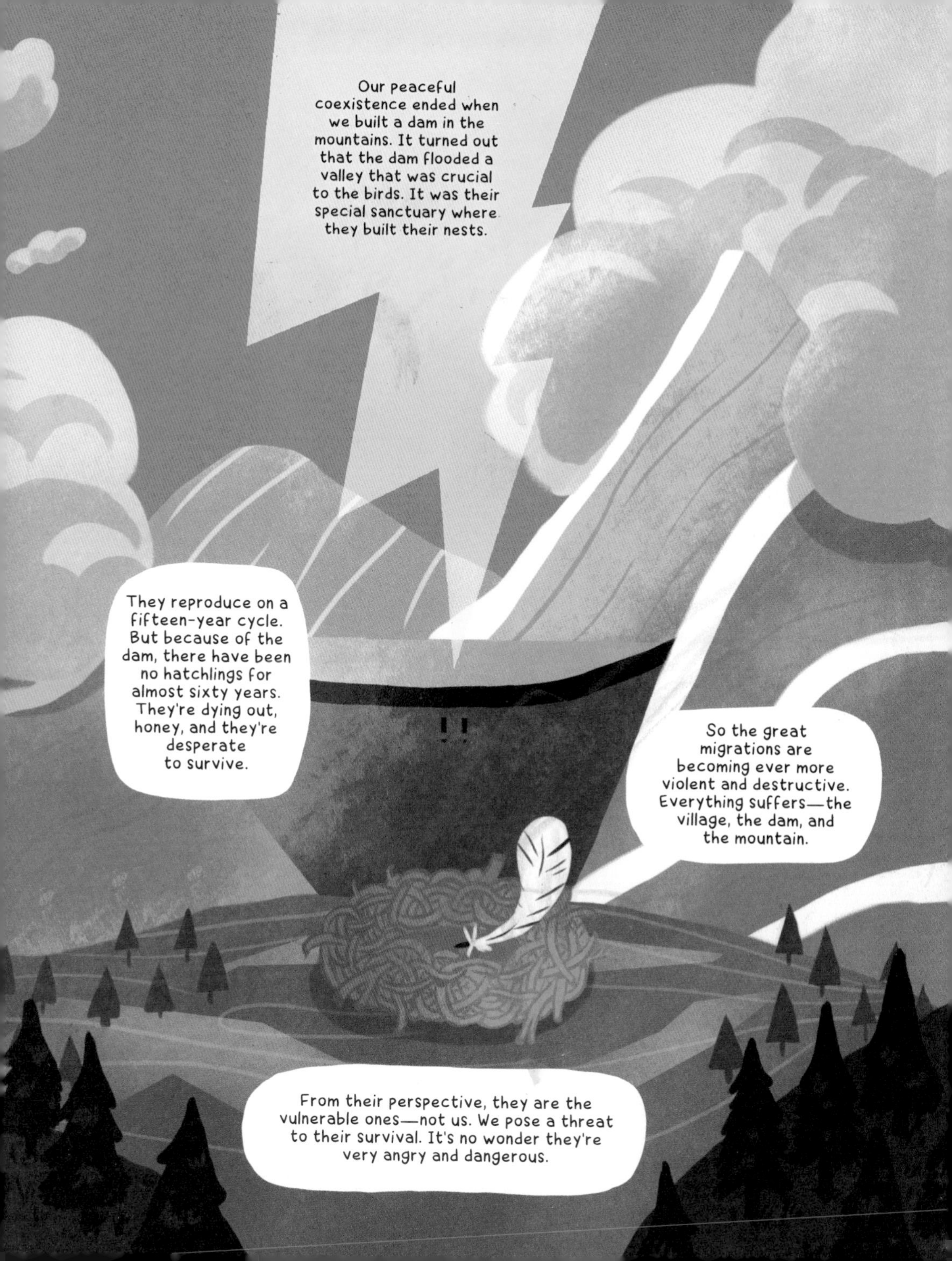
Our peaceful coexistence ended when we built a dam in the mountains. It turned out that the dam flooded a valley that was crucial to the birds. It was their special sanctuary where they built their nests.
They reproduce on a fifteen-year cycle. But because of the dam, there have been no hatchlings for almost sixty years. They're dying out, honey, and they're desperate to survive.
So the great migrations are becoming ever more violent and destructive. Everything suffers—the village, the dam, and the mountain.
From their perspective, they are the vulnerable ones—not us. We pose a threat to their survival. It's no wonder they're very angry and dangerous.

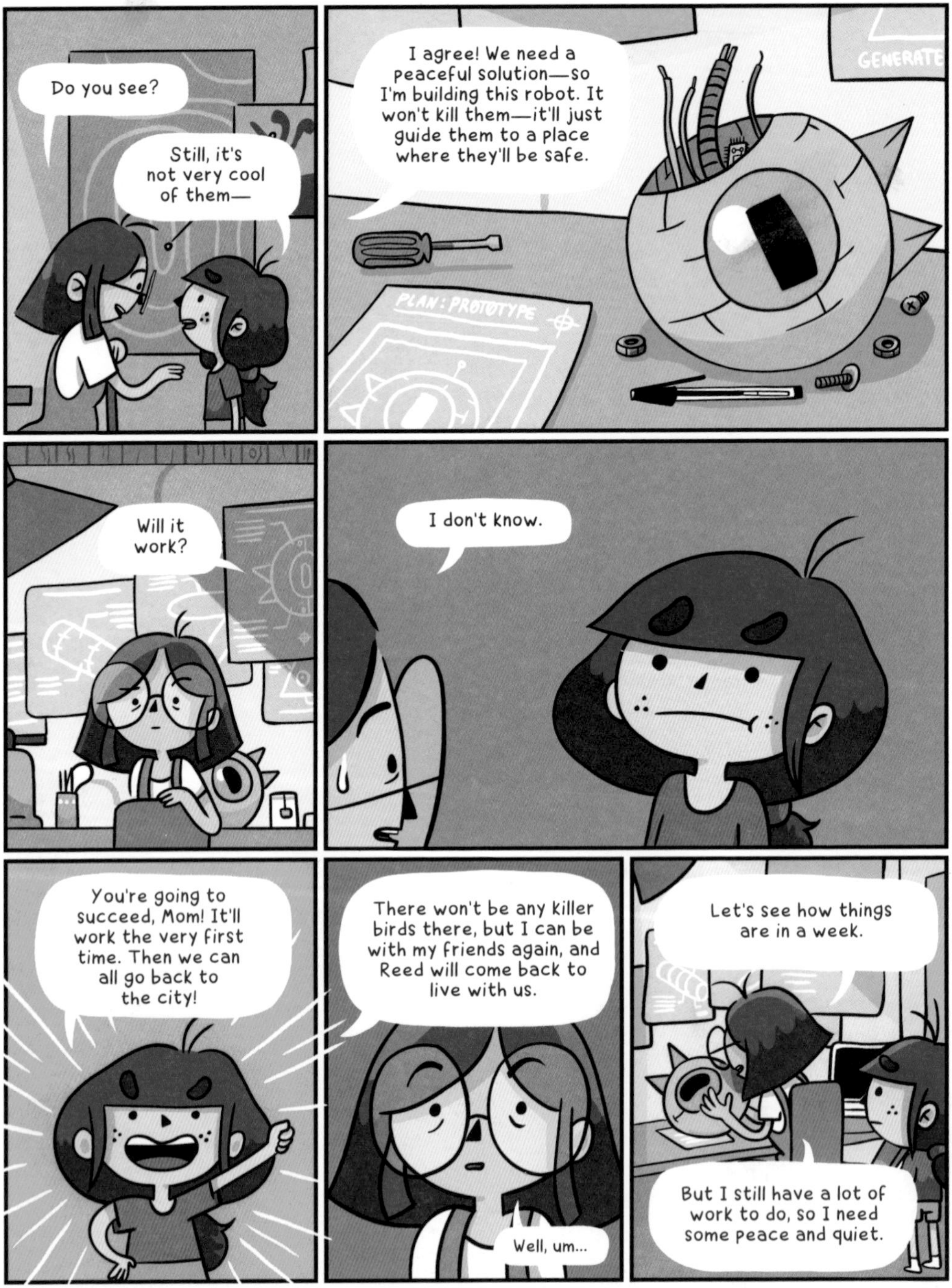
Do you see?
Still, it's not very cool of them—
I agree! We need a peaceful solution—so I'm building this robot. It won't kill them—it'll just guide them to a place where they'll be safe.
GENERATE
PLAN: PROTOTYPE
Will it work?
I don't know.
You're going to succeed, Mom! It'll work the very first time. Then we can all go back to the city!
There won't be any killer birds there, but I can be with my friends again, and Reed will come back to live with us.
Well, um...
Let's see how things are in a week.
But I still have a lot of work to do, so I need some peace and quiet.

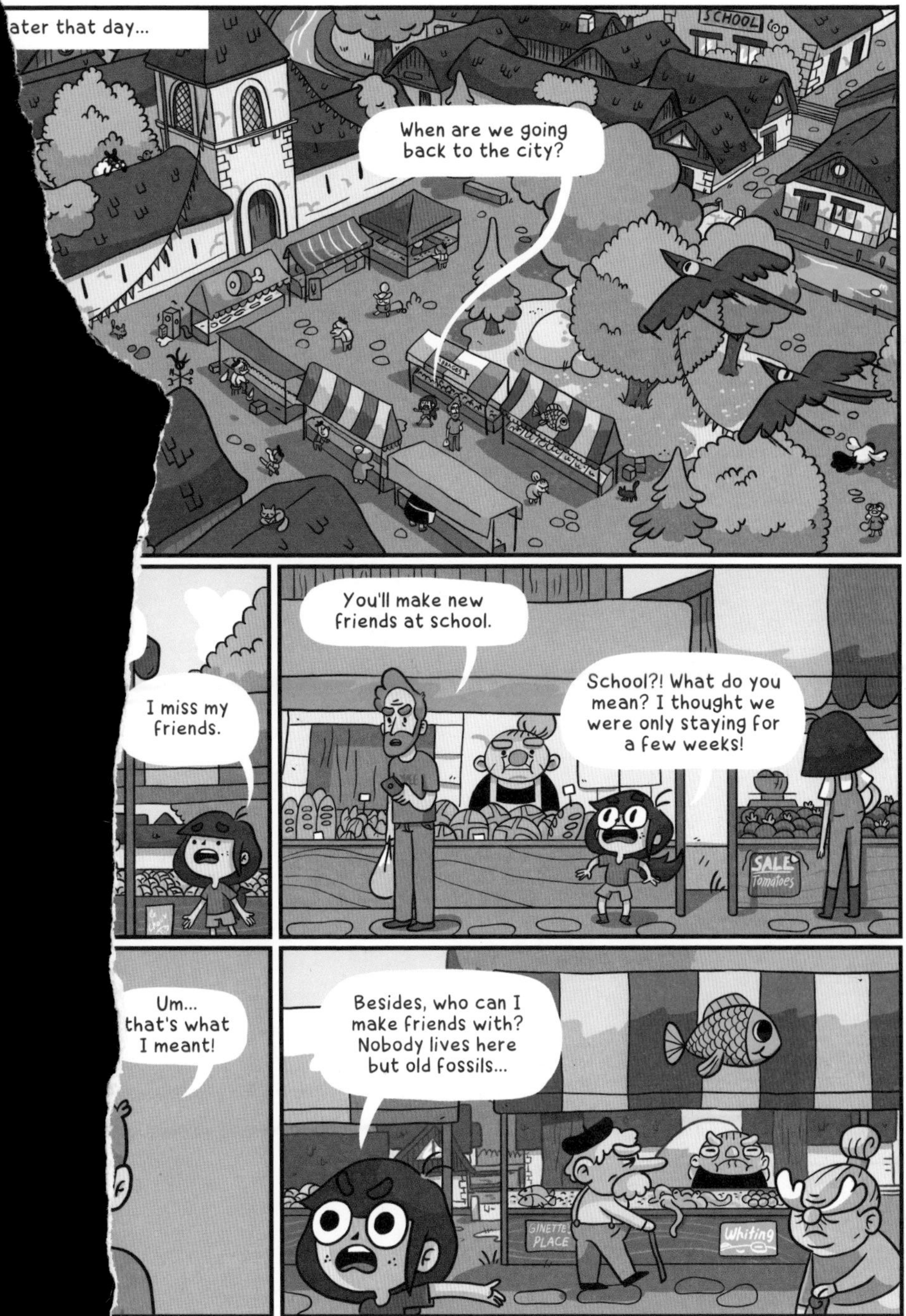
ater that day...
SCHOOL
When are we going back to the city?
I miss my friends.
You'll make new friends at school.
School?! What do you mean? I thought we were only staying for a few weeks!
SALE
Tomatoes
Um... that's what I meant!
Besides, who can I make friends with? Nobody lives here but old fossils...
GINETTE PLACE
Whiting

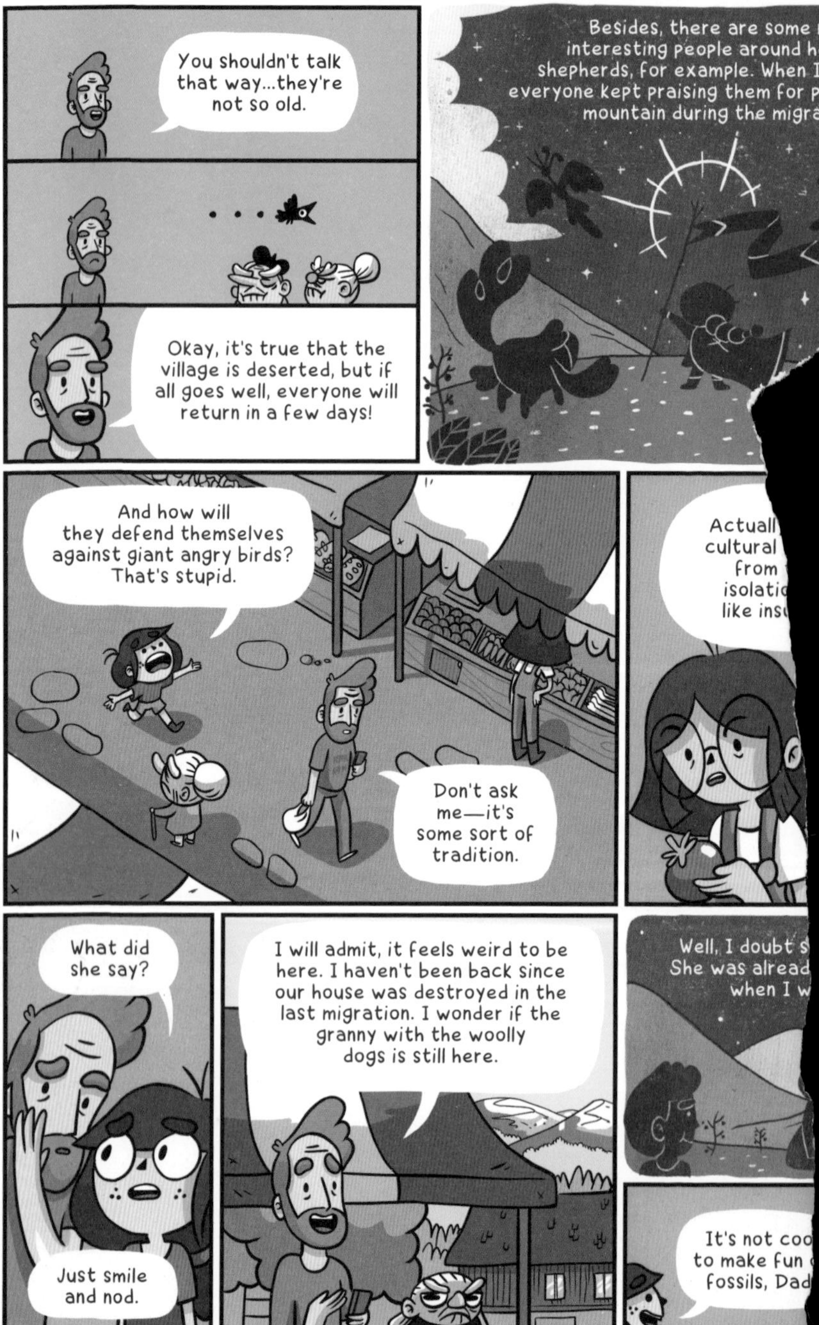
You shouldn't talk that way...they're not so old.
Okay, it's true that the village is deserted, but if all goes well, everyone will return in a few days!
Besides, there are some really interesting people around here. The shepherds, for example. When I was littl
everyone kept praising them for protectin
mountain during the migrations.
And how will they defend themselves against giant angry birds? That's stupid.
Don't ask me—it's some sort of tradition.
Actuall
cultural
from
isolatio
like ins
What did she say?
Just smile and nod.
I will admit, it feels weird to be here. I haven't been back since our house was destroyed in the last migration. I wonder if the granny with the woolly dogs is still here.
Well, I doubt s
She was alread
when I w
It's not coo
to make fun
fossils, Dad

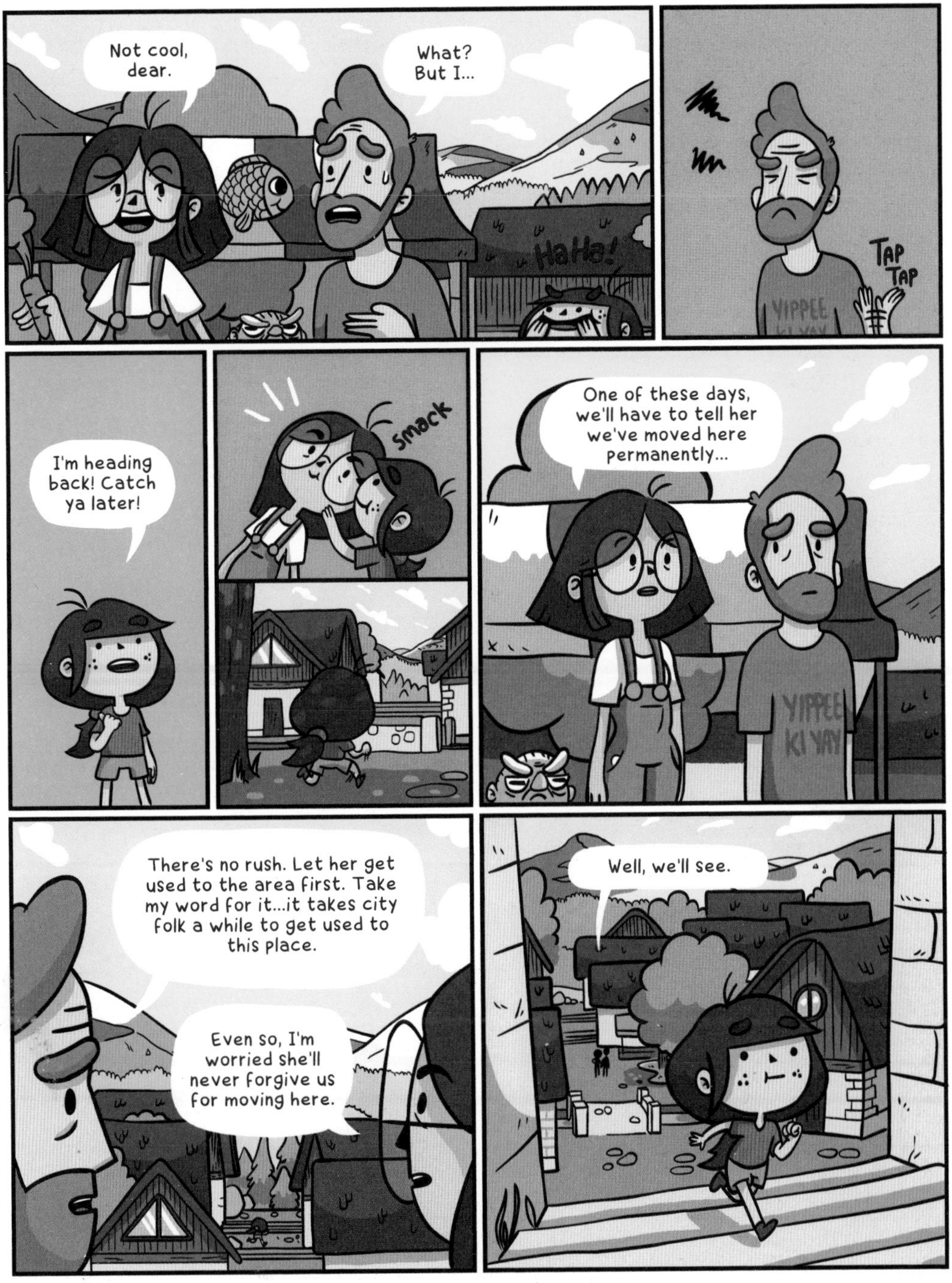
Not cool, dear.
What? But I...
HaHa!
TAP TAP
YIPPEE KI YAY
I'm heading back! Catch ya later!
SMACK
One of these days, we'll have to tell her we've moved here permanently...
YIPPEE KI YAY
There's no rush. Let her get used to the area first. Take my word for it...it takes city folk a while to get used to this place.
Even so, I'm worried she'll never forgive us for moving here.
Well, we'll see.

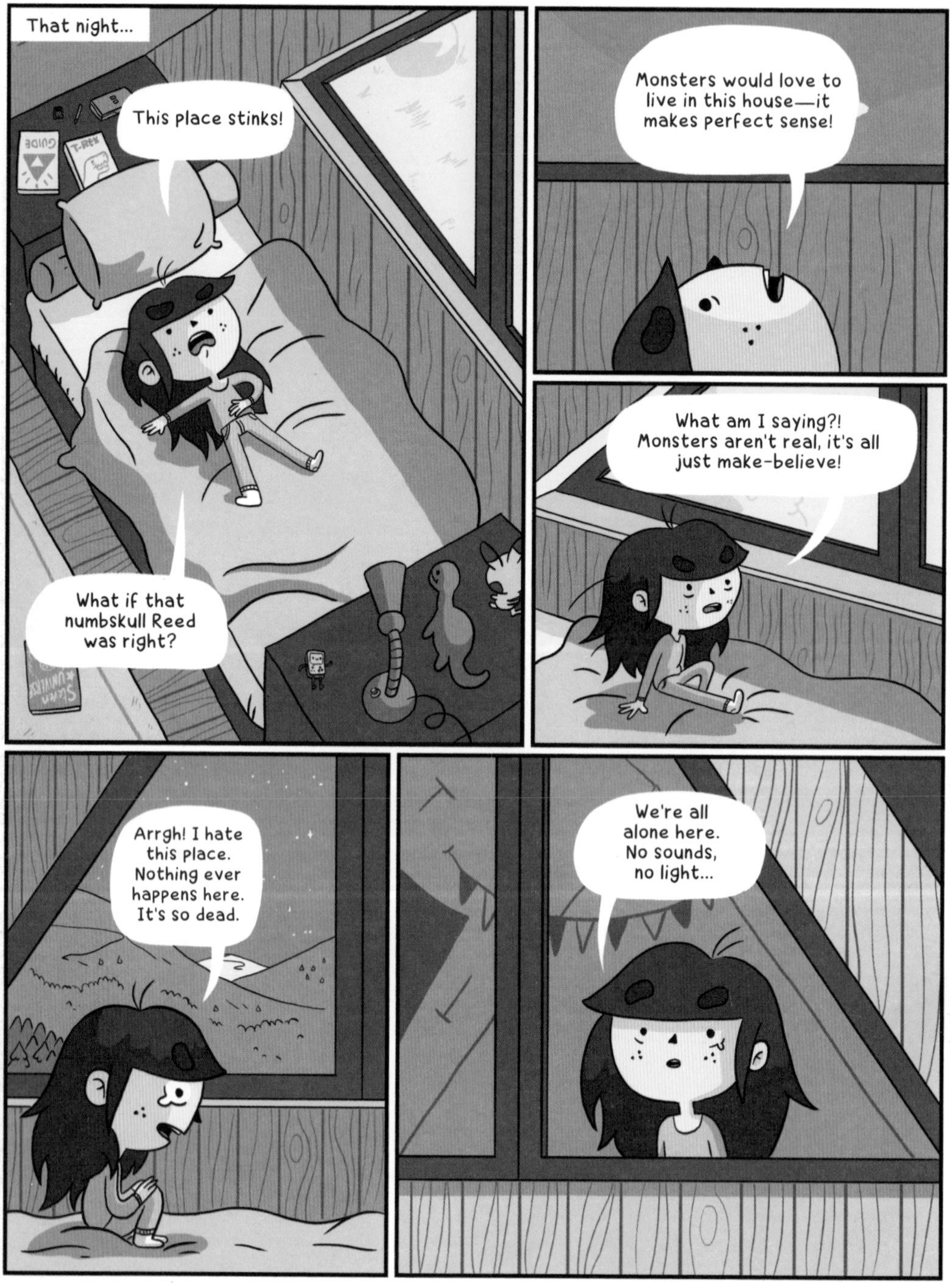
That night...
This place stinks!
What if that numbskull Reed was right?
Monsters would love to live in this house—it makes perfect sense!
What am I saying?! Monsters aren't real, it's all just make-believe!
Arrgh! I hate this place. Nothing ever happens here. It's so dead.
We're all alone here. No sounds, no light...

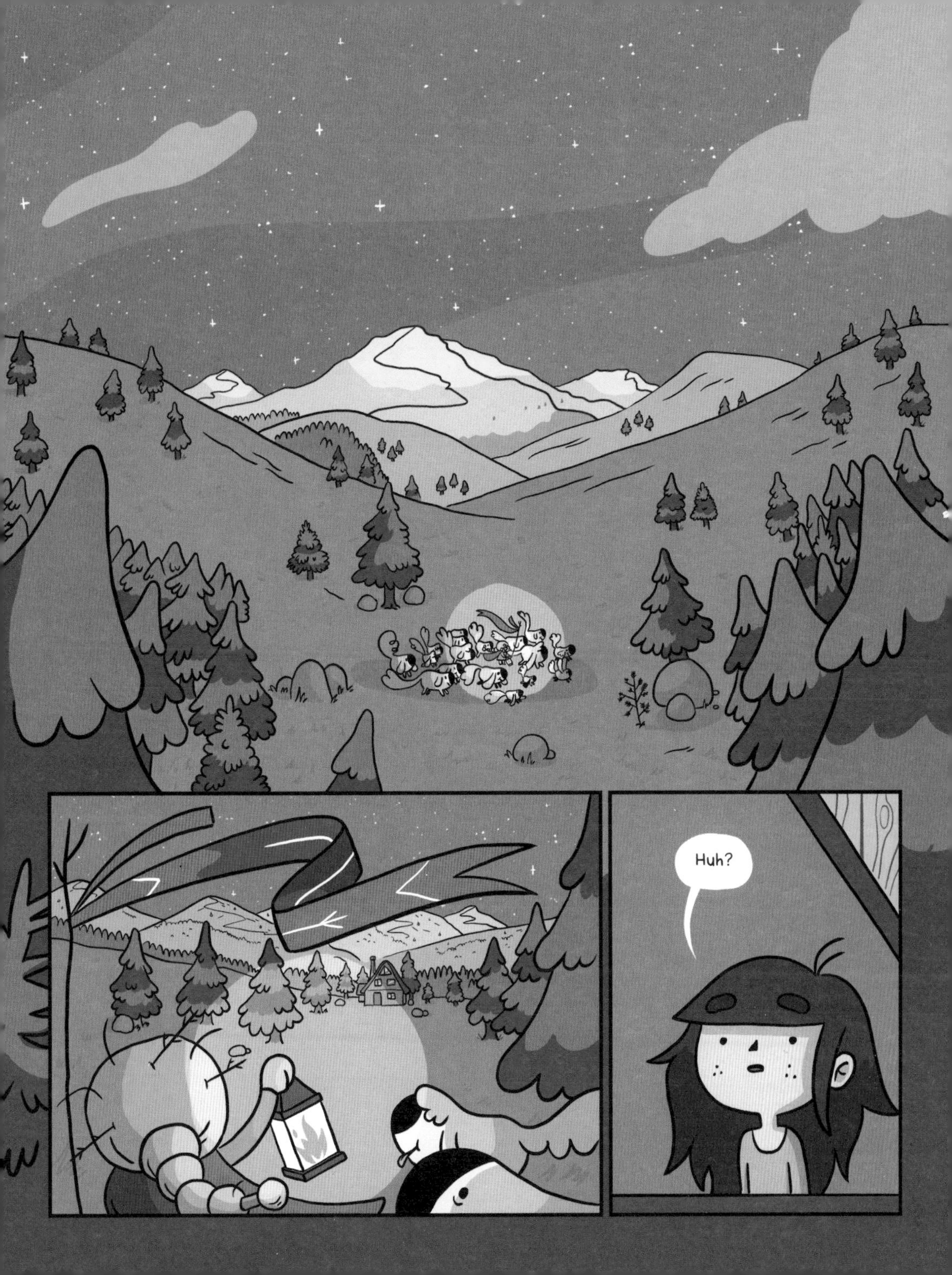
Huh?

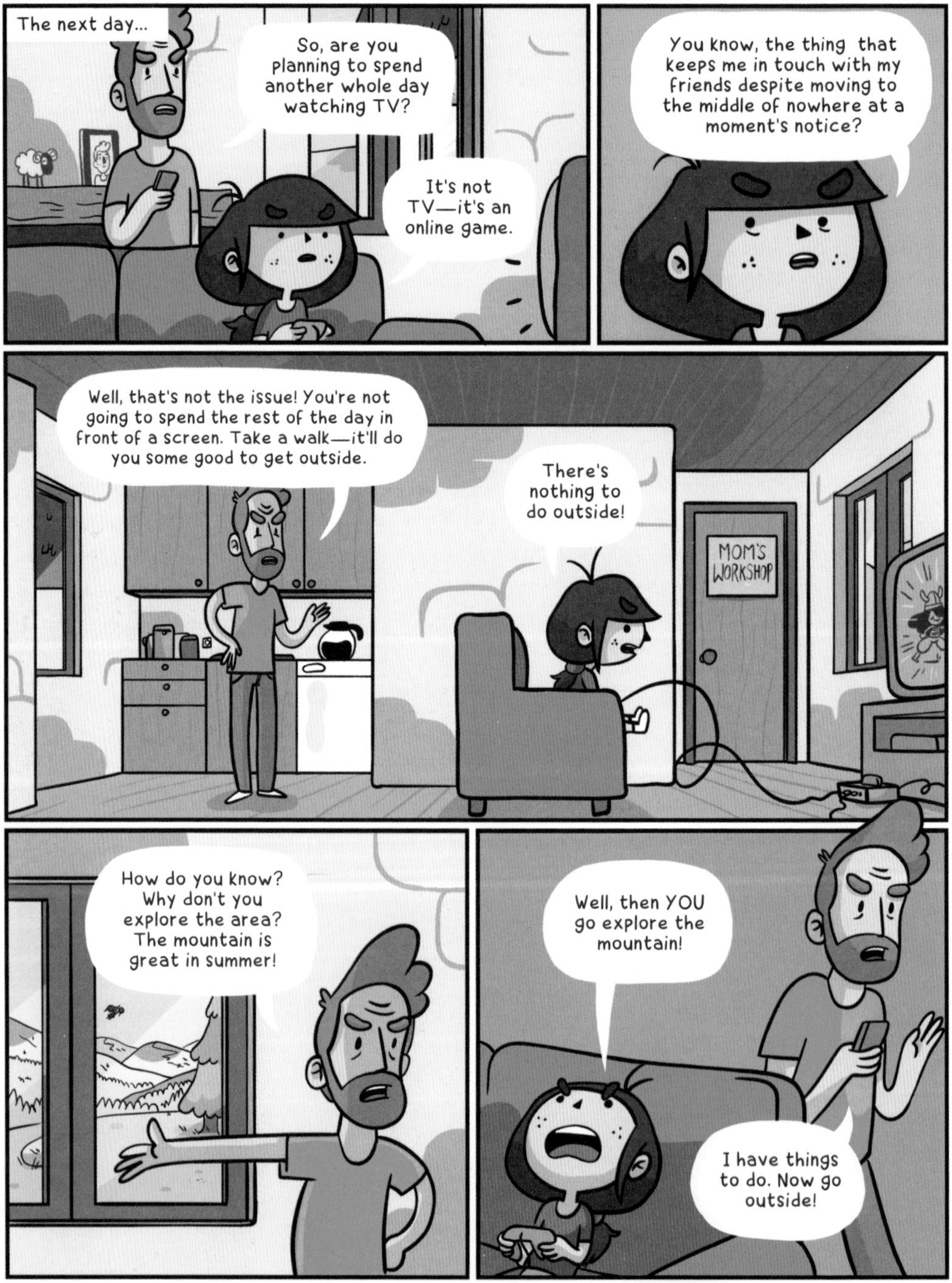
The next day...
So, are you planning to spend another whole day watching TV?
It's not TV—it's an online game.
You know, the thing that keeps me in touch with my friends despite moving to the middle of nowhere at a moment's notice?
Well, that's not the issue! You're not going to spend the rest of the day in front of a screen. Take a walk—it'll do you some good to get outside.
There's nothing to do outside!
MOM'S WORKSHOP
How do you know? Why don't you explore the area? The mountain is great in summer!
Well, then YOU go explore the mountain!
I have things to do. Now go outside!

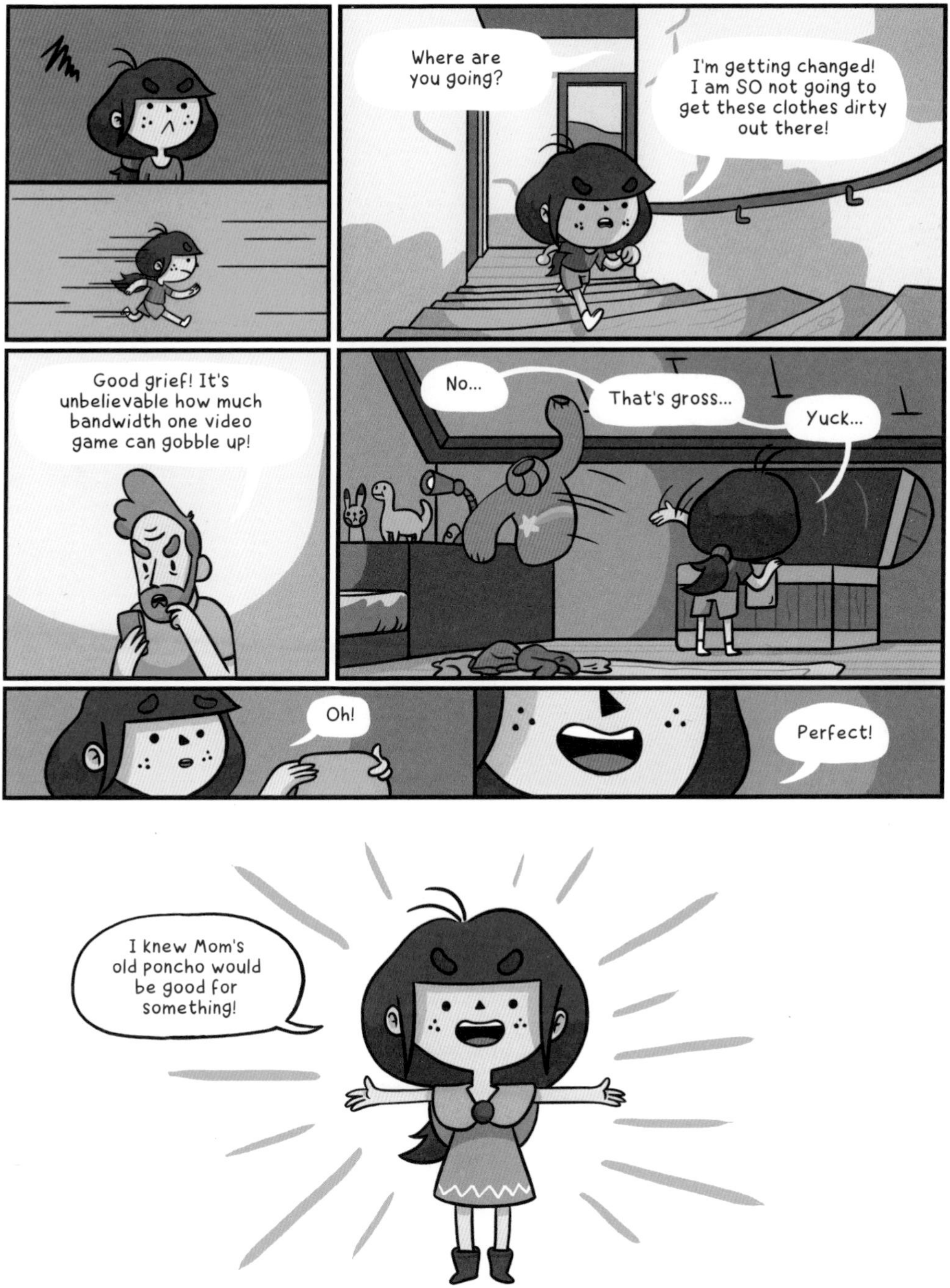
Where are you going?
I'm getting changed! I am SO not going to get these clothes dirty out there!
Good grief! It's unbelievable how much bandwidth one video game can gobble up!
No...
That's gross...
Yuck...
Oh!
Perfect!
I knew Mom's old poncho would be good for something!

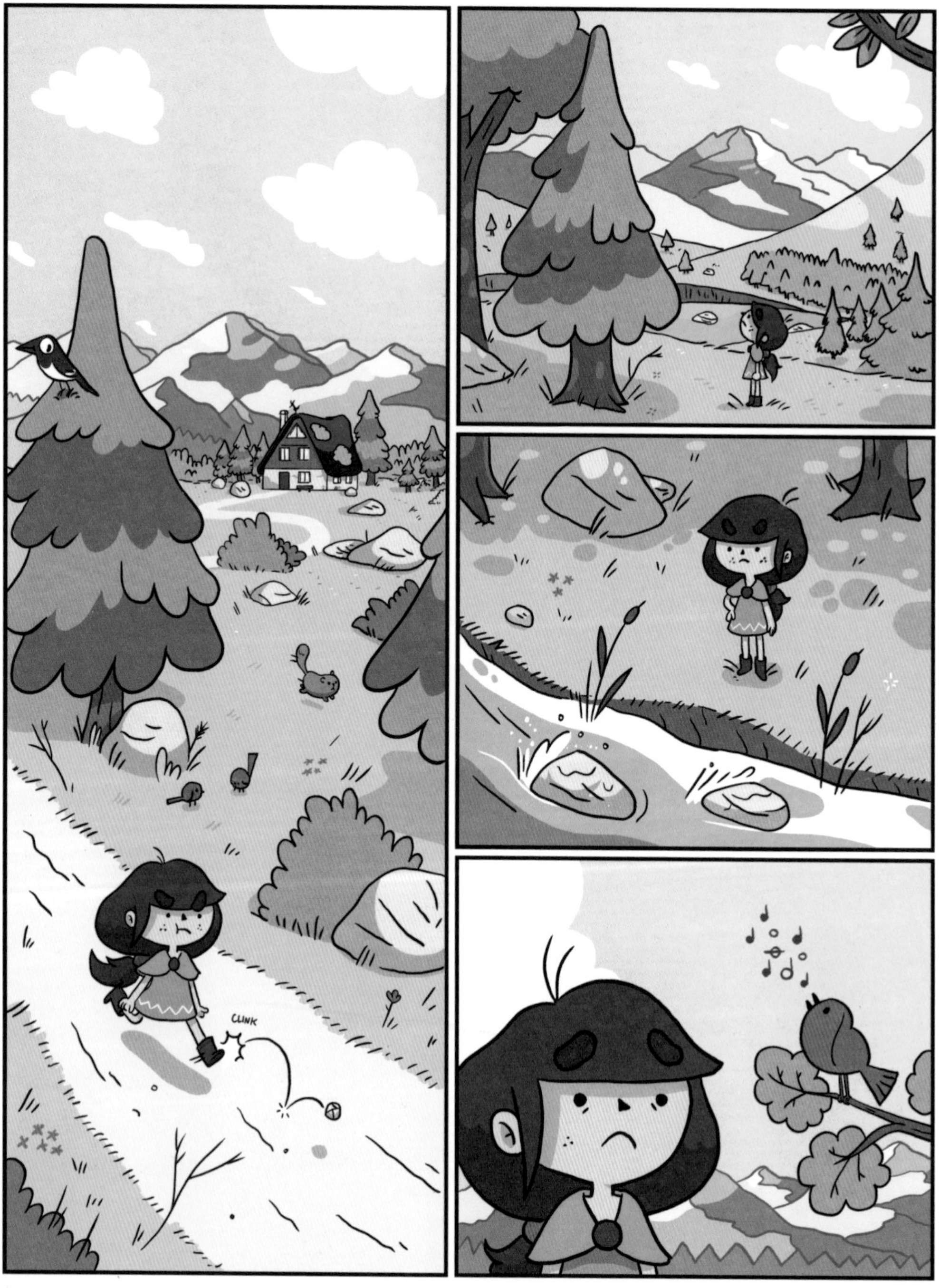
CLINK

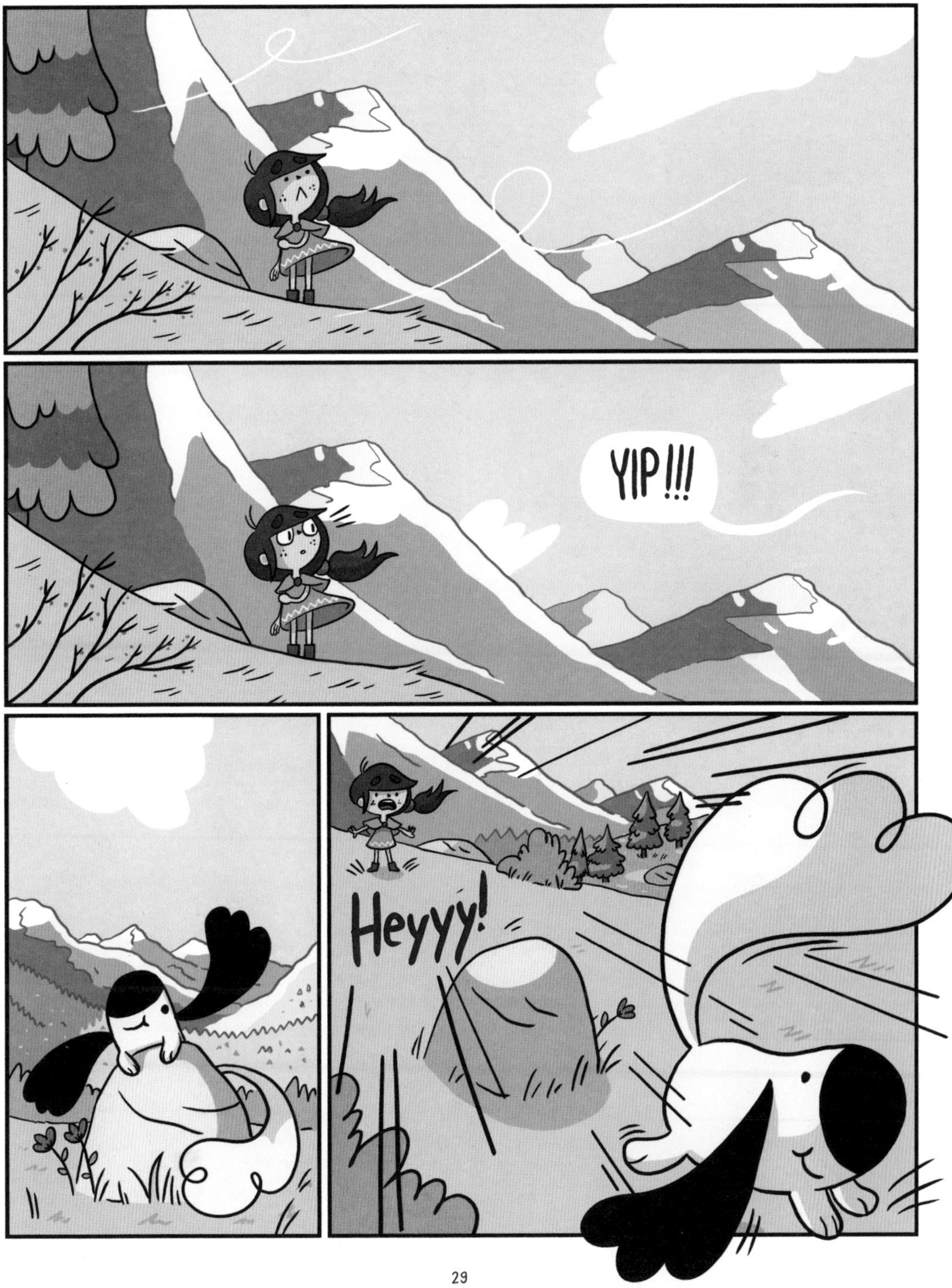
YIP!!!
Heyyy!

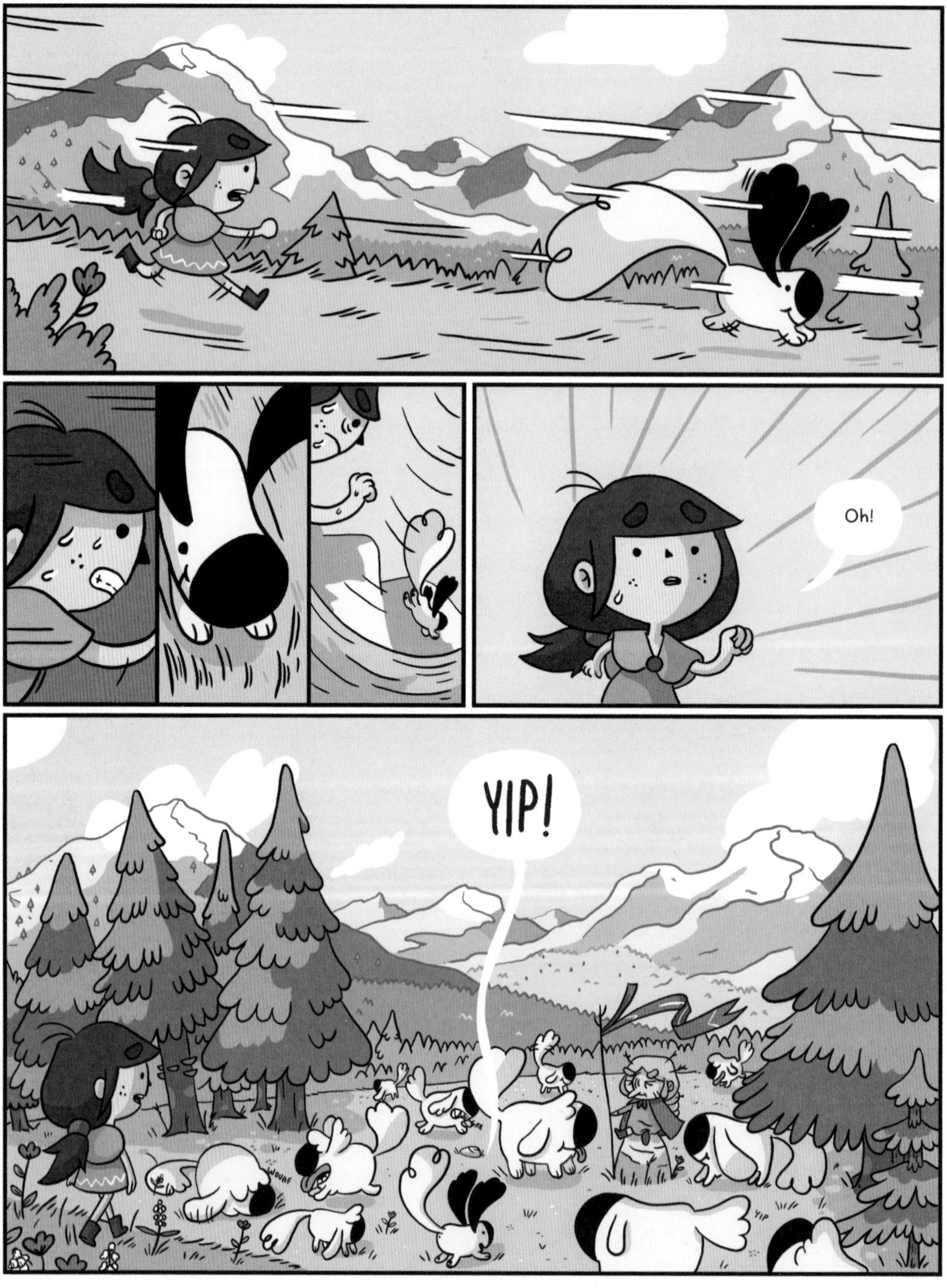
Oh!
YIP!
WOUAF
YIP

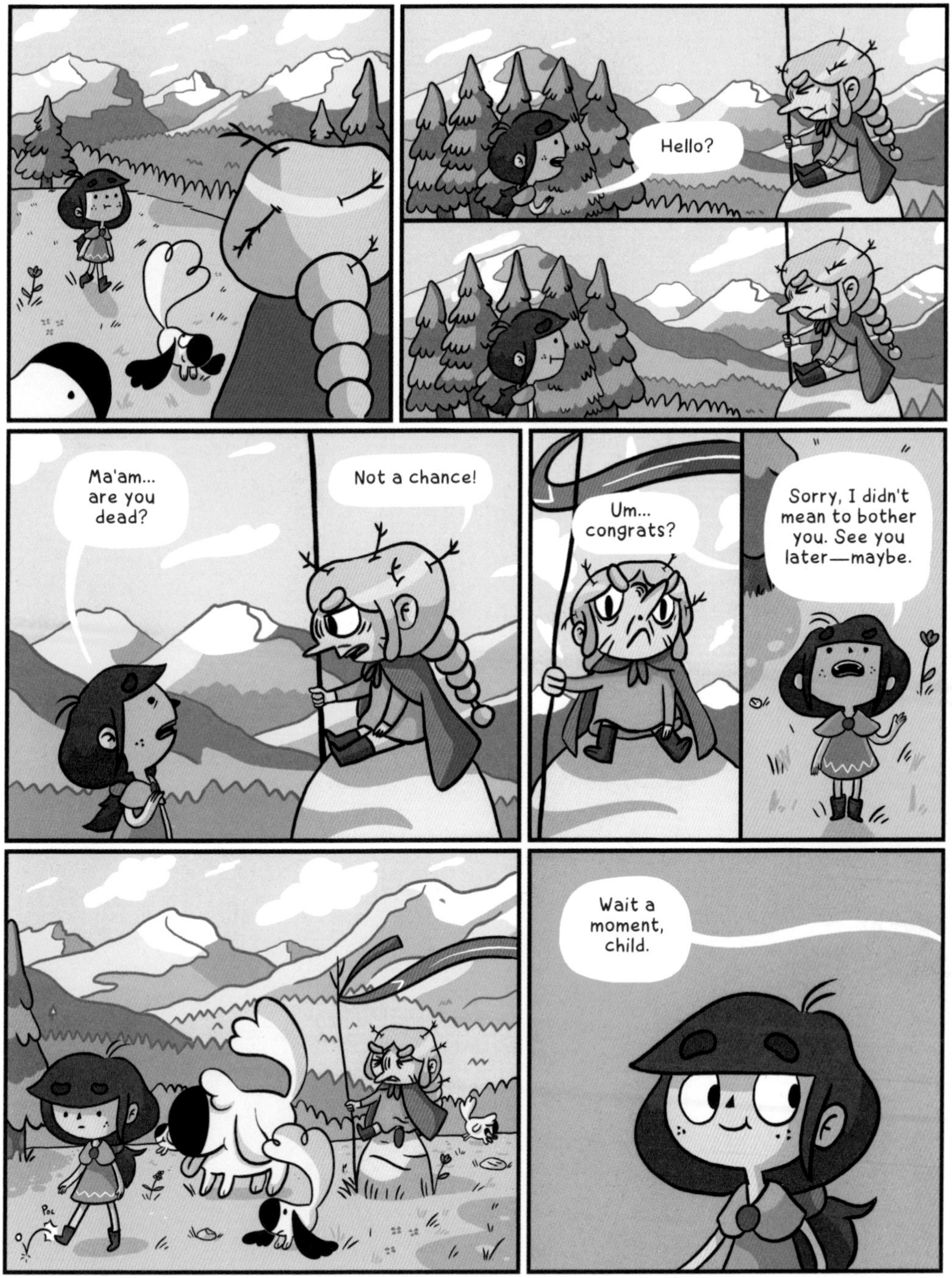
Hello?
Ma'am... are you dead?
Not a chance!
Um... congrats?
Sorry, I didn't mean to bother you. See you later—maybe.
Poc
Wait a moment, child.

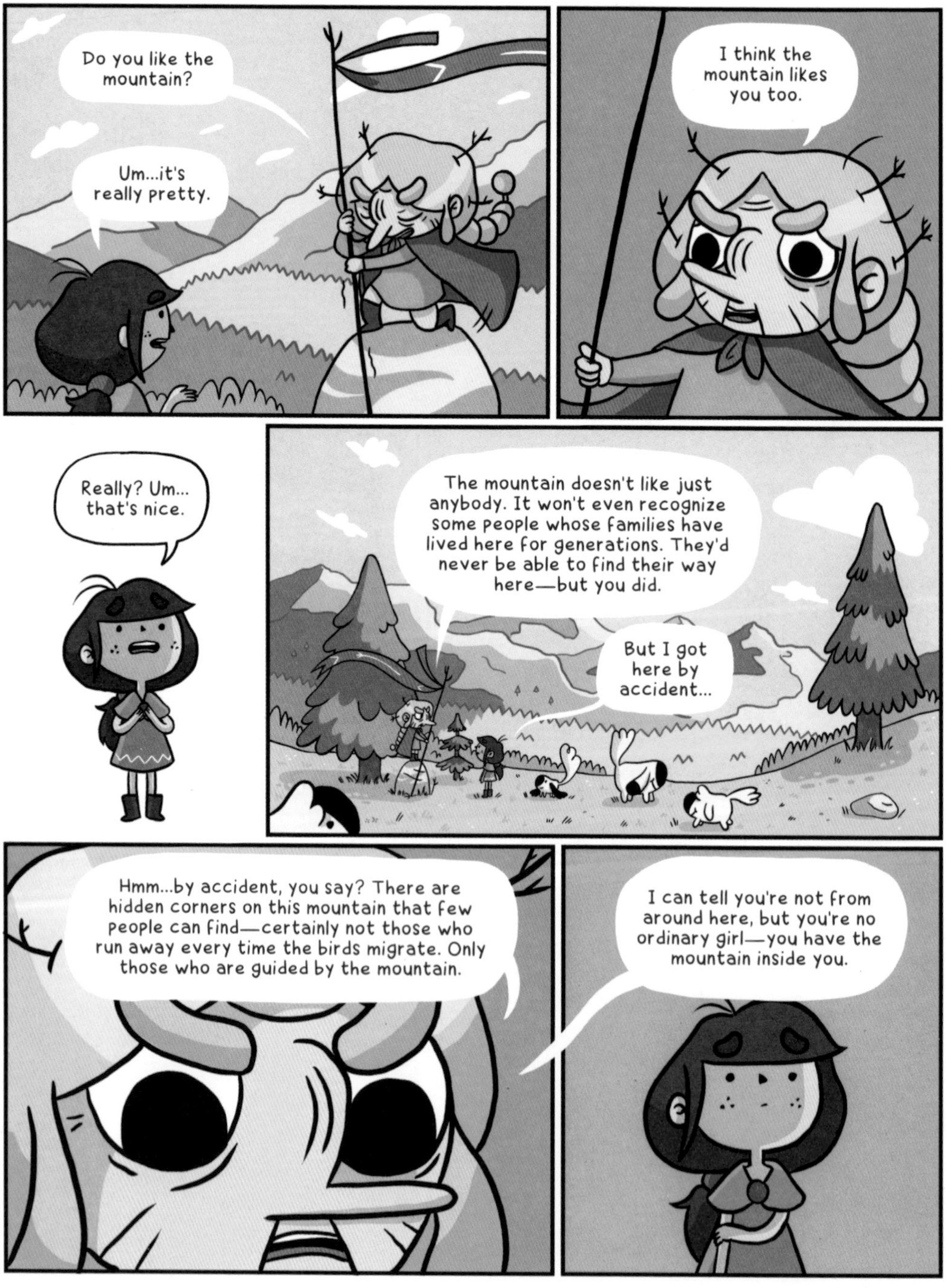
Do you like the mountain?
Um...it's really pretty.
I think the mountain likes you too.
Really? Um... that's nice.
The mountain doesn't like just anybody. It won't even recognize some people whose families have lived here for generations. They'd never be able to find their way here—but you did.
But I got here by accident...
Hmm...by accident, you say? There are hidden corners on this mountain that few people can find—certainly not those who run away every time the birds migrate. Only those who are guided by the mountain.
I can tell you're not from around here, but you're no ordinary girl—you have the mountain inside you.

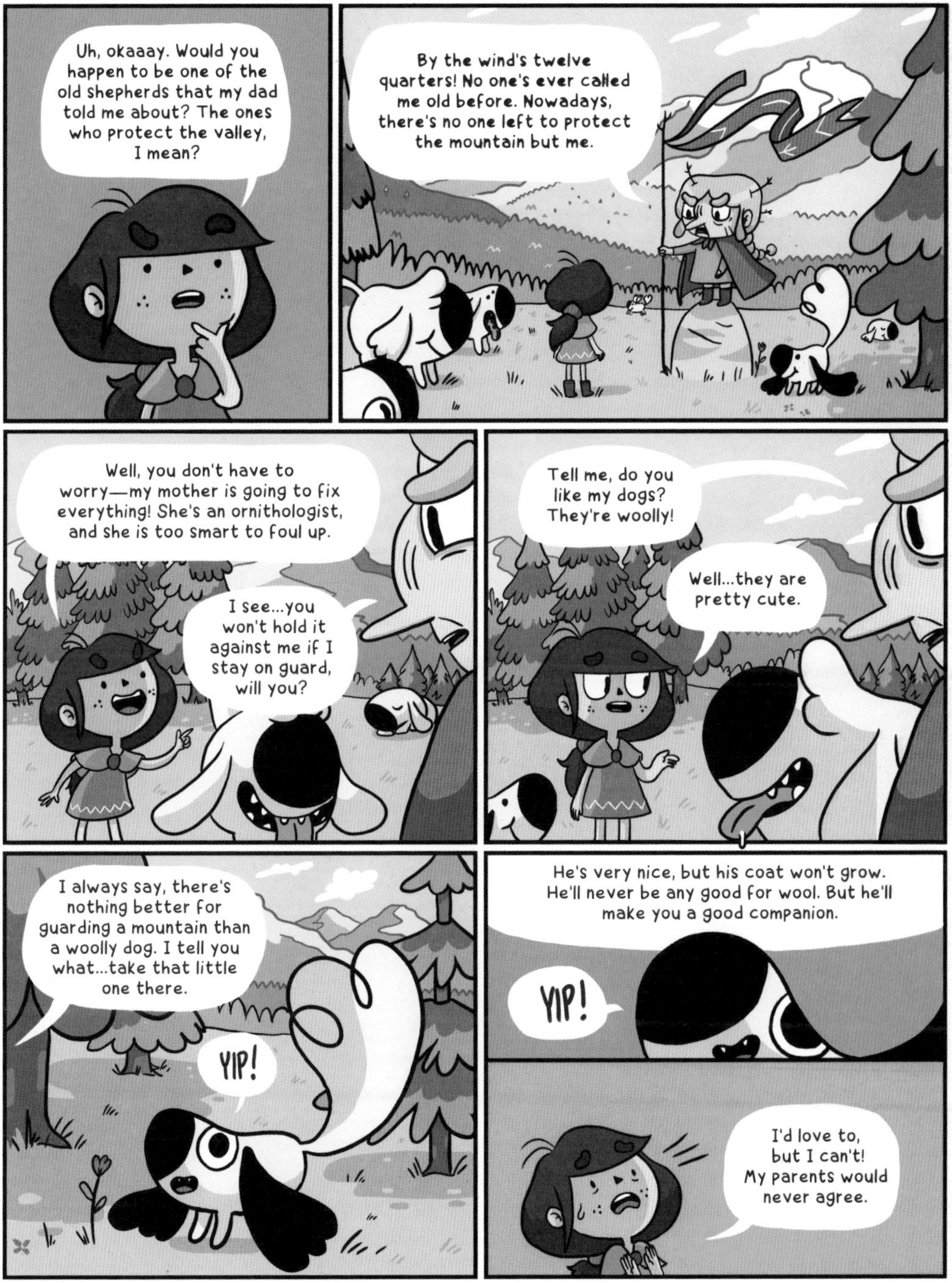

Uh, okaaay. Would you happen to be one of the old shepherds that my dad told me about? The ones who protect the valley, I mean?
By the wind's twelve quarters! No one's ever called me old before. Nowadays, there's no one left to protect the mountain but me.
Well, you don't have to worry—my mother is going to fix everything! She's an ornithologist, and she is too smart to foul up.
I see...you won't hold it against me if I stay on guard, will you?
Tell me, do you like my dogs? They're woolly!
Well...they are pretty cute.
I always say, there's nothing better for guarding a mountain than a woolly dog. I tell you what...take that little one there.
YIP!
He's very nice, but his coat won't grow. He'll never be any good for wool. But he'll make you a good companion.
YIP!
I'd love to, but I can't! My parents would never agree.

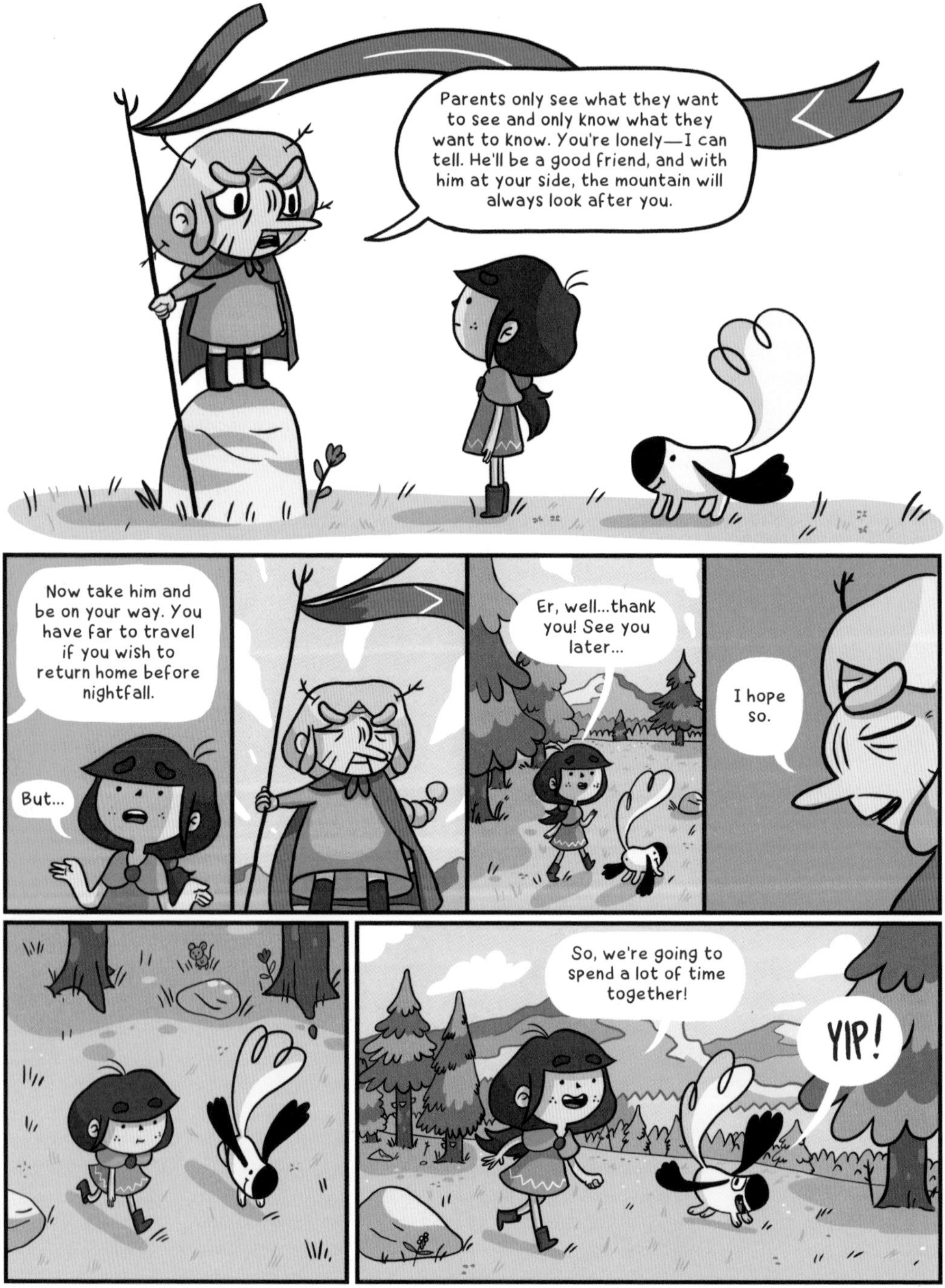
Parents only see what they want to see and only know what they want to know. You're lonely—I can tell. He'll be a good friend, and with him at your side, the mountain will always look after you.
Now take him and be on your way. You have far to travel if you wish to return home before nightfall.
But...
Er, well...thank you! See you later...
I hope so.
So, we're going to spend a lot of time together!
YIP!

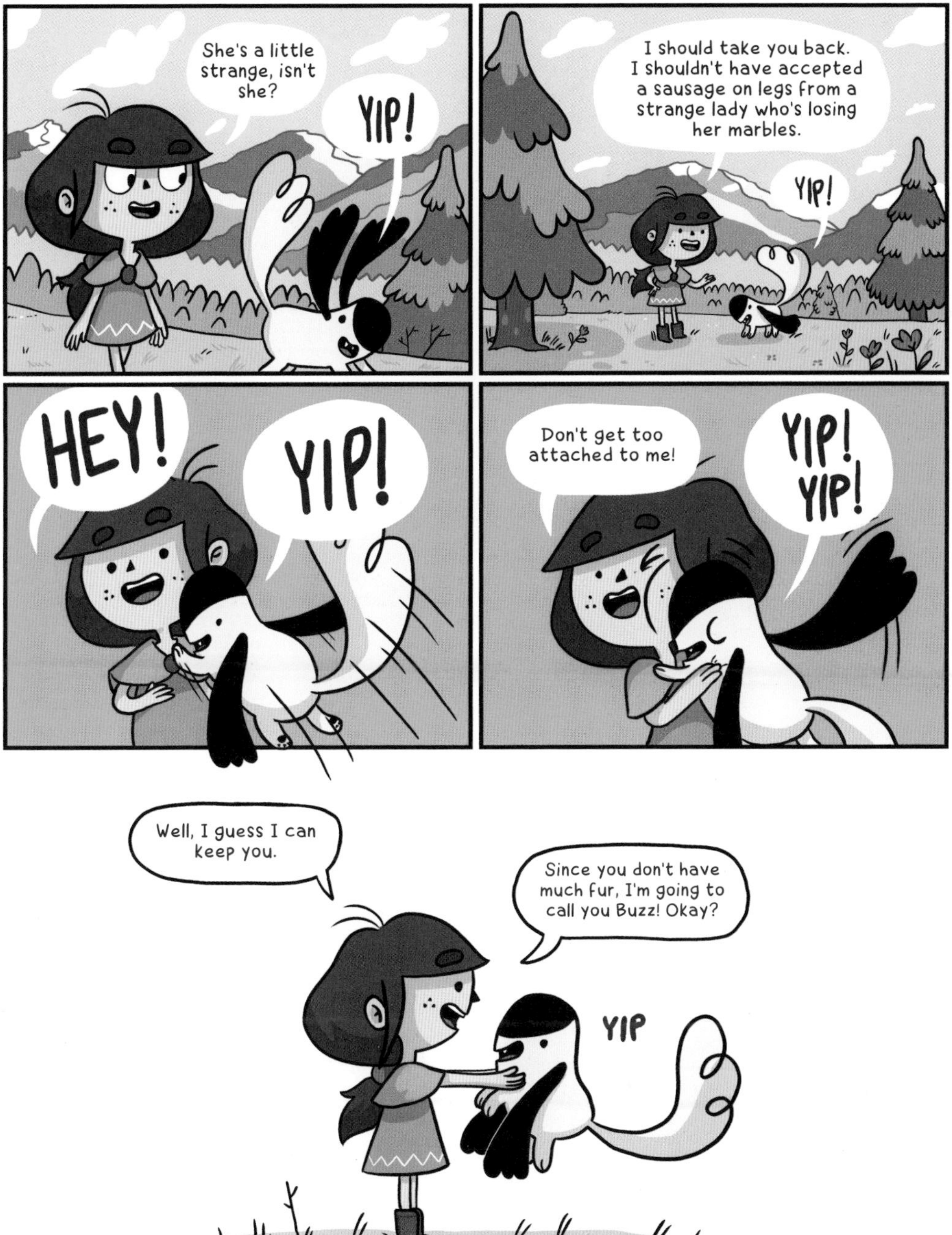
She's a little strange, isn't she?
YIP!
I should take you back. I shouldn't have accepted a sausage on legs from a strange lady who's losing her marbles.
YIP!
HEY!
YIP!
Don't get too attached to me!
YIP! YIP!
Well, I guess I can keep you.
Since you don't have much fur, I'm going to call you Buzz! Okay?
YIP

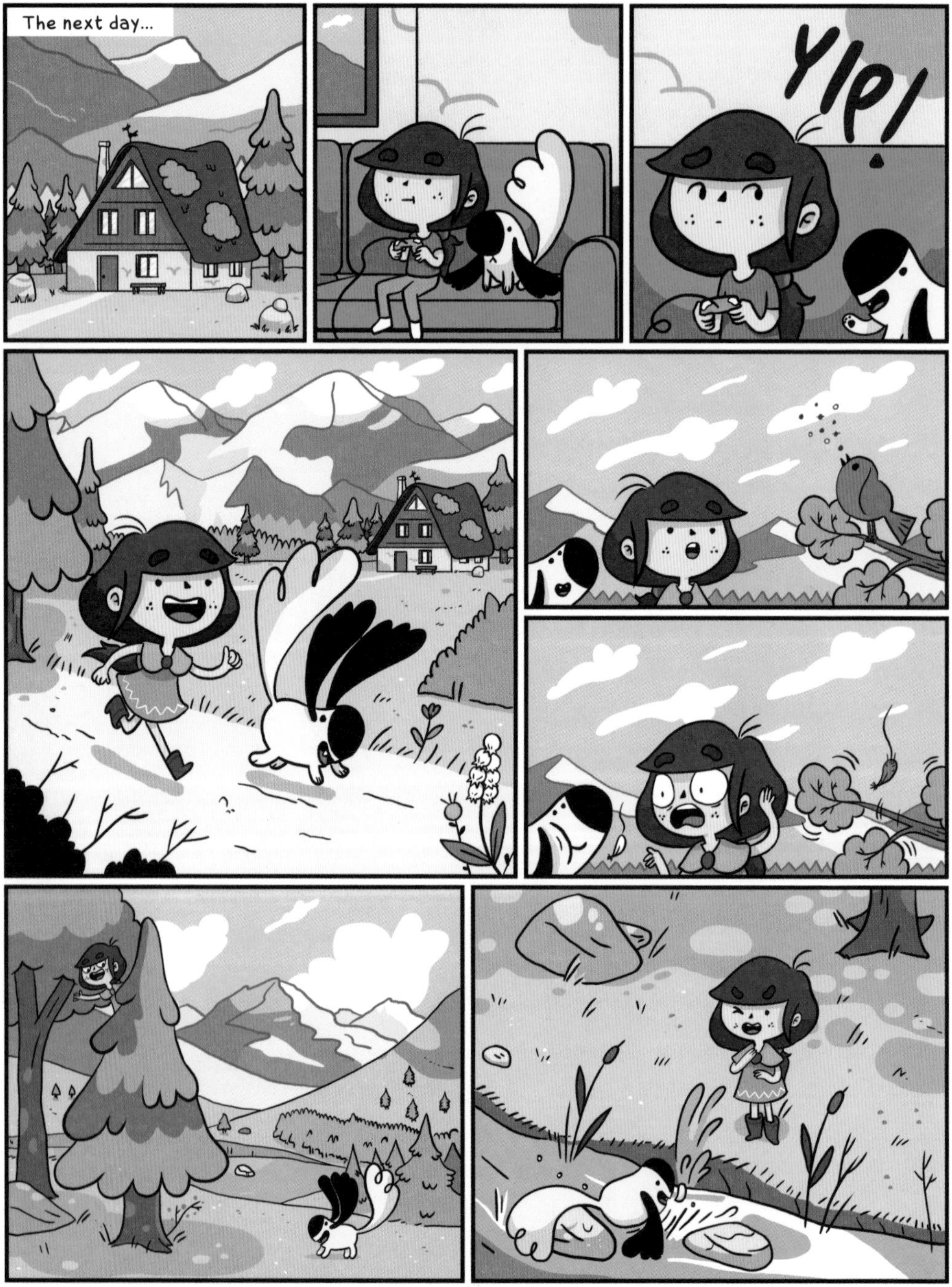
The next day...
YIP!

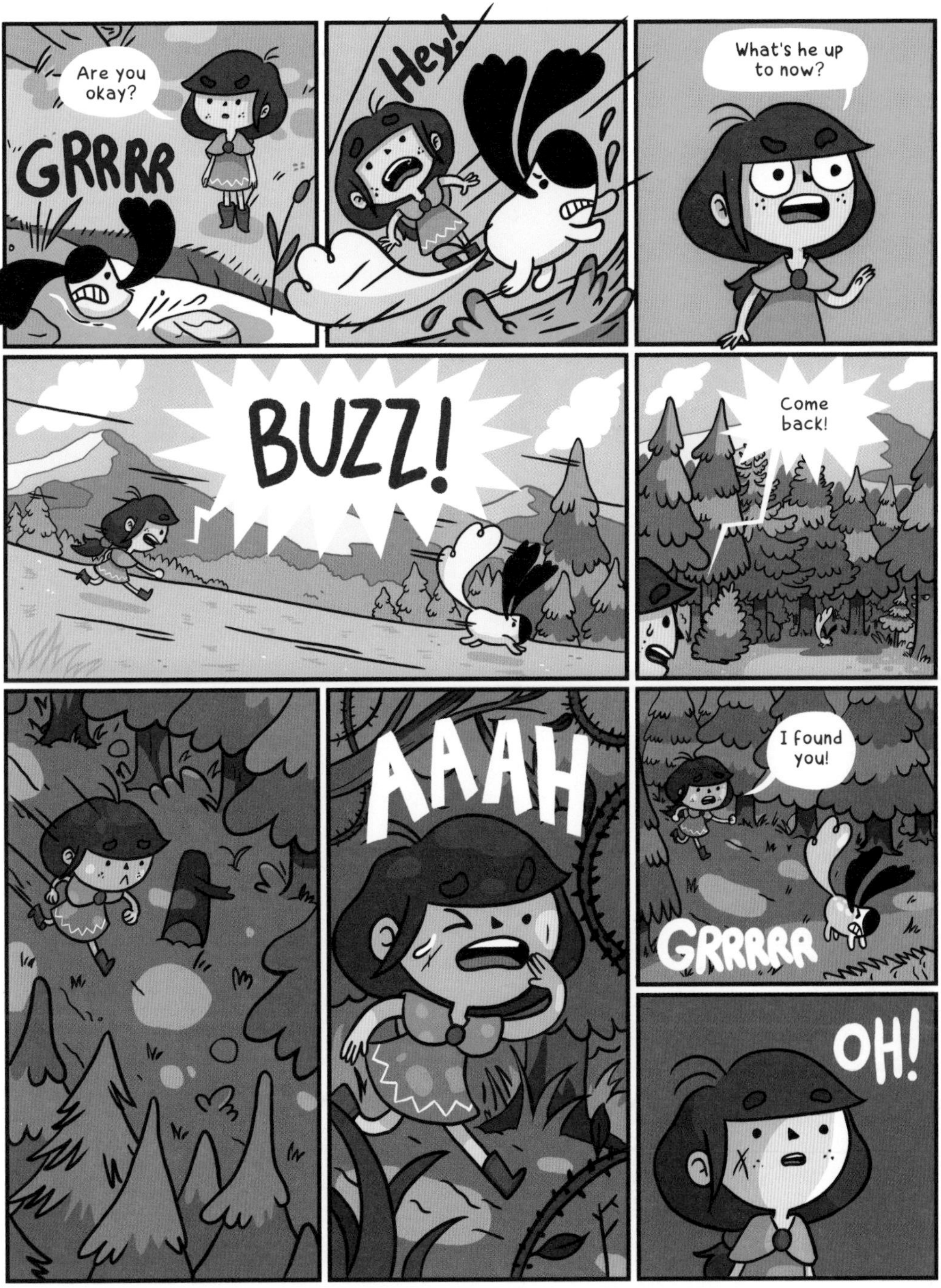
Are you okay?
GRRRR
Hey!
What's he up to now?
BUZZ!
Come back!
AAAH
I found you!
GRRRRR
OH!

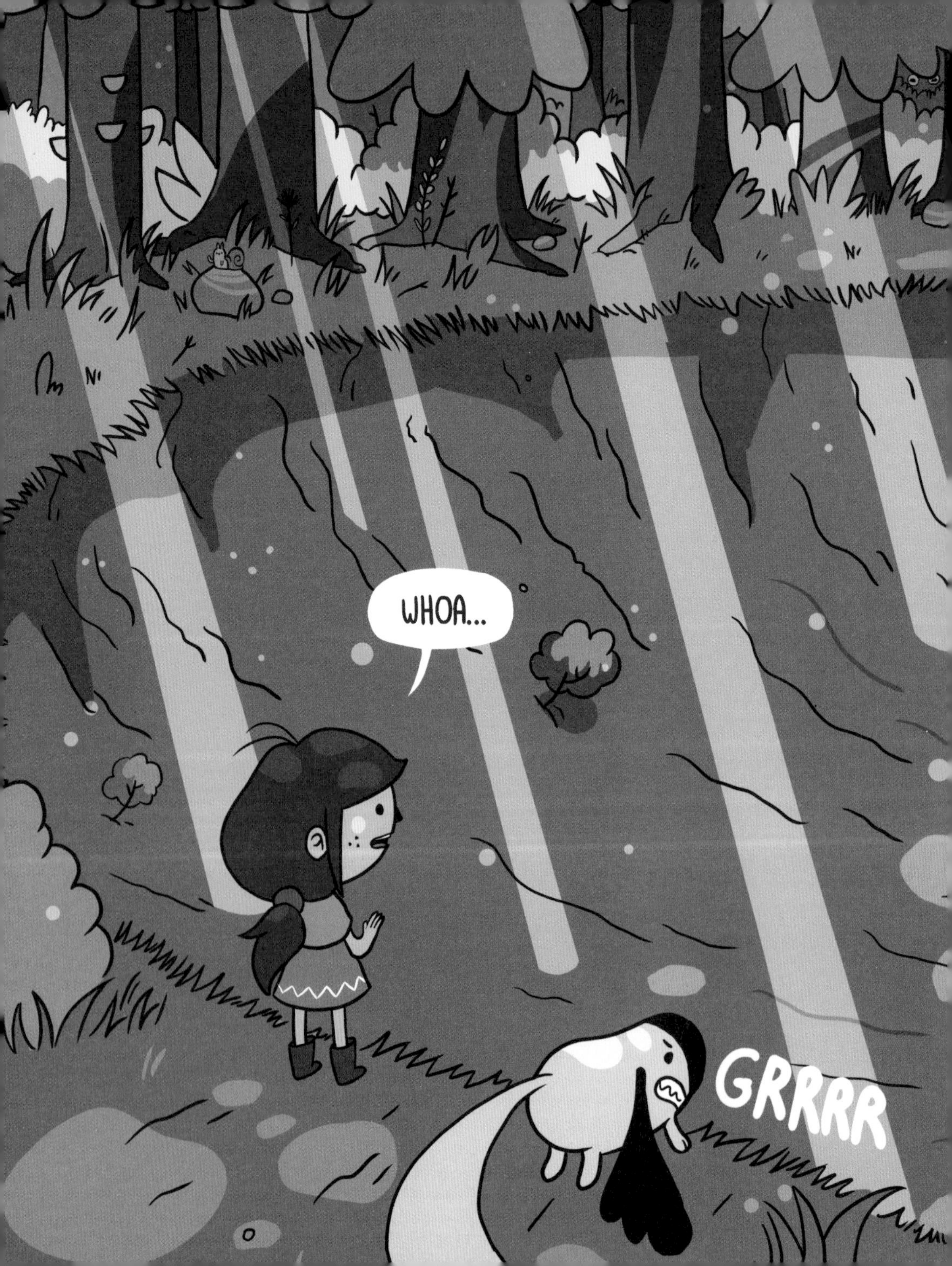
WHOA...
GRRRR

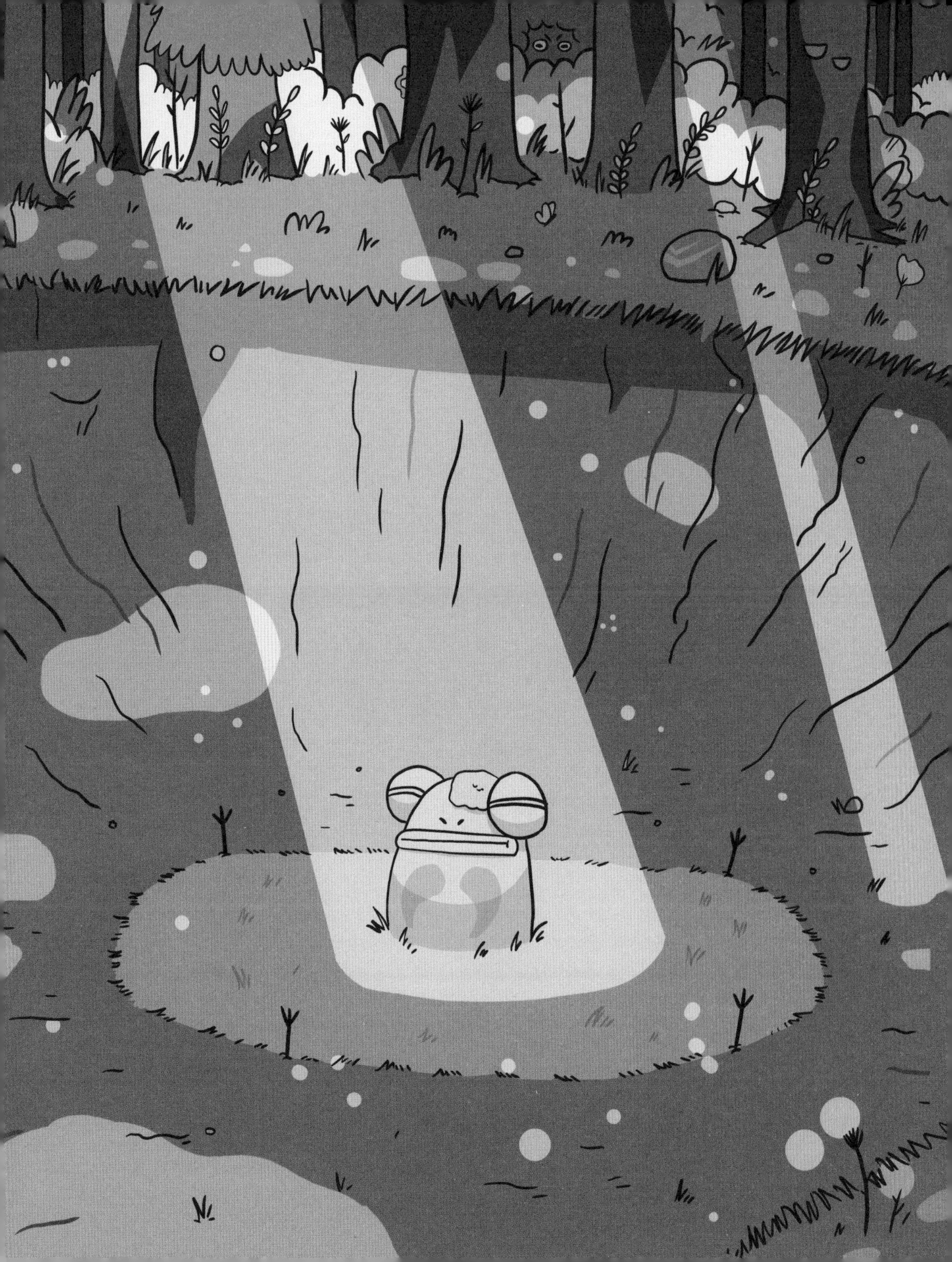

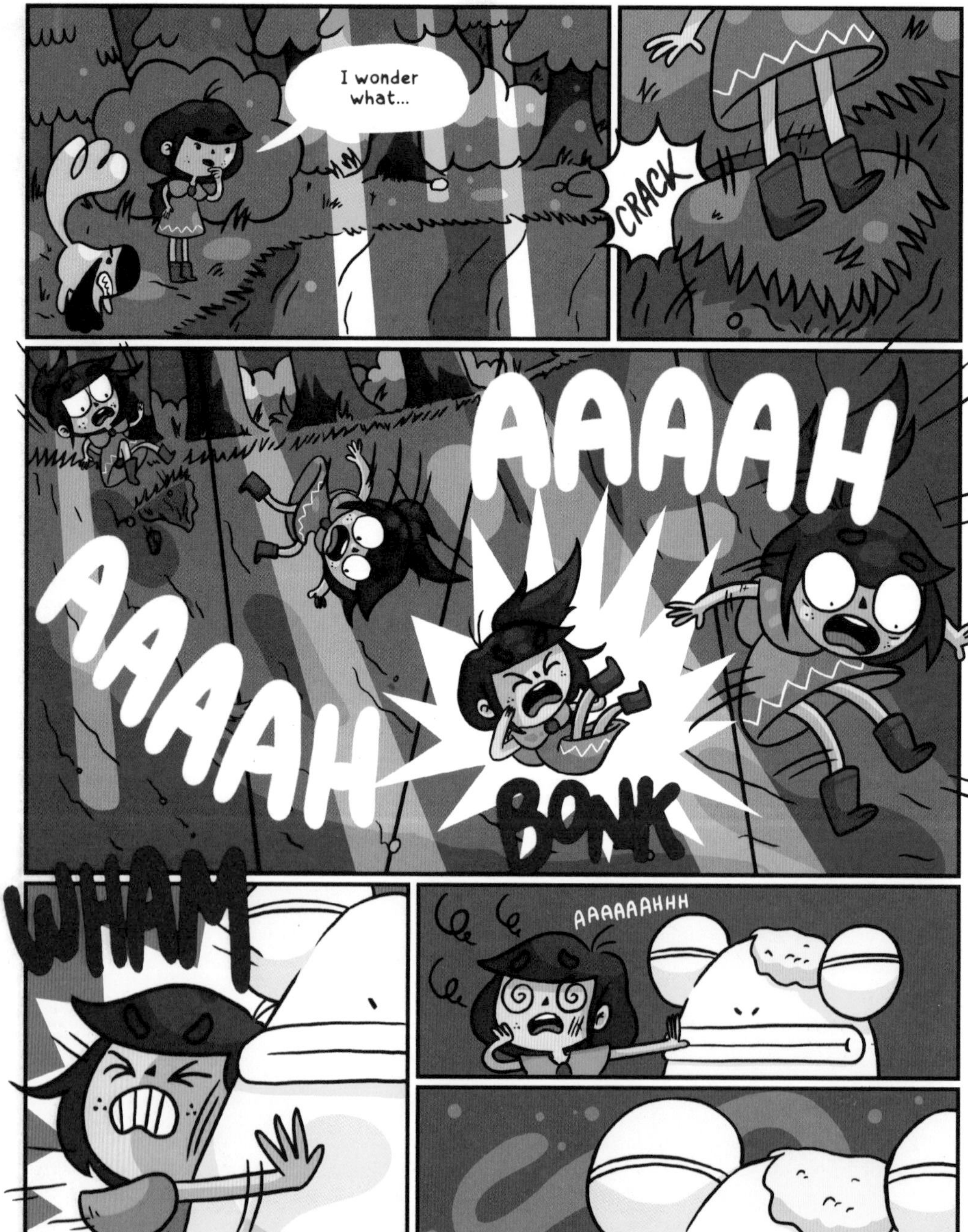
I wonder what...
CRACK
AAAAAH
AAAAAH
BONK
WHAM
AAAAAAHHH

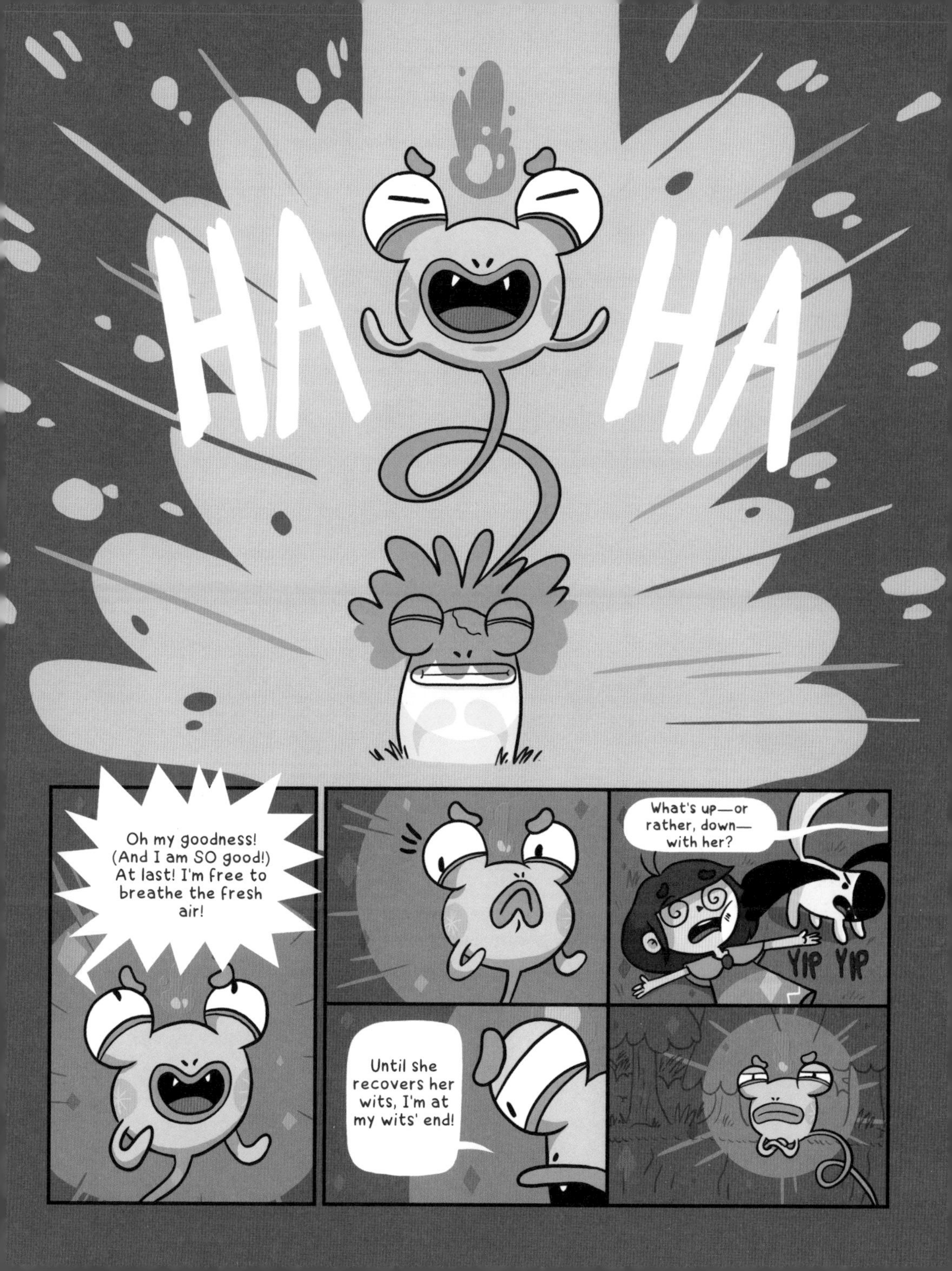
HA HA
Oh my goodness! (And I am SO good!) At last! I'm free to breathe the fresh air!
What's up—or rather, down—with her?
YIP YIP
Until she recovers her wits, I'm at my wits' end!

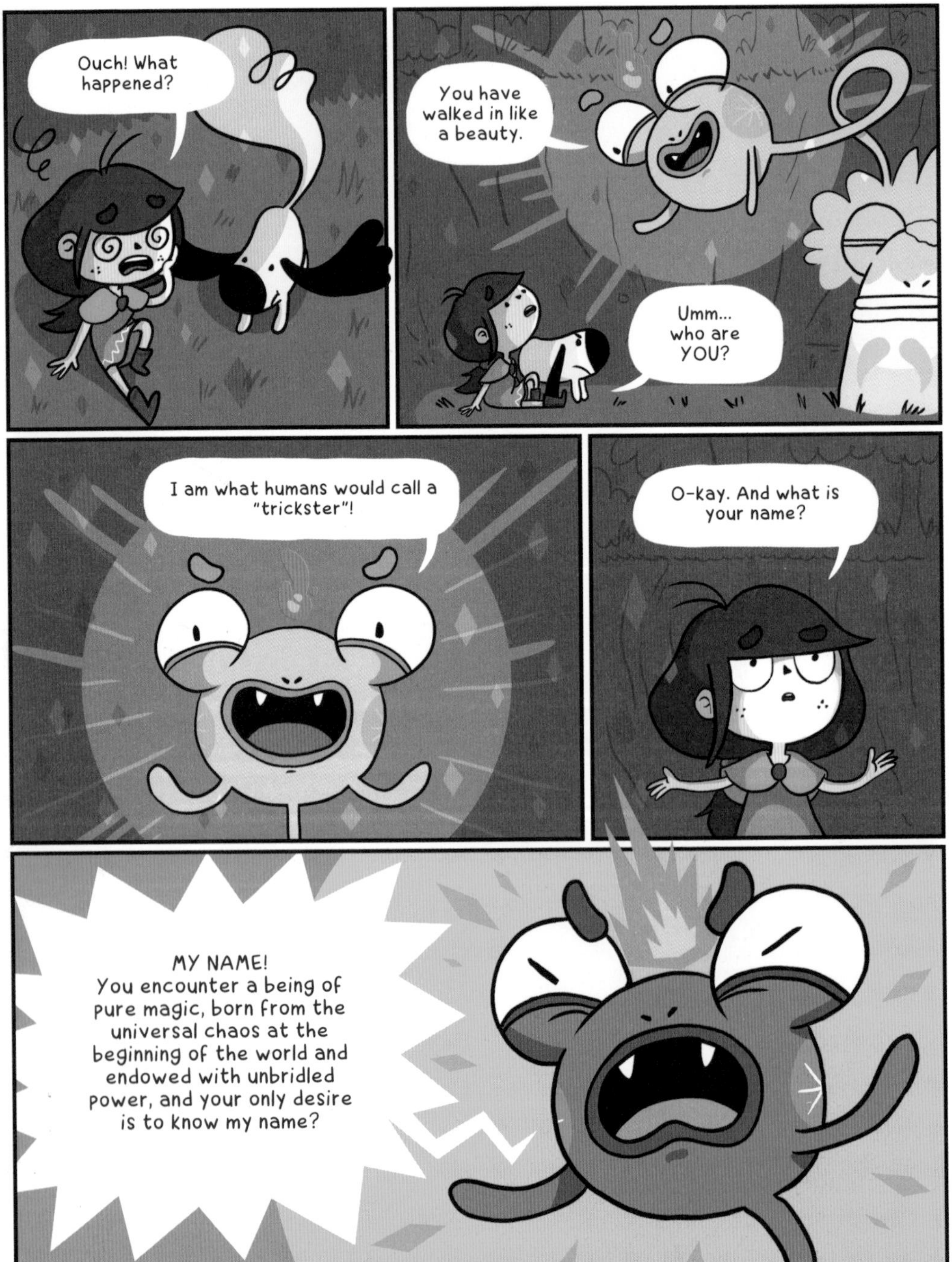
Ouch! What happened?
You have walked in like a beauty.
Umm... who are YOU?
I am what humans would call a "trickster"!
O-kay. And what is your name?
MY NAME! You encounter a being of pure magic, born from the universal chaos at the beginning of the world and endowed with unbridled power, and your only desire is to know my name?

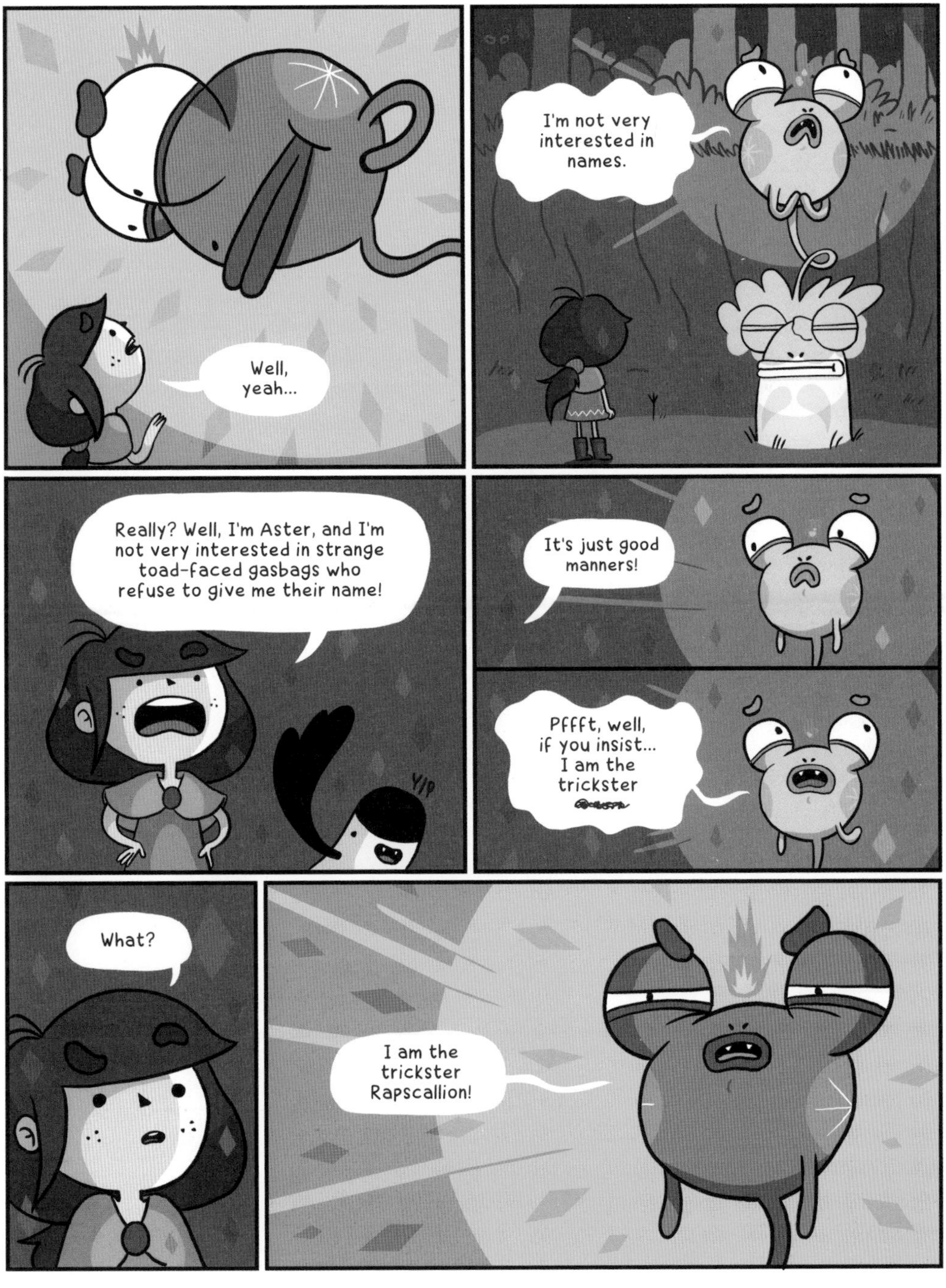
Well, yeah...
I'm not very interested in names.
Really? Well, I'm Aster, and I'm not very interested in strange toad-faced gasbags who refuse to give me their name!
YIP
It's just good manners!
Pfffft, well, if you insist... I am the trickster
What?
I am the trickster Rapscallion!

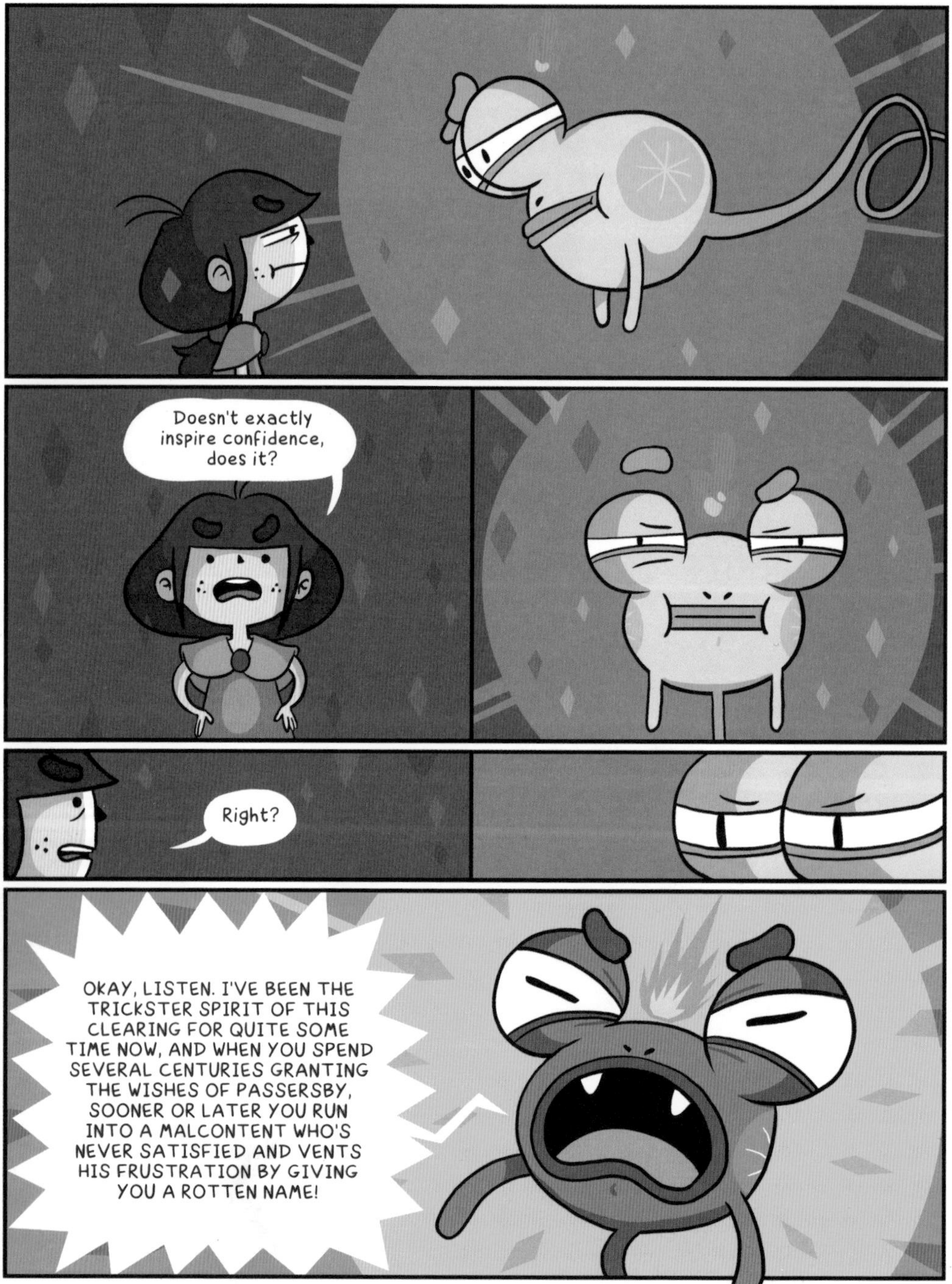
Doesn't exactly inspire confidence, does it?
Right?
OKAY, LISTEN. I'VE BEEN THE TRICKSTER SPIRIT OF THIS CLEARING FOR QUITE SOME TIME NOW, AND WHEN YOU SPEND SEVERAL CENTURIES GRANTING THE WISHES OF PASSERSBY, SOONER OR LATER YOU RUN INTO A MALCONTENT WHO'S NEVER SATISFIED AND VENTS HIS FRUSTRATION BY GIVING YOU A ROTTEN NAME!

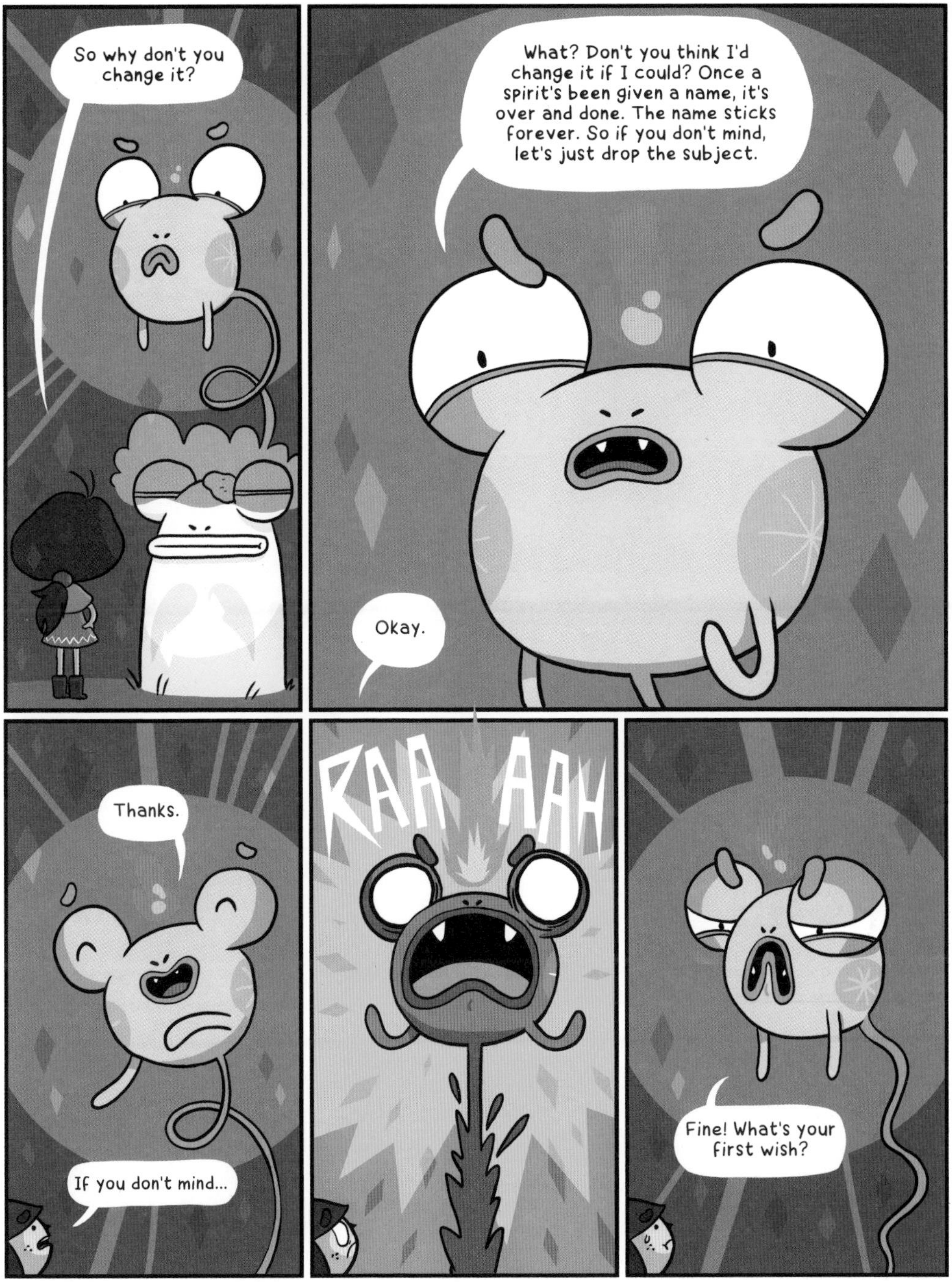
So why don't you change it?
What? Don't you think I'd change it if I could? Once a spirit's been given a name, it's over and done. The name sticks forever. So if you don't mind, let's just drop the subject.
Okay.
Thanks.
If you don't mind...
RAAAAH
Fine! What's your first wish?

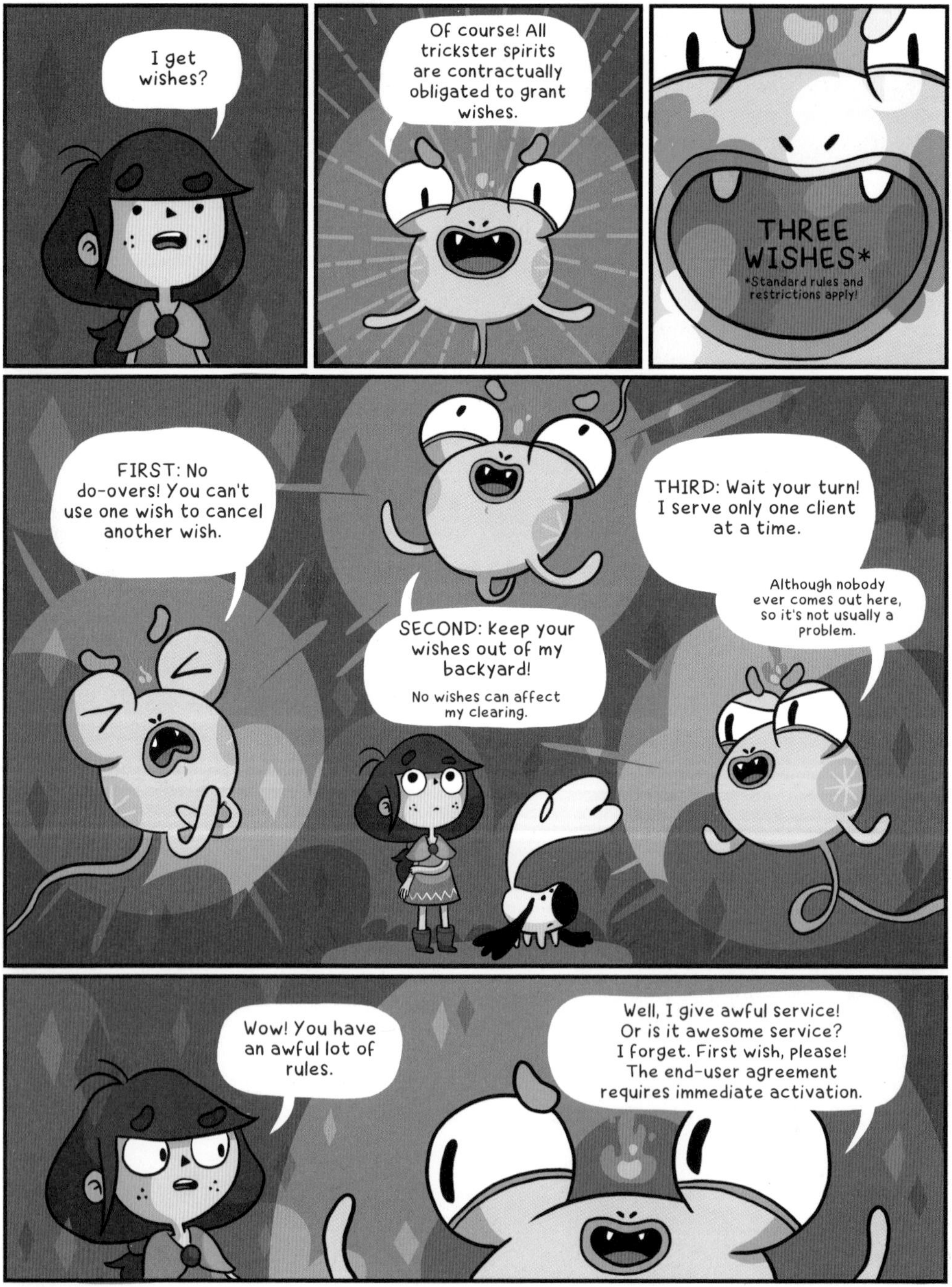
I get wishes?
Of course! All trickster spirits are contractually obligated to grant wishes.
THREE WISHES*
*Standard rules and restrictions apply!
FIRST: No do-overs! You can't use one wish to cancel another wish.
SECOND: Keep your wishes out of my backyard!
No wishes can affect my clearing.
THIRD: Wait your turn! I serve only one client at a time.
Although nobody ever comes out here, so it's not usually a problem.
Wow! You have an awful lot of rules.
Well, I give awful service! Or is it awesome service? I forget. First wish, please! The end-user agreement requires immediate activation.

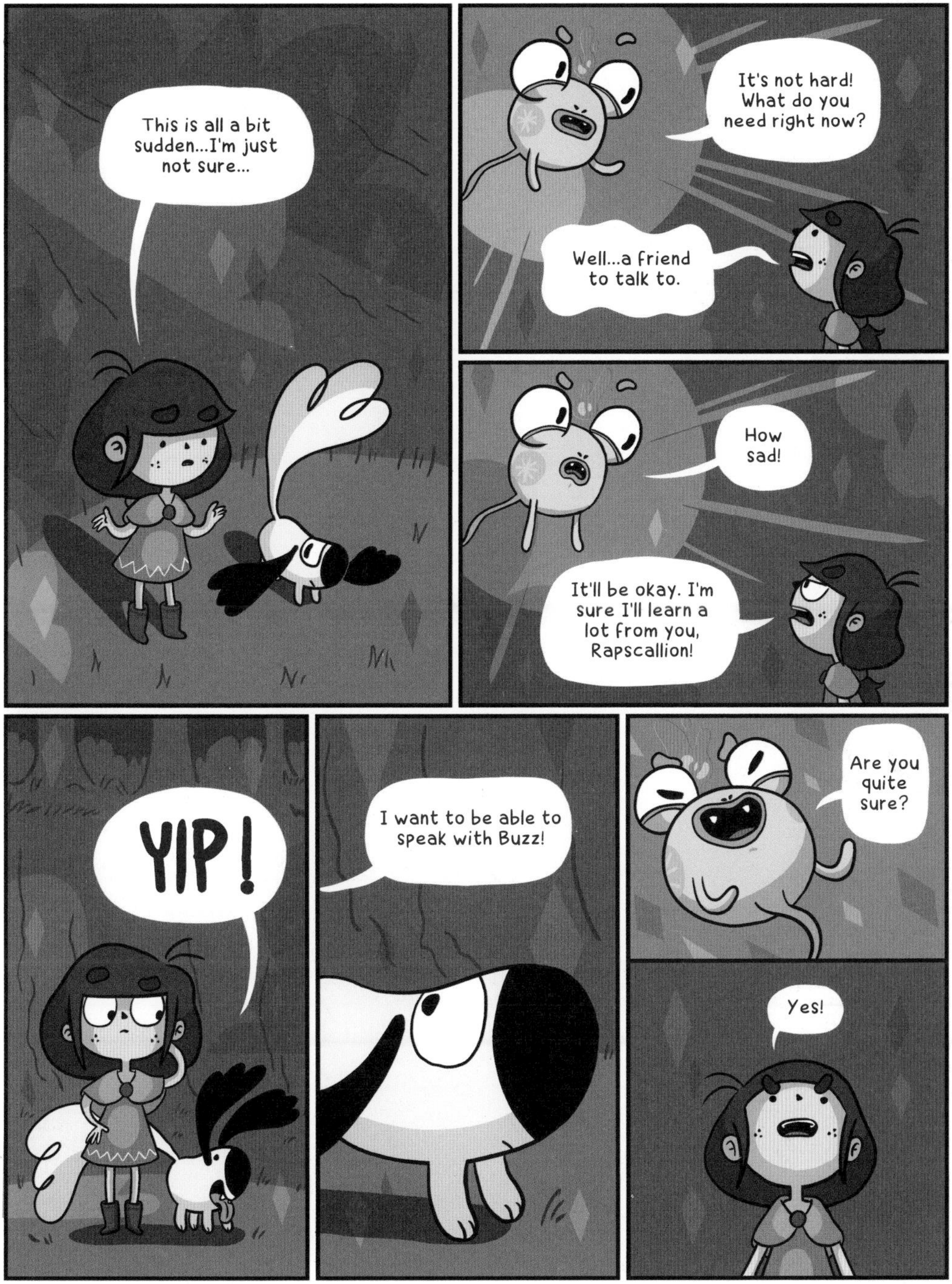
This is all a bit sudden...I'm just not sure...
It's not hard! What do you need right now?
Well...a friend to talk to.
How sad!
It'll be okay. I'm sure I'll learn a lot from you, Rapscallion!
YIP!
I want to be able to speak with Buzz!
Are you quite sure?
Yes!

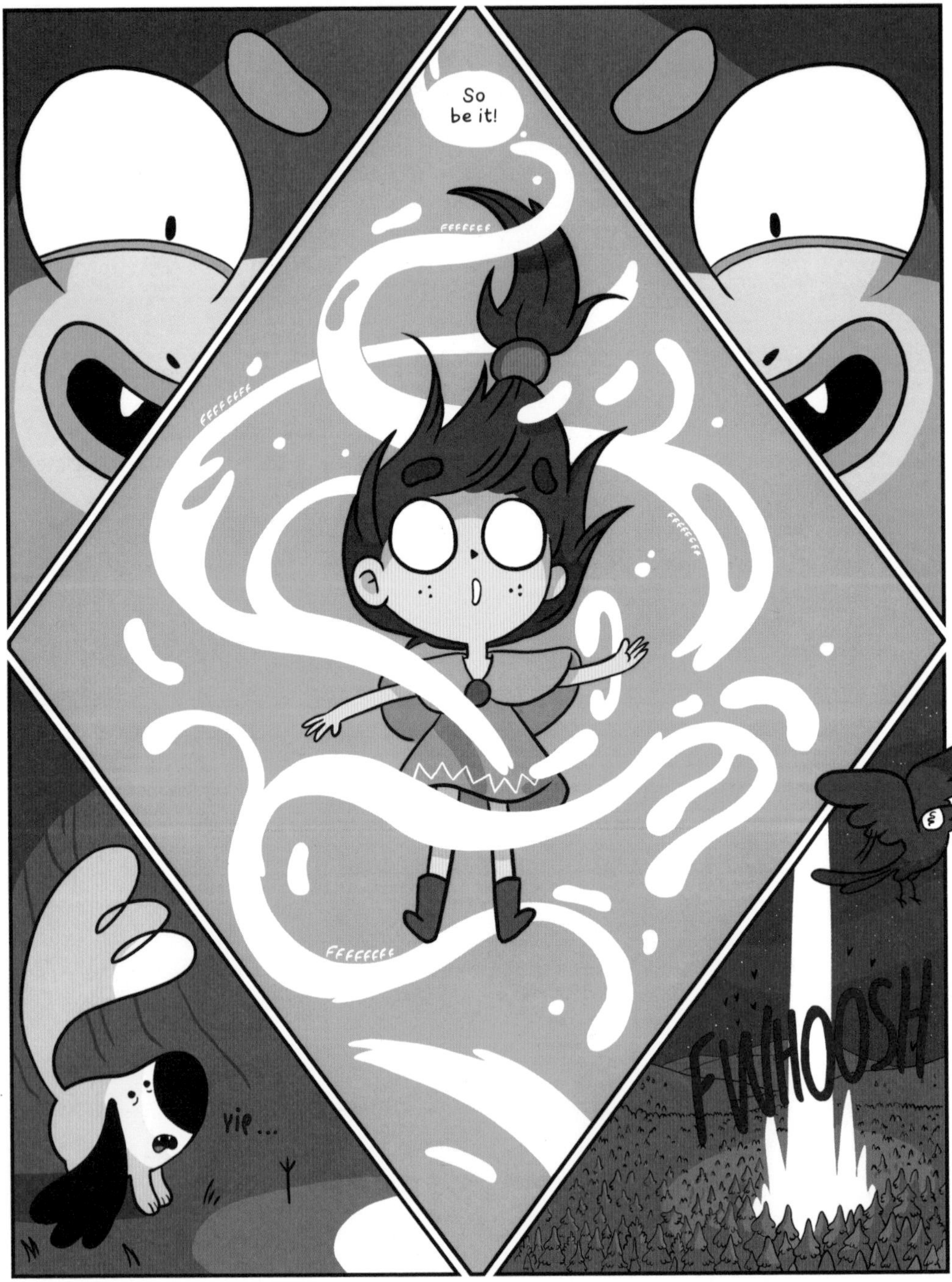

So be it!
FFFFFFF
FFFFFFFF
FFFFFFFF
FFFFFFFF
FWHOOSH
yip...

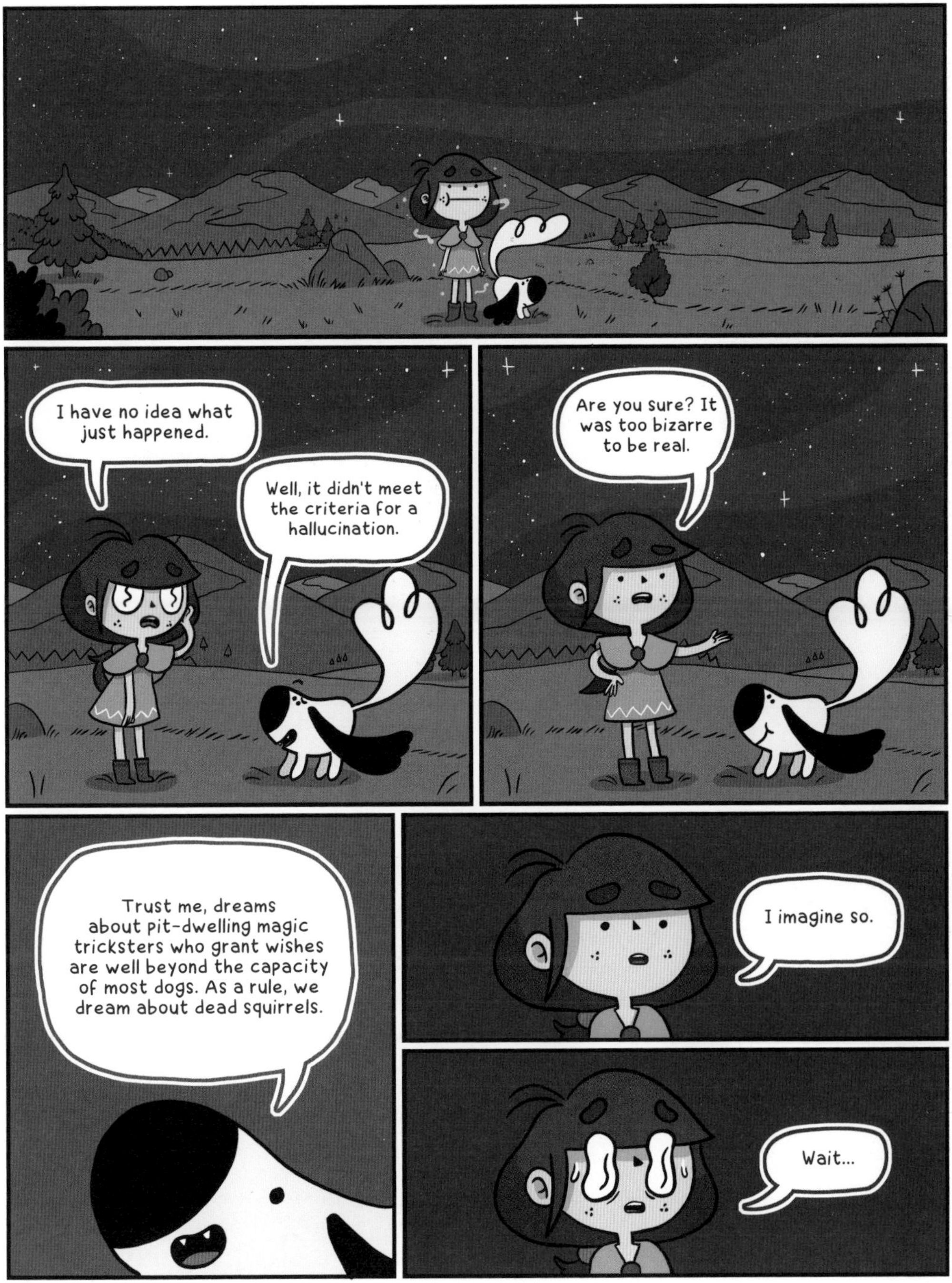
I have no idea what just happened.
Well, it didn't meet the criteria for a hallucination.
Are you sure? It was too bizarre to be real.
Trust me, dreams about pit-dwelling magic tricksters who grant wishes are well beyond the capacity of most dogs. As a rule, we dream about dead squirrels.
I imagine so.
Wait...

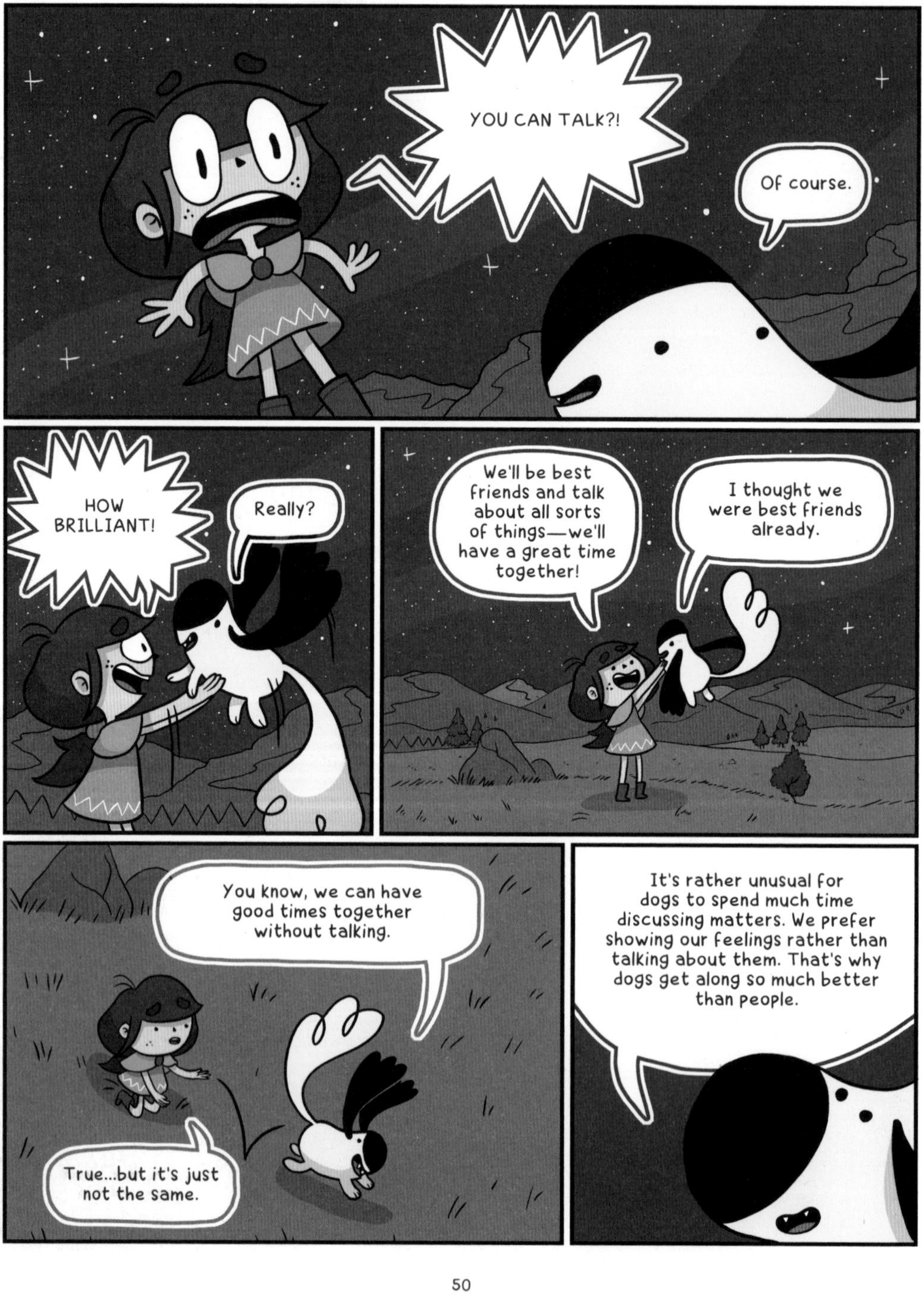

YOU CAN TALK?!
Of course.
HOW BRILLIANT!
Really?
We'll be best friends and talk about all sorts of things—we'll have a great time together!
I thought we were best friends already.
You know, we can have good times together without talking.
True...but it's just not the same.
It's rather unusual for dogs to spend much time discussing matters. We prefer showing our feelings rather than talking about them. That's why dogs get along so much better than people.

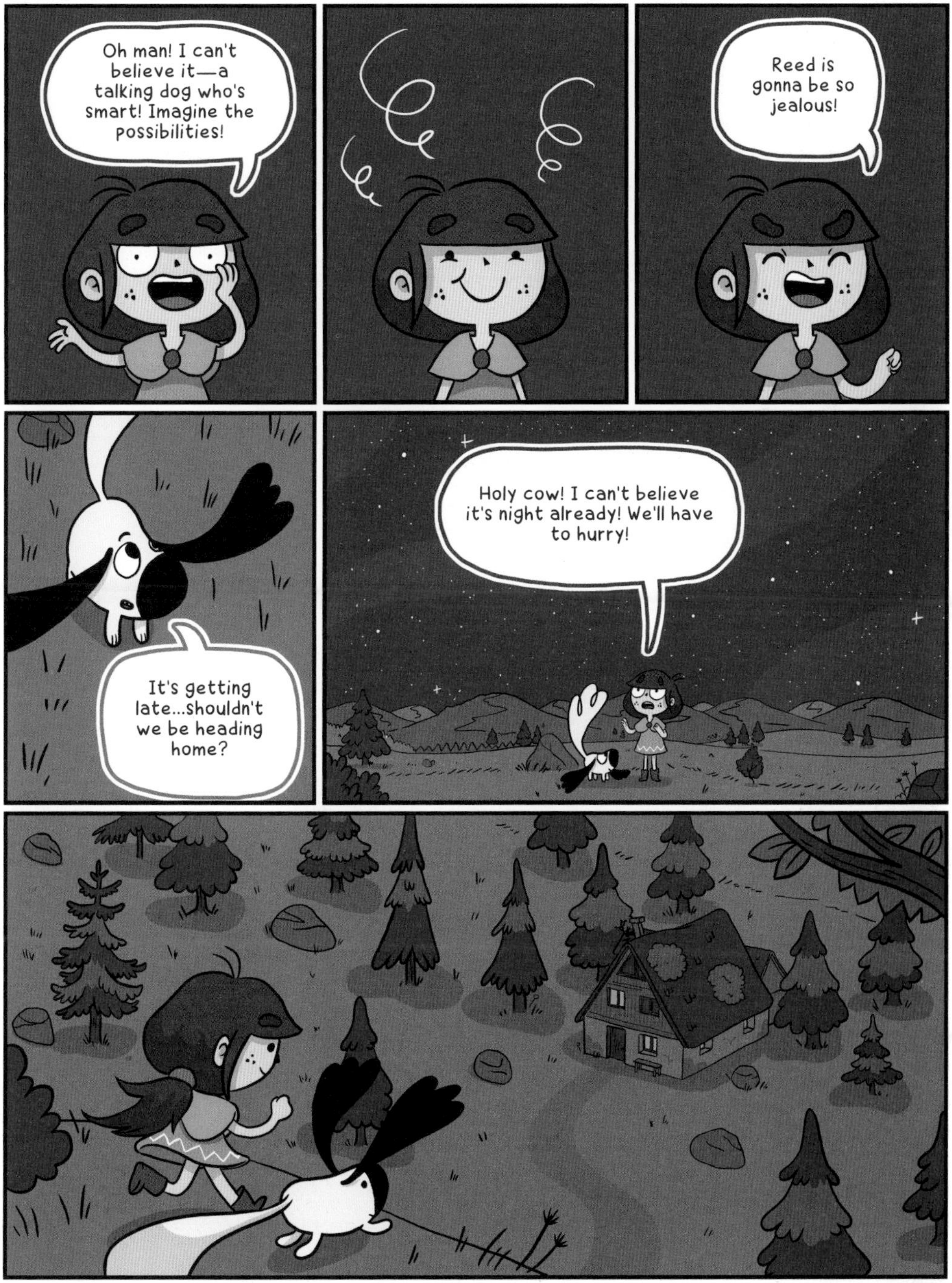
Oh man! I can't believe it—a talking dog who's smart! Imagine the possibilities!
Reed is gonna be so jealous!
It's getting late...shouldn't we be heading home?
Holy cow! I can't believe it's night already! We'll have to hurry!

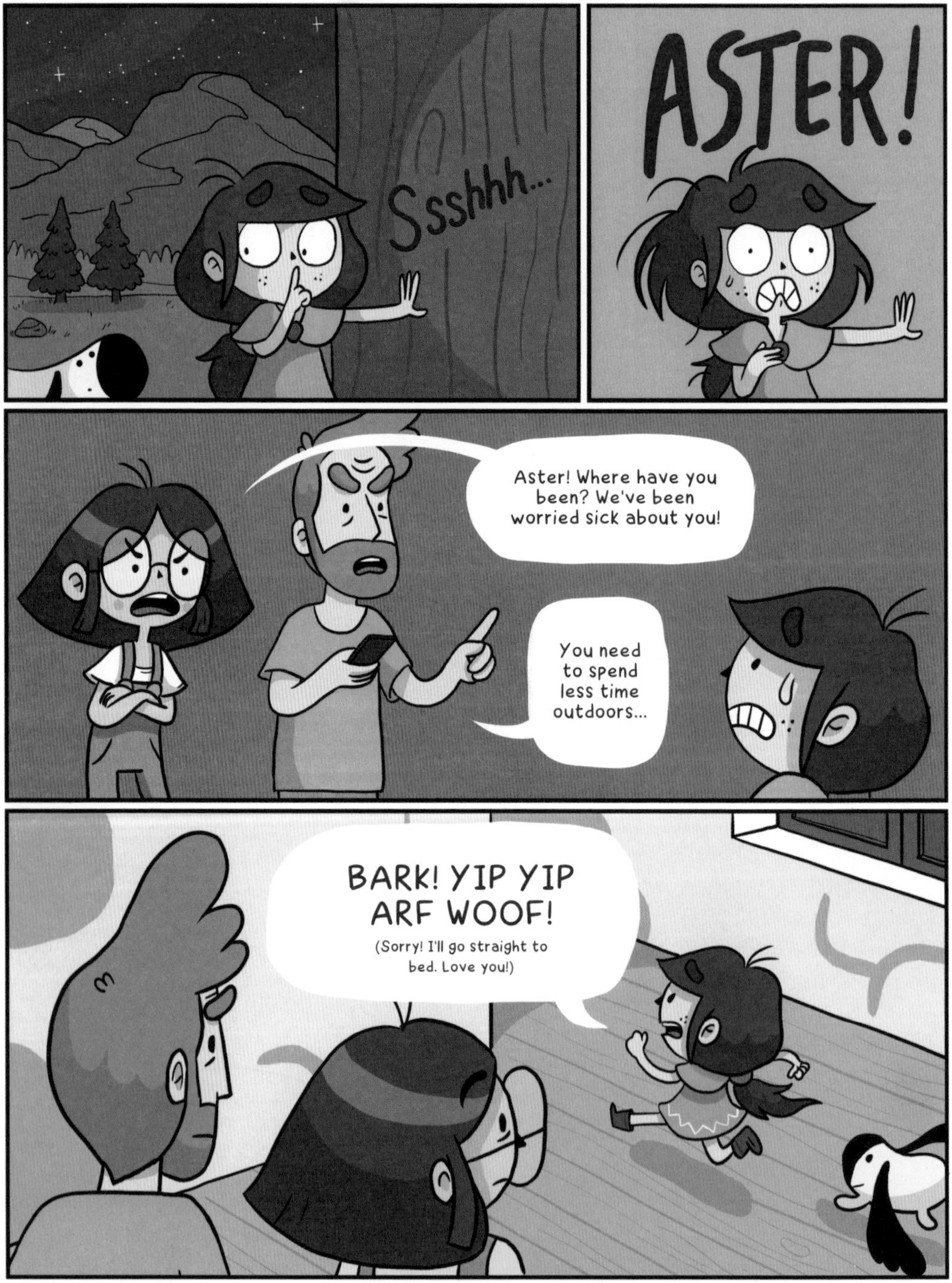
Ssshhh...
ASTER!
Aster! Where have you been? We've been worried sick about you!
You need to spend less time outdoors...
BARK! YIP YIP ARF WOOF!
(Sorry! I'll go straight to bed. Love you!)

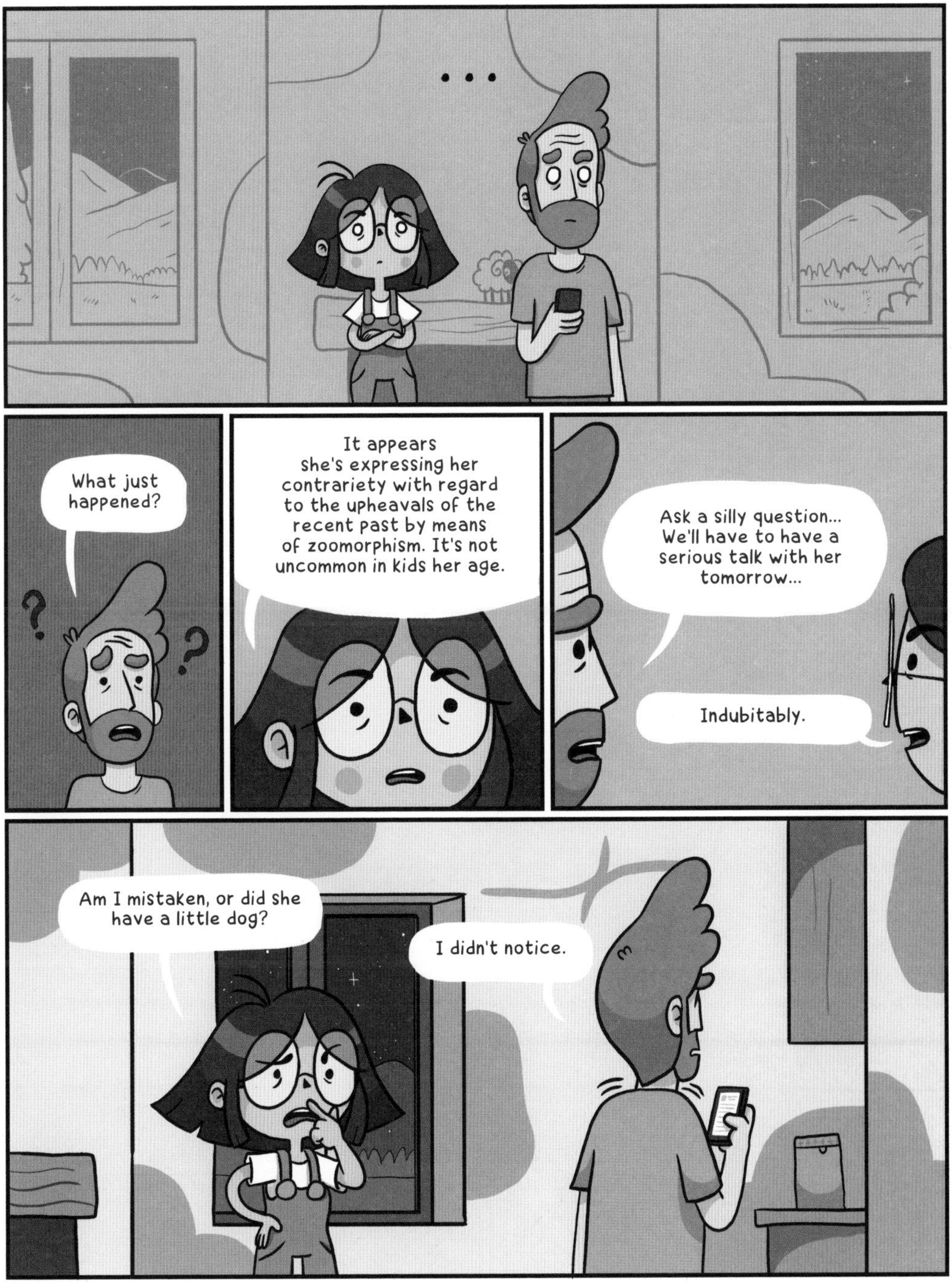
...
What just happened?
It appears she's expressing her contrariety with regard to the upheavals of the recent past by means of zoomorphism. It's not uncommon in kids her age.
Ask a silly question... We'll have to have a serious talk with her tomorrow...
Indubitably.
Am I mistaken, or did she have a little dog?
I didn't notice.

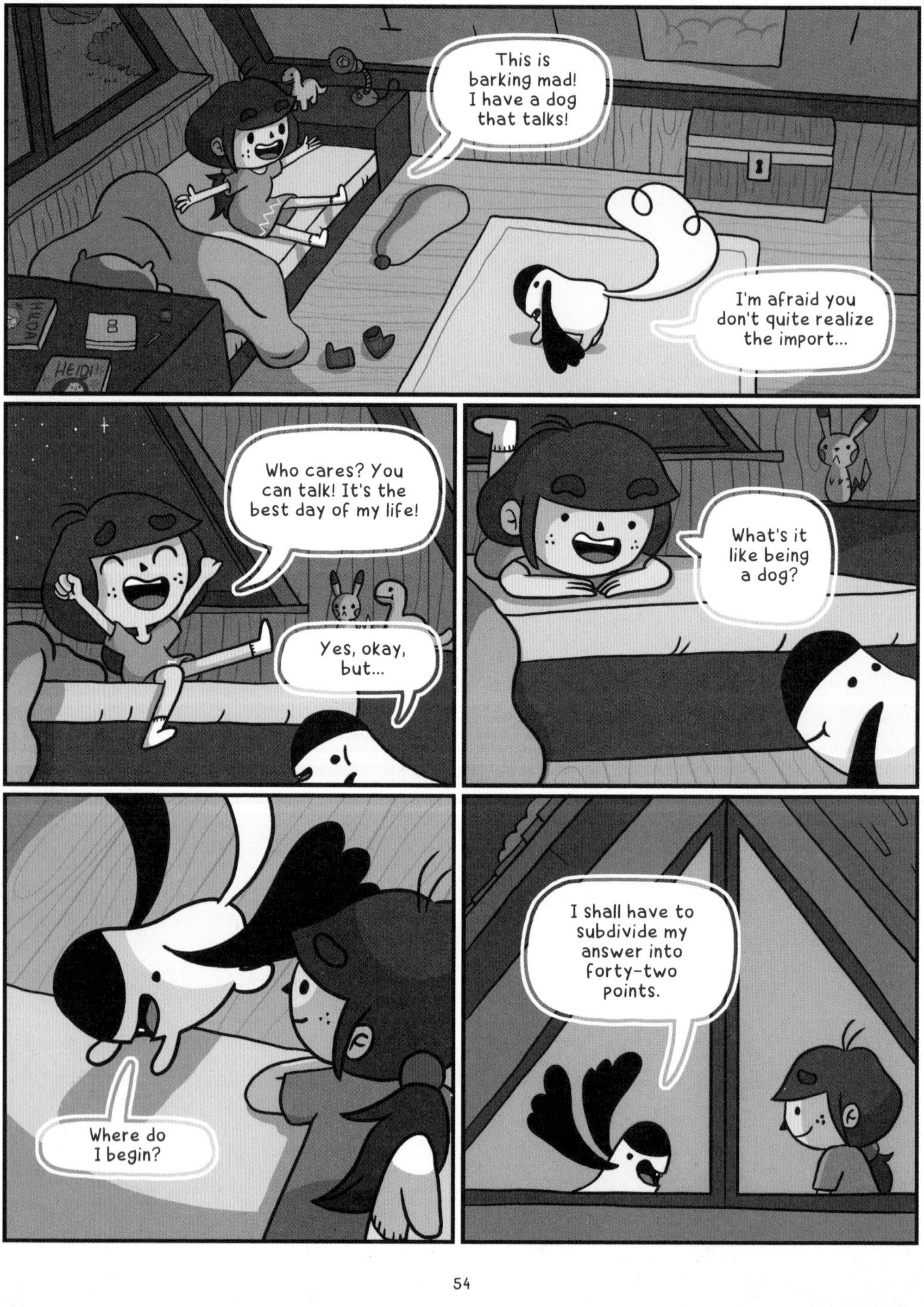
This is barking mad! I have a dog that talks!
I'm afraid you don't quite realize the import...
HILDA
HEIDI
Who cares? You can talk! It's the best day of my life!
Yes, okay, but...
What's it like being a dog?
Where do I begin?
I shall have to subdivide my answer into forty-two points.

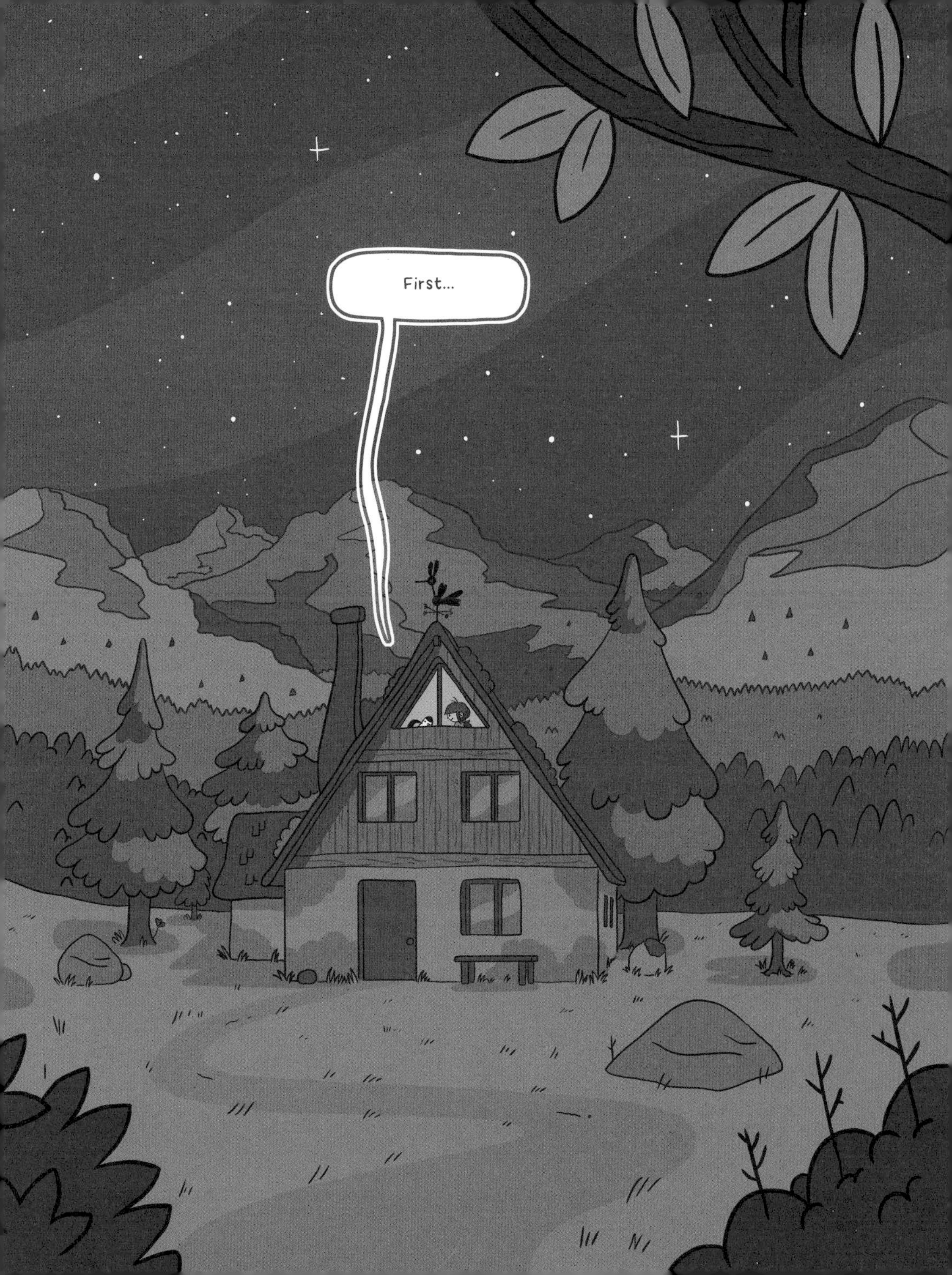
First...

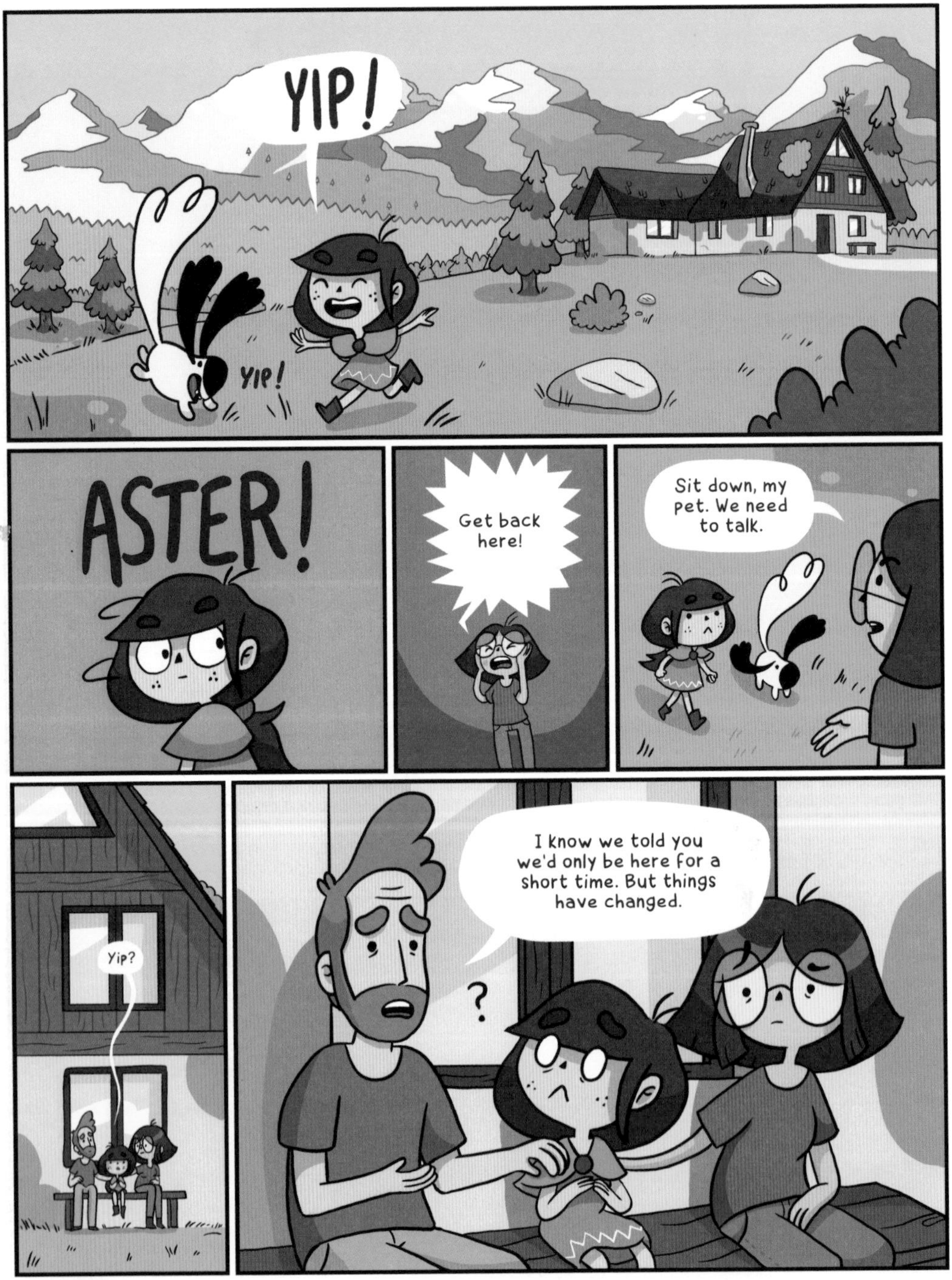
YIP!
YIP!
ASTER!
Get back here!
Sit down, my pet. We need to talk.
Yip?
I know we told you we'd only be here for a short time. But things have changed.
?

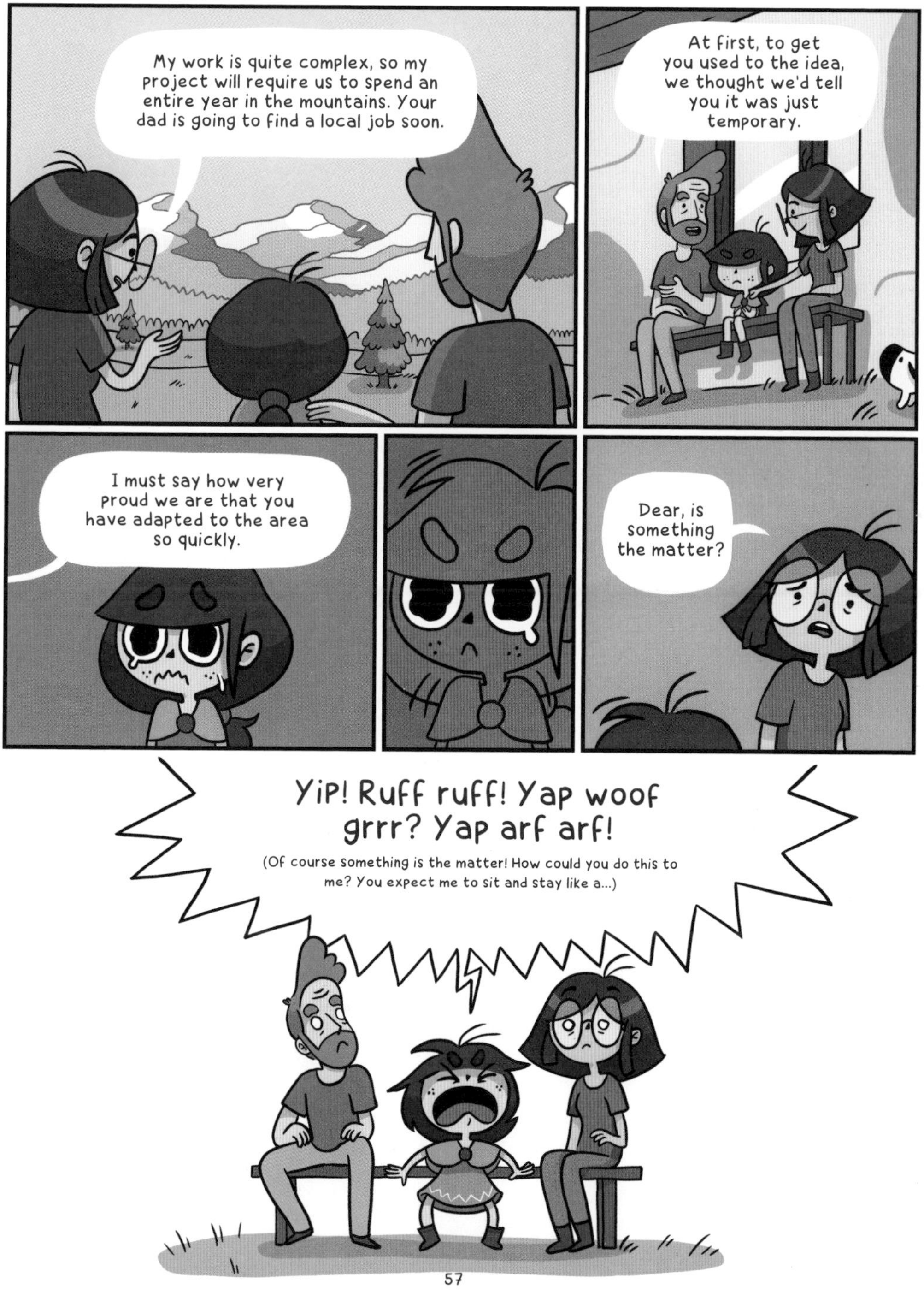
My work is quite complex, so my project will require us to spend an entire year in the mountains. Your dad is going to find a local job soon.
At first, to get you used to the idea, we thought we'd tell you it was just temporary.
I must say how very proud we are that you have adapted to the area so quickly.
Dear, is something the matter?
Yip! Ruff ruff! Yap woof grrr? Yap arf arf!
(Of course something is the matter! How could you do this to me? You expect me to sit and stay like a...)

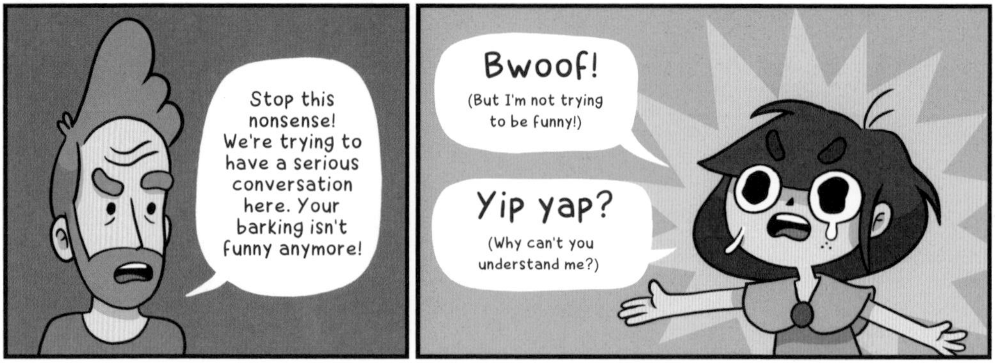
Stop this nonsense! We're trying to have a serious conversation here. Your barking isn't funny anymore!
Bwoof!
(But I'm not trying to be funny!)
Yip yap?
(Why can't you understand me?)

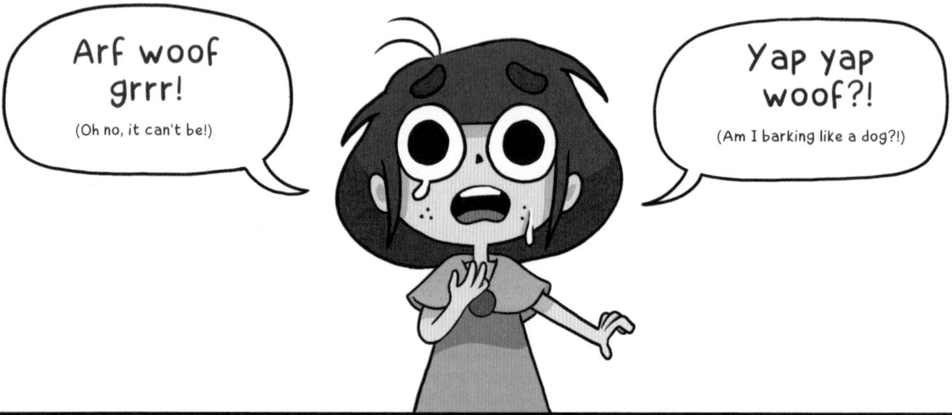
Arf woof grrr!
(Oh no, it can't be!)
Yap yap woof?!
(Am I barking like a dog?!)

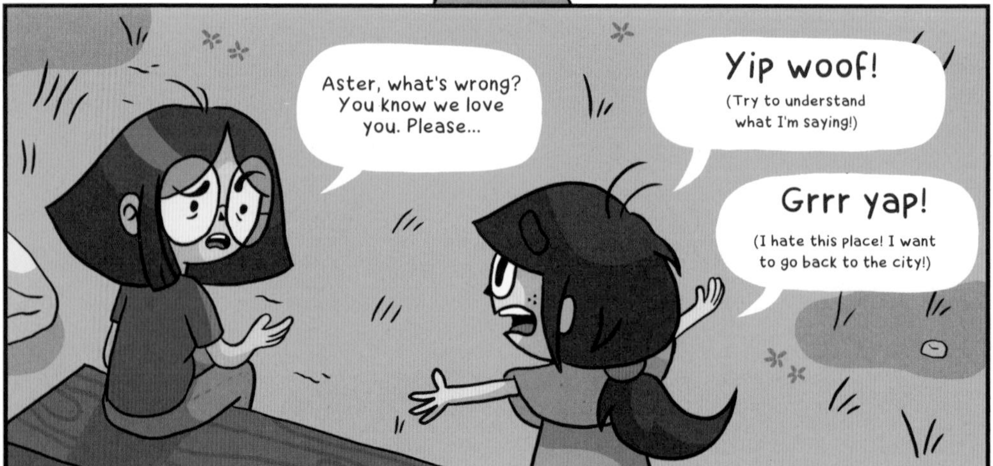
Aster, what's wrong? You know we love you. Please...
Yip woof!
(Try to understand what I'm saying!)
Grrr yap!
(I hate this place! I want to go back to the city!)

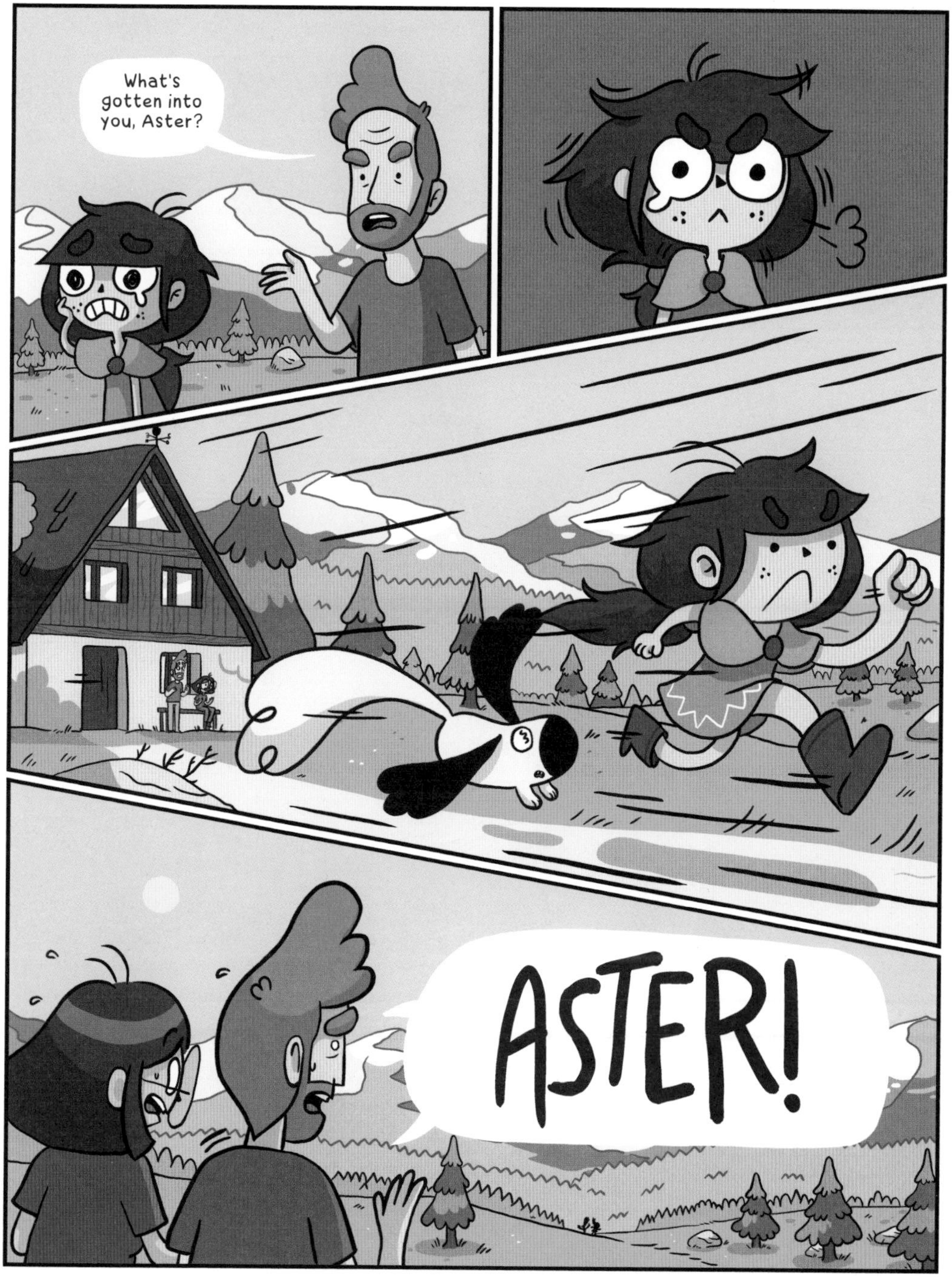
What's gotten into you, Aster?
ASTER!

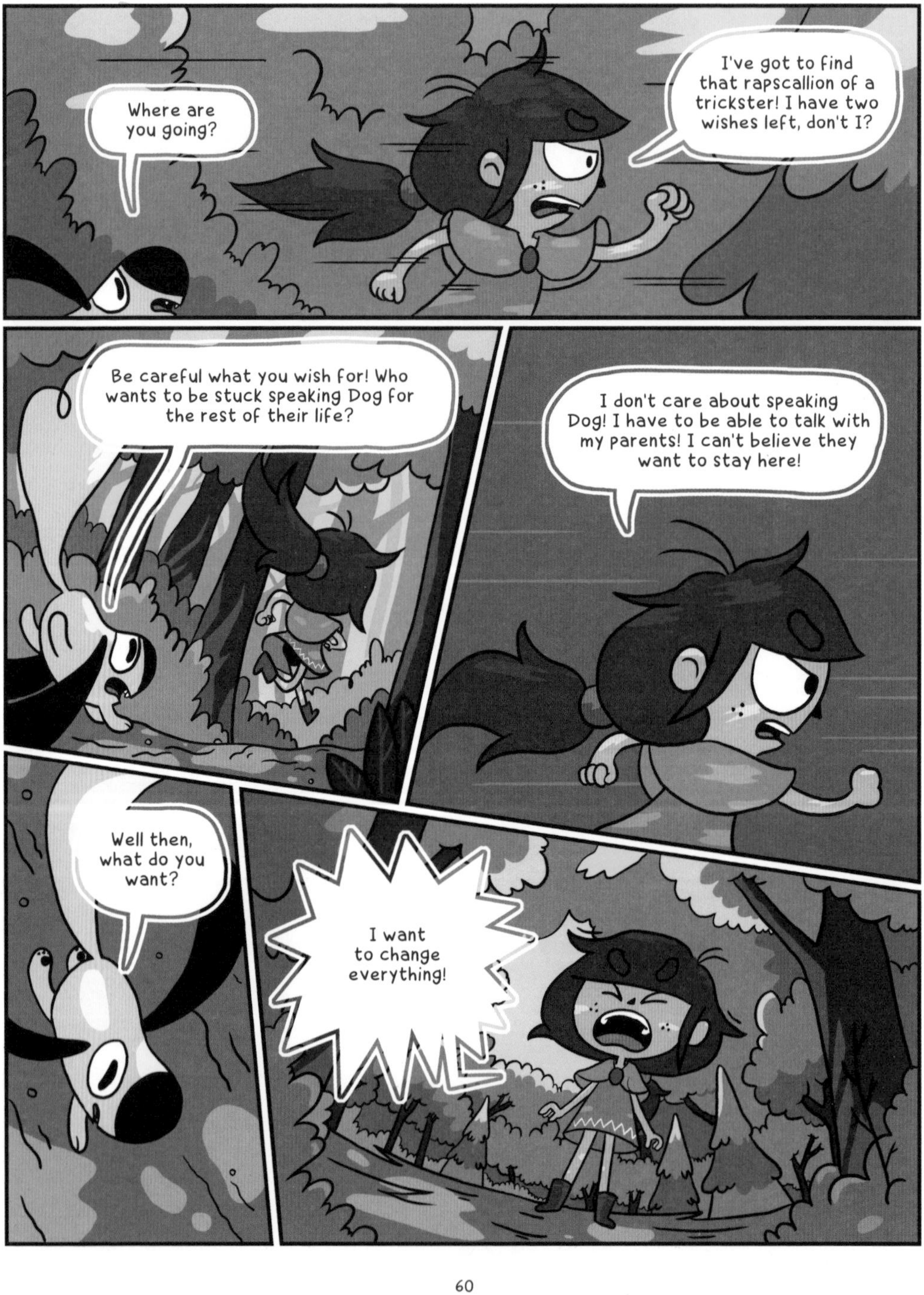
Where are you going?
I've got to find that rapscallion of a trickster! I have two wishes left, don't I?
Be careful what you wish for! Who wants to be stuck speaking Dog for the rest of their life?
I don't care about speaking Dog! I have to be able to talk with my parents! I can't believe they want to stay here!
Well then, what do you want?
I want to change everything!

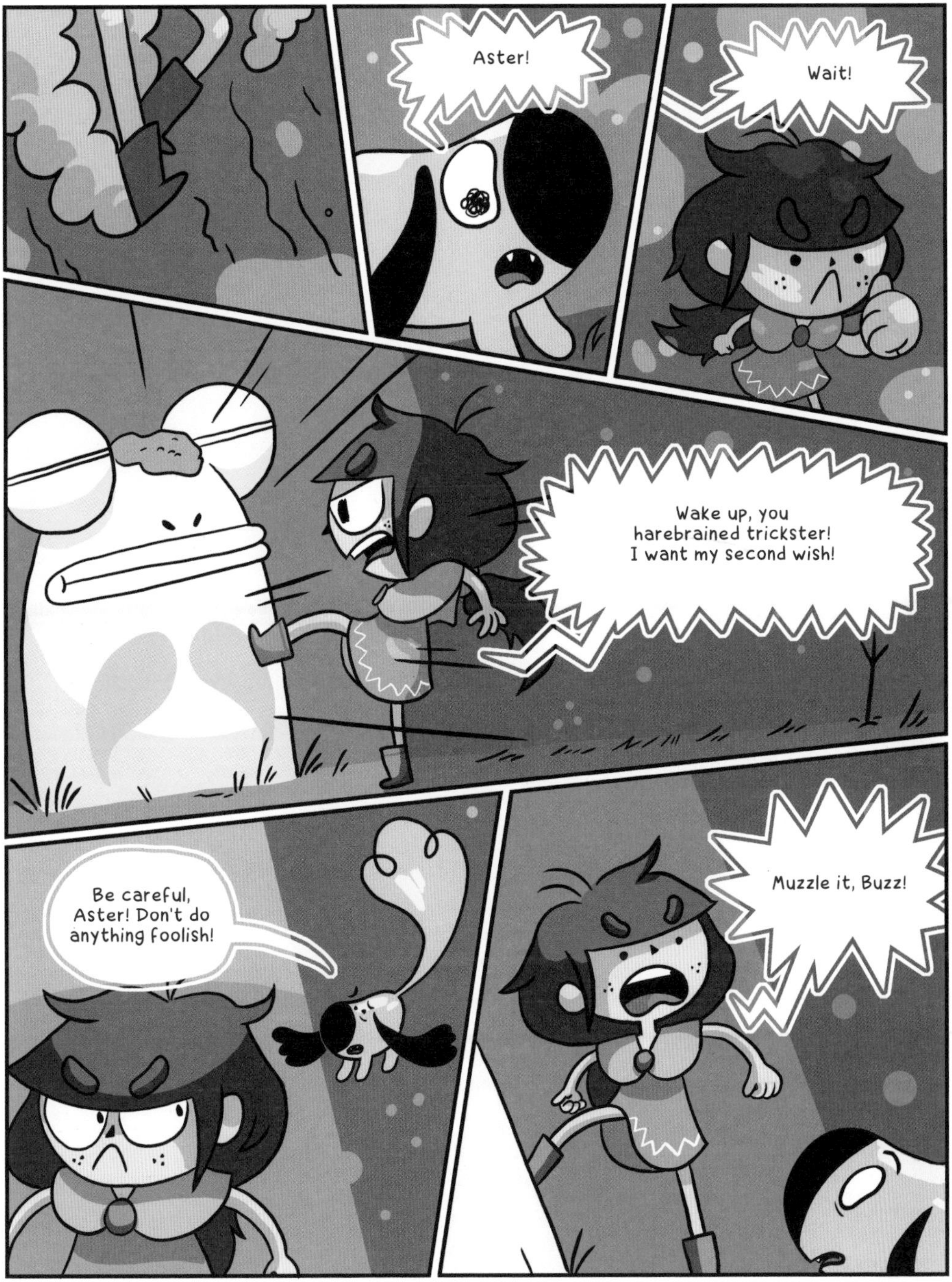
Aster!
Wait!
Wake up, you harebrained trickster! I want my second wish!
Be careful, Aster! Don't do anything foolish!
Muzzle it, Buzz!

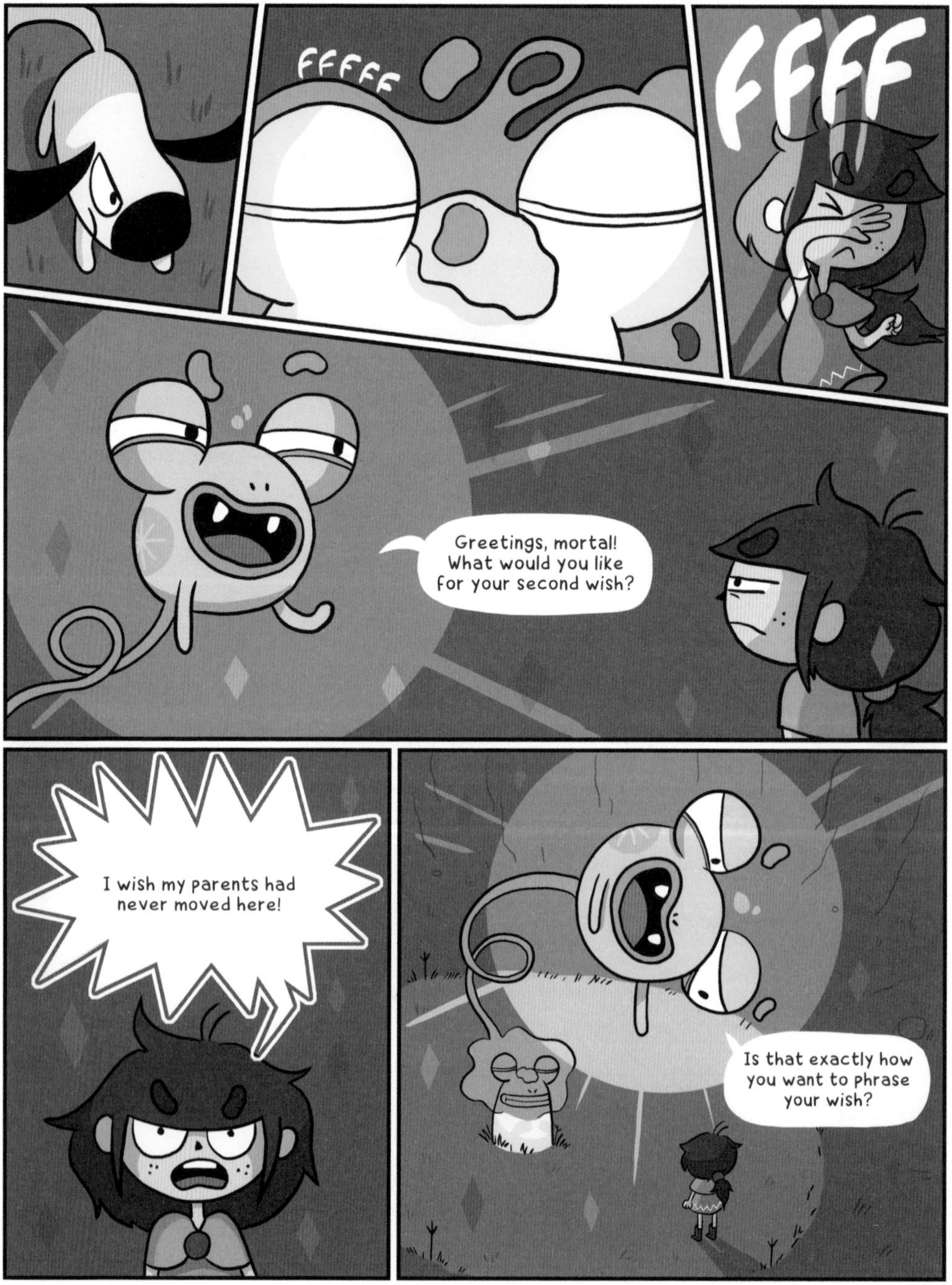
FFFFF
FFFF
Greetings, mortal! What would you like for your second wish?
I wish my parents had never moved here!
Is that exactly how you want to phrase your wish?

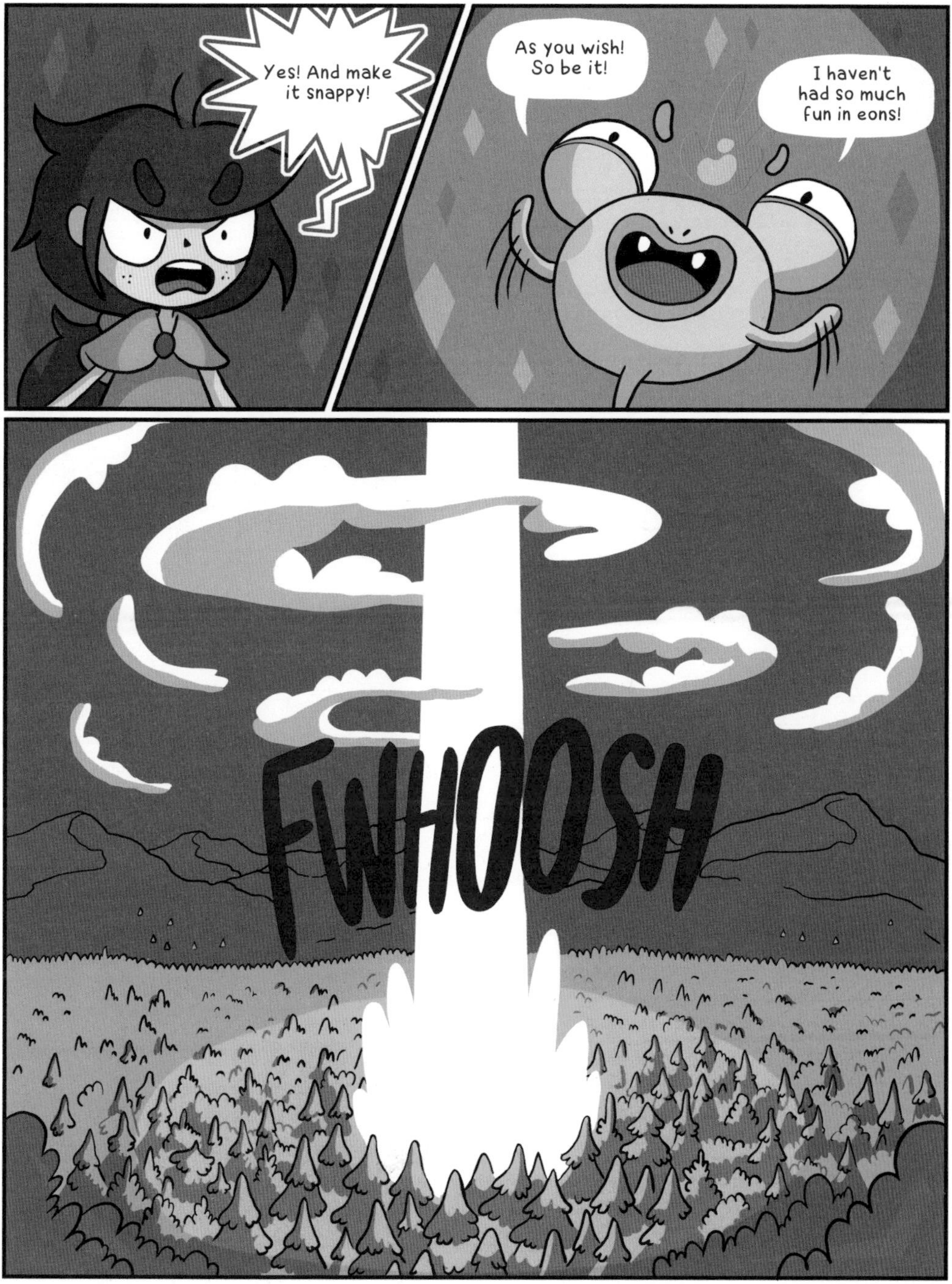
Yes! And make it snappy!
As you wish! So be it!
I haven't had so much fun in eons!
FWHOOSH

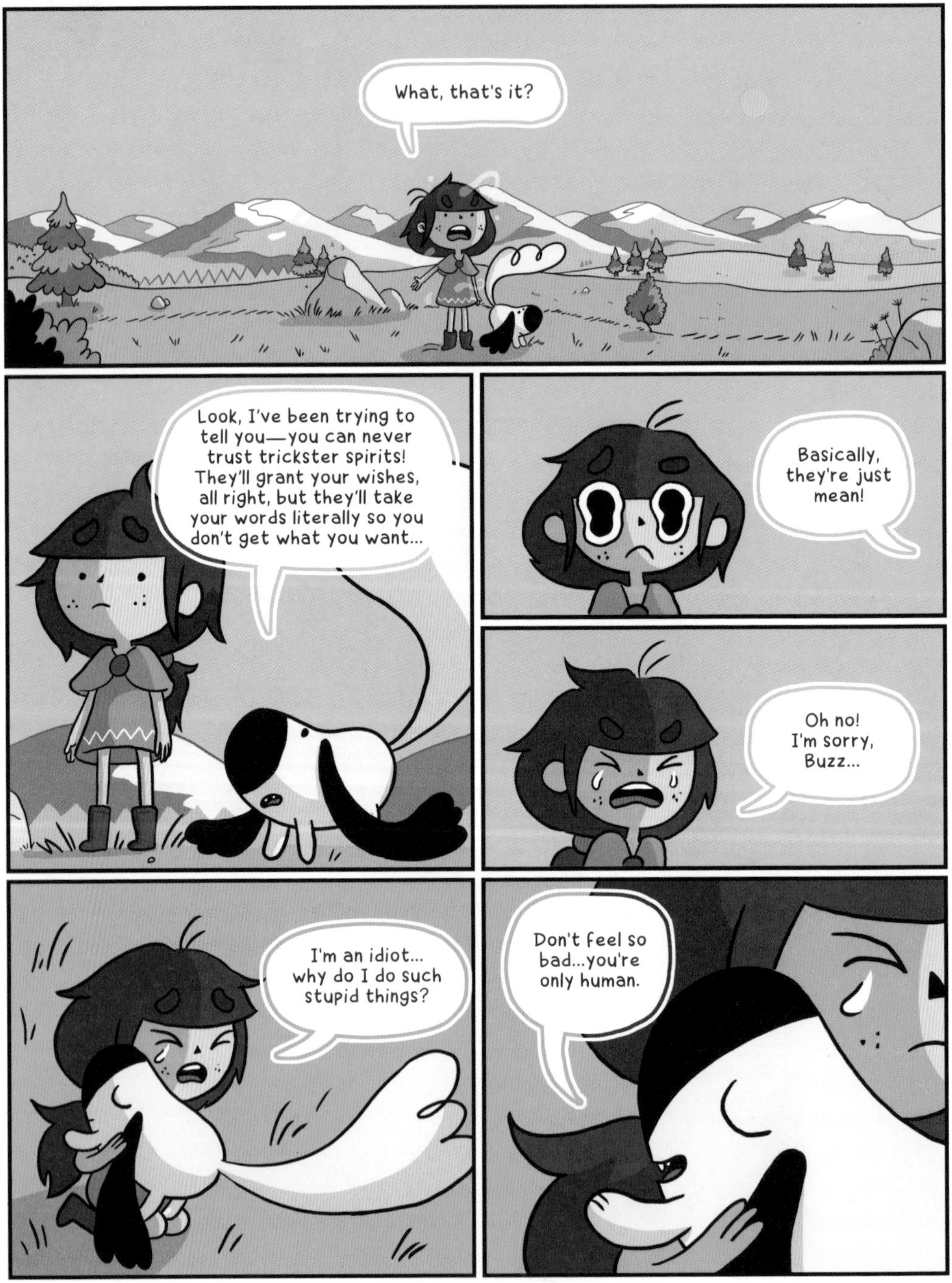
What, that's it?
Look, I've been trying to tell you—you can never trust trickster spirits! They'll grant your wishes, all right, but they'll take your words literally so you don't get what you want...
Basically, they're just mean!
Oh no! I'm sorry, Buzz...
I'm an idiot... why do I do such stupid things?
Don't feel so bad...you're only human.

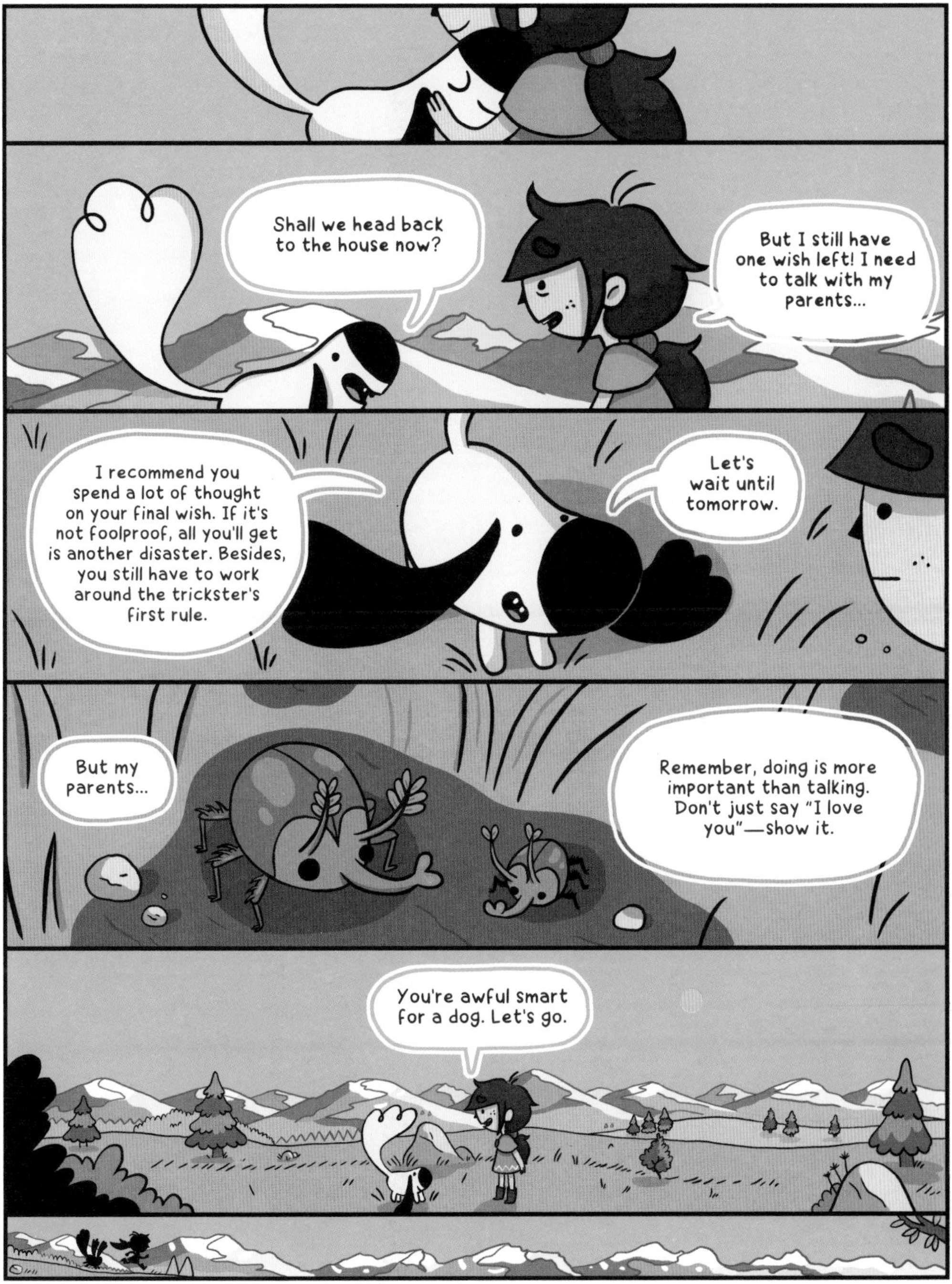
Shall we head back to the house now?
But I still have one wish left! I need to talk with my parents...
I recommend you spend a lot of thought on your final wish. If it's not foolproof, all you'll get is another disaster. Besides, you still have to work around the trickster's first rule.
Let's wait until tomorrow.
But my parents...
Remember, doing is more important than talking. Don't just say "I love you"—show it.
You're awful smart for a dog. Let's go.

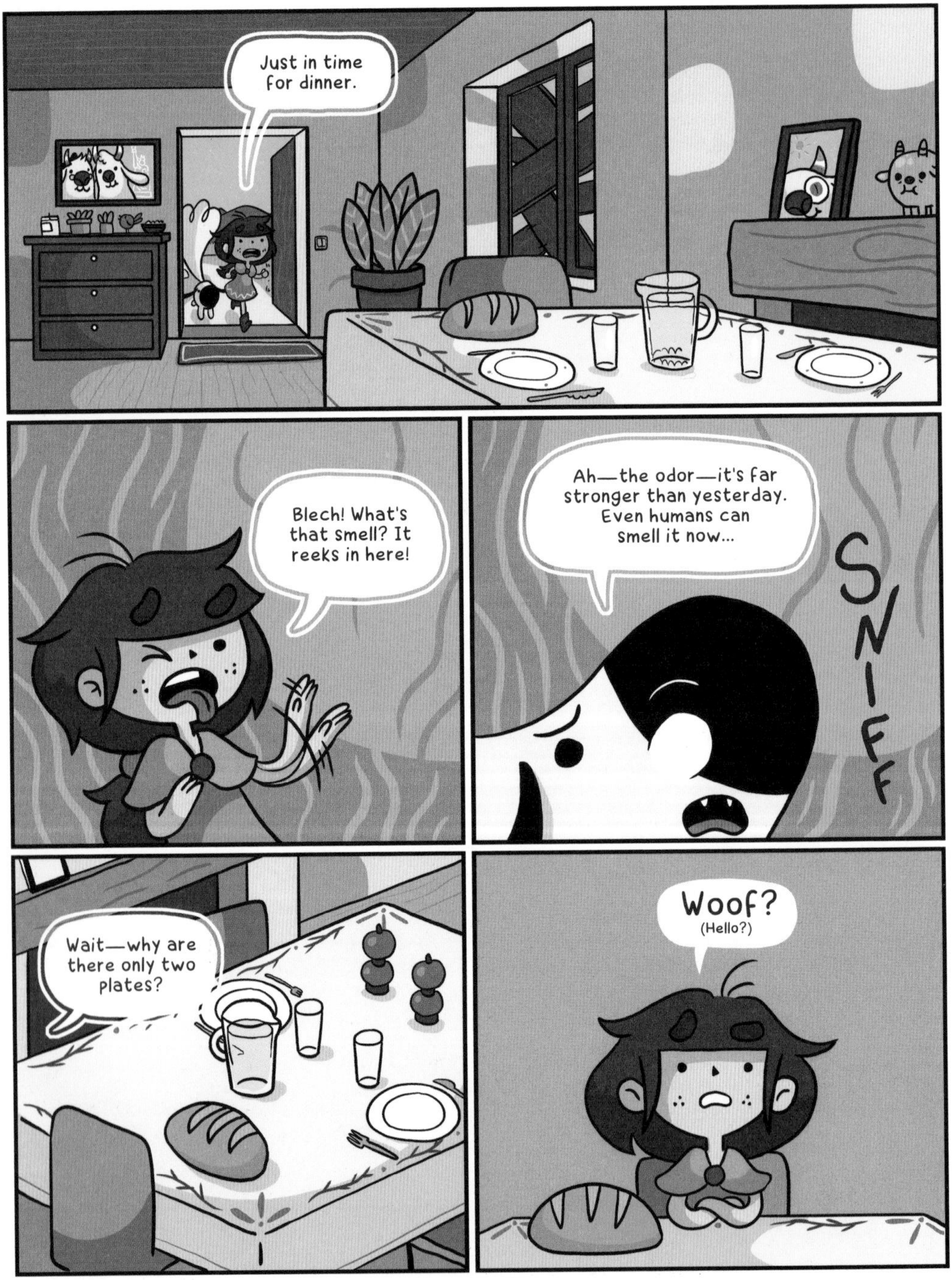
Just in time for dinner.
Blech! What's that smell? It reeks in here!
Ah—the odor—it's far stronger than yesterday. Even humans can smell it now...
SNIFF
Wait—why are there only two plates?
Woof?
(Hello?)

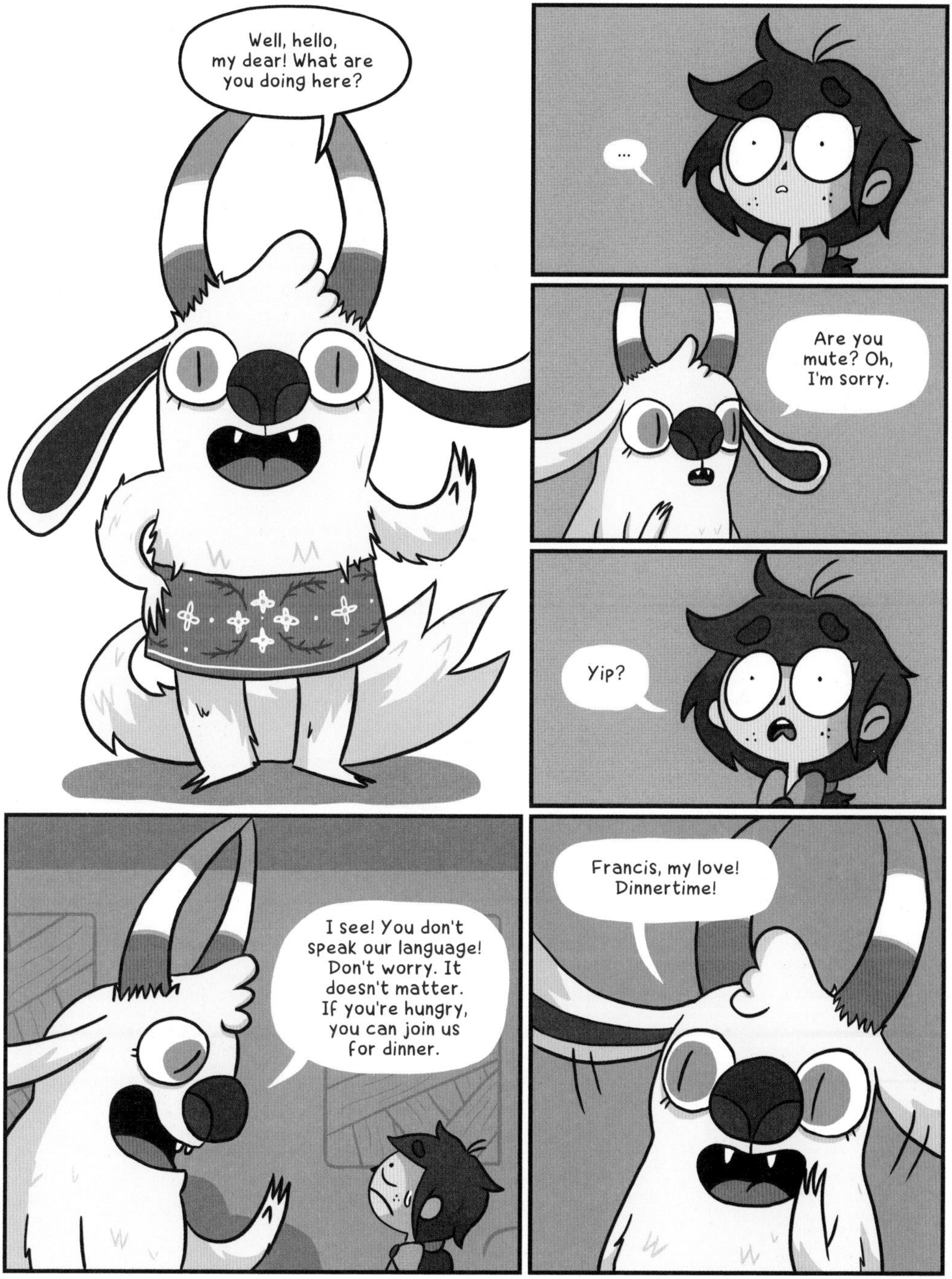
Well, hello, my dear! What are you doing here?
...
Are you mute? Oh, I'm sorry.
Yip?
I see! You don't speak our language! Don't worry. It doesn't matter. If you're hungry, you can join us for dinner.
Francis, my love! Dinnertime!

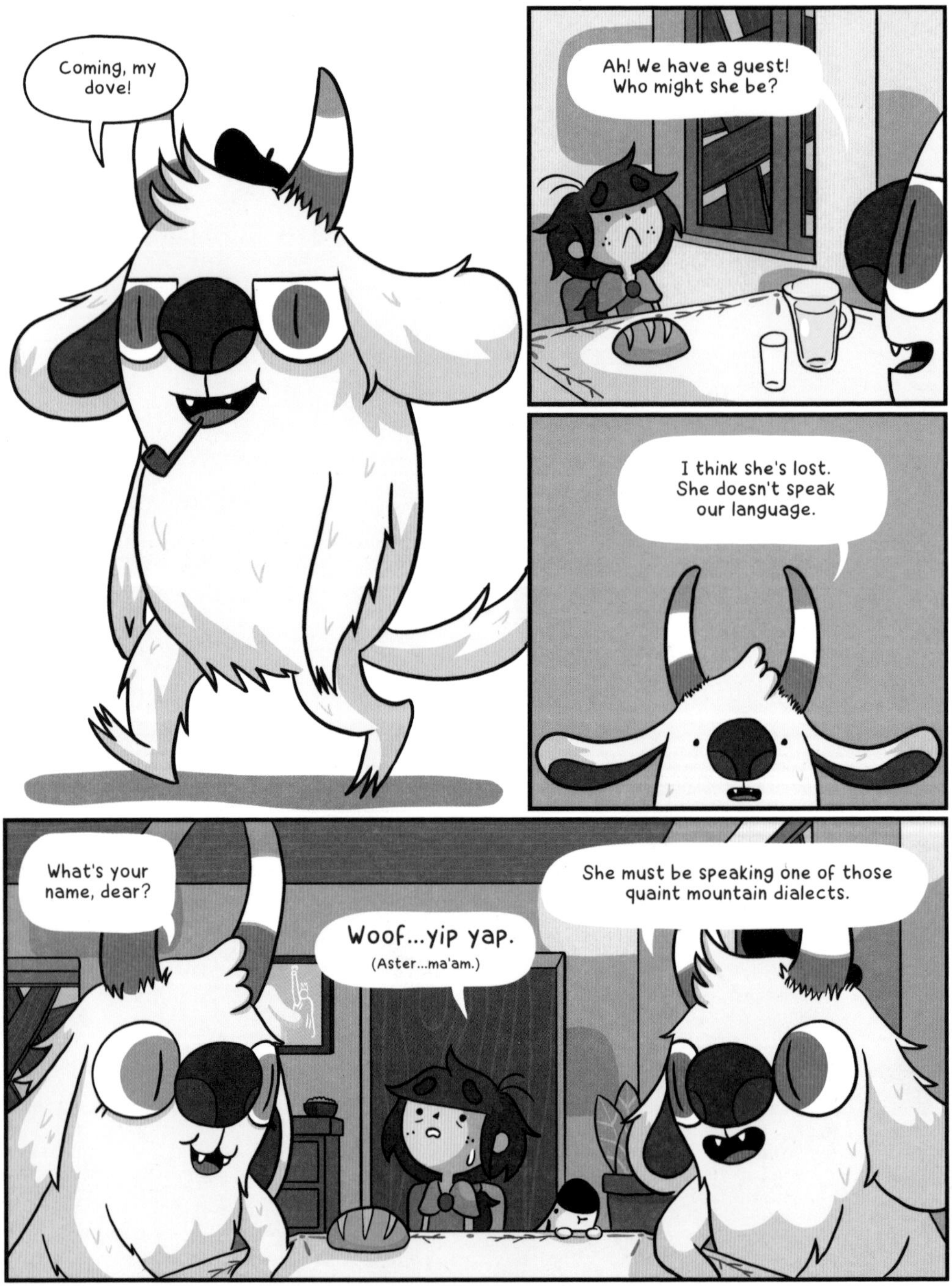

Coming, my dove!
Ah! We have a guest! Who might she be?
I think she's lost. She doesn't speak our language.
What's your name, dear?
Woof...yip yap.
(Aster...ma'am.)
She must be speaking one of those quaint mountain dialects.

I must say, it's curiously refreshing to have a nice conversation with one of the natives. Usually, they run away with bloodcurdling shrieks!

Come now, Francis, we said we weren't going to mention that incident again.

I know we can't do anything about it, but it's still rather irksome.

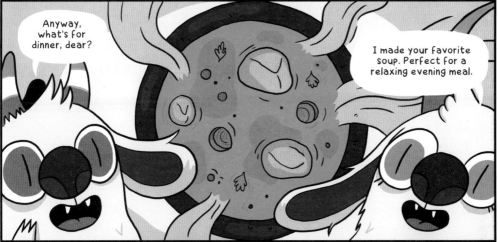

Anyway, what's for dinner, dear?

I made your favorite soup. Perfect for a relaxing evening meal.

Buzz, what's going on here?

Well, since your wish has been granted, these must be the former occupants of your house.

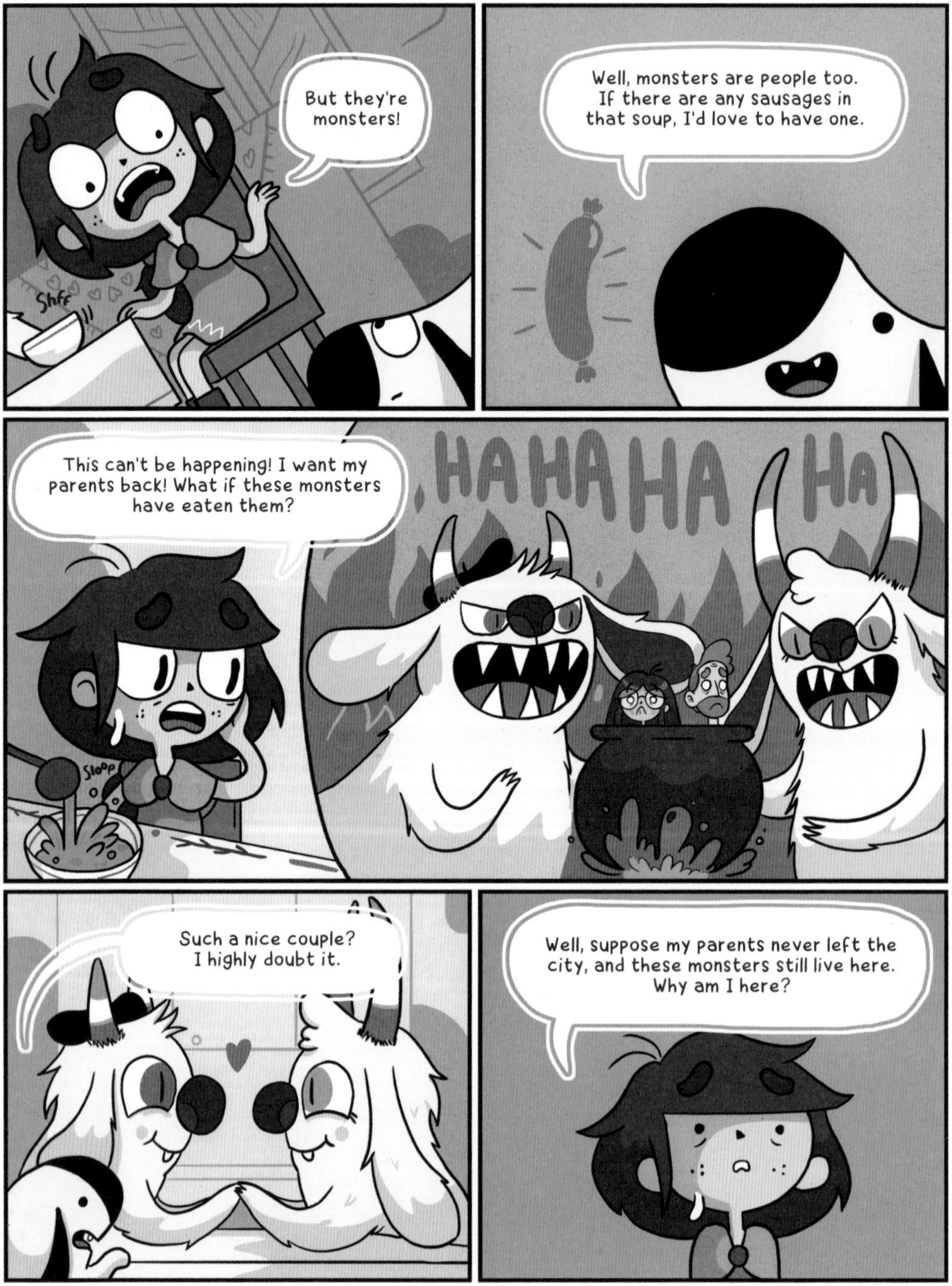
But they're monsters!
Shff
Well, monsters are people too. If there are any sausages in that soup, I'd love to have one.
This can't be happening! I want my parents back! What if these monsters have eaten them?
HAHAHA HA
Slopp
Such a nice couple? I highly doubt it.
Well, suppose my parents never left the city, and these monsters still live here. Why am I here?

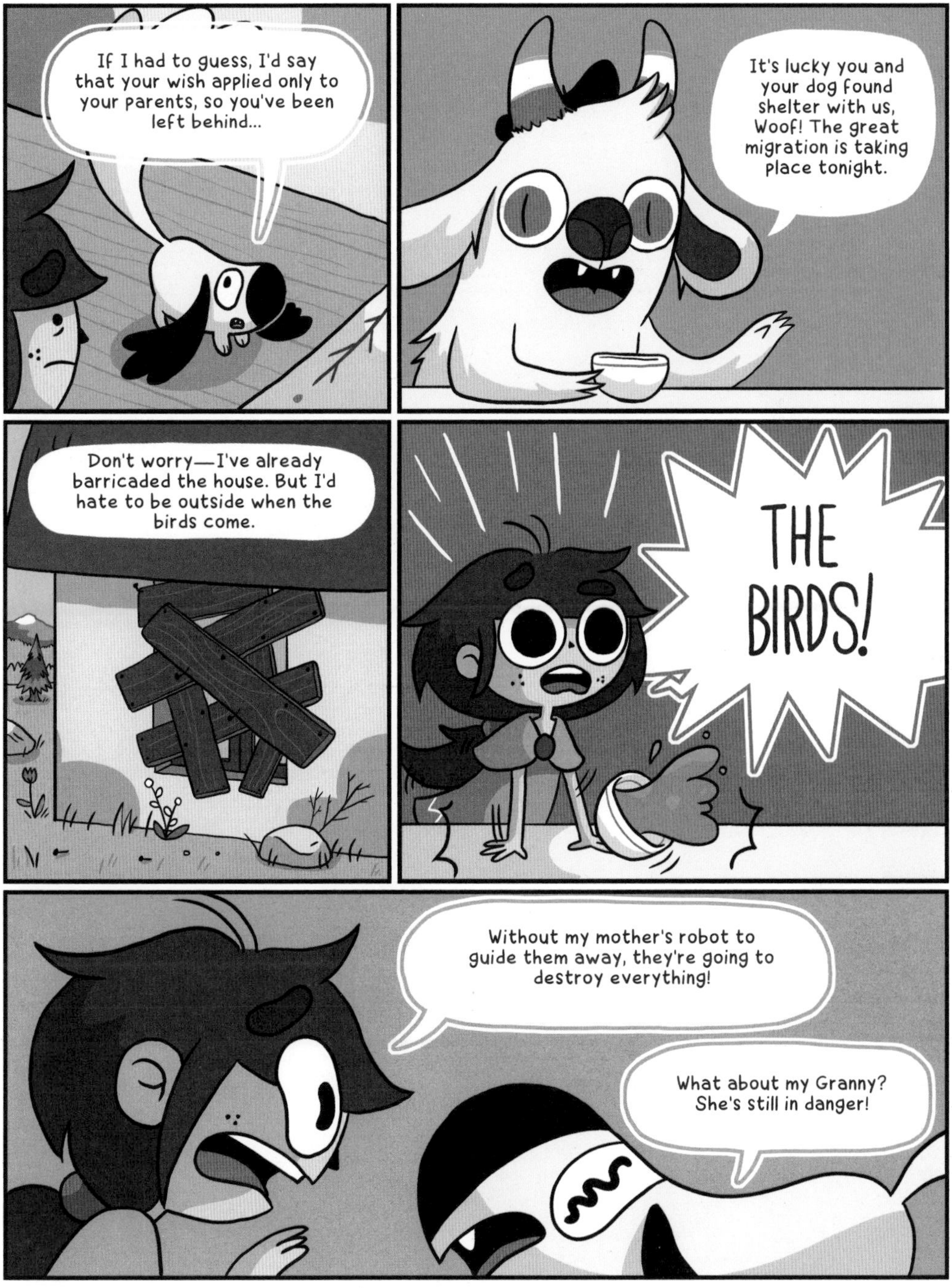
If I had to guess, I'd say that your wish applied only to your parents, so you've been left behind...
It's lucky you and your dog found shelter with us, Woof! The great migration is taking place tonight.
Don't worry—I've already barricaded the house. But I'd hate to be outside when the birds come.
THE BIRDS!
Without my mother's robot to guide them away, they're going to destroy everything!
What about my Granny? She's still in danger!

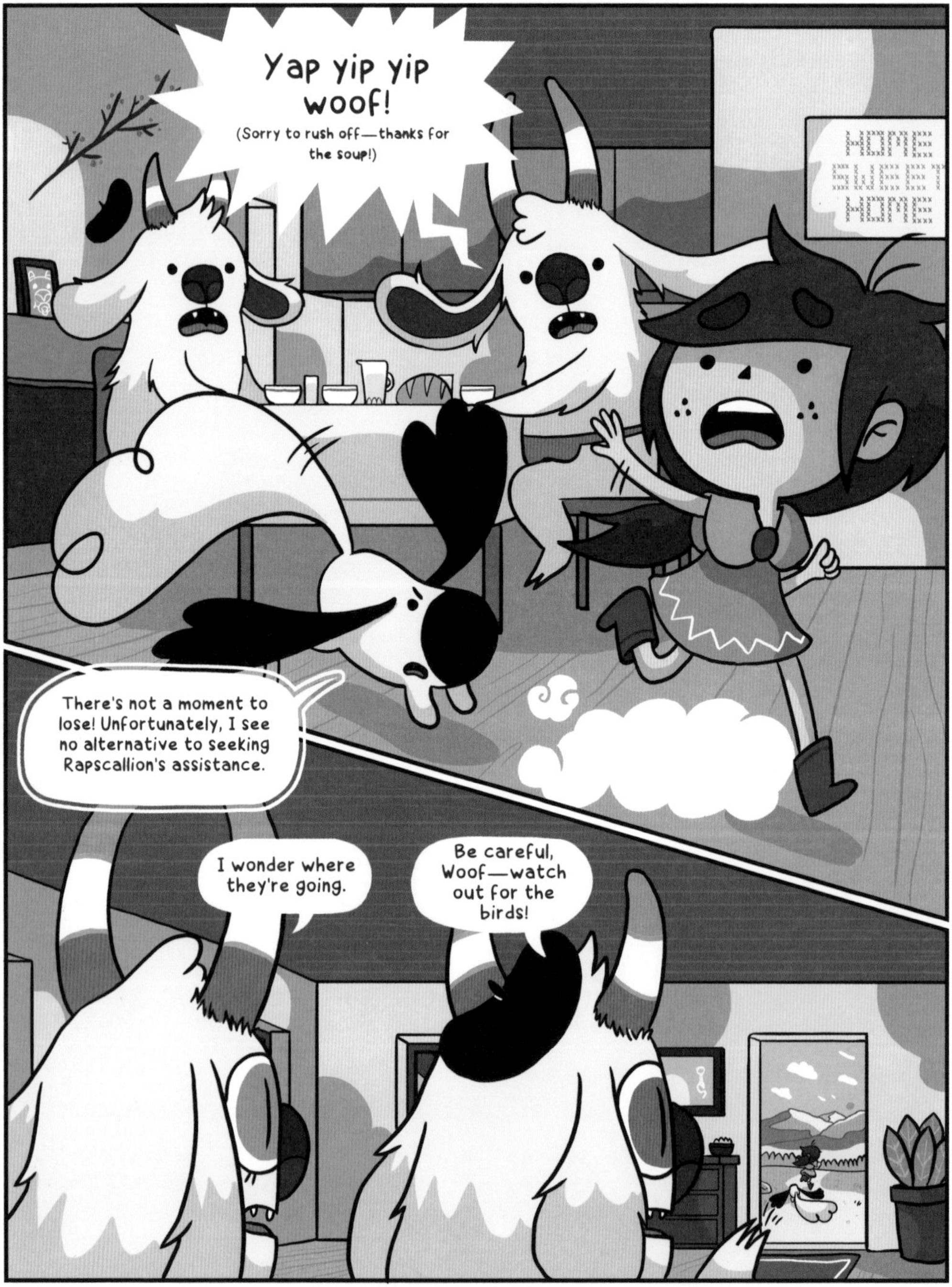

Yap yip yip woof!
(Sorry to rush off—thanks for the soup!)
There's not a moment to lose! Unfortunately, I see no alternative to seeking Rapscallion's assistance.
I wonder where they're going.
Be careful, Woof—watch out for the birds!

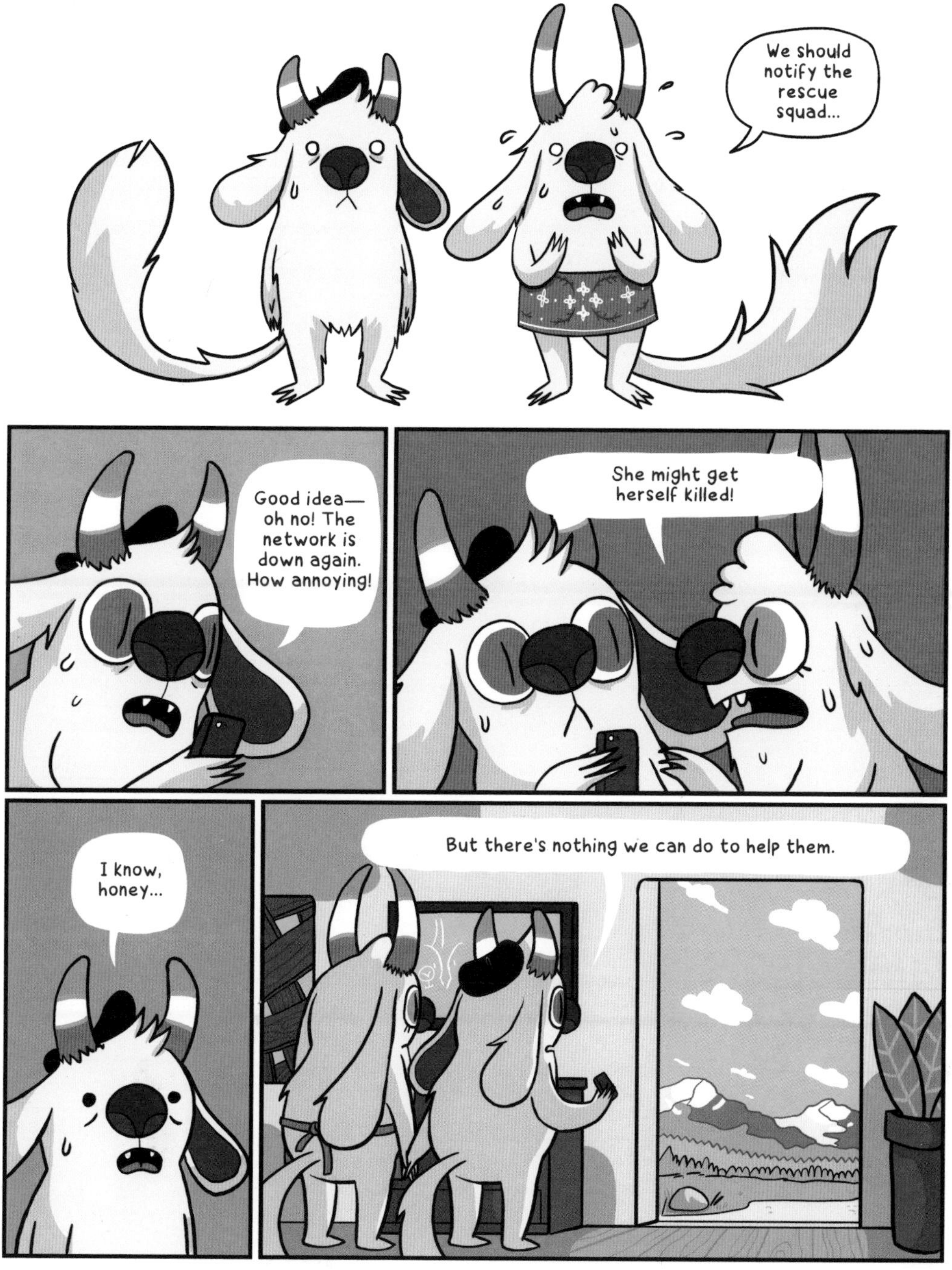

We should notify the rescue squad...
Good idea— oh no! The network is down again. How annoying!
She might get herself killed!
I know, honey...
But there's nothing we can do to help them.

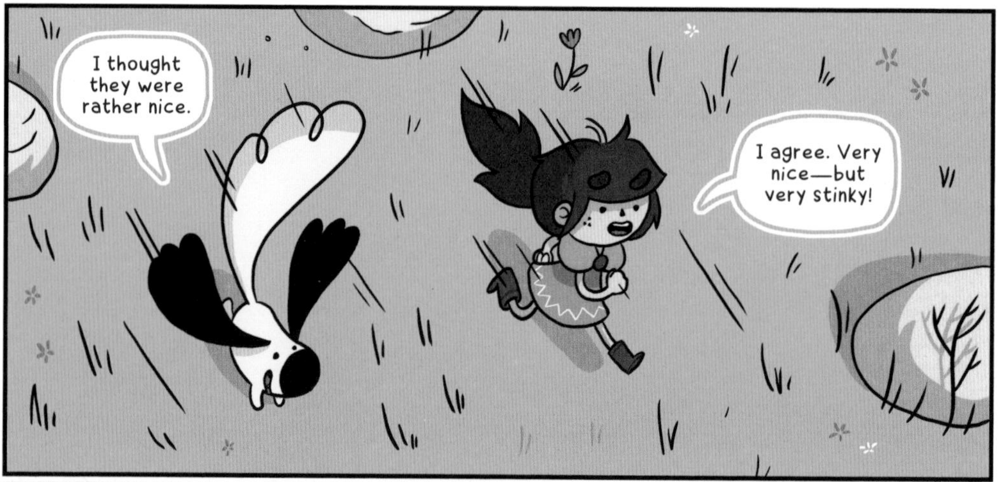
I thought they were rather nice.
I agree. Very nice—but very stinky!

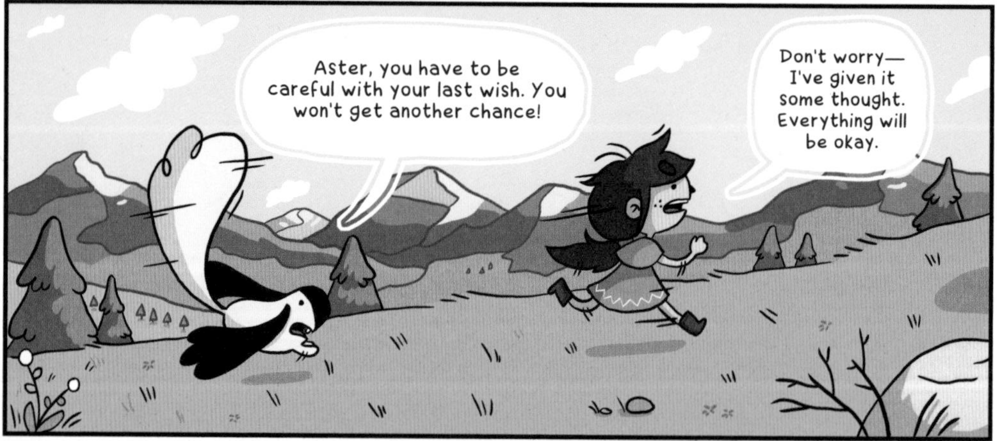
Aster, you have to be careful with your last wish. You won't get another chance!
Don't worry— I've given it some thought. Everything will be okay.

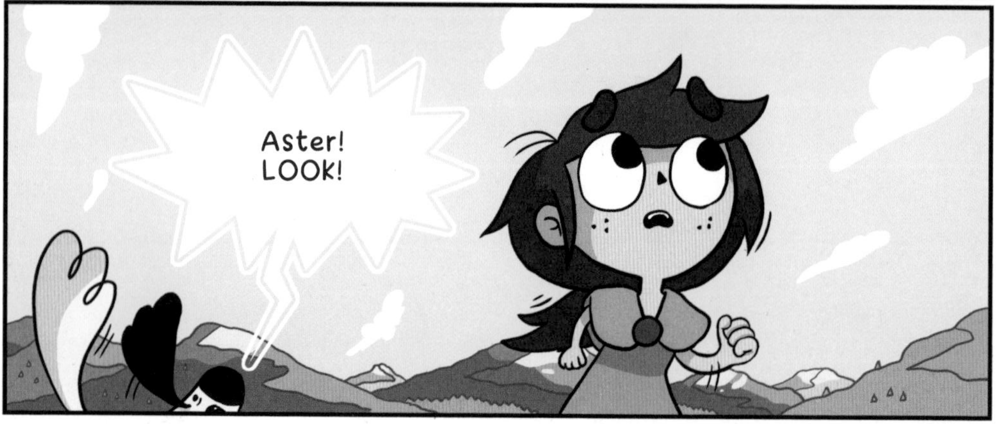
Aster! LOOK!

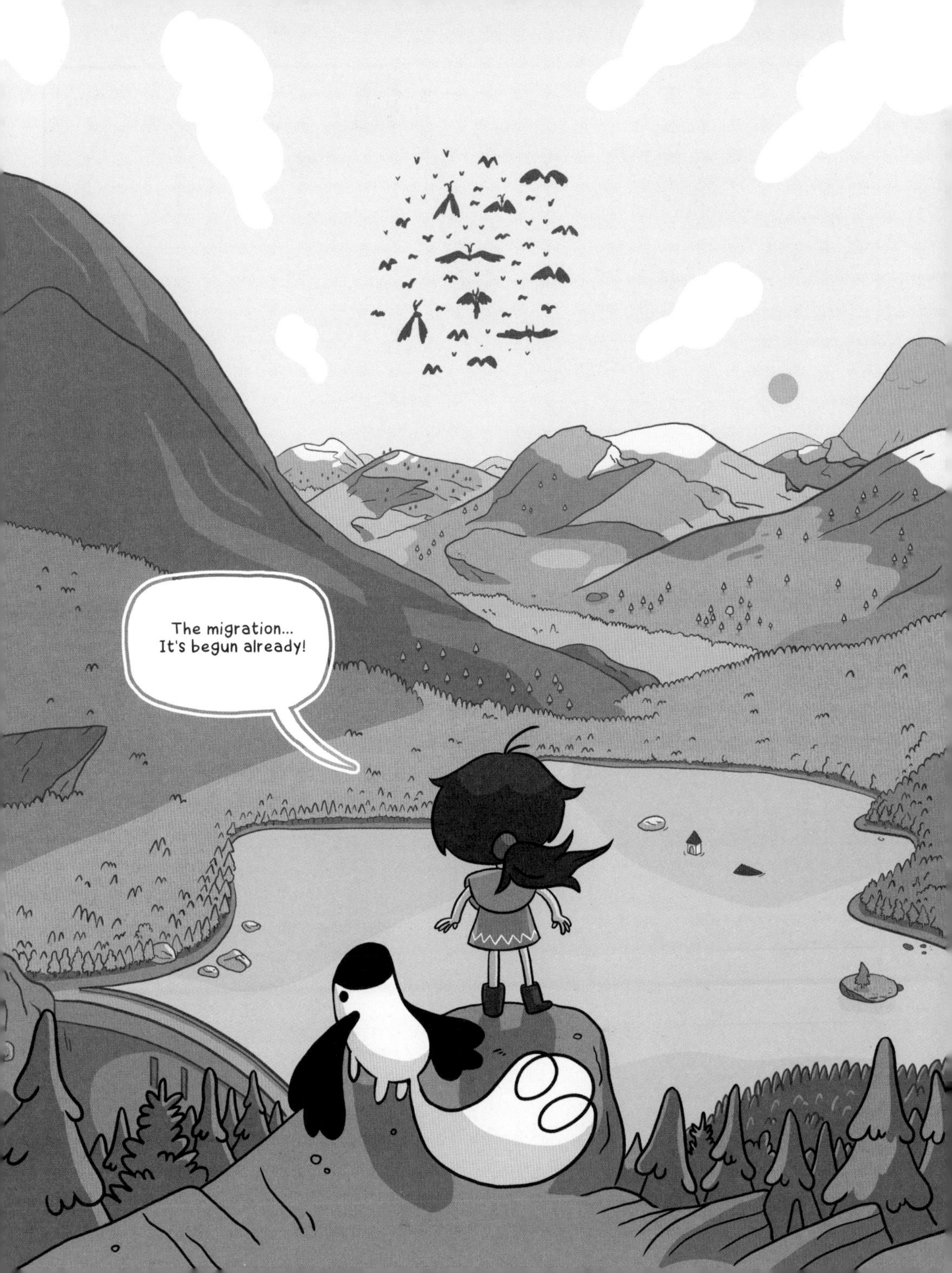
The migration... It's begun already!

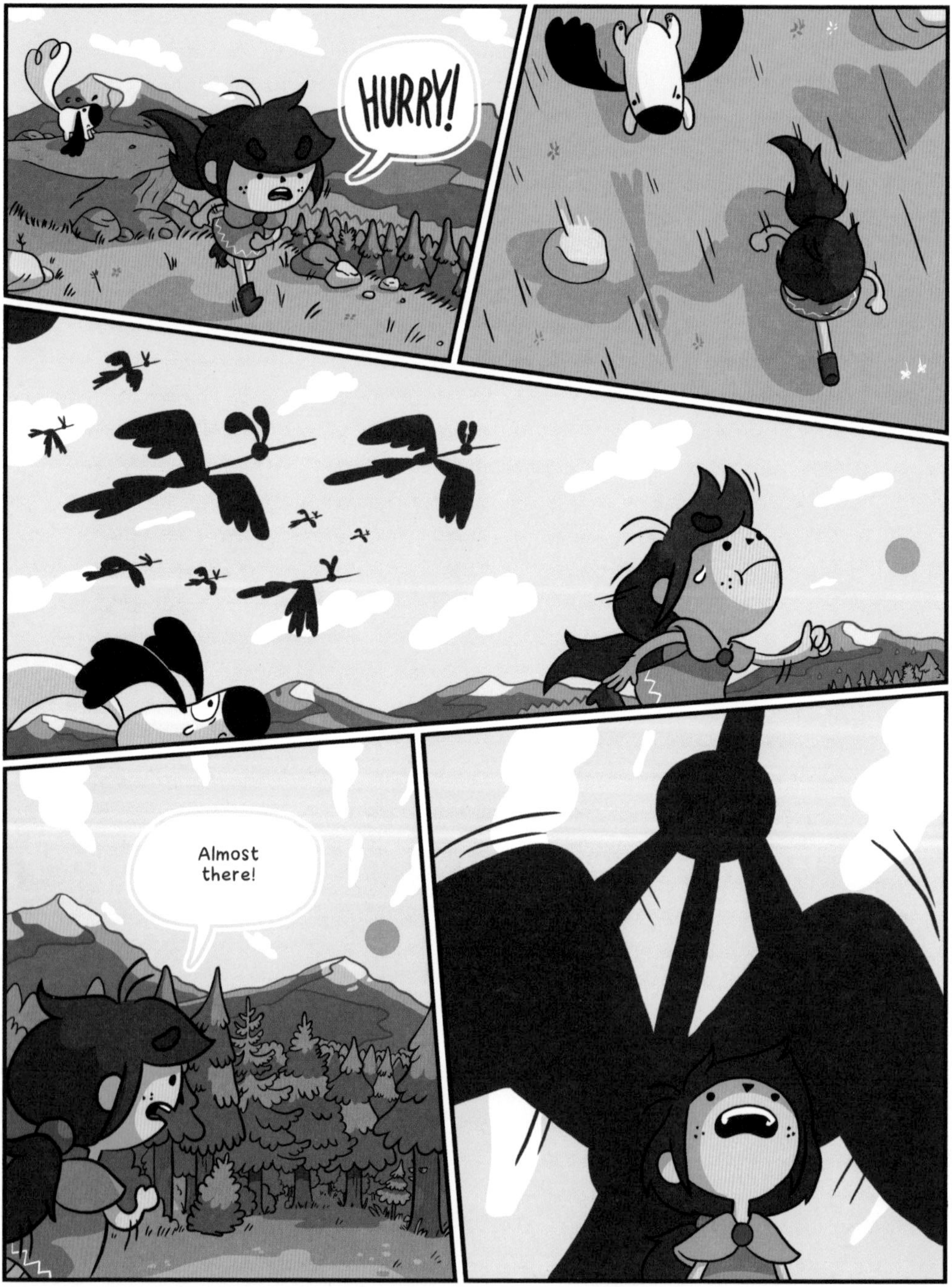
HURRY!
Almost there!

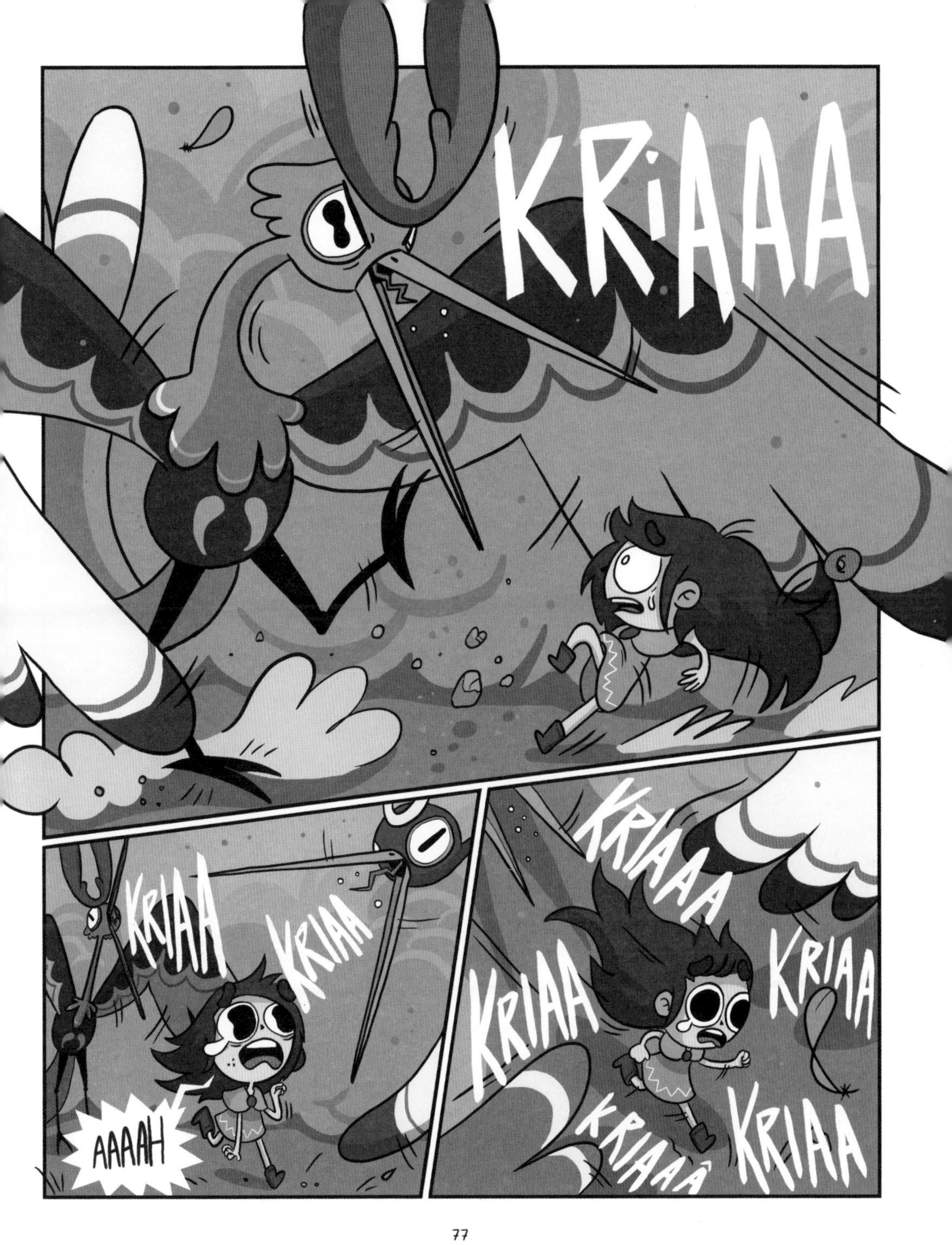
KRIAAA
KRIAA
KRIAA
AAAAH
KRIAAA
KRIAA
KRIAA
KRIAA
KRIAAÂ
KRIAA

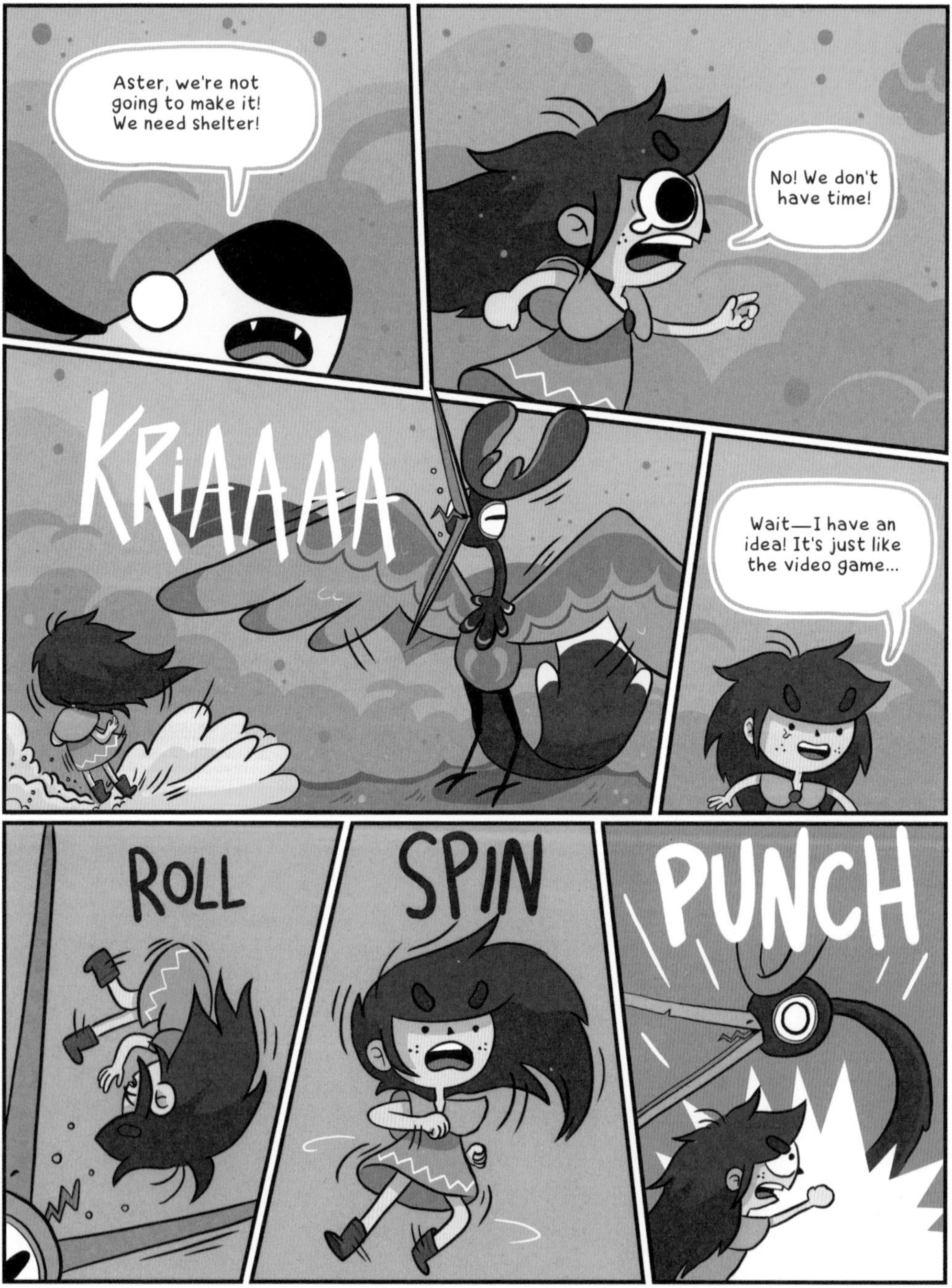
Aster, we're not going to make it! We need shelter!
No! We don't have time!
KRiAAAA
Wait—I have an idea! It's just like the video game...
ROLL
SPIN
PUNCH

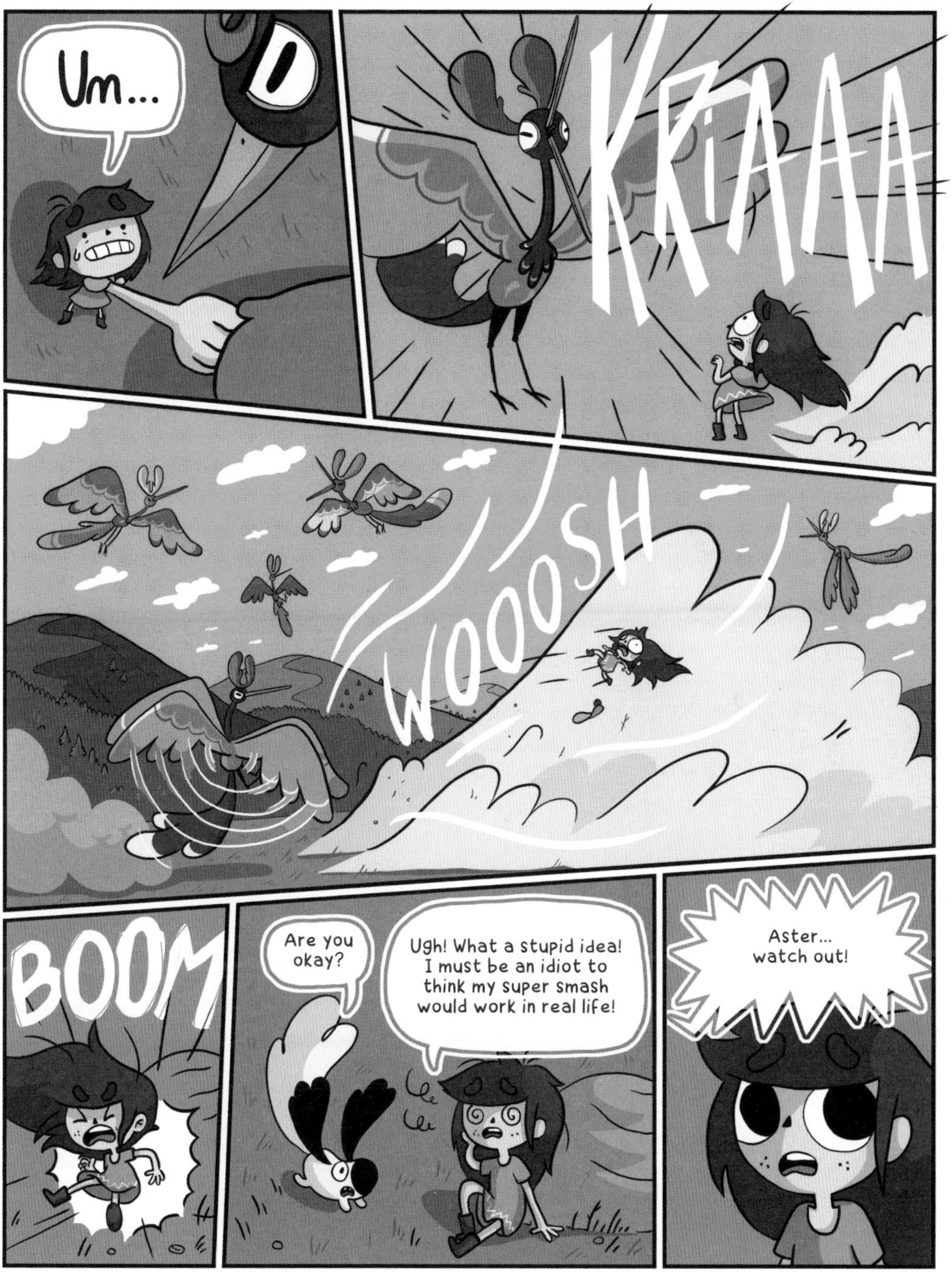
Um...
KRIAAA
WOOOSH
BOOM
Are you okay?
Ugh! What a stupid idea! I must be an idiot to think my super smash would work in real life!
Aster... watch out!

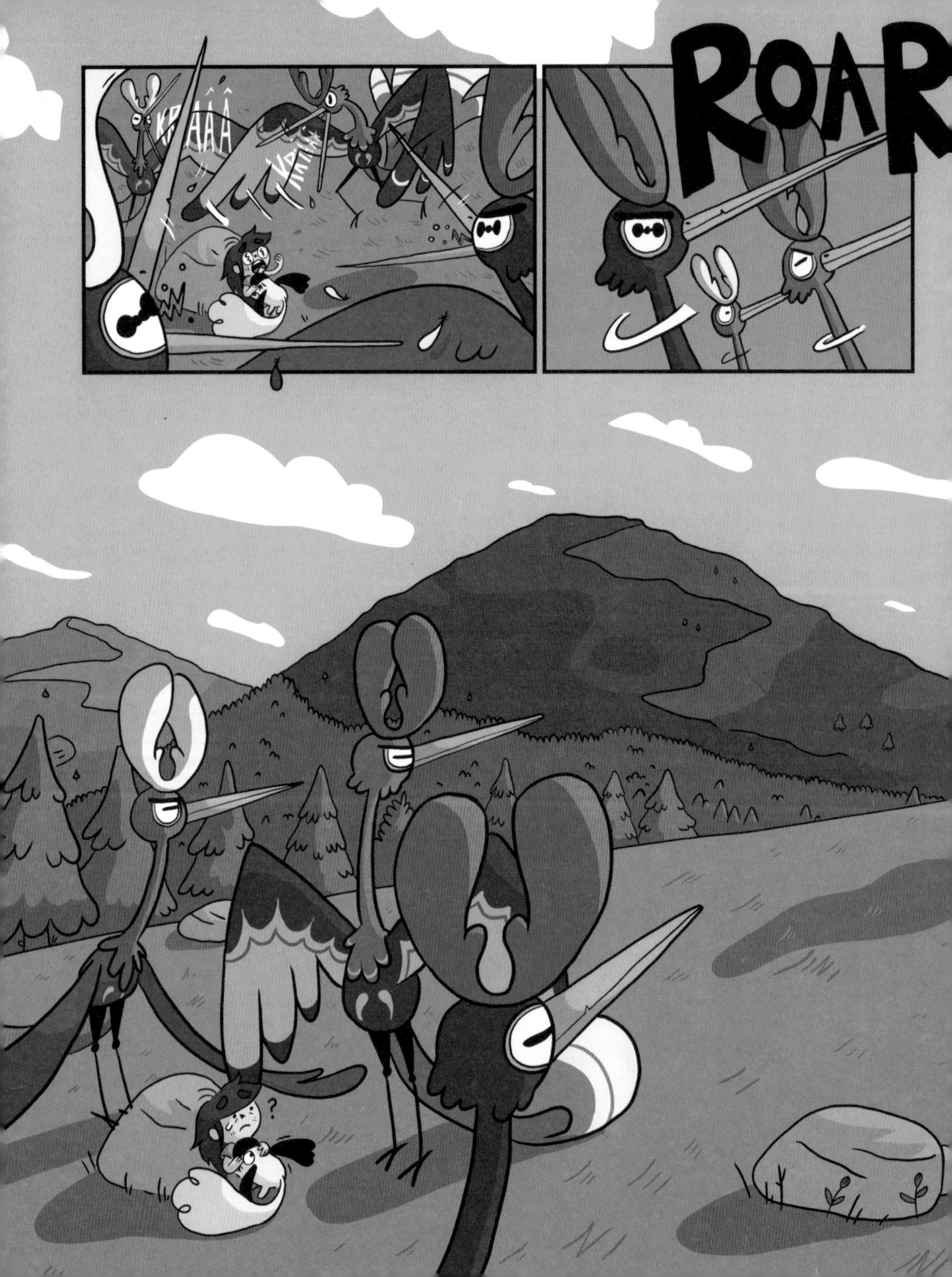
ROAR

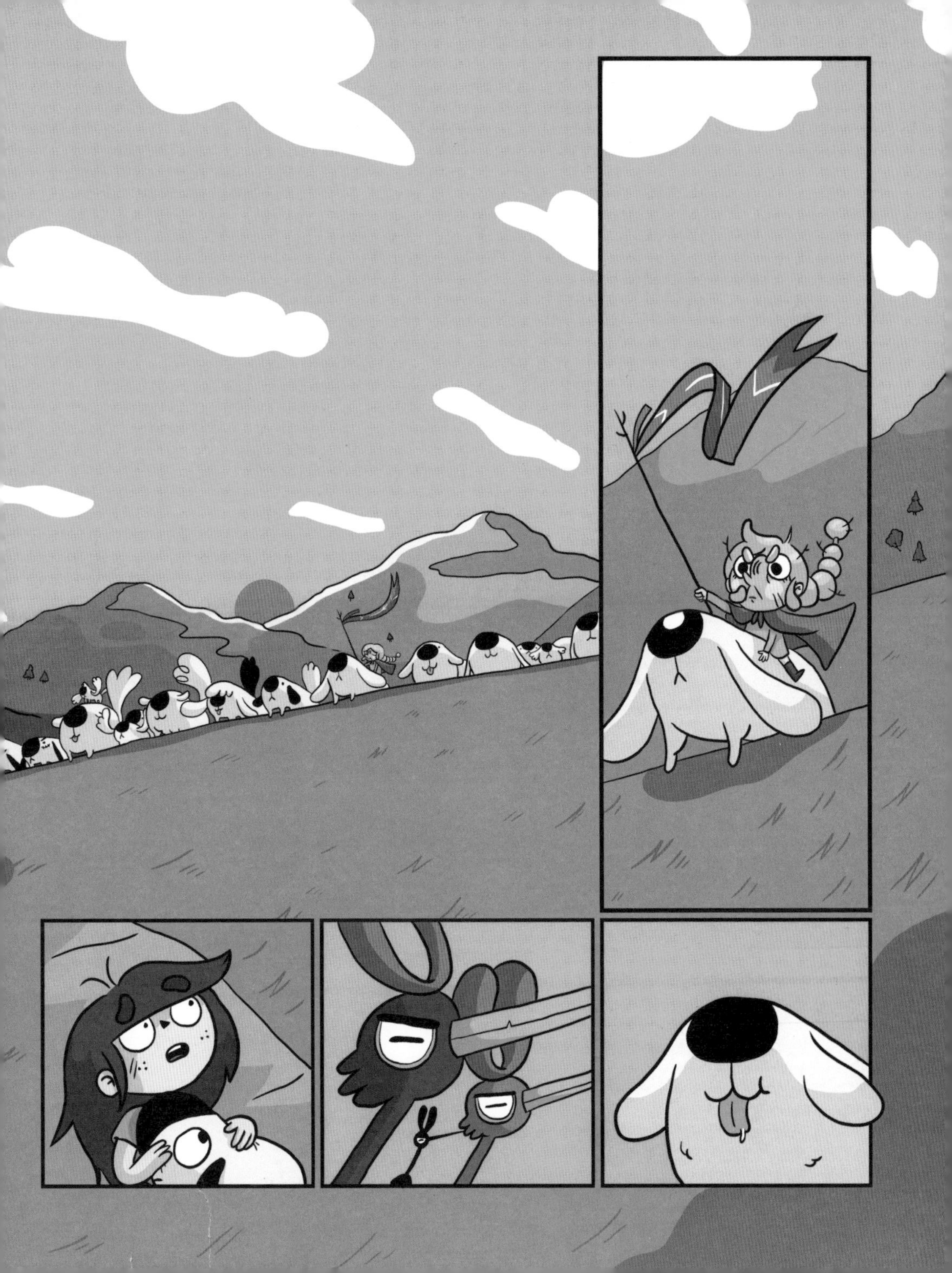

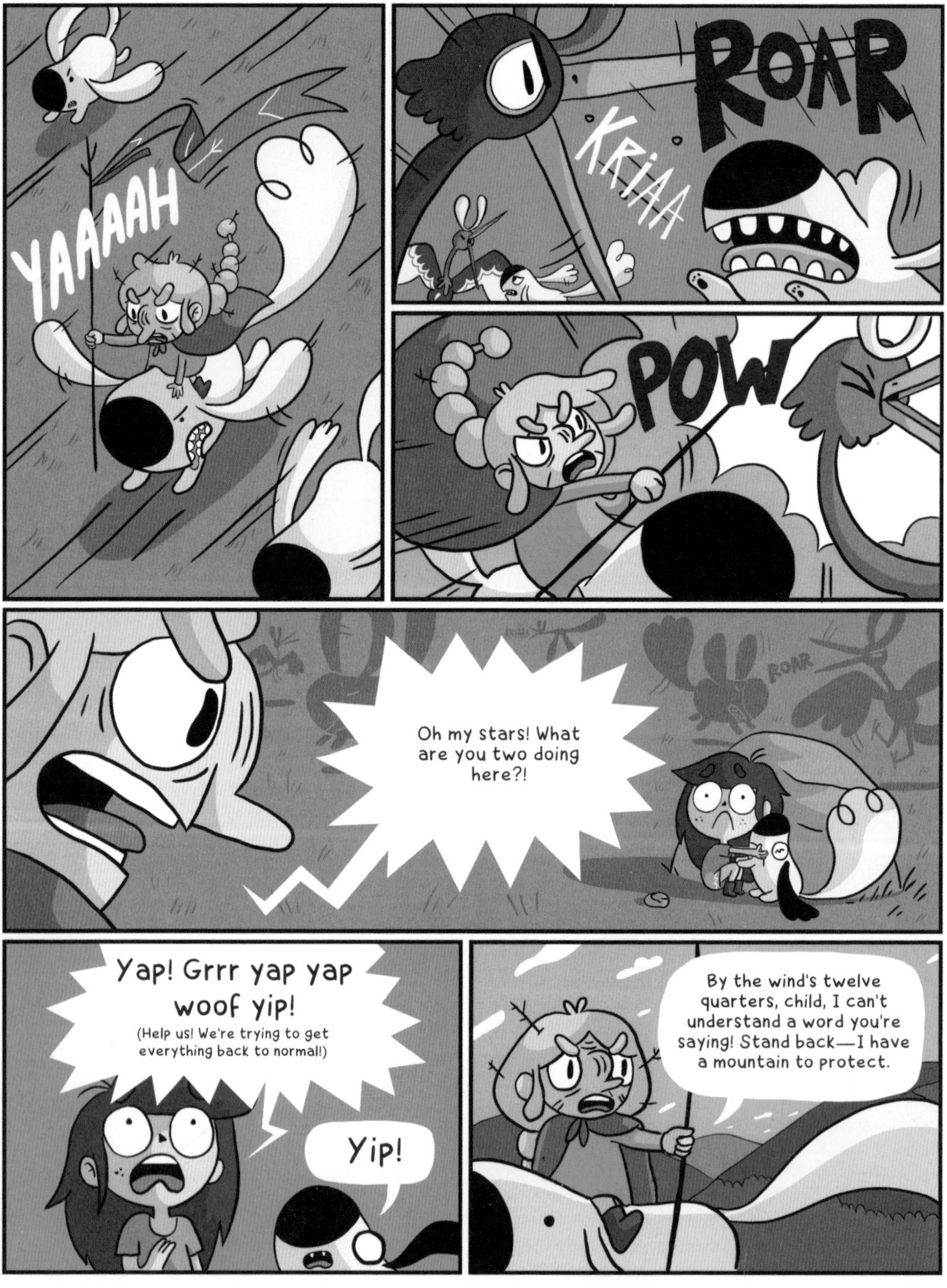
YAAAAH
ROAR
KRiAA
POW
ROAR
Oh my stars! What are you two doing here?!
Yap! Grrr yap yap woof yip!
(Help us! We're trying to get everything back to normal!)
Yip!
By the wind's twelve quarters, child, I can't understand a word you're saying! Stand back—I have a mountain to protect.

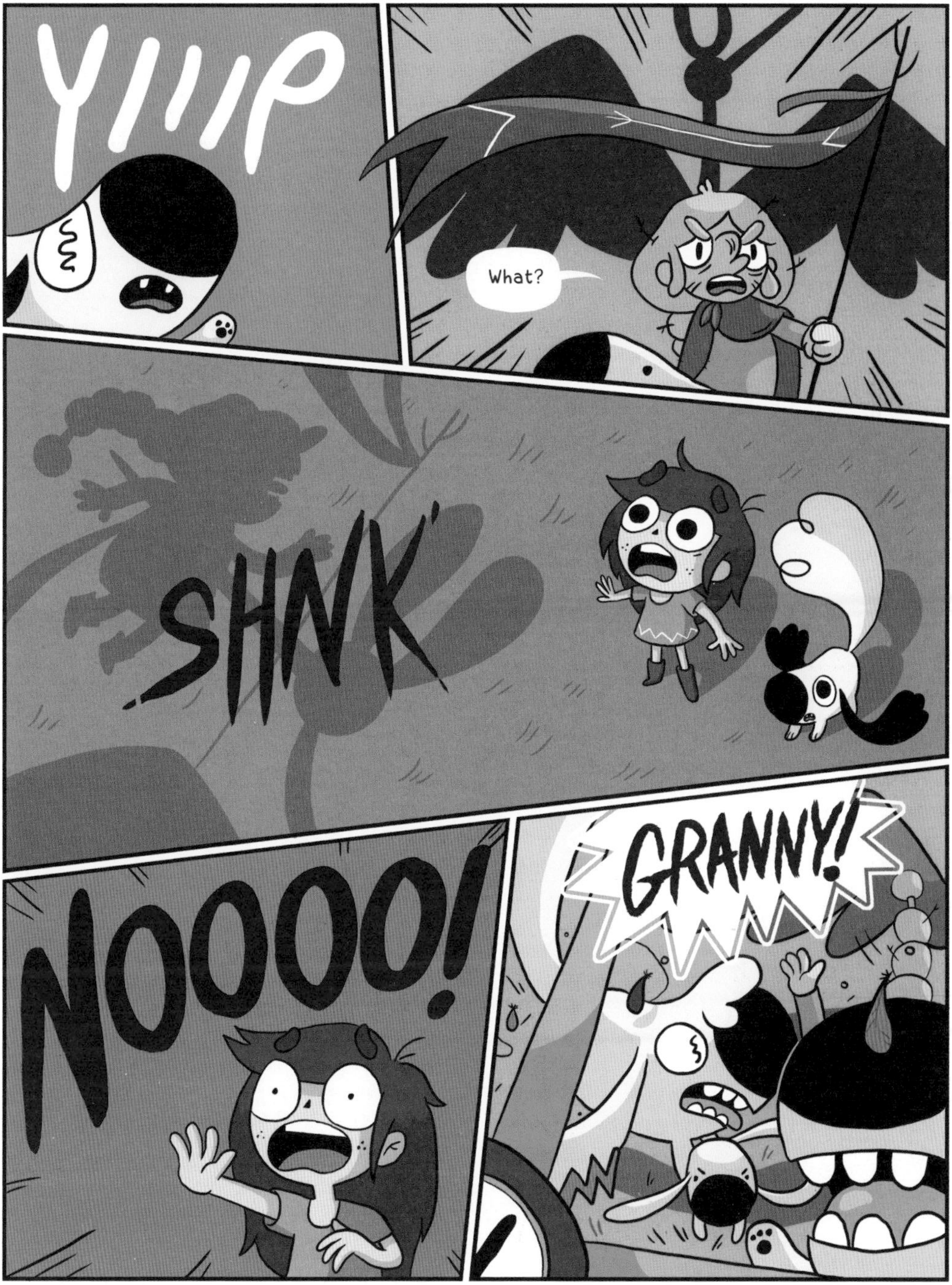
YIIIP
What?
SHNK
NOOOO!
GRANNY!

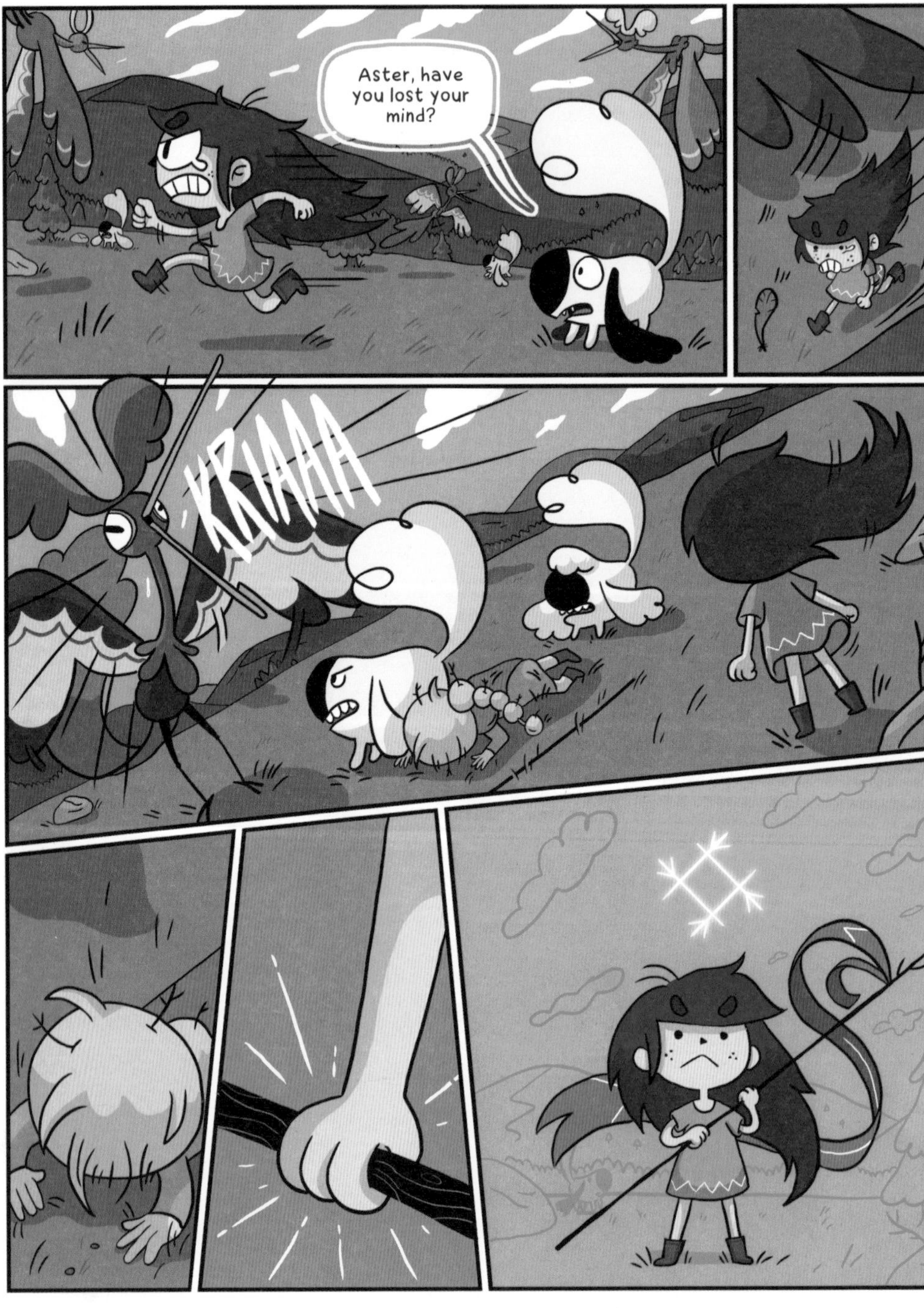
Aster, have you lost your mind?
KRIAAA

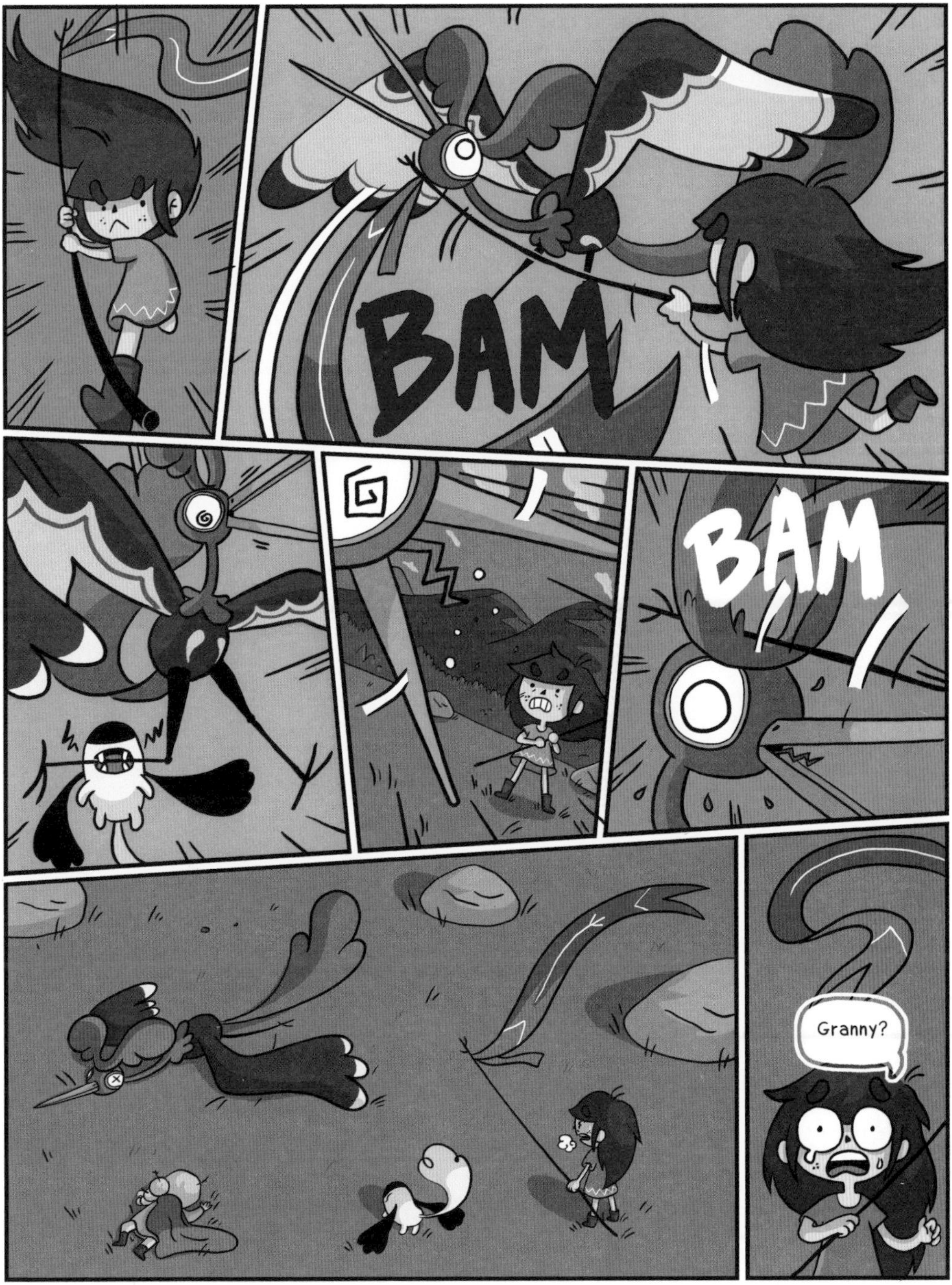
BAM
BAM
Granny?

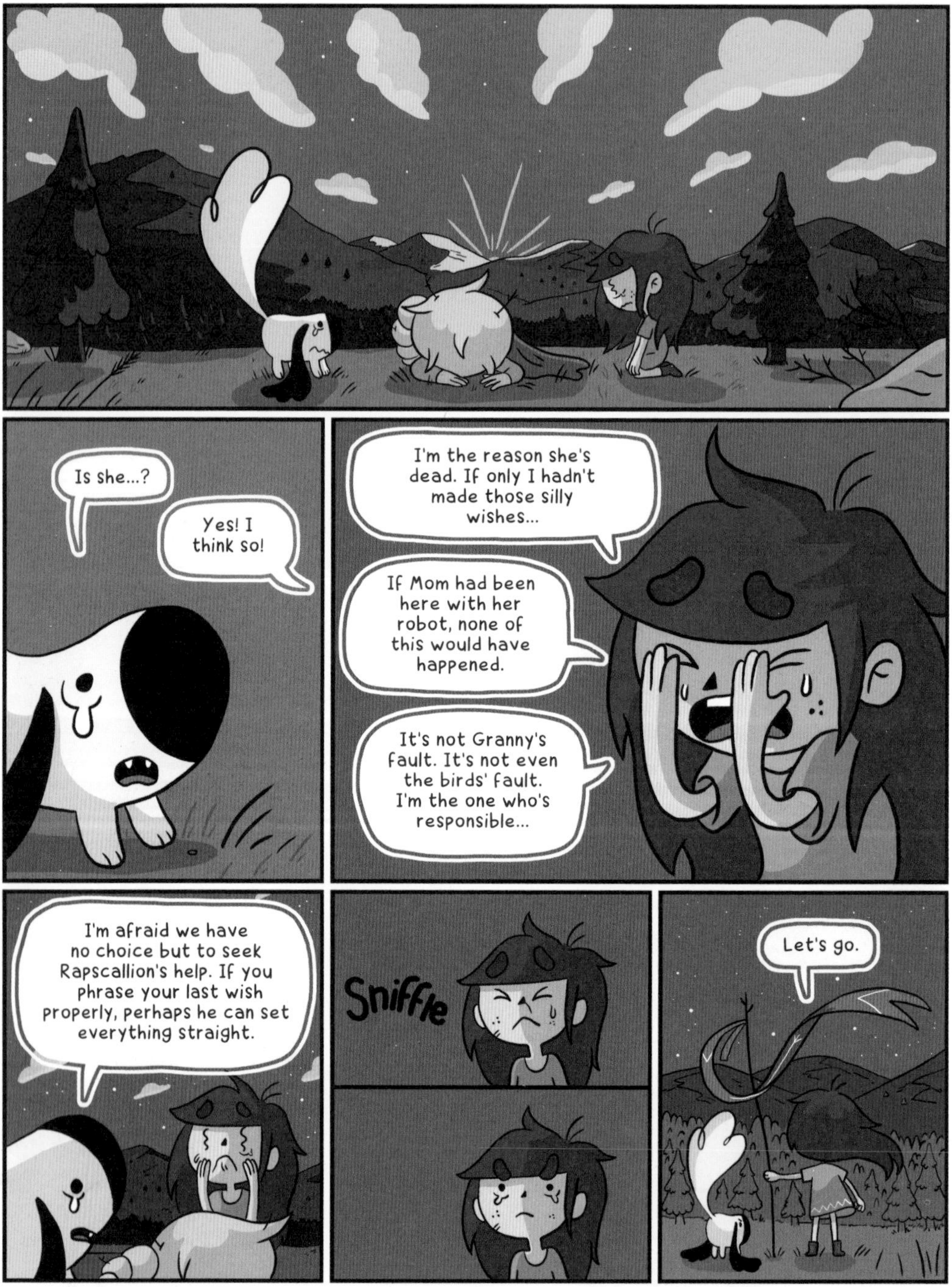
Is she...?
Yes! I think so!
I'm the reason she's dead. If only I hadn't made those silly wishes...
If Mom had been here with her robot, none of this would have happened.
It's not Granny's fault. It's not even the birds' fault. I'm the one who's responsible...
I'm afraid we have no choice but to seek Rapscallion's help. If you phrase your last wish properly, perhaps he can set everything straight.
Sniffle
Let's go.

Well, well, well. Once again, the chosen one graces me with her presence. Has everything gone as you wished?

Stop making fun of me!

Me? Make fun of you? Never! All I did was give you exactly what you wished for.

You must have read stories about tricksters—we all behave the same way. It's not our fault humans never remember what they read.

Nothing turned out the way I wanted!

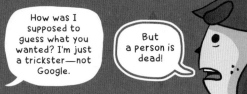

How was I supposed to guess what you wanted? I'm just a trickster—not Google.

But a person is dead!

87

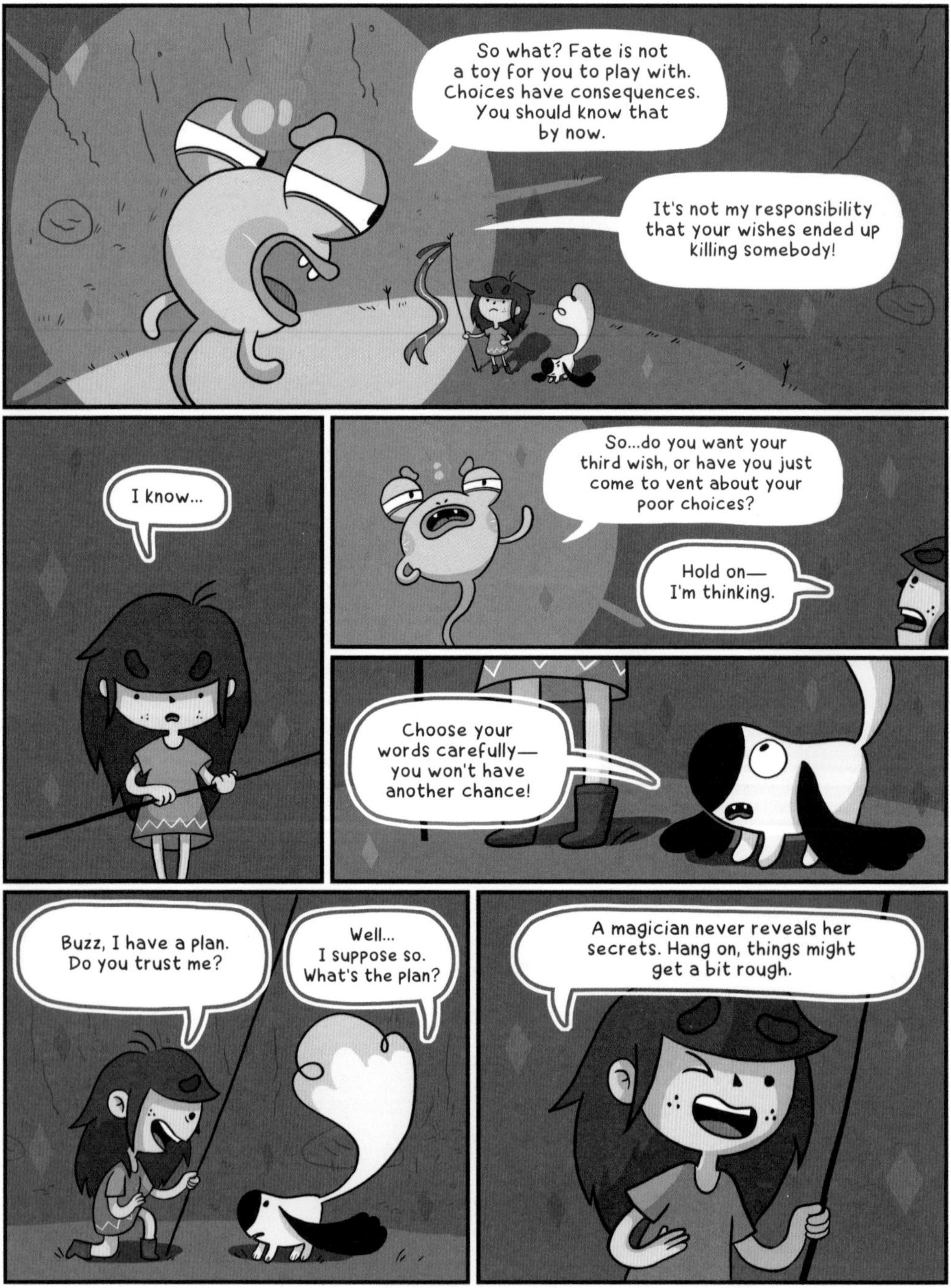
So what? Fate is not a toy for you to play with. Choices have consequences. You should know that by now.
It's not my responsibility that your wishes ended up killing somebody!
I know...
So...do you want your third wish, or have you just come to vent about your poor choices?
Hold on— I'm thinking.
Choose your words carefully— you won't have another chance!
Buzz, I have a plan. Do you trust me?
Well... I suppose so. What's the plan?
A magician never reveals her secrets. Hang on, things might get a bit rough.

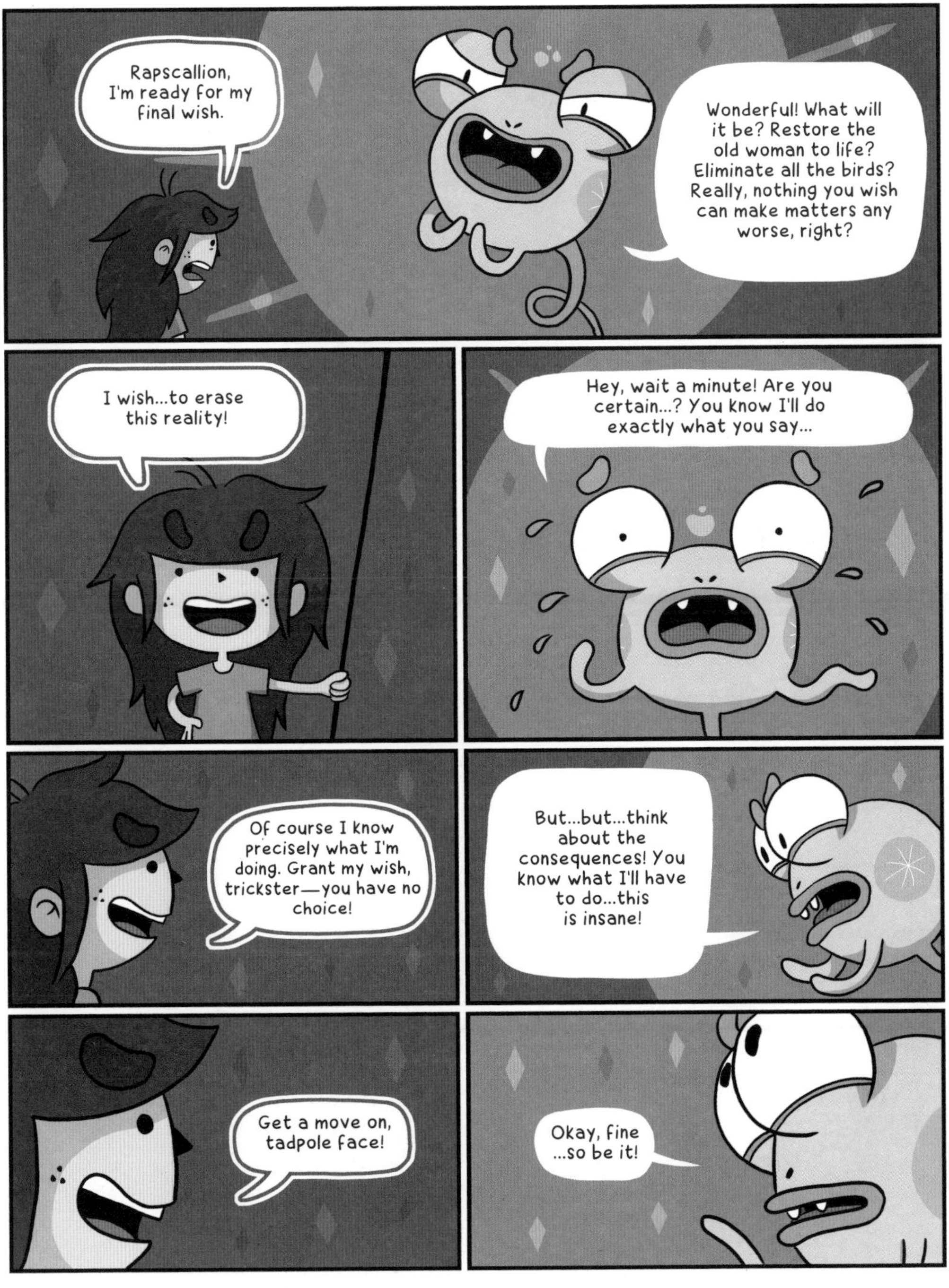
Rapscallion, I'm ready for my final wish.
Wonderful! What will it be? Restore the old woman to life? Eliminate all the birds? Really, nothing you wish can make matters any worse, right?
I wish...to erase this reality!
Hey, wait a minute! Are you certain...? You know I'll do exactly what you say...
Of course I know precisely what I'm doing. Grant my wish, trickster—you have no choice!
But...but...think about the consequences! You know what I'll have to do...this is insane!
Get a move on, tadpole face!
Okay, fine ...so be it!

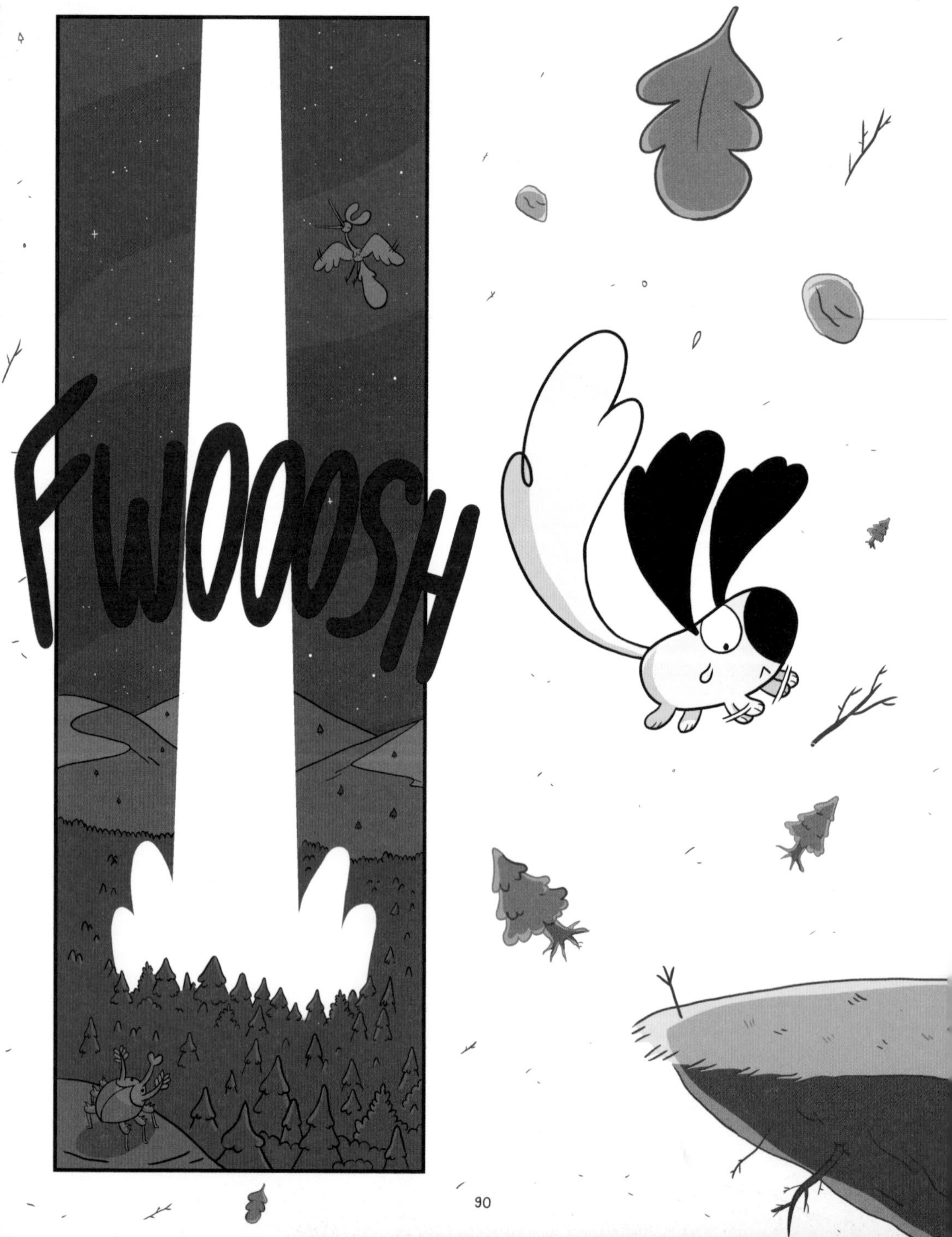
FWOOOSH

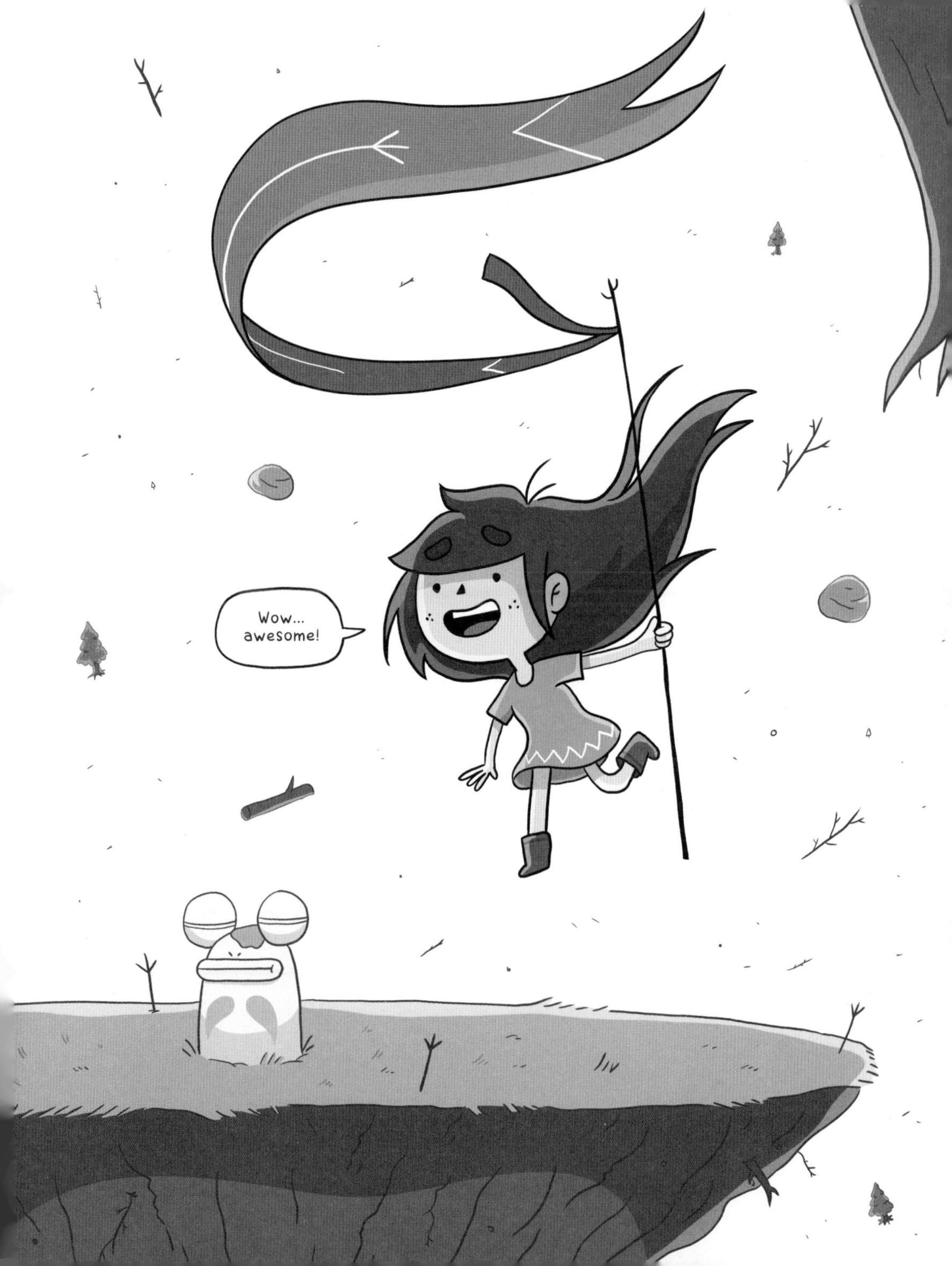
Wow... awesome!

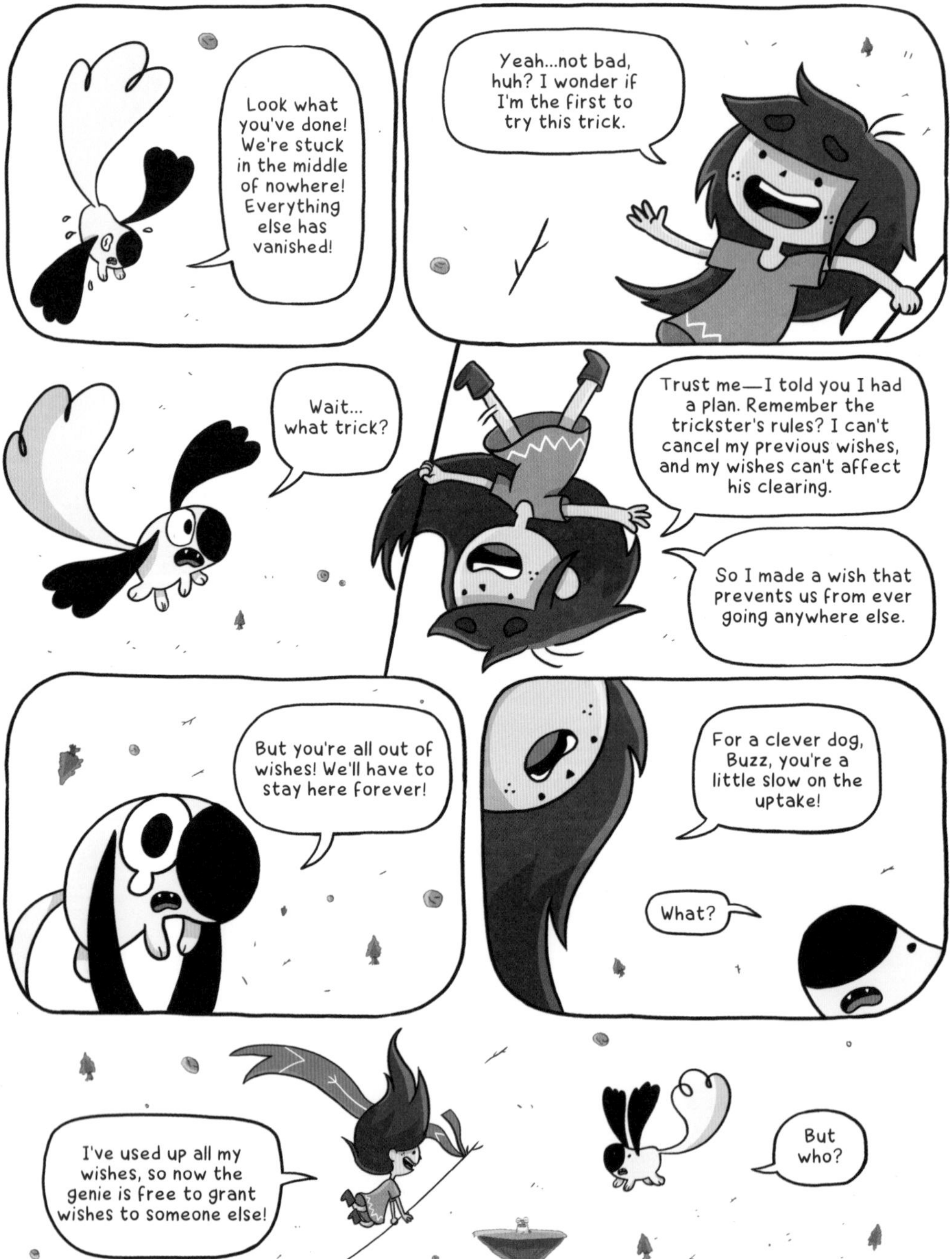

Look what you've done! We're stuck in the middle of nowhere! Everything else has vanished!
Yeah...not bad, huh? I wonder if I'm the first to try this trick.
Wait... what trick?
Trust me—I told you I had a plan. Remember the trickster's rules? I can't cancel my previous wishes, and my wishes can't affect his clearing.
So I made a wish that prevents us from ever going anywhere else.
But you're all out of wishes! We'll have to stay here forever!
For a clever dog, Buzz, you're a little slow on the uptake!
What?
I've used up all my wishes, so now the genie is free to grant wishes to someone else!
But who?

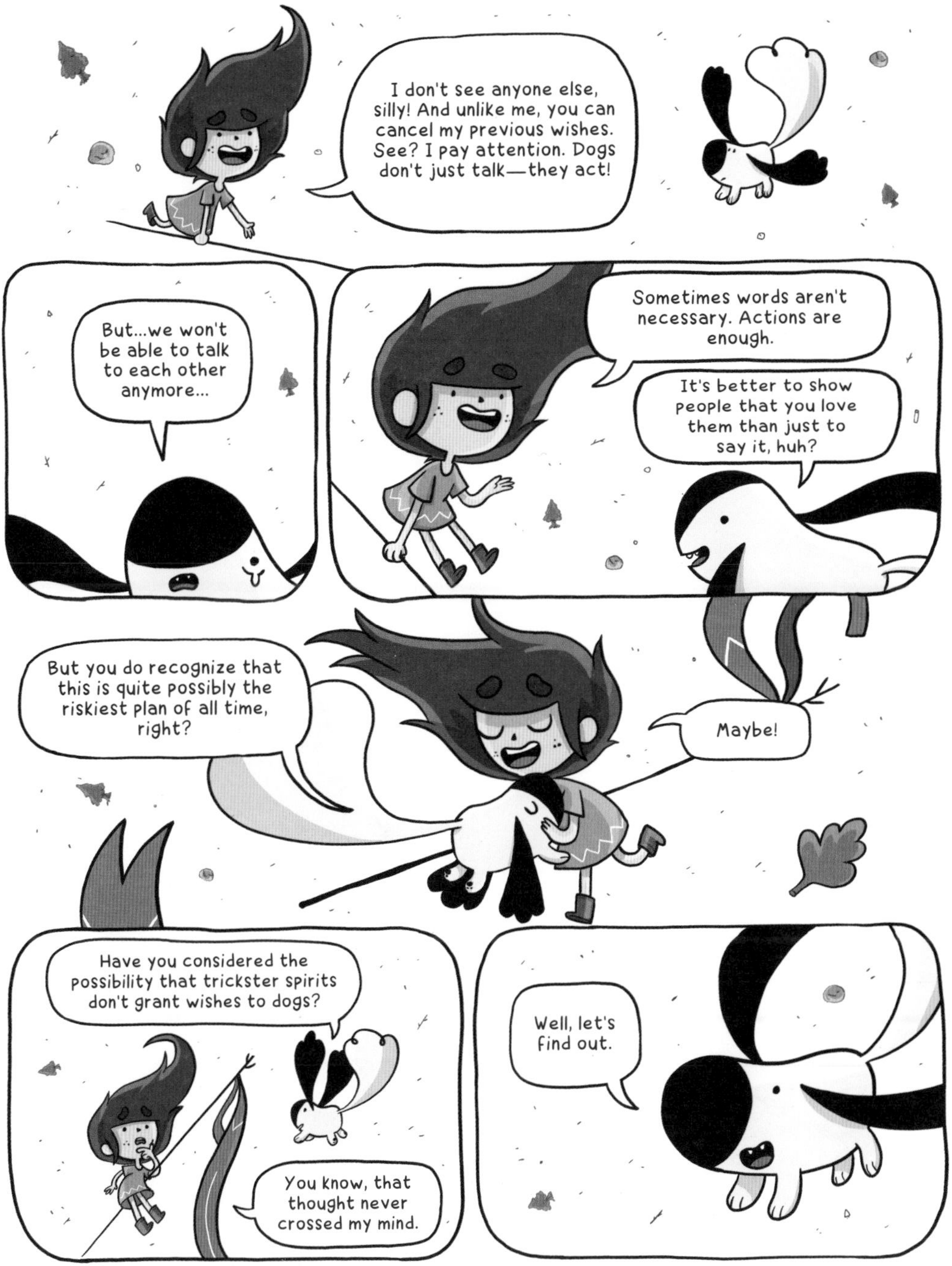
I don't see anyone else, silly! And unlike me, you can cancel my previous wishes. See? I pay attention. Dogs don't just talk—they act!
But...we won't be able to talk to each other anymore...
Sometimes words aren't necessary. Actions are enough.
It's better to show people that you love them than just to say it, huh?
But you do recognize that this is quite possibly the riskiest plan of all time, right?
Maybe!
Have you considered the possibility that trickster spirits don't grant wishes to dogs?
You know, that thought never crossed my mind.
Well, let's find out.

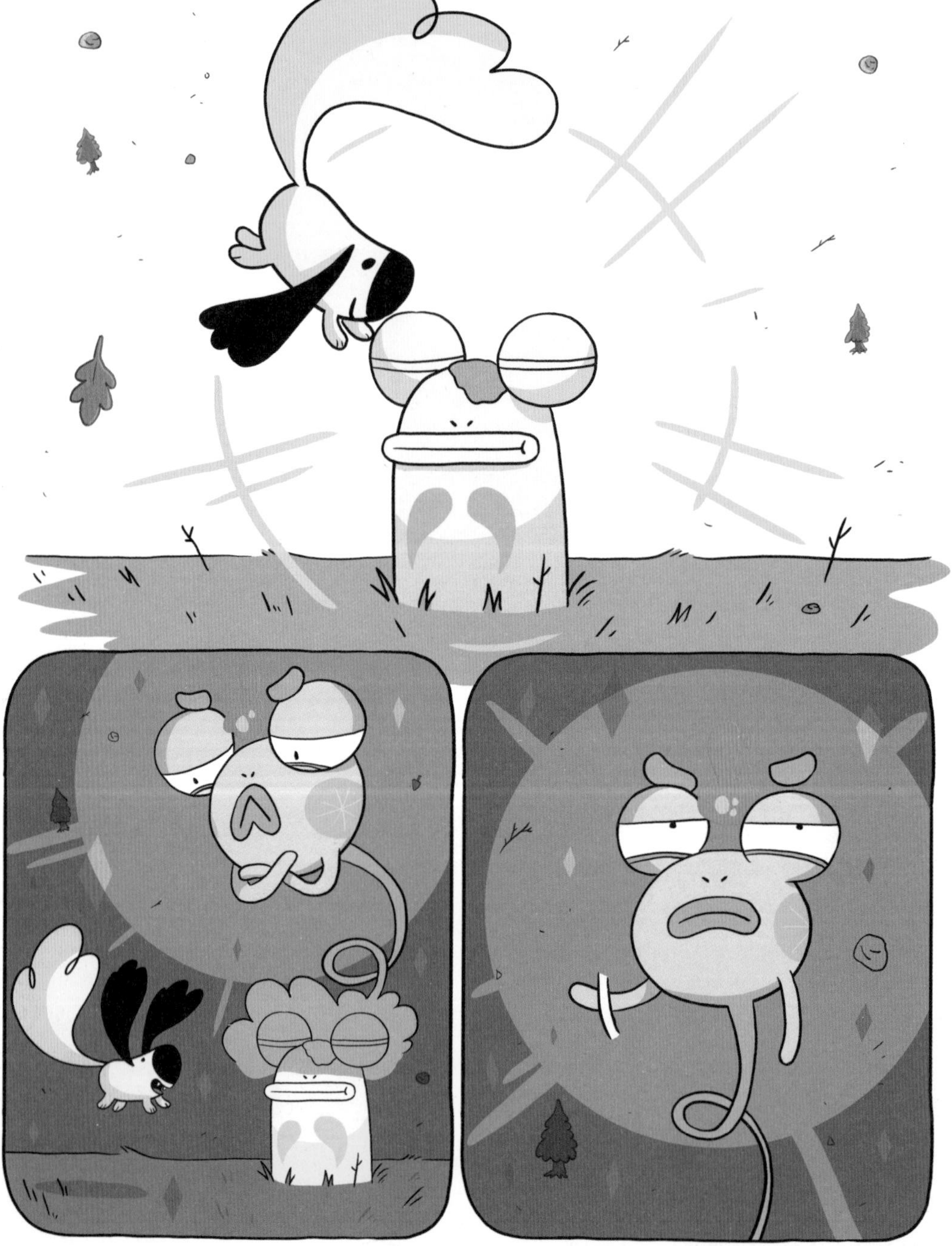

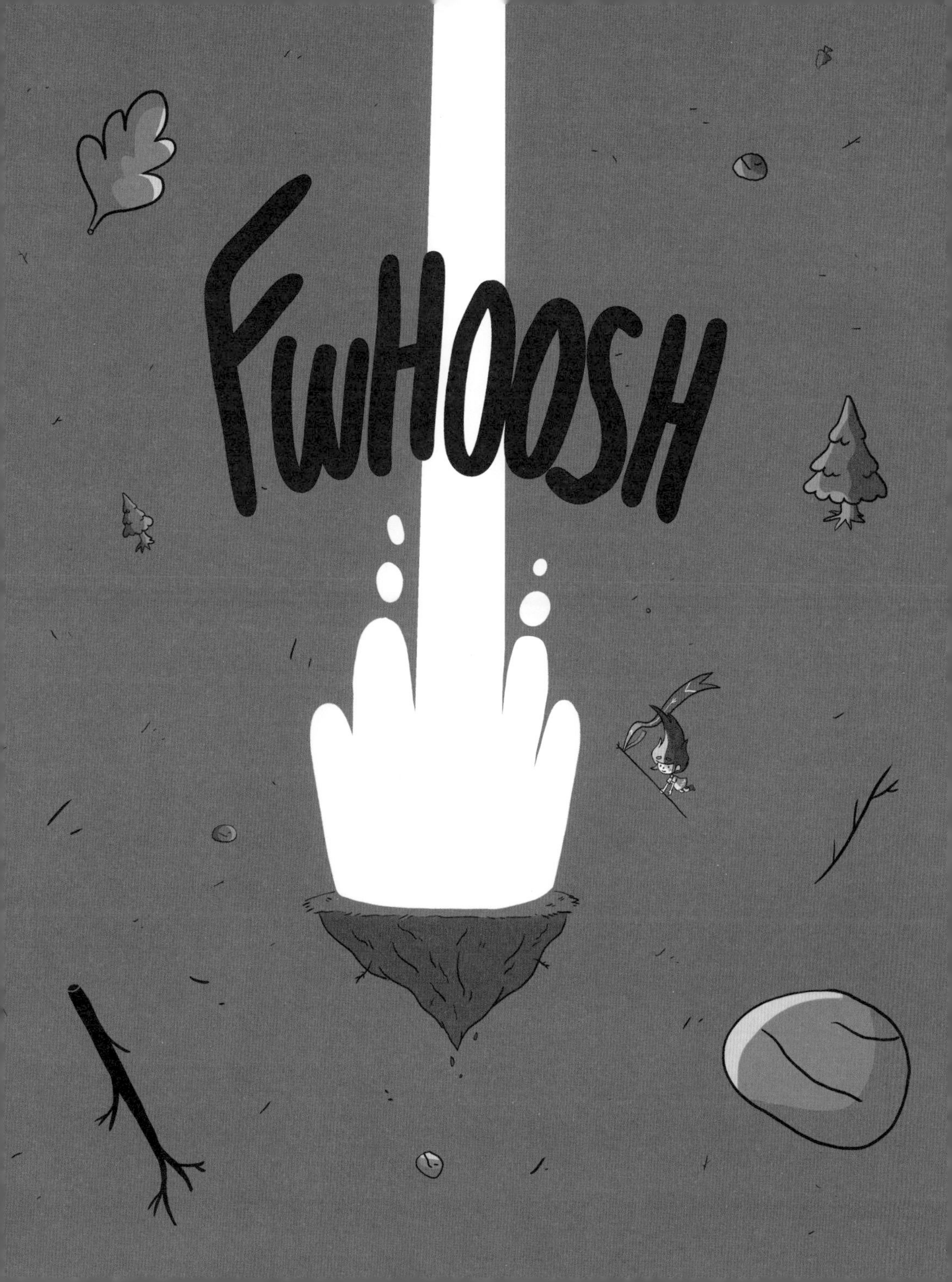
FWHOOSH

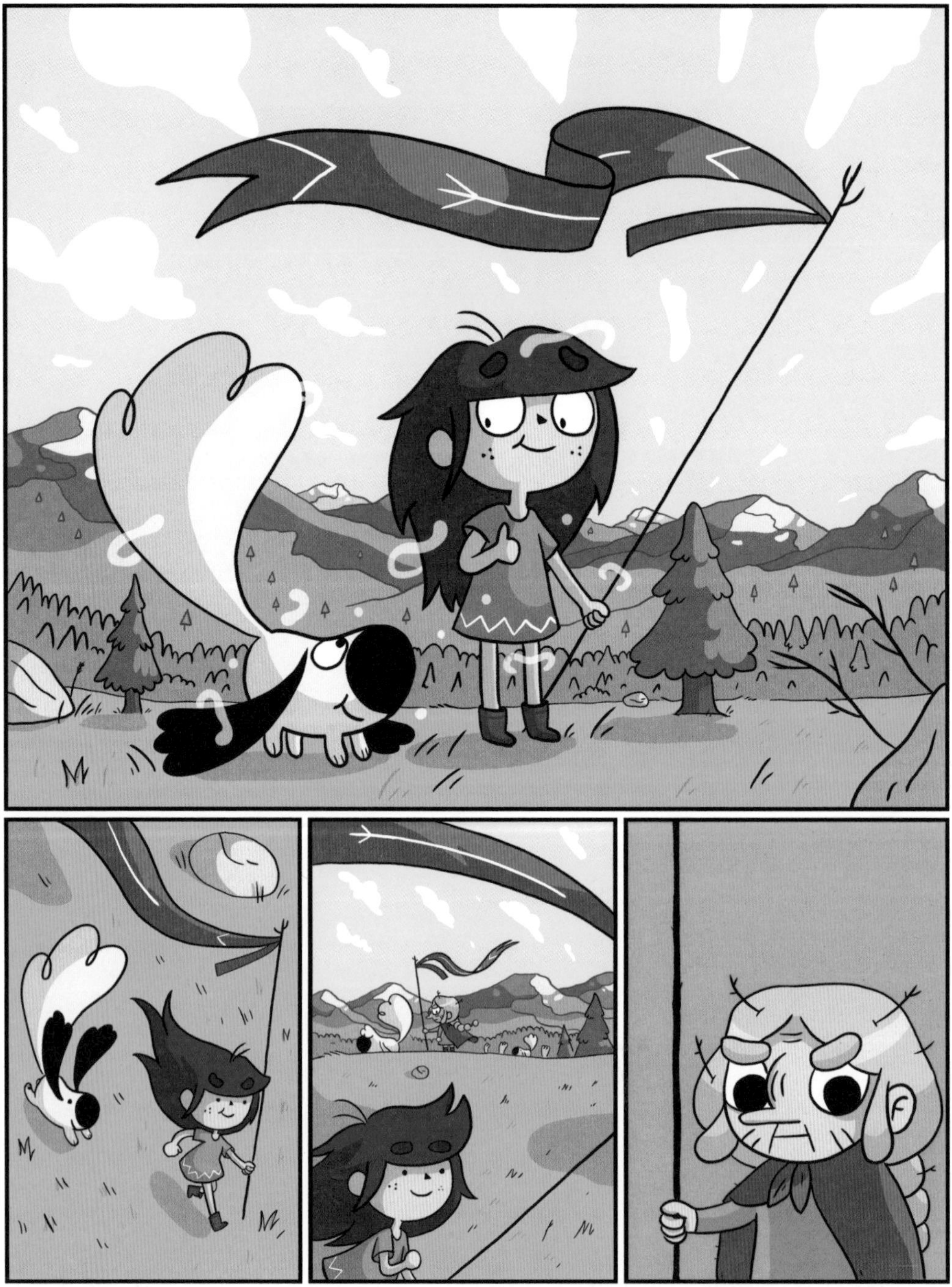

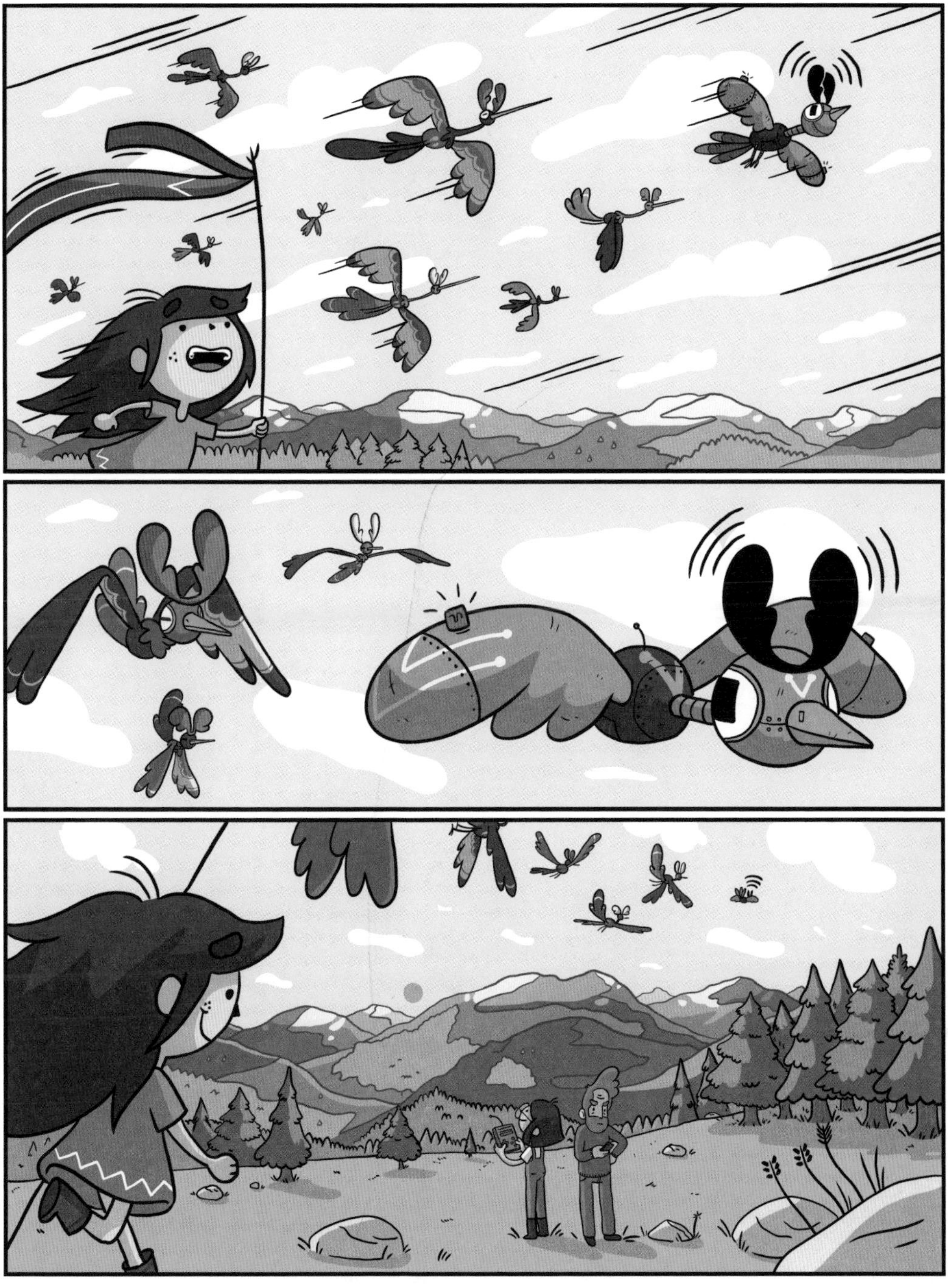

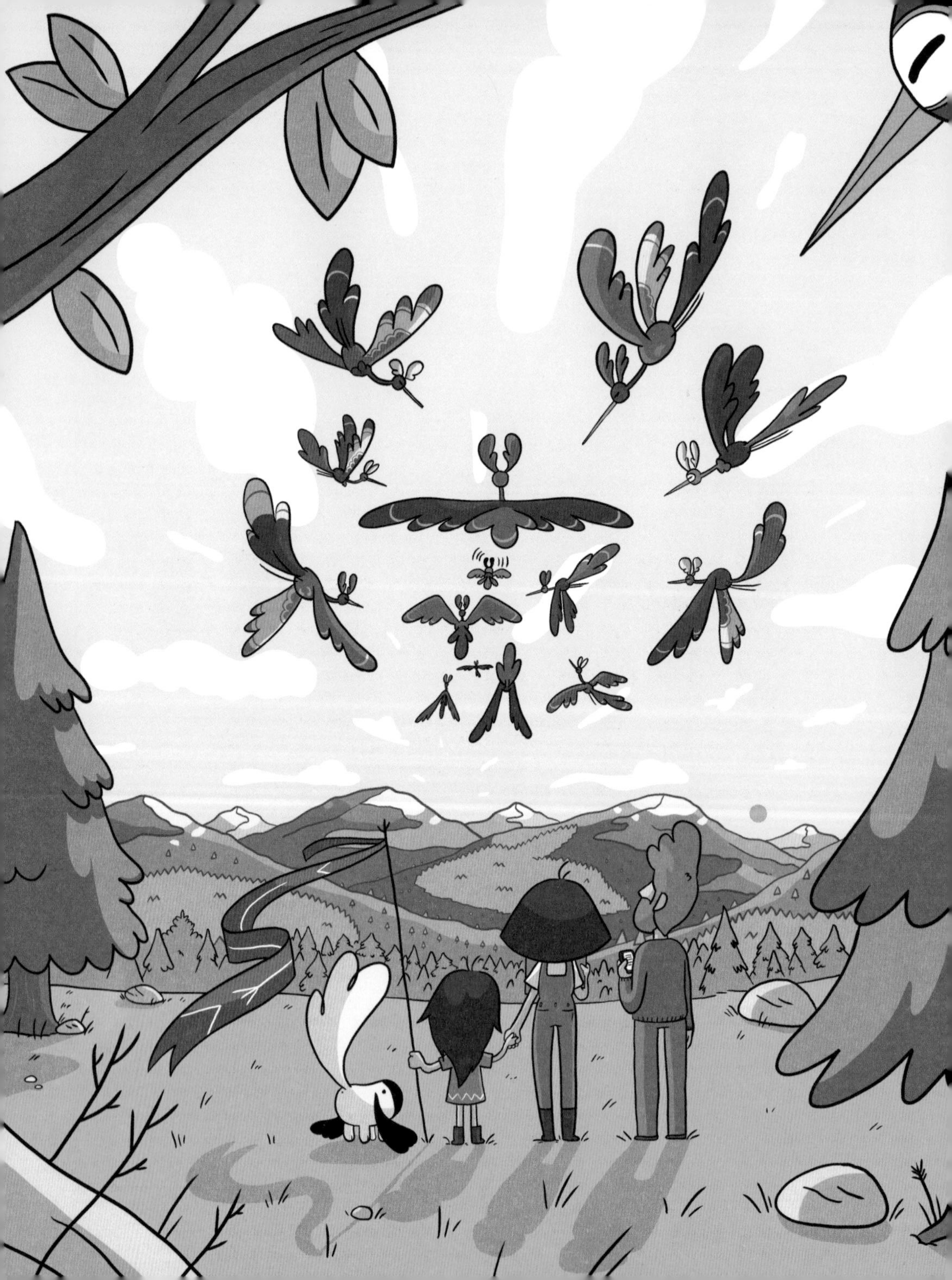

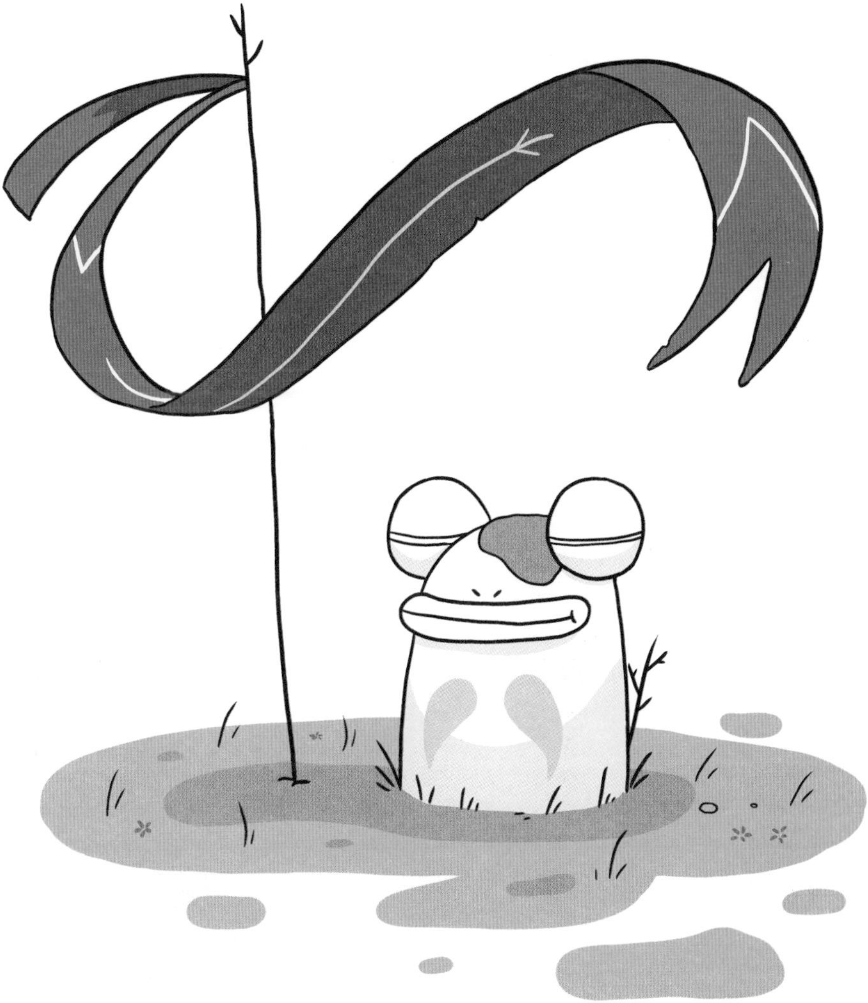

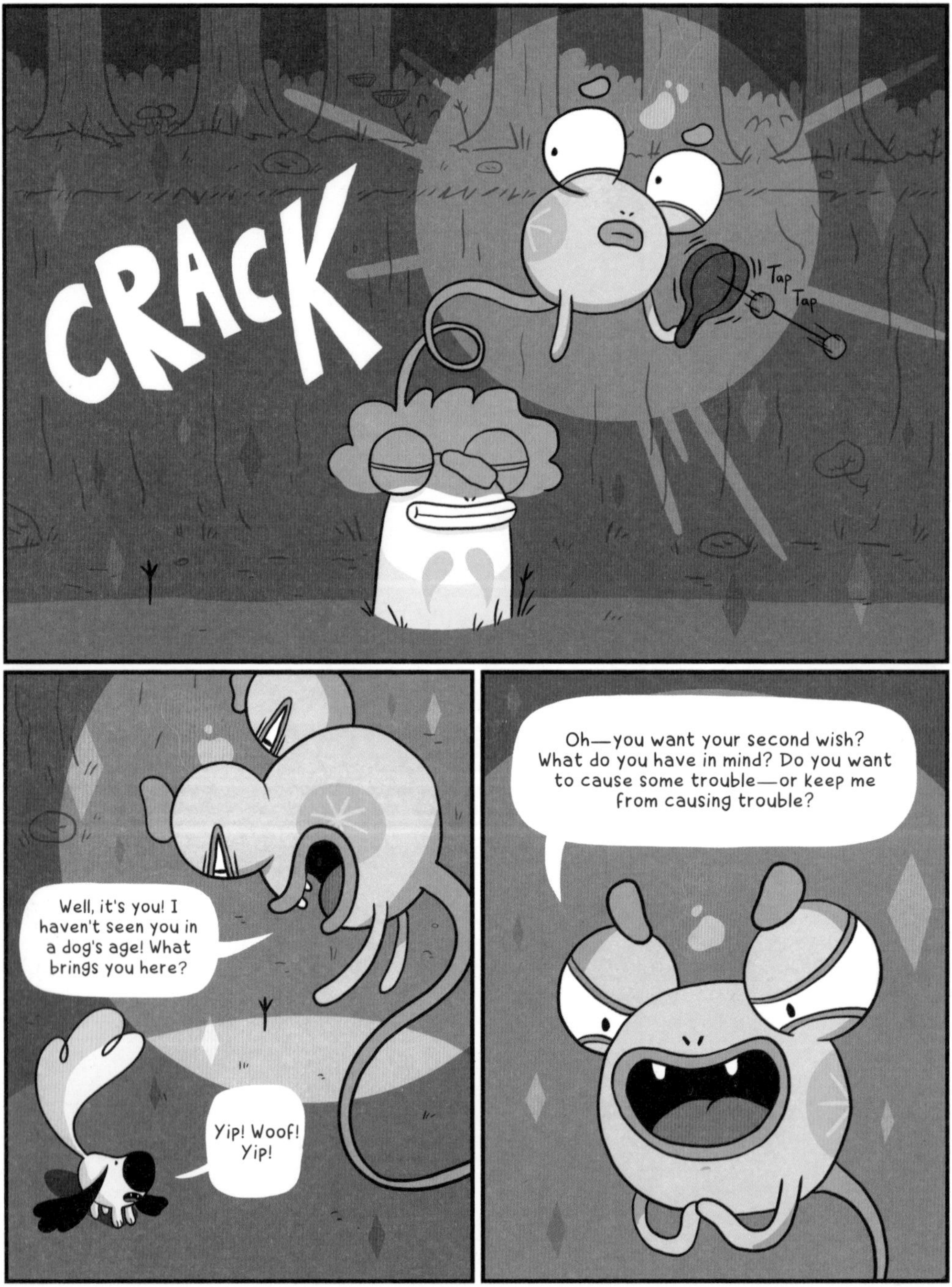
CRACK
Tap
Tap
Well, it's you! I haven't seen you in a dog's age! What brings you here?
Yip! Woof! Yip!
Oh—you want your second wish? What do you have in mind? Do you want to cause some trouble—or keep me from causing trouble?

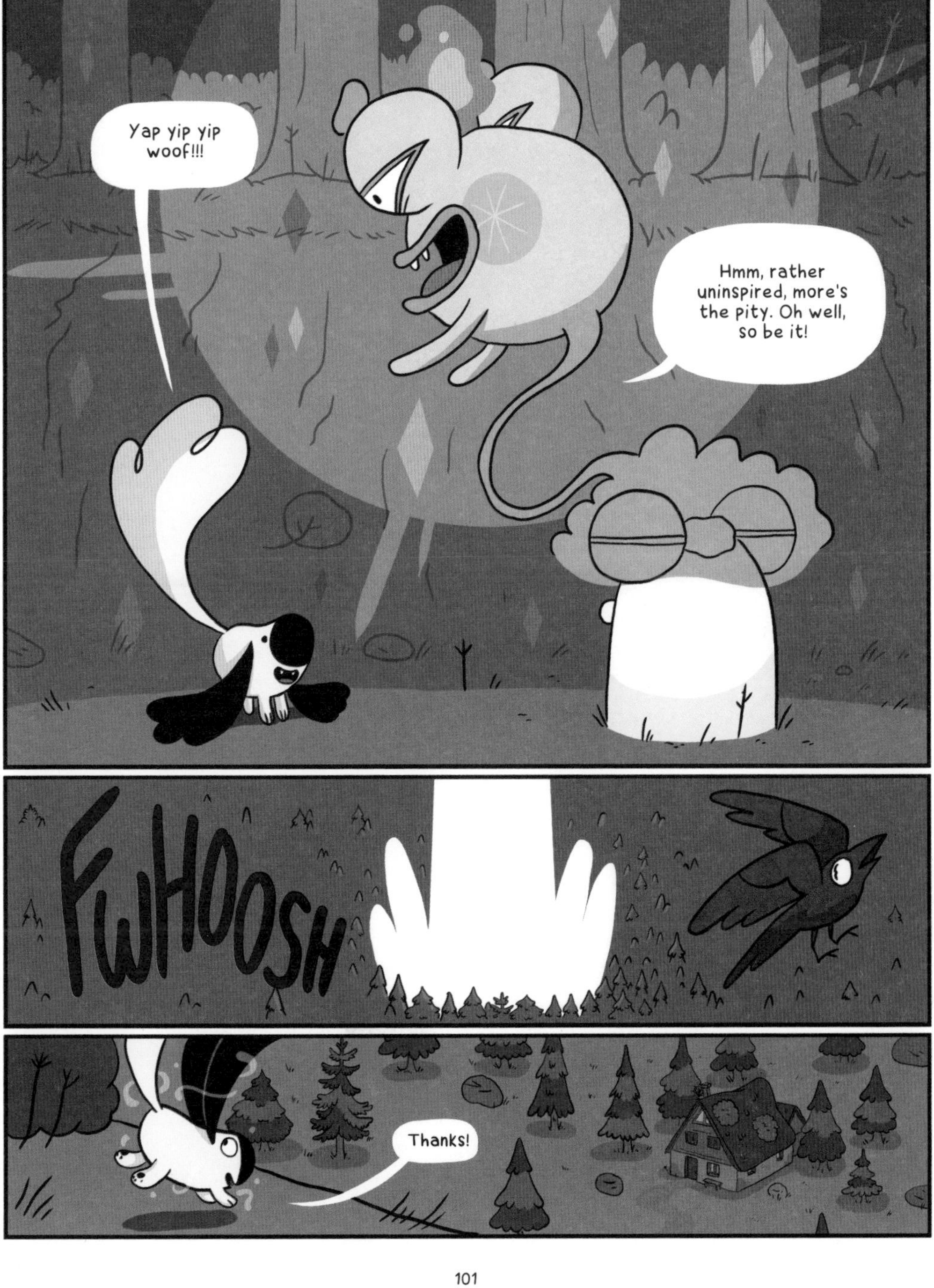
Yap yip yip woof!!!
Hmm, rather uninspired, more's the pity. Oh well, so be it!
FWHOOSH
Thanks!

ASTER + BUZZ'S
Map of the Valley
Forest
DANGER
GRANNY
STILL LAME

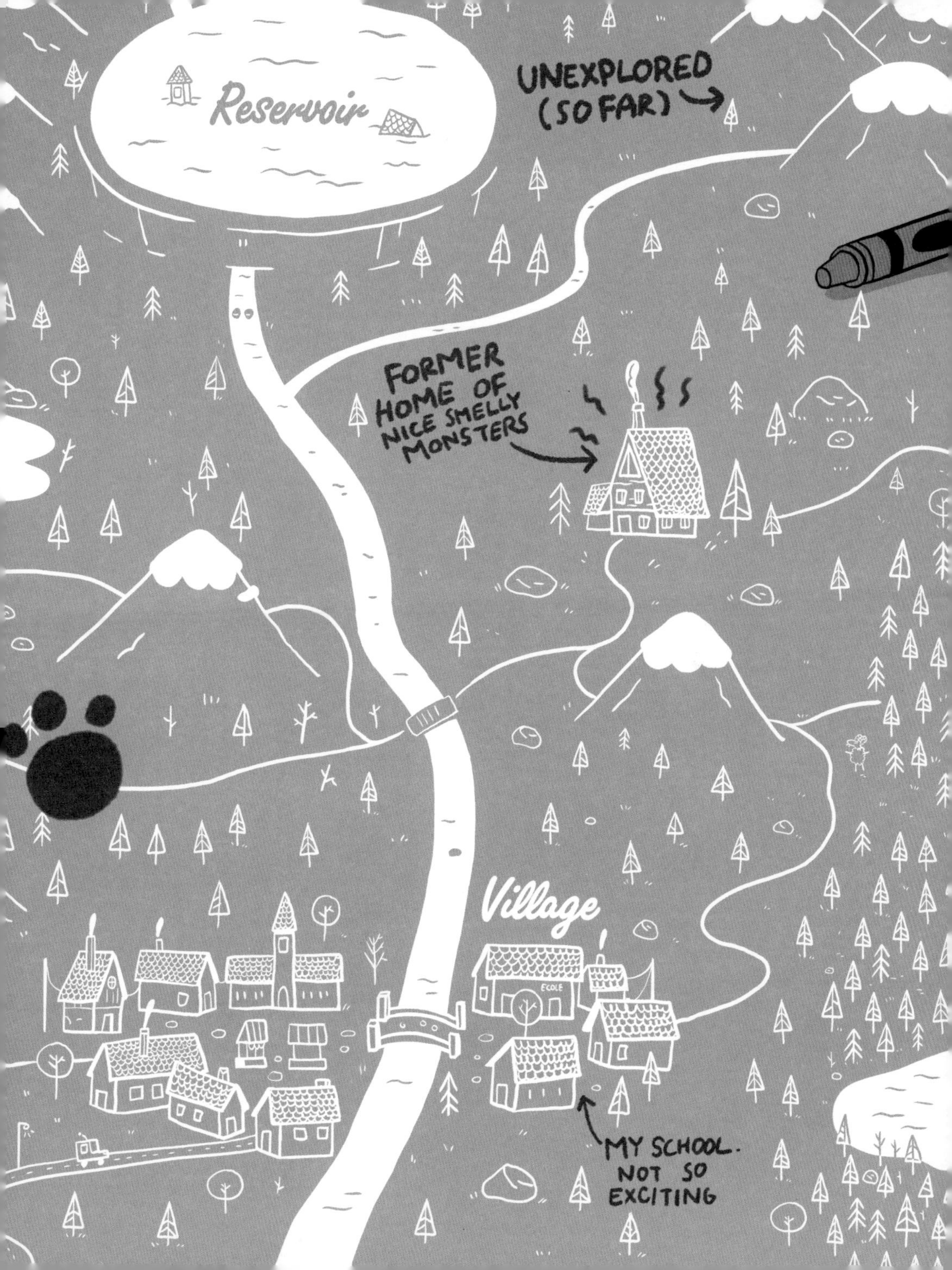
Reservoir
UNEXPLORED (SO FAR)
FORMER HOME OF NICE SMELLY MONSTERS
Village
ECOLE
MY SCHOOL. NOT SO EXCITING

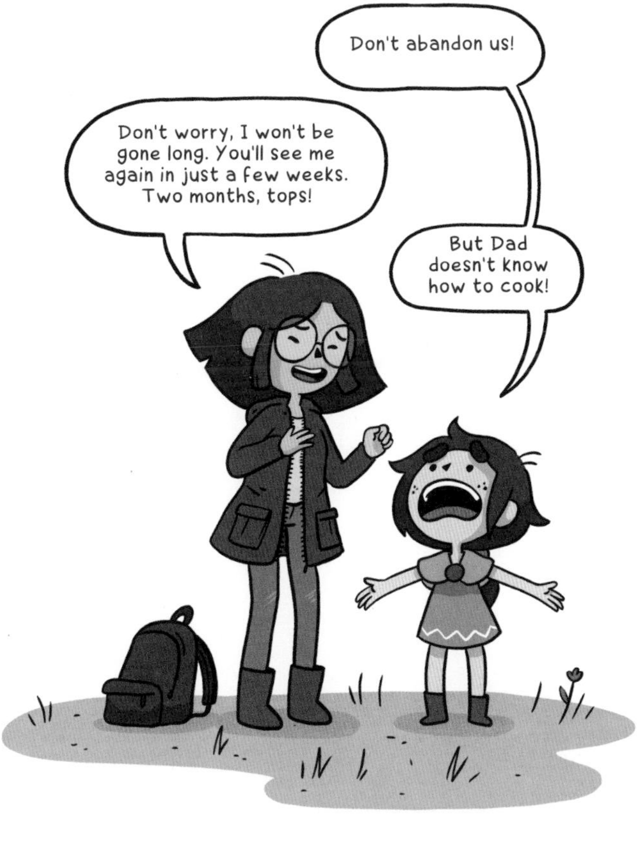
Don't worry, I won't be gone long. You'll see me again in just a few weeks. Two months, tops!
Don't abandon us!
But Dad doesn't know how to cook!

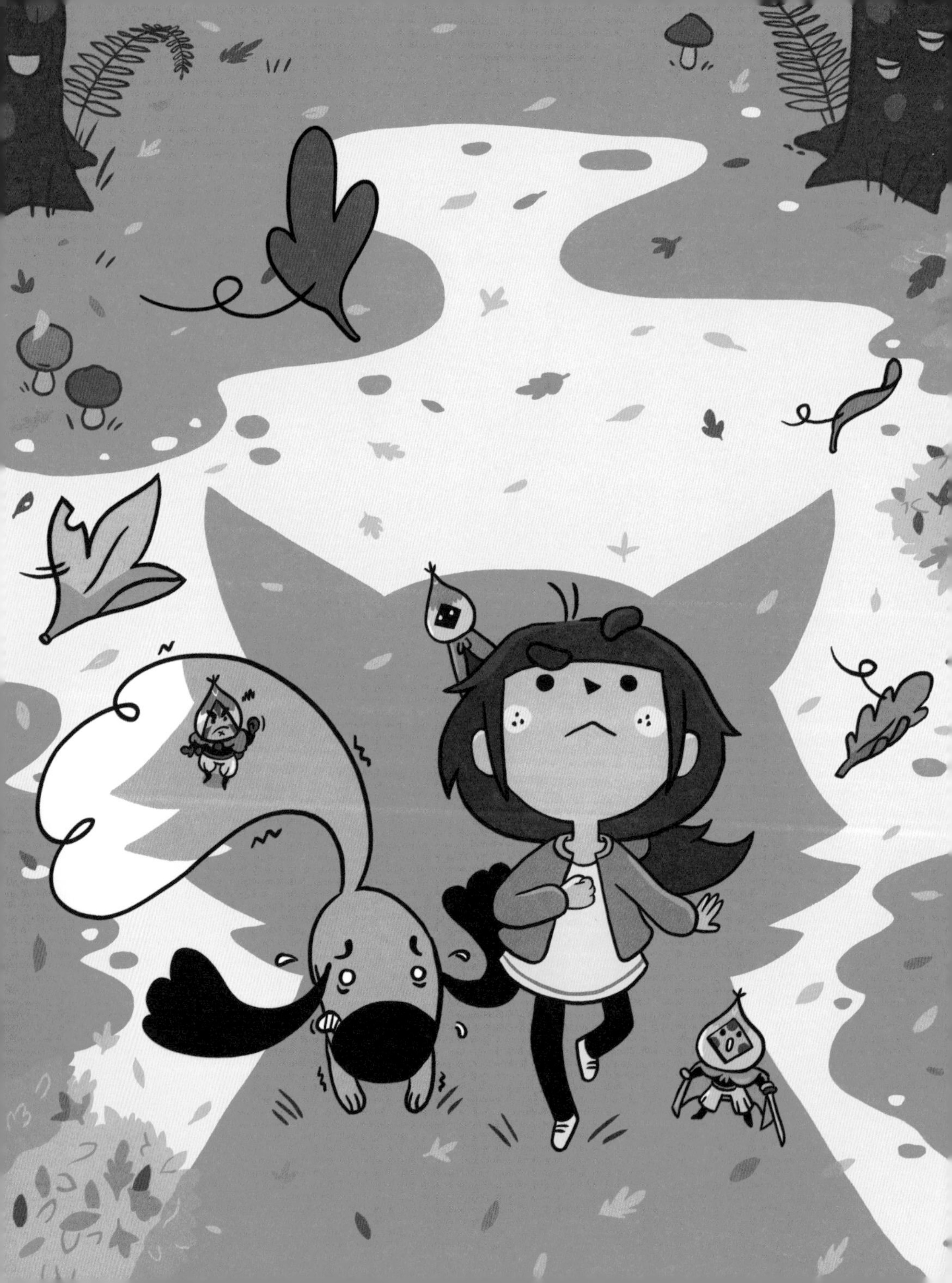

GETS A MAGICAL FOX
EXCEEDINGLY UPSET

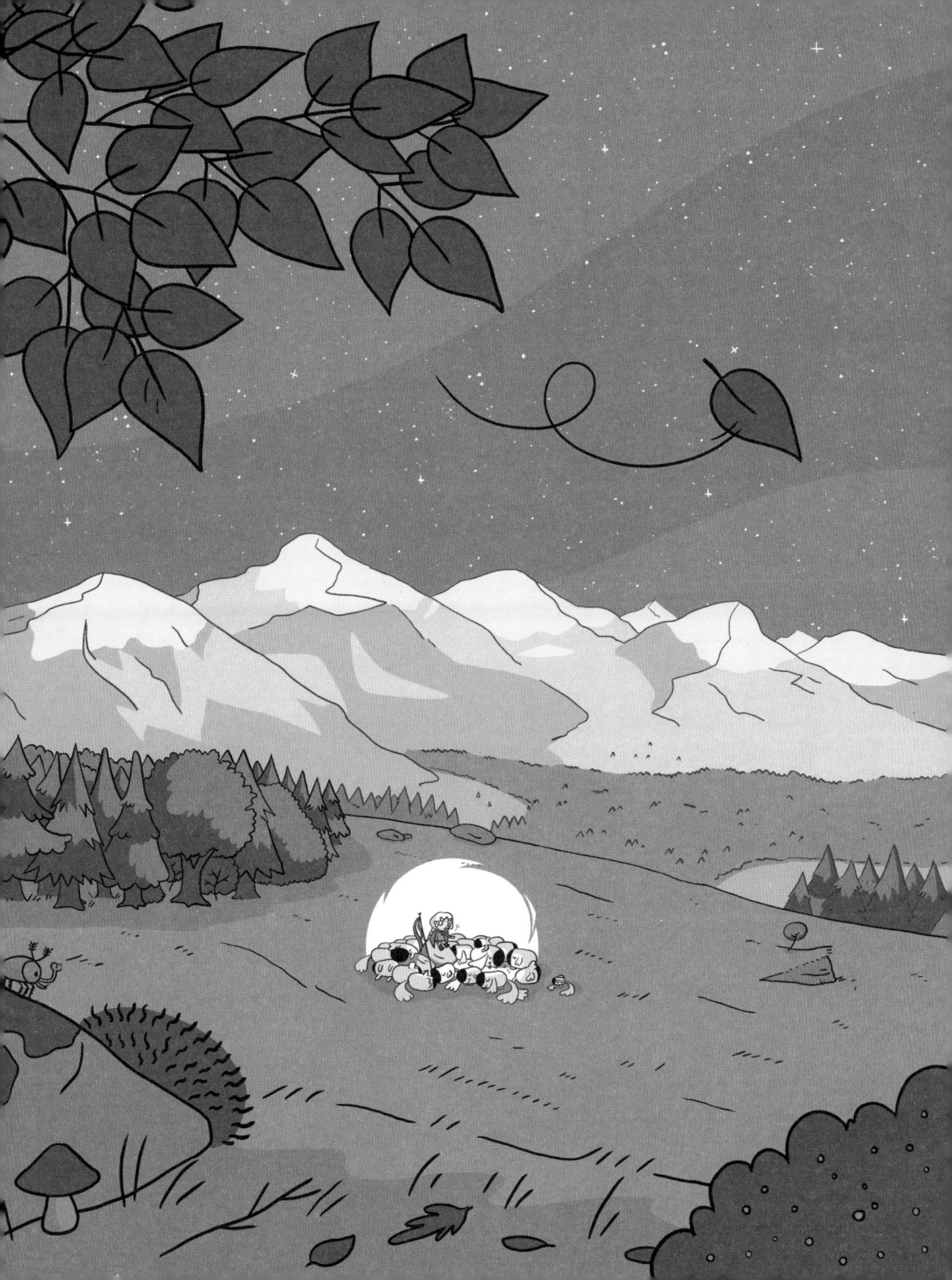

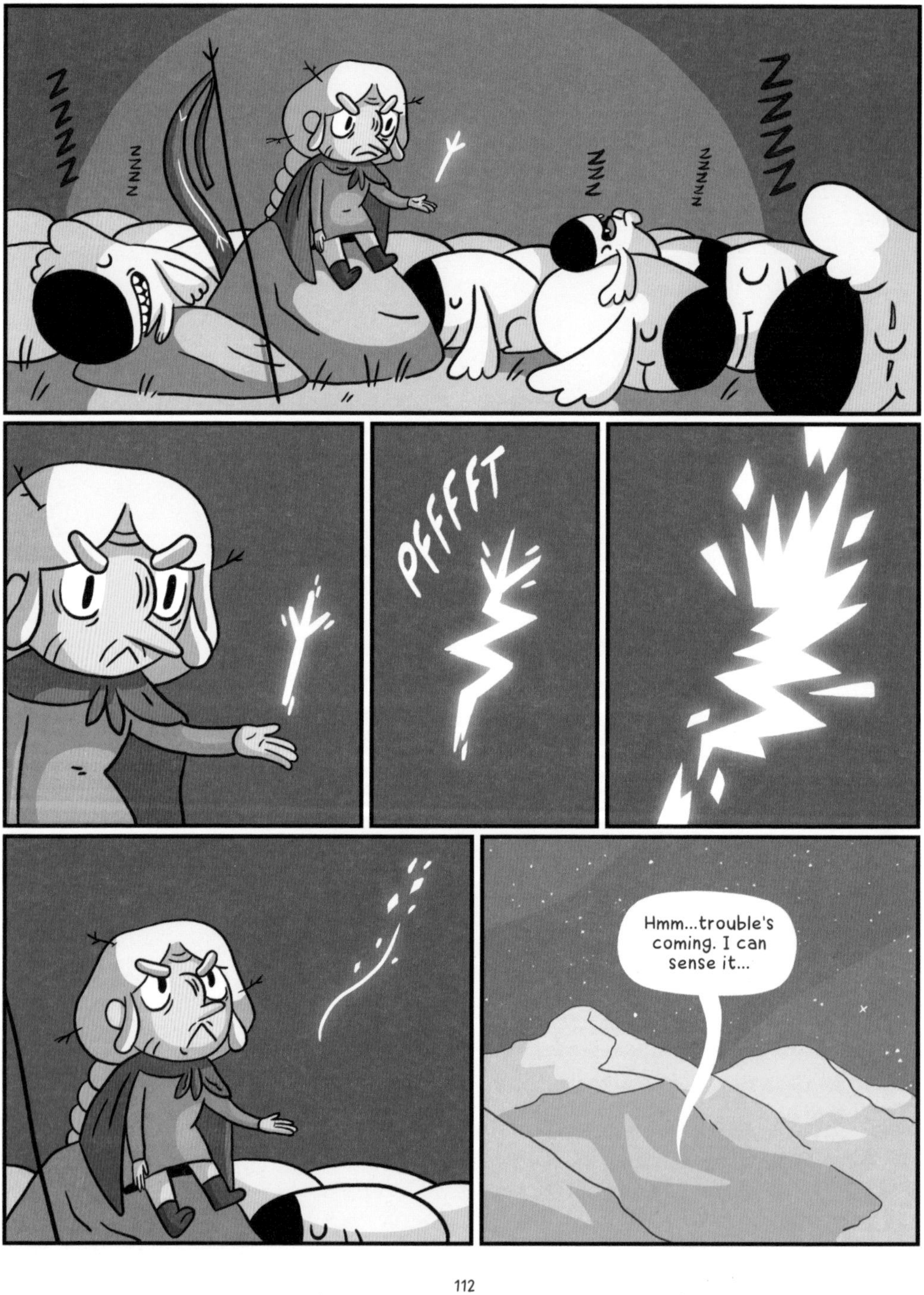
ZZZZ
ZZZZ
ZZZ
ZZZZZ
ZZZZZ
PFFFFT
Hmm...trouble's coming. I can sense it...

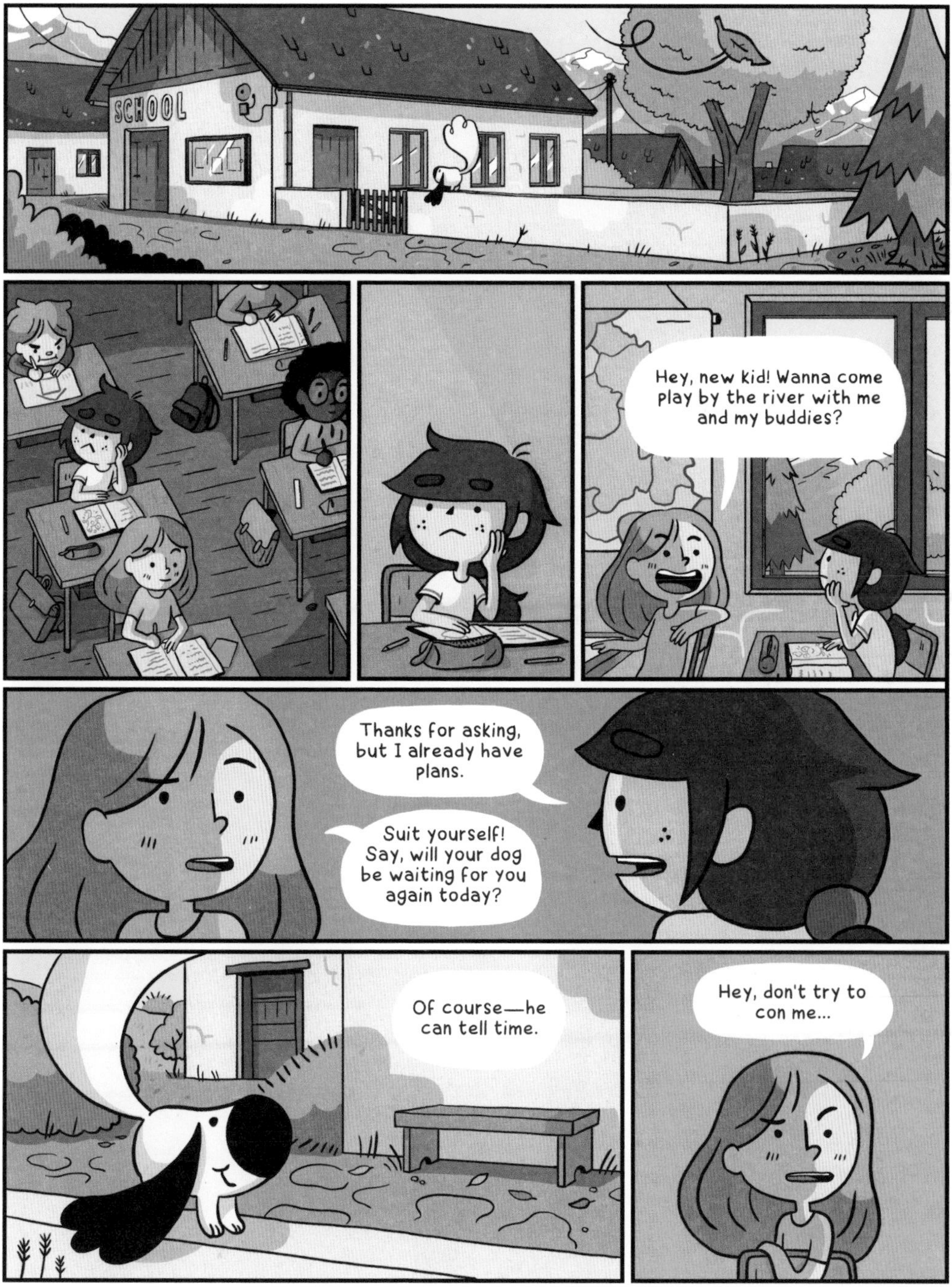
SCHOOL
Hey, new kid! Wanna come play by the river with me and my buddies?
Thanks for asking, but I already have plans.
Suit yourself! Say, will your dog be waiting for you again today?
Of course—he can tell time.
Hey, don't try to con me...

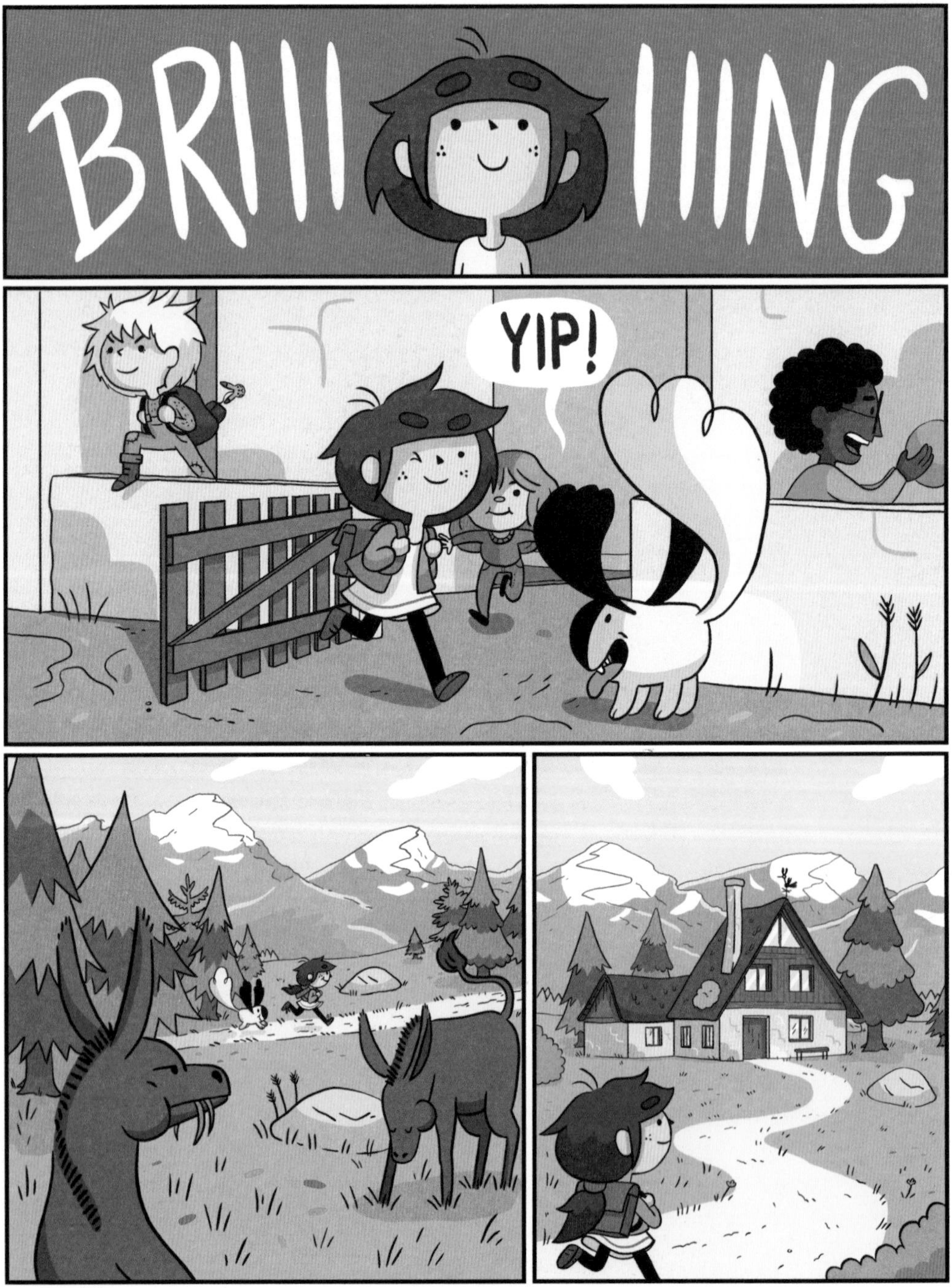
BRIIIIING
YIP!

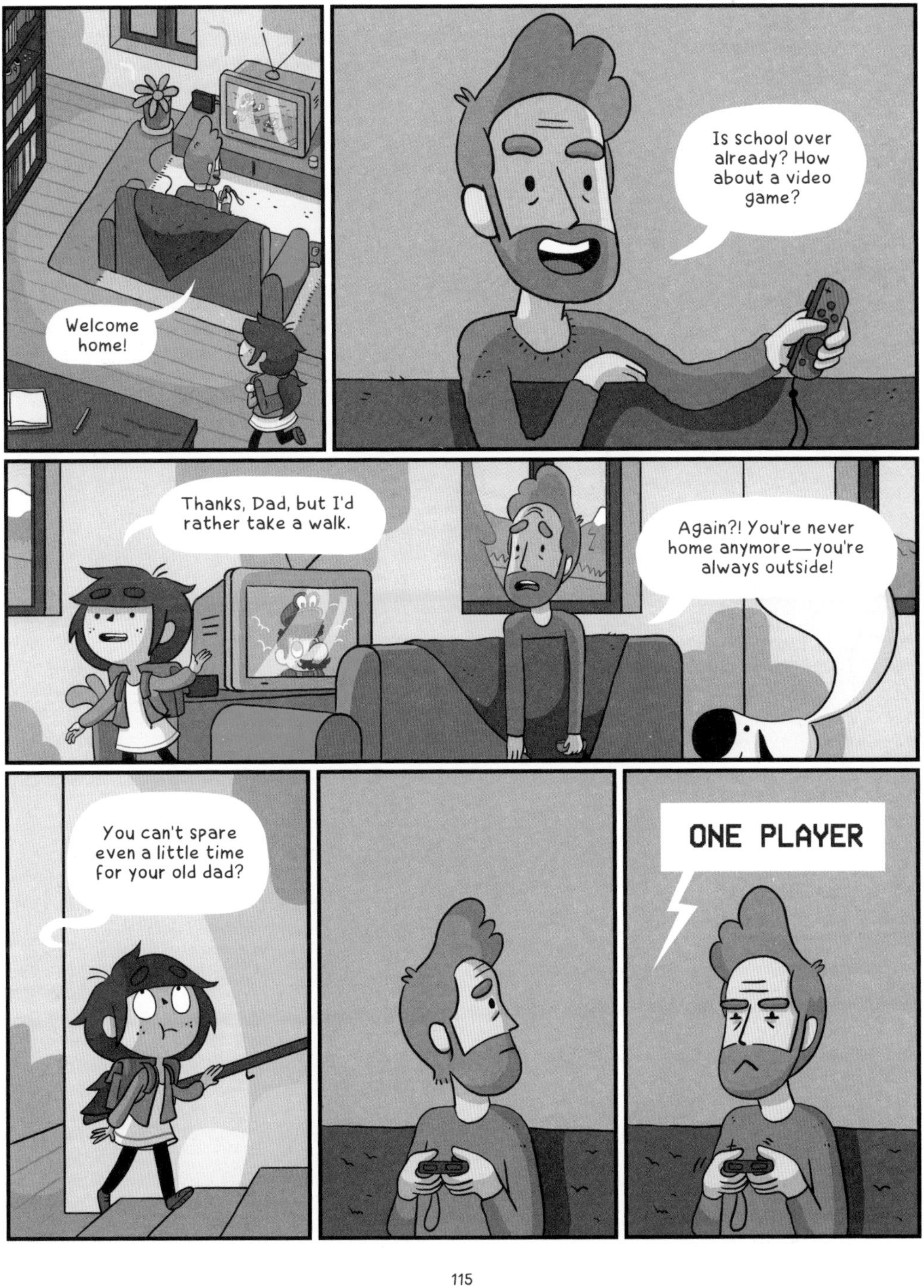
Welcome home!
Is school over already? How about a video game?
Thanks, Dad, but I'd rather take a walk.
Again?! You're never home anymore—you're always outside!
You can't spare even a little time for your old dad?
ONE PLAYER

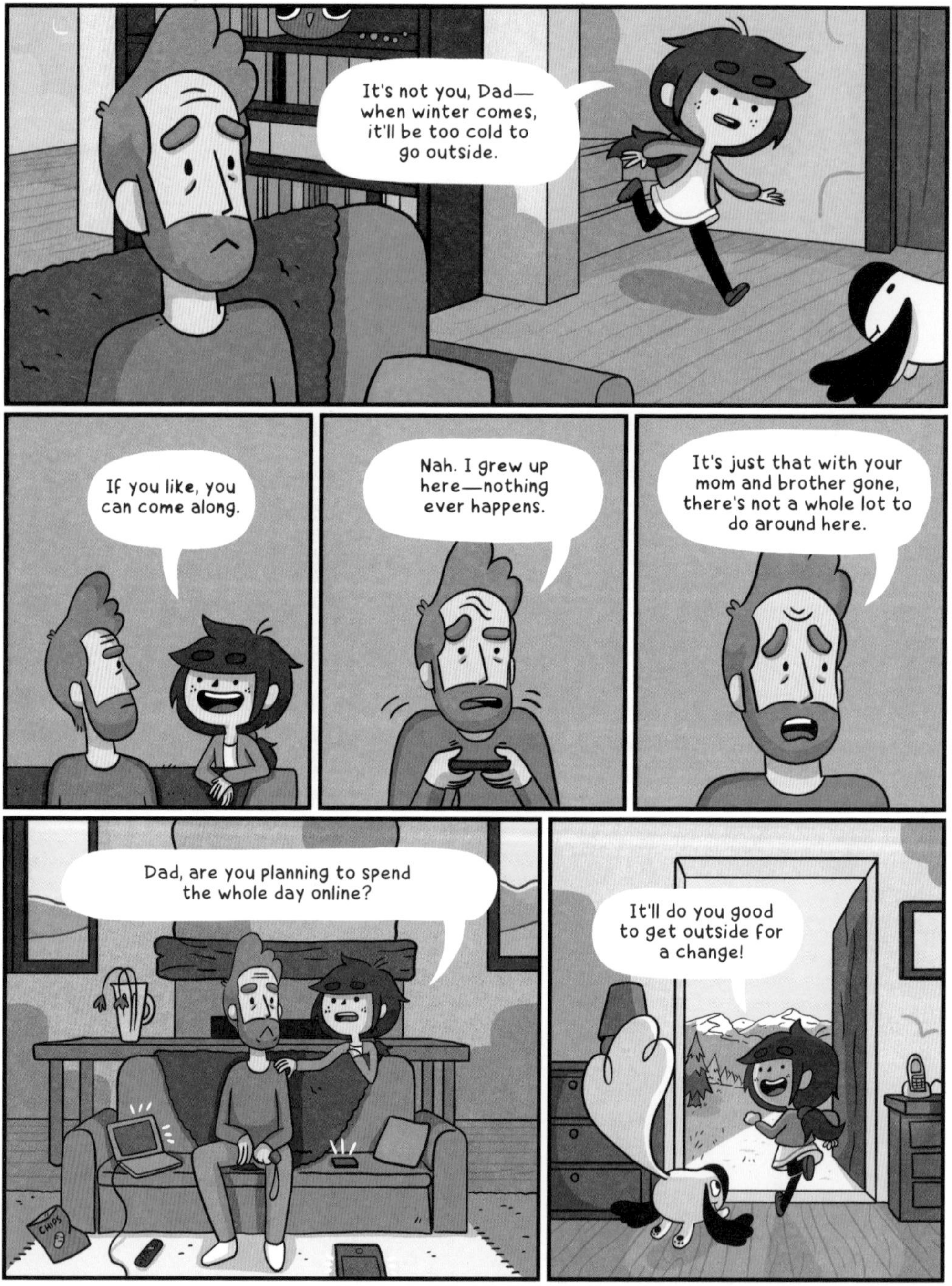
It's not you, Dad— when winter comes, it'll be too cold to go outside.
If you like, you can come along.
Nah. I grew up here—nothing ever happens.
It's just that with your mom and brother gone, there's not a whole lot to do around here.
Dad, are you planning to spend the whole day online?
It'll do you good to get outside for a change!
CHIPS

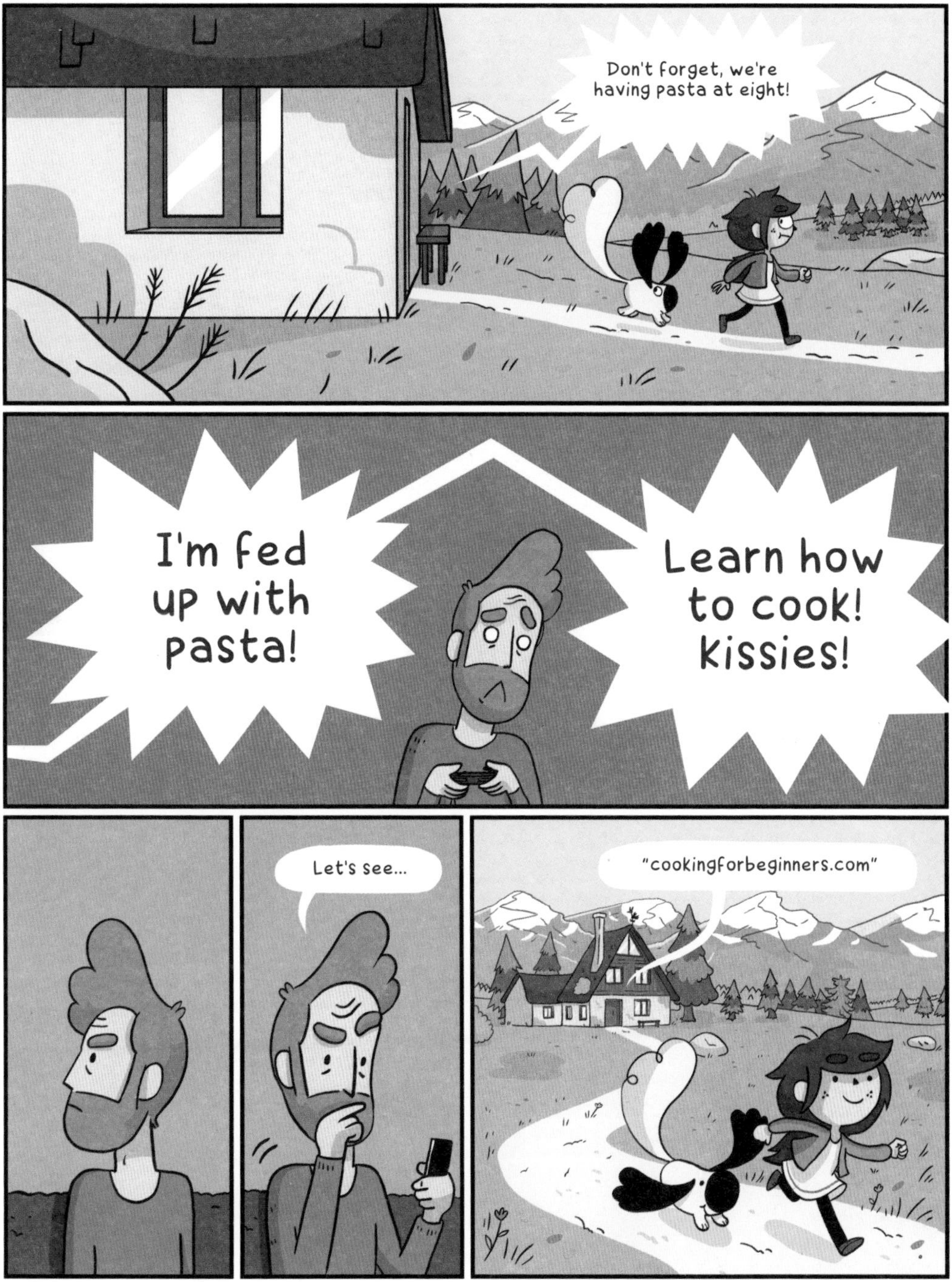
Don't forget, we're having pasta at eight!
I'm fed up with pasta!
Learn how to cook! Kissies!
Let's see...
"cookingforbeginners.com"

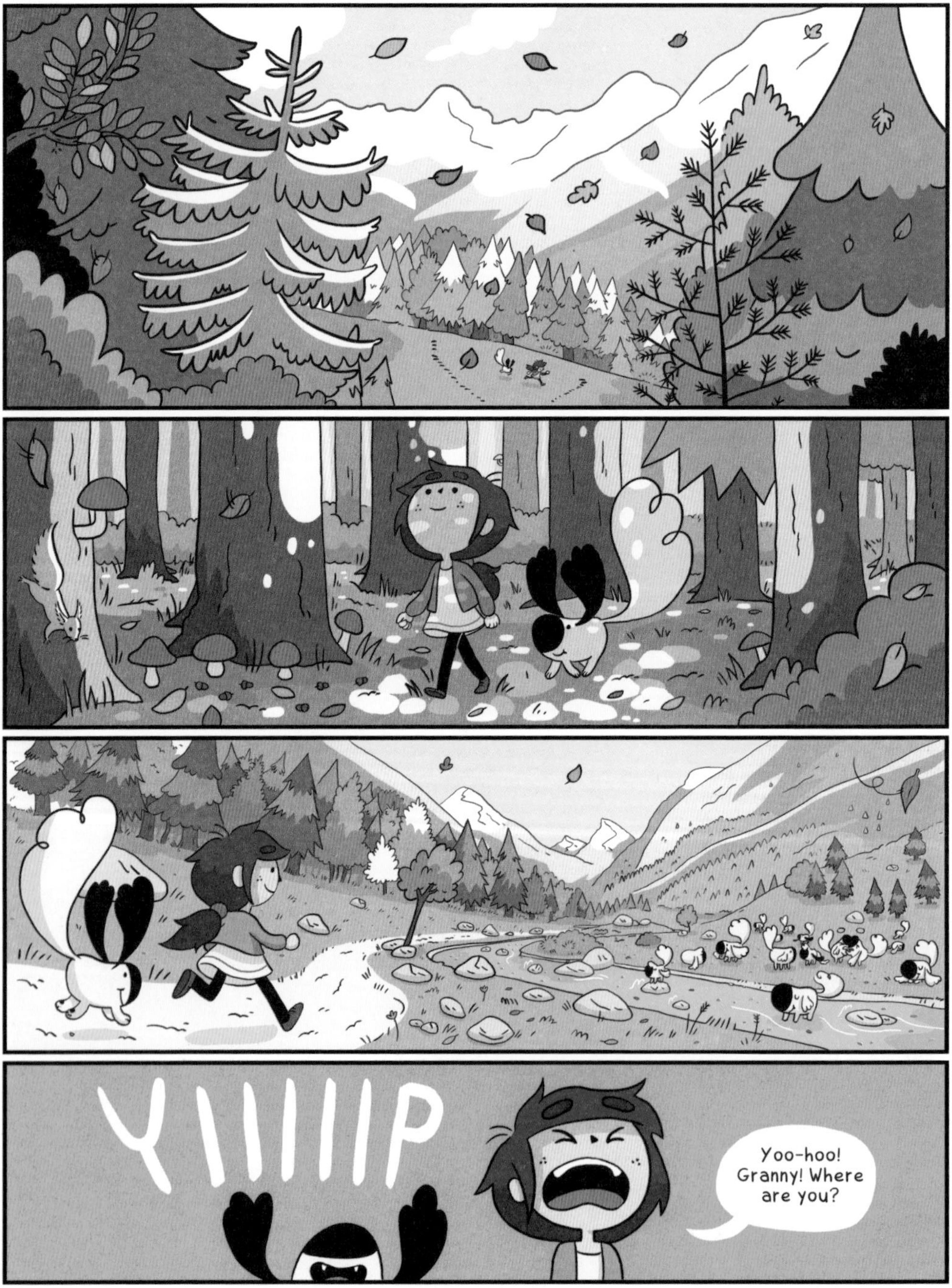
YIIIIIP
Yoo-hoo! Granny! Where are you?

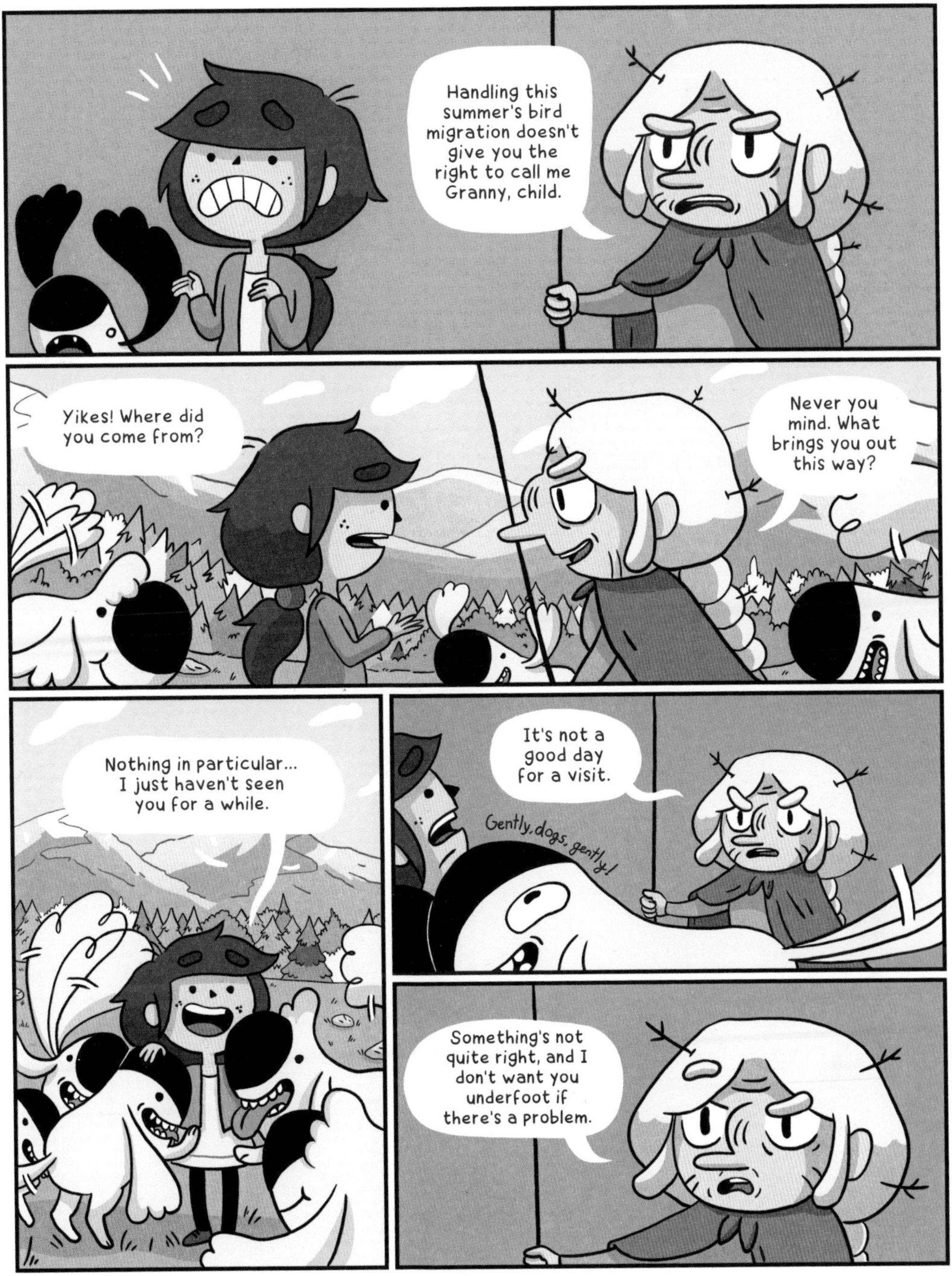
Handling this summer's bird migration doesn't give you the right to call me Granny, child.
Yikes! Where did you come from?
Never you mind. What brings you out this way?
Nothing in particular... I just haven't seen you for a while.
It's not a good day for a visit.
Gently, dogs, gently!
Something's not quite right, and I don't want you underfoot if there's a problem.

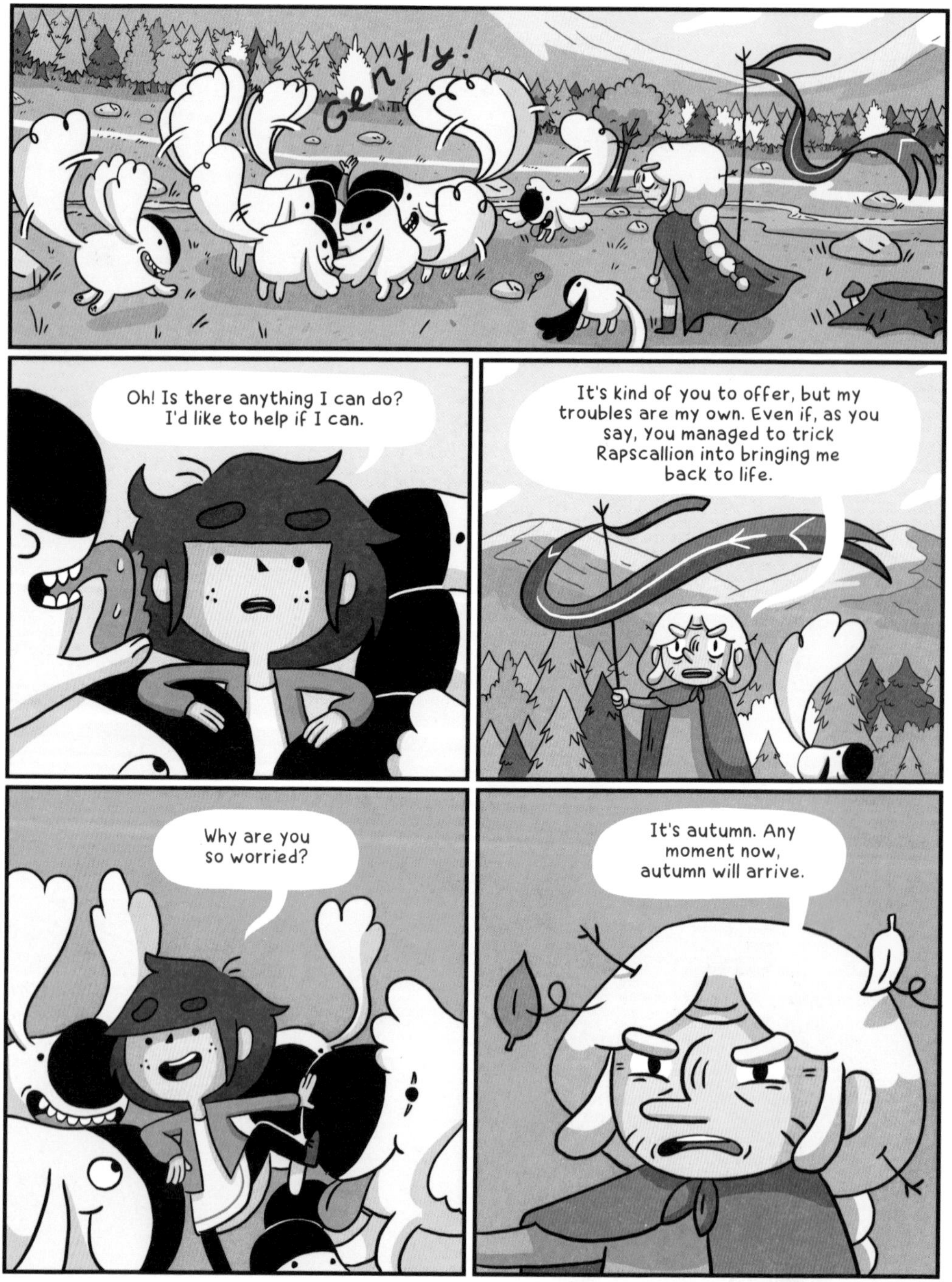
Gently!
Oh! Is there anything I can do? I'd like to help if I can.
It's kind of you to offer, but my troubles are my own. Even if, as you say, you managed to trick Rapscallion into bringing me back to life.
Why are you so worried?
It's autumn. Any moment now, autumn will arrive.

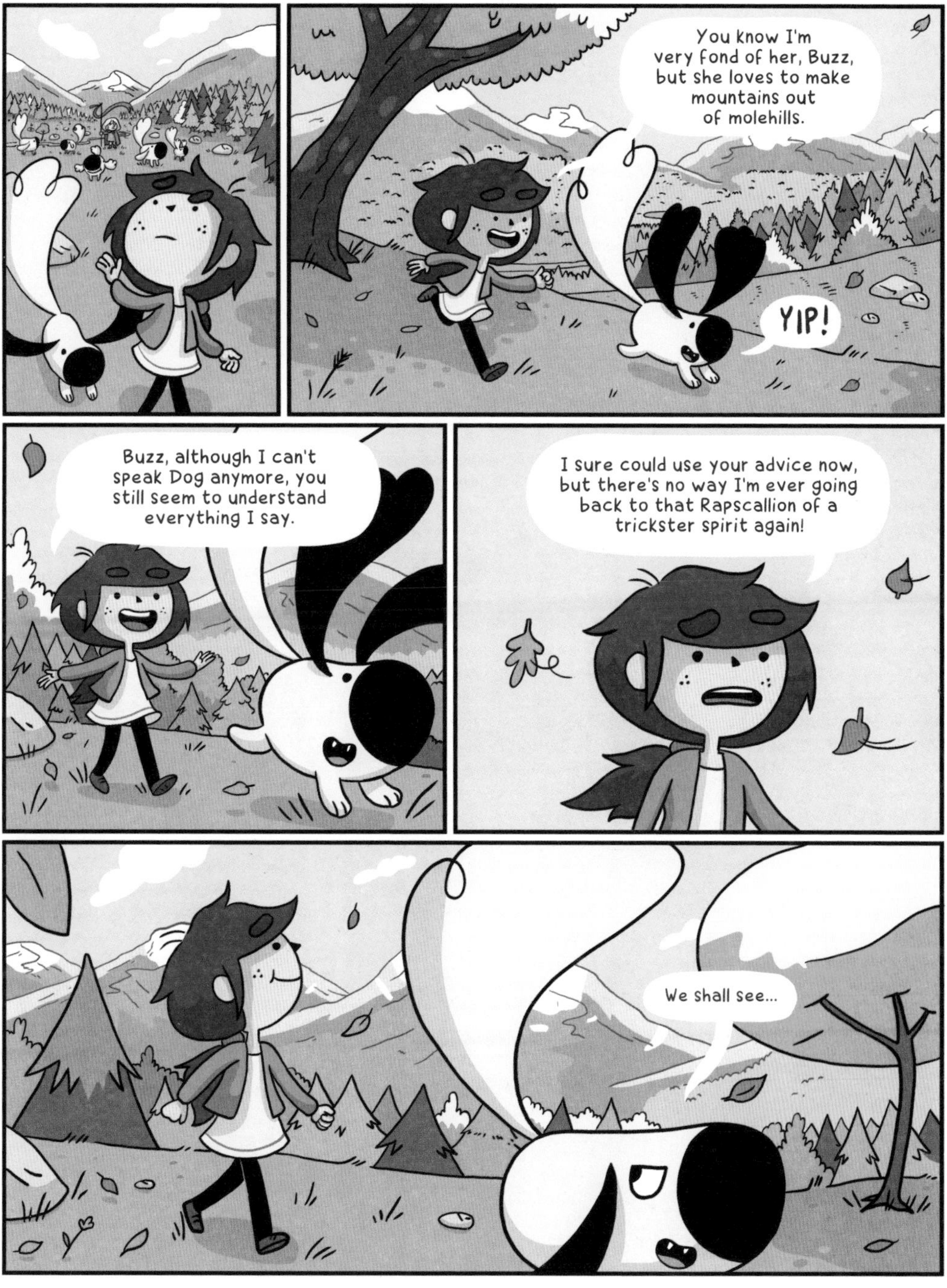
You know I'm very fond of her, Buzz, but she loves to make mountains out of molehills.
YIP!
Buzz, although I can't speak Dog anymore, you still seem to understand everything I say.
I sure could use your advice now, but there's no way I'm ever going back to that Rapscallion of a trickster spirit again!
We shall see...

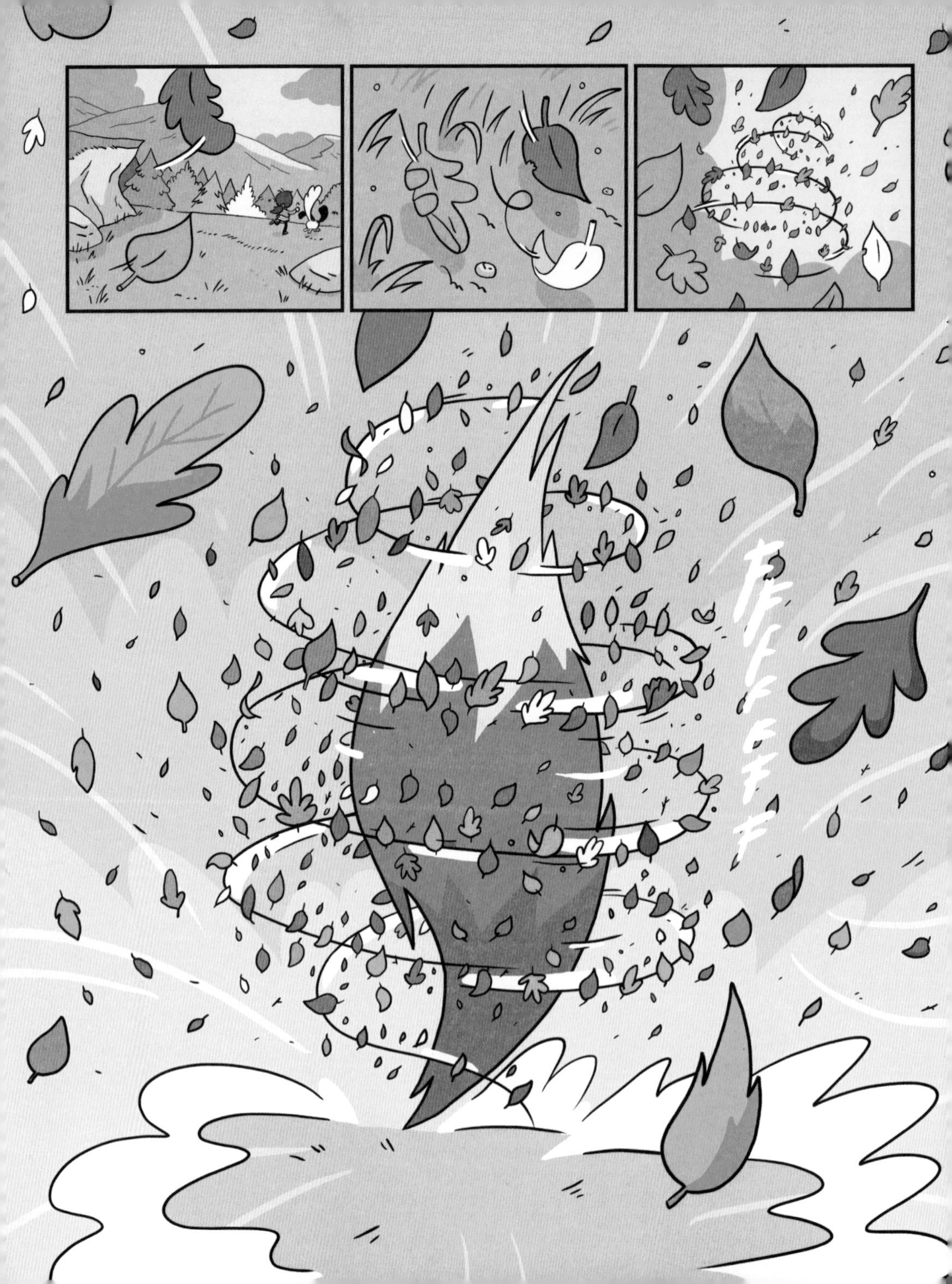
FFFFFFFF

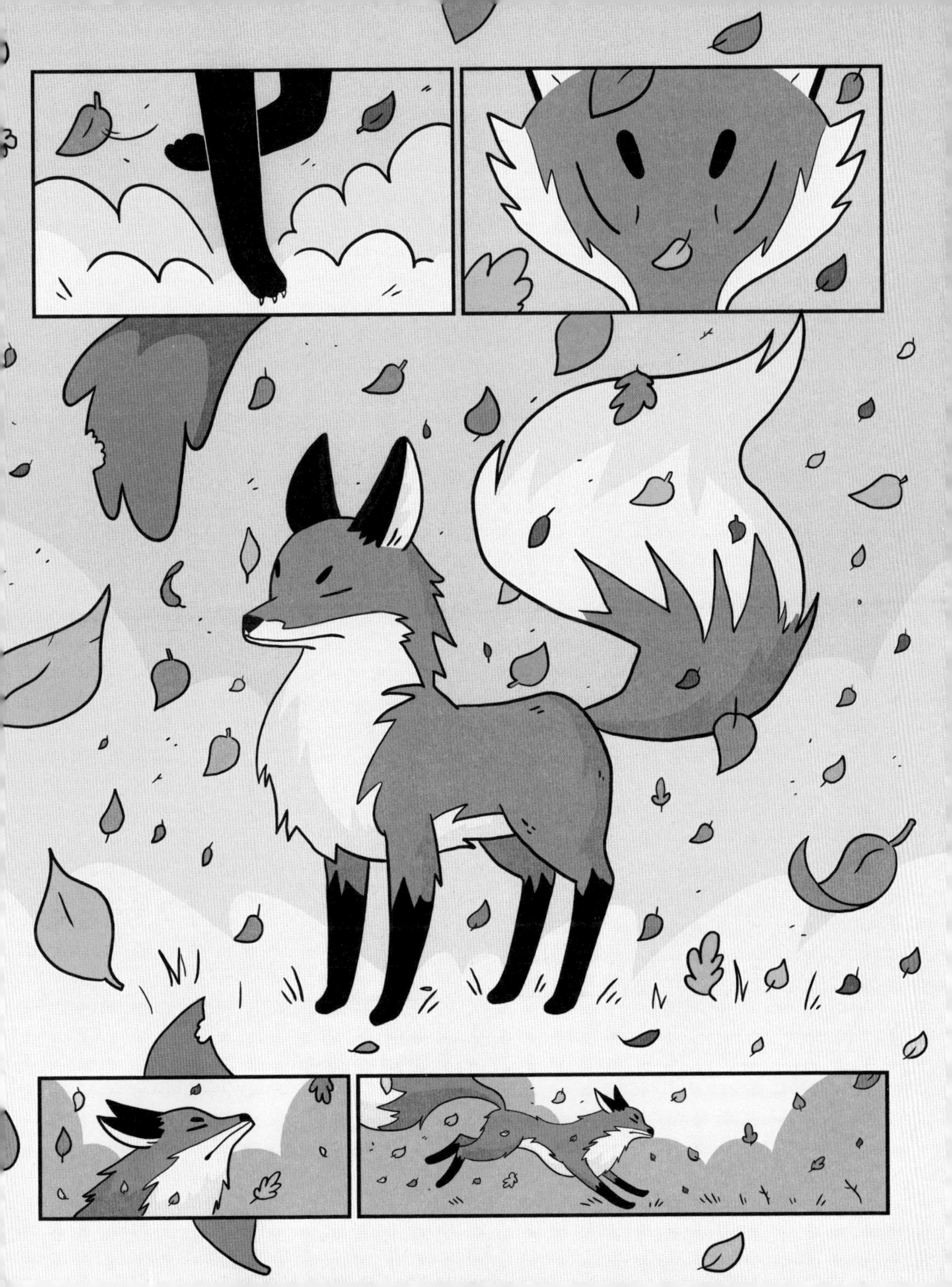

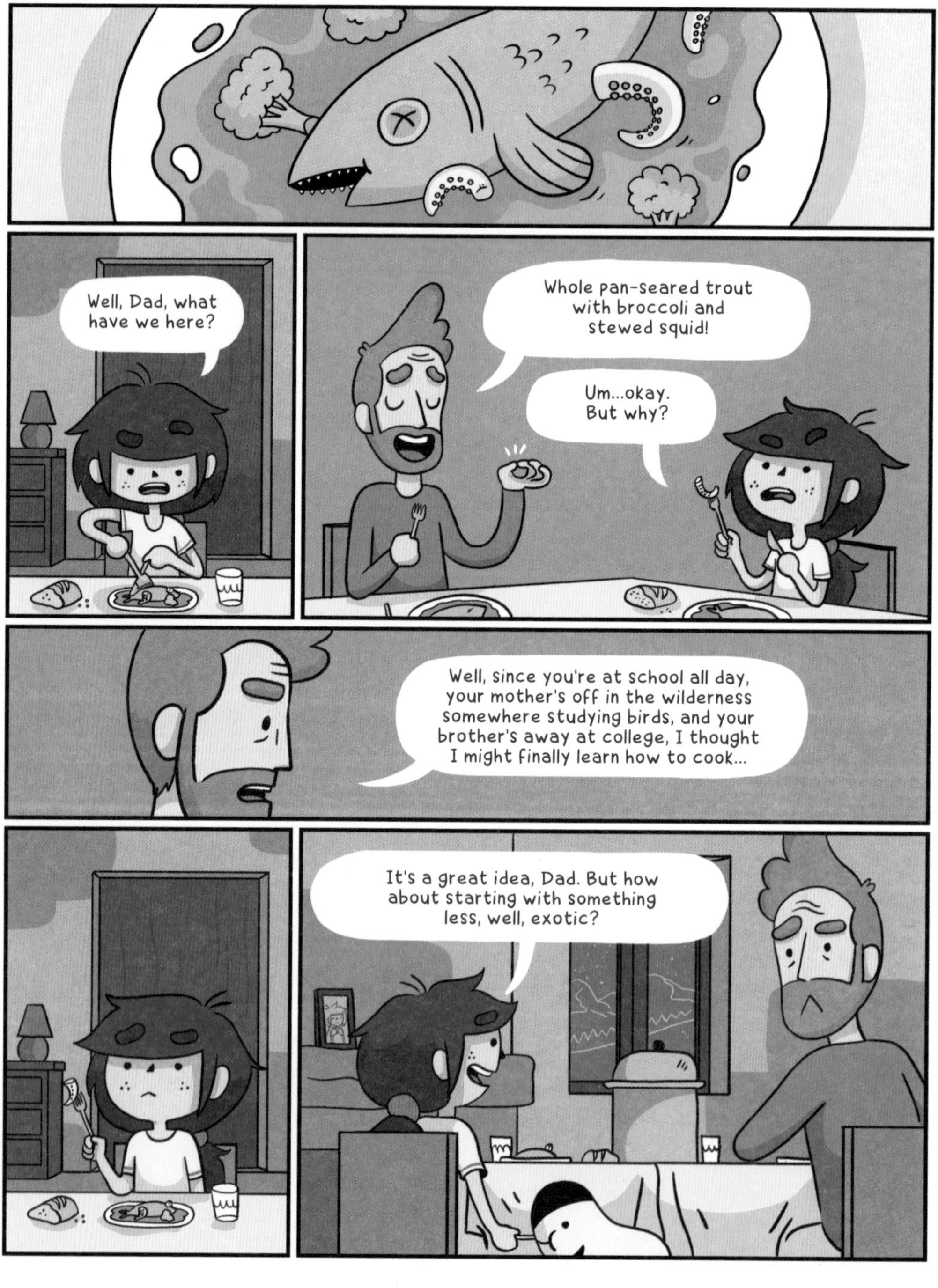
Well, Dad, what have we here?
Whole pan-seared trout with broccoli and stewed squid!
Um...okay. But why?
Well, since you're at school all day, your mother's off in the wilderness somewhere studying birds, and your brother's away at college, I thought I might finally learn how to cook...
It's a great idea, Dad. But how about starting with something less, well, exotic?

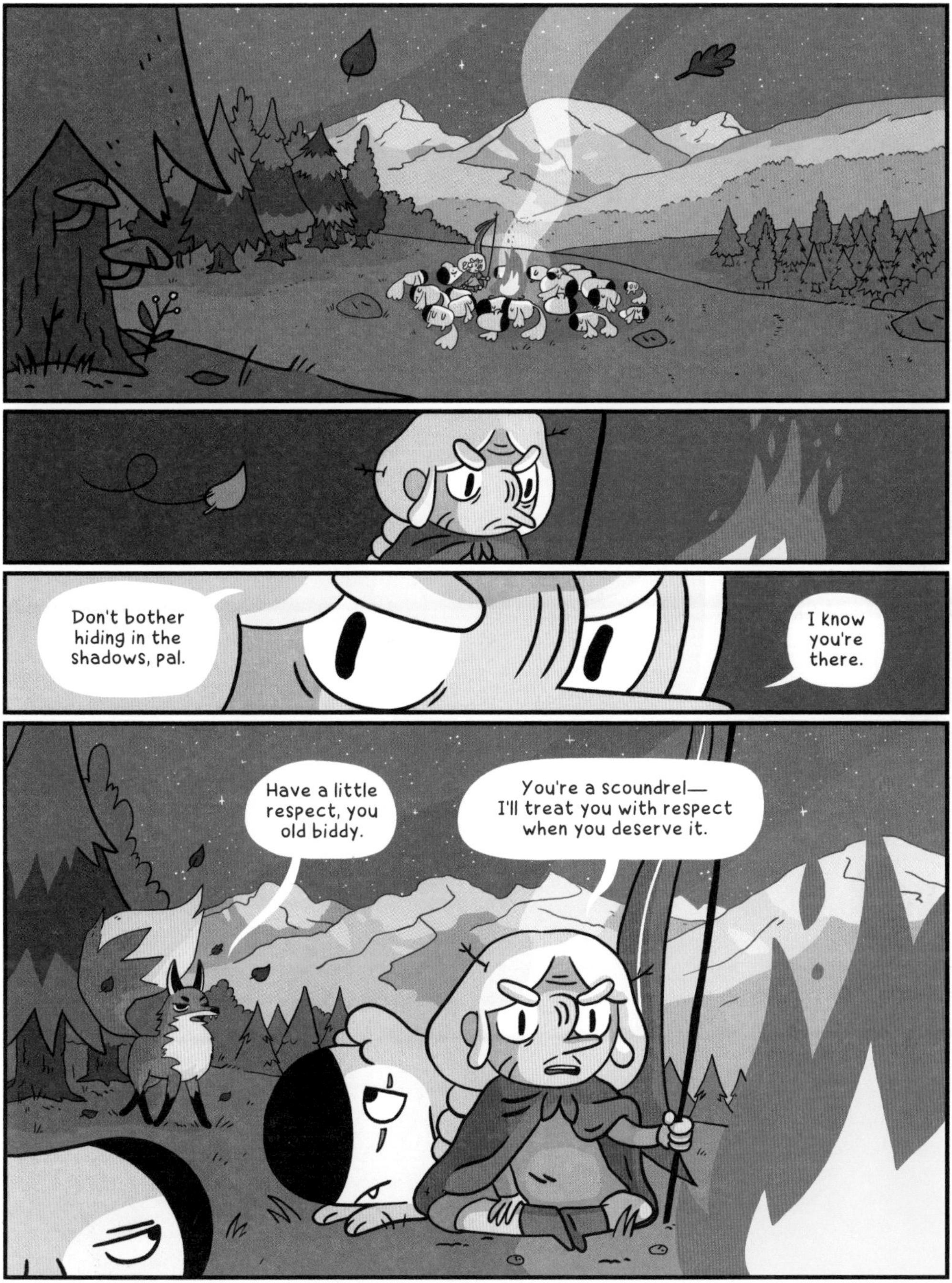

Don't bother hiding in the shadows, pal.
I know you're there.
Have a little respect, you old biddy.
You're a scoundrel—I'll treat you with respect when you deserve it.

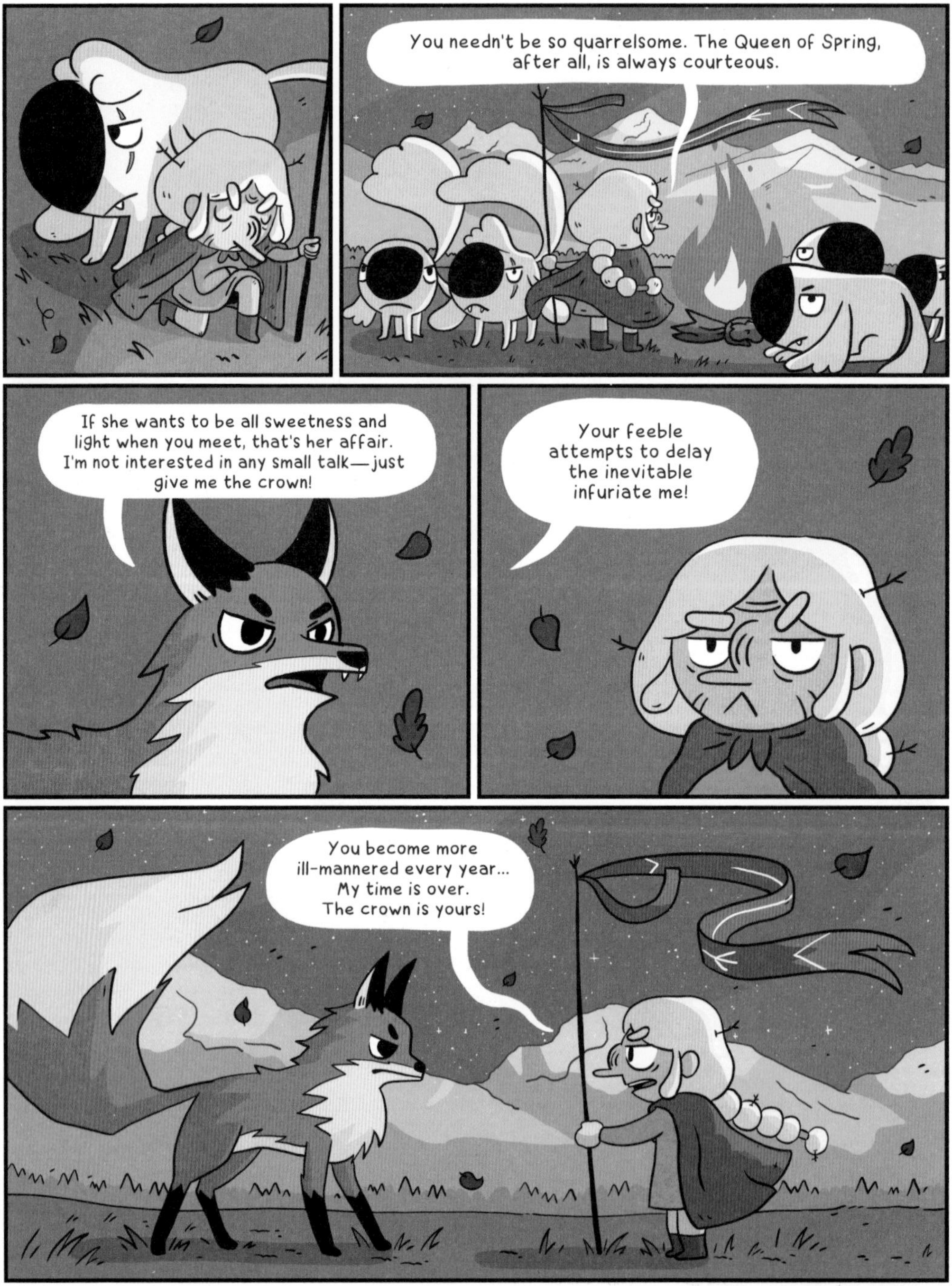
You needn't be so quarrelsome. The Queen of Spring, after all, is always courteous.
If she wants to be all sweetness and light when you meet, that's her affair. I'm not interested in any small talk—just give me the crown!
Your feeble attempts to delay the inevitable infuriate me!
You become more ill-mannered every year... My time is over. The crown is yours!

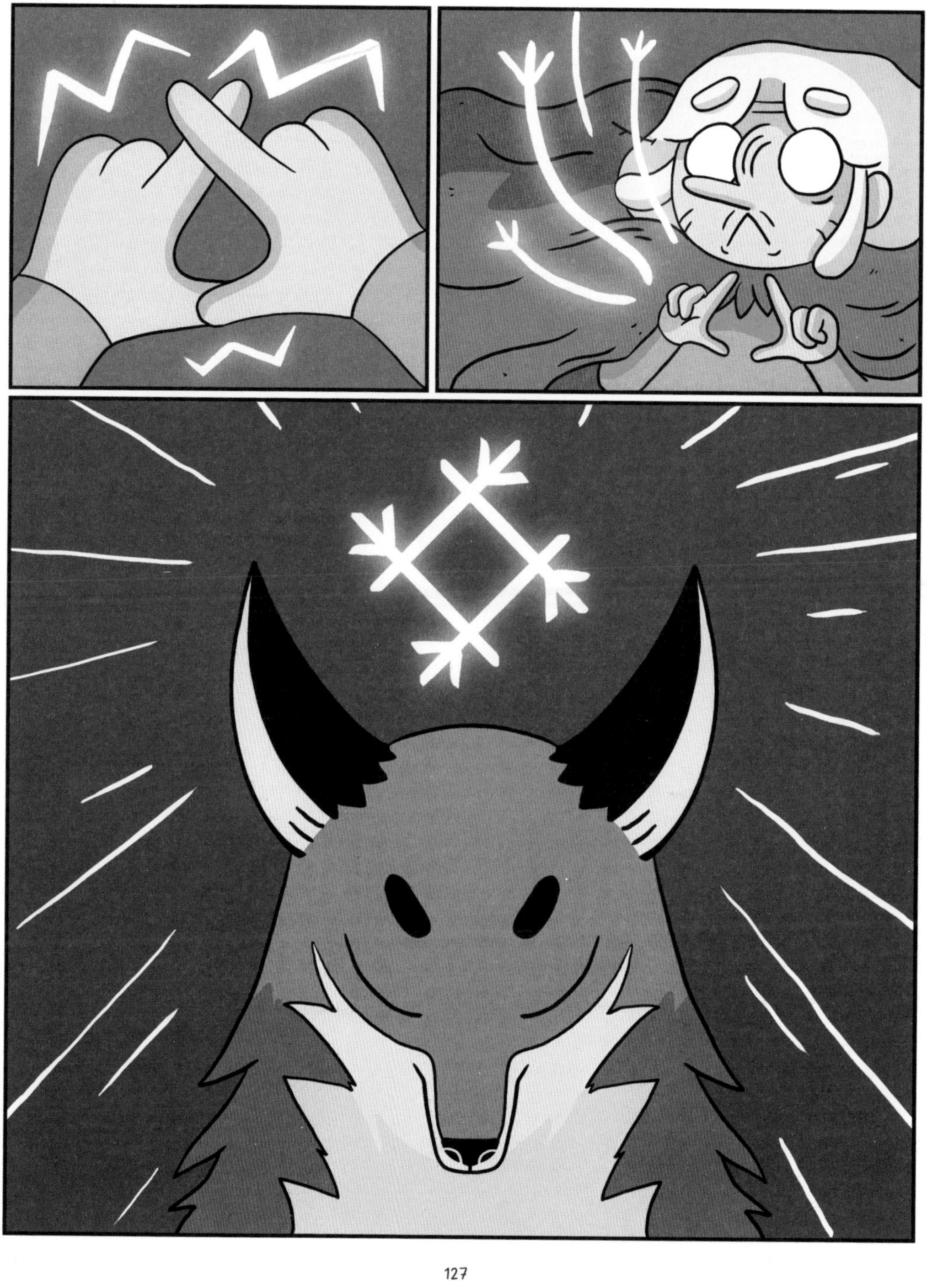

At last!

CRRRK

What?

FFFFFFF

128

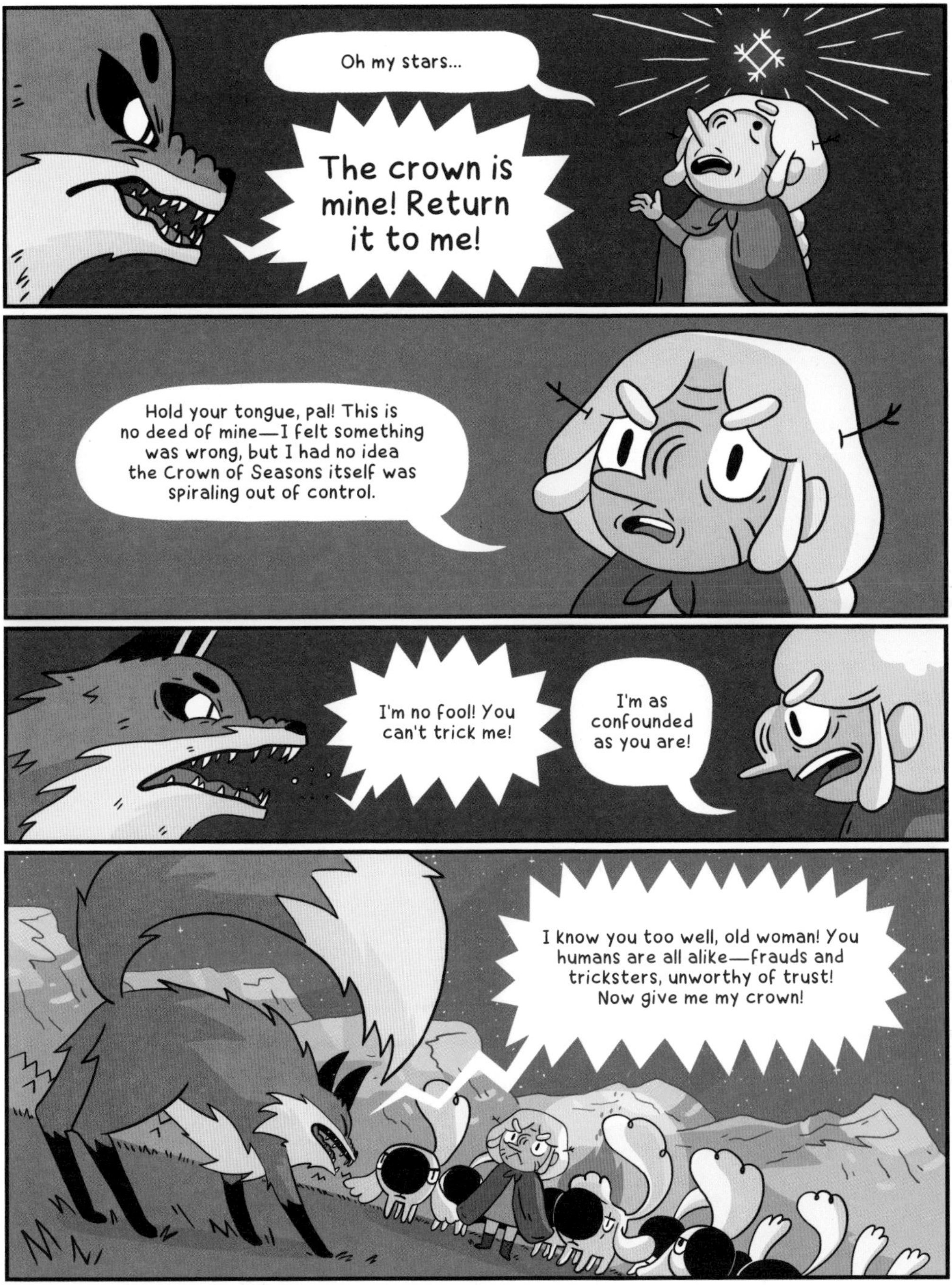
Oh my stars...
The crown is mine! Return it to me!
Hold your tongue, pal! This is no deed of mine—I felt something was wrong, but I had no idea the Crown of Seasons itself was spiraling out of control.
I'm no fool! You can't trick me!
I'm as confounded as you are!
I know you too well, old woman! You humans are all alike—frauds and tricksters, unworthy of trust! Now give me my crown!

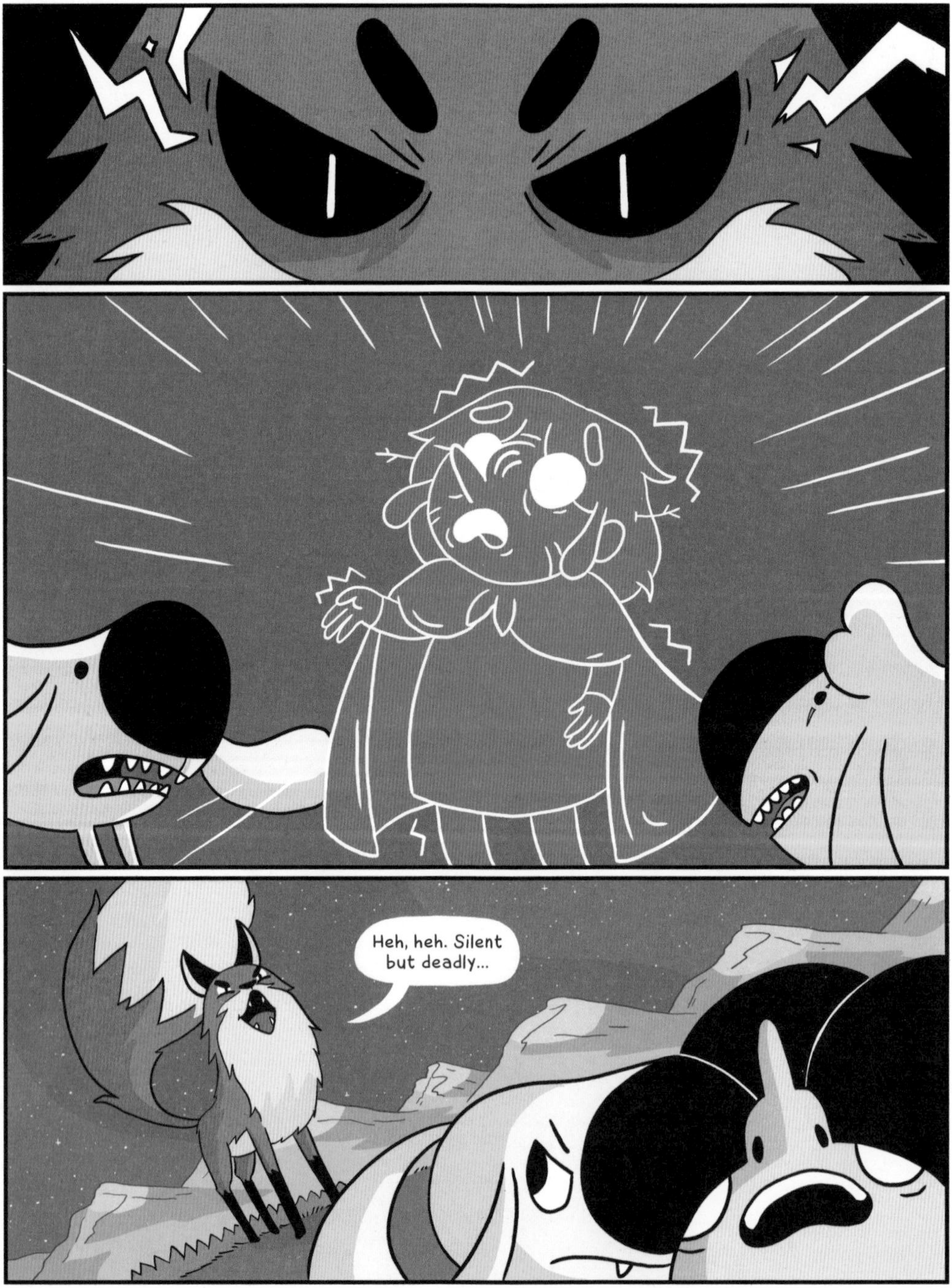
Heh, heh. Silent but deadly...

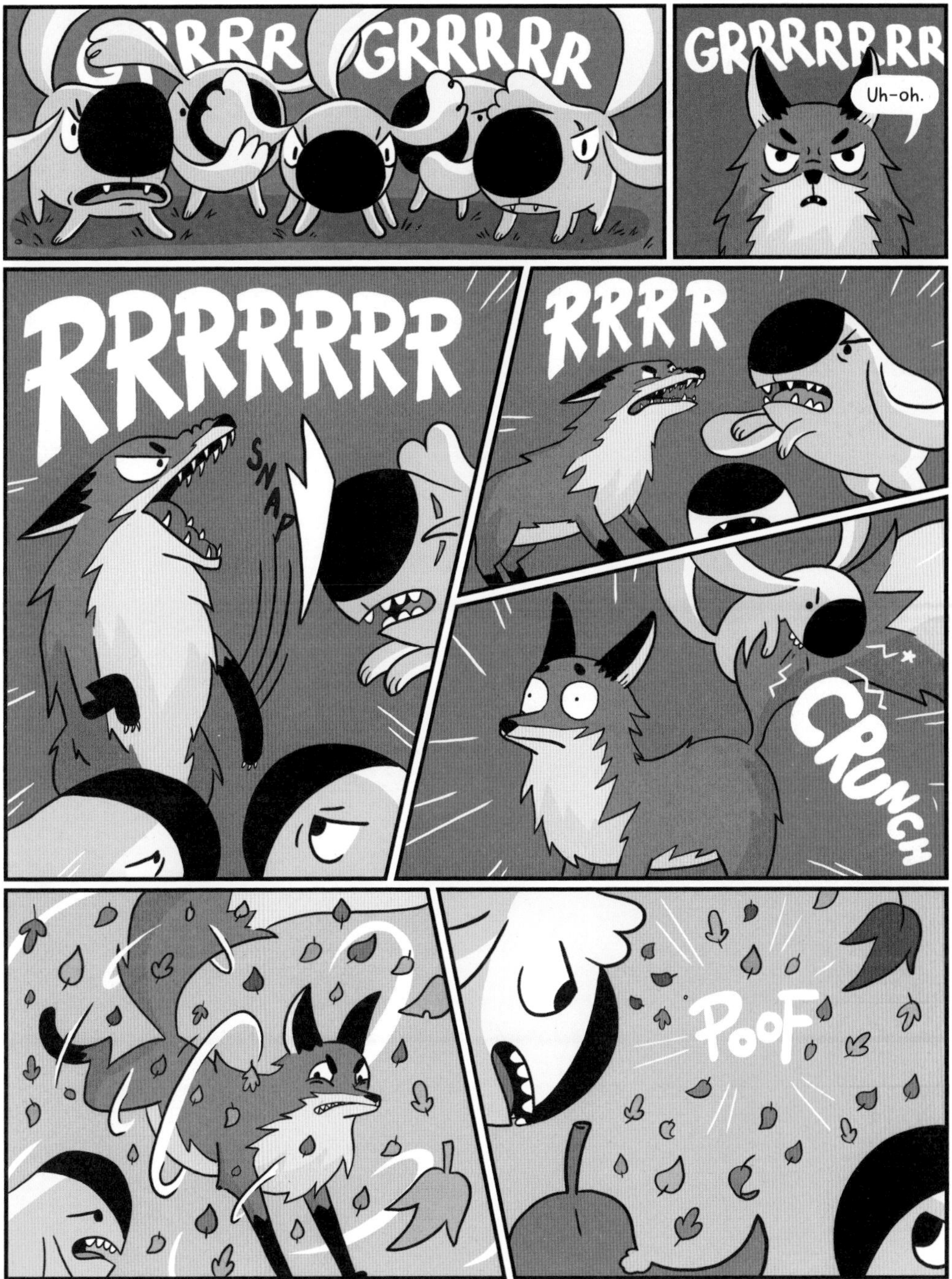
GRRRR GRRRRRR
GRRRRRRRR
Uh-oh.
RRRRRRRR
SNAP
RRRR
CRUNCH
POOF

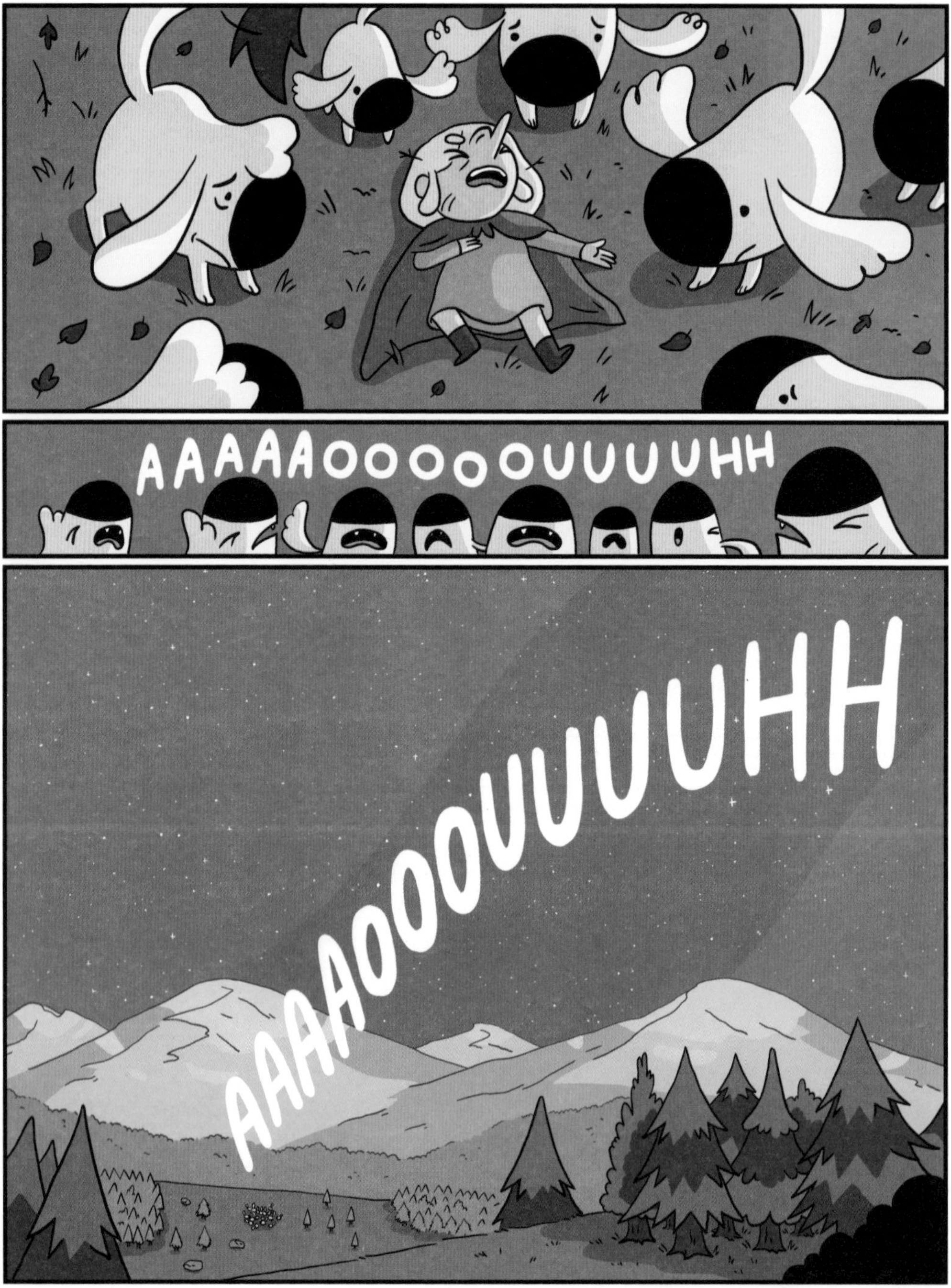
AAAAAOOOOOUUUUUHH
AAAAOOOOUUUUUHH

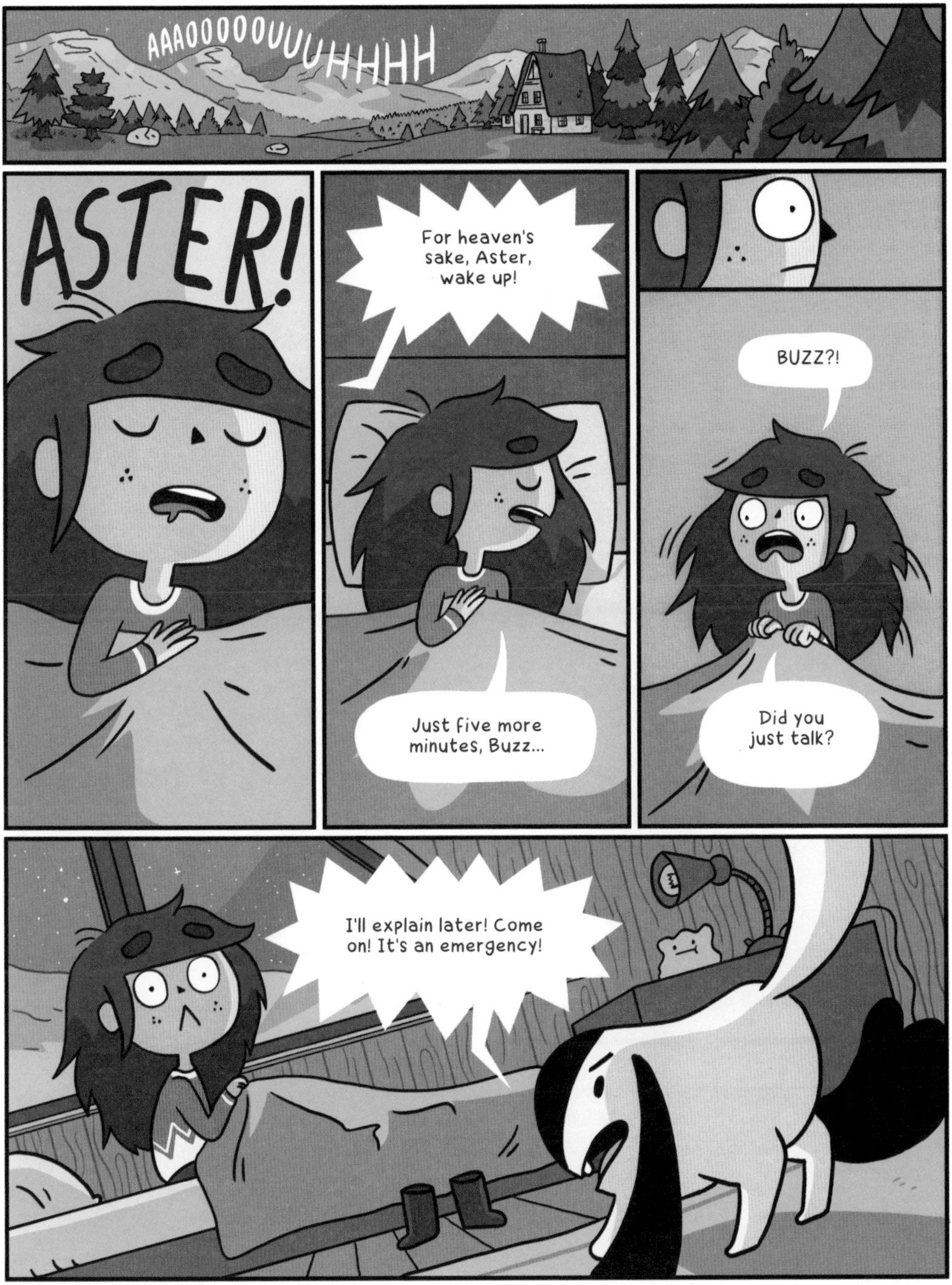
AAAOOOOOUUUHHHHH
ASTER!
For heaven's sake, Aster, wake up!
Just five more minutes, Buzz...
BUZZ?!
Did you just talk?
I'll explain later! Come on! It's an emergency!

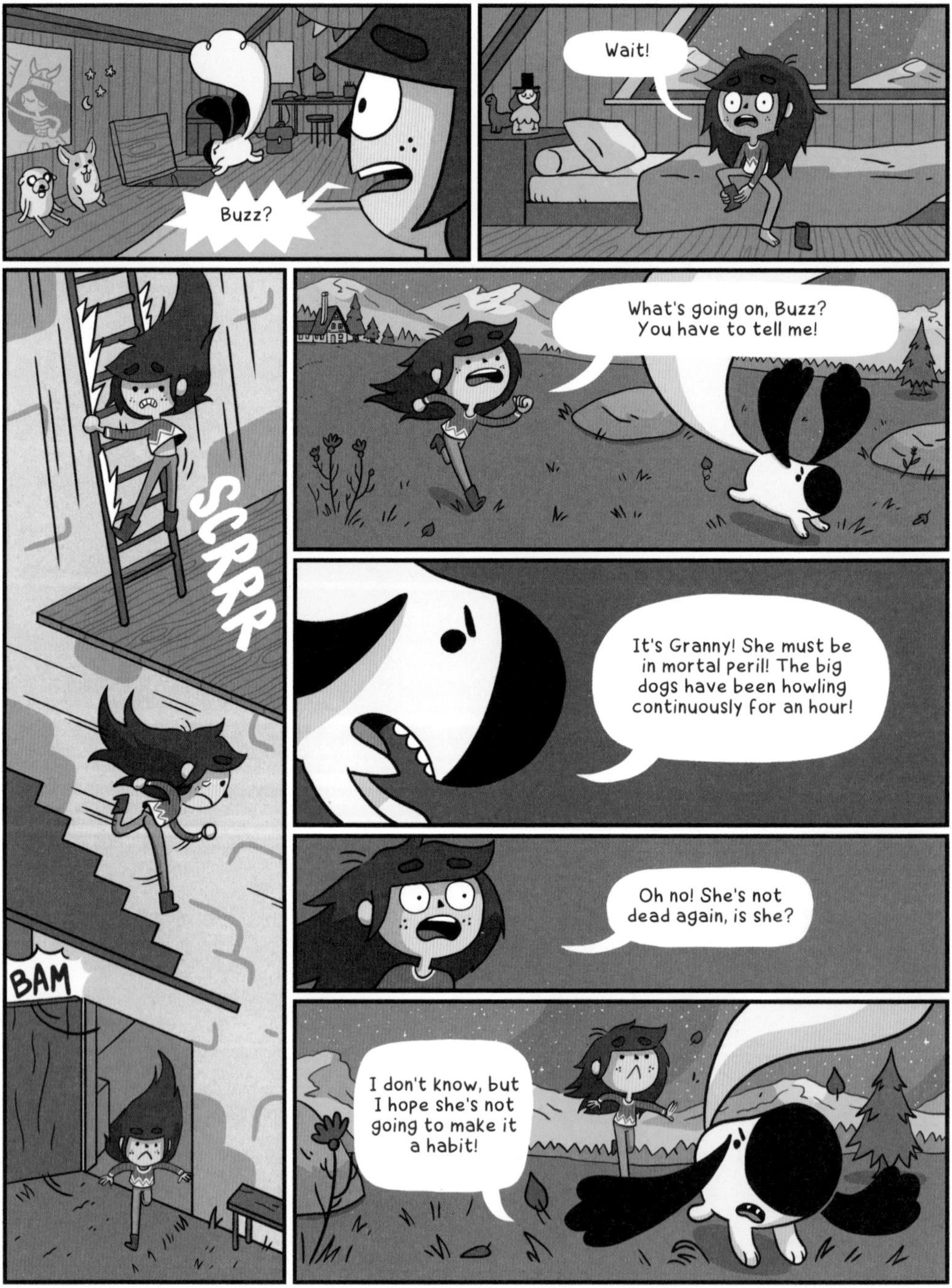
Buzz?
Wait!
SCRRR
BAM
What's going on, Buzz? You have to tell me!
It's Granny! She must be in mortal peril! The big dogs have been howling continuously for an hour!
Oh no! She's not dead again, is she?
I don't know, but I hope she's not going to make it a habit!

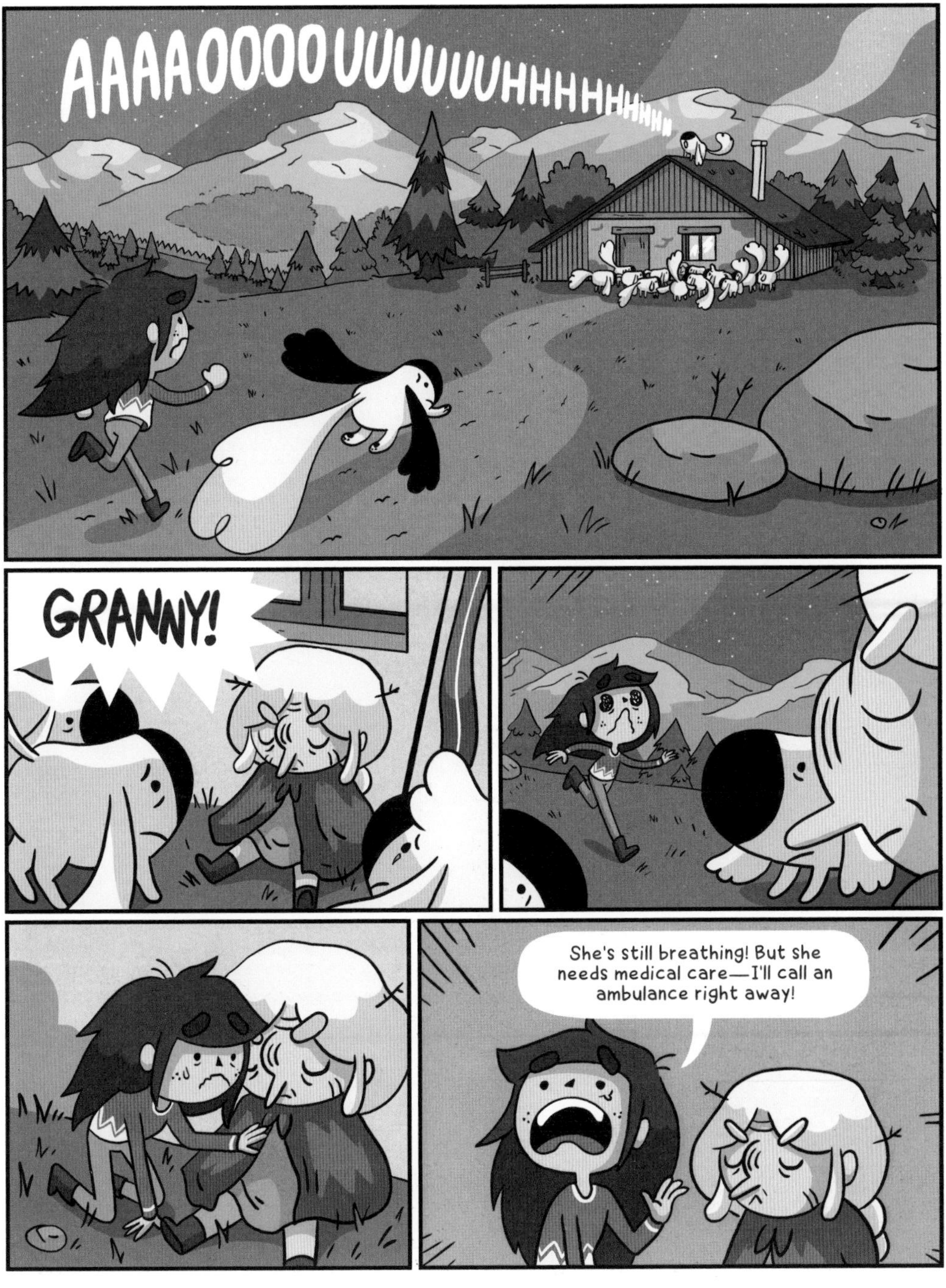
AAAAOOOOUUUUUUUHHHHHHHH
GRANNY!
She's still breathing! But she needs medical care—I'll call an ambulance right away!

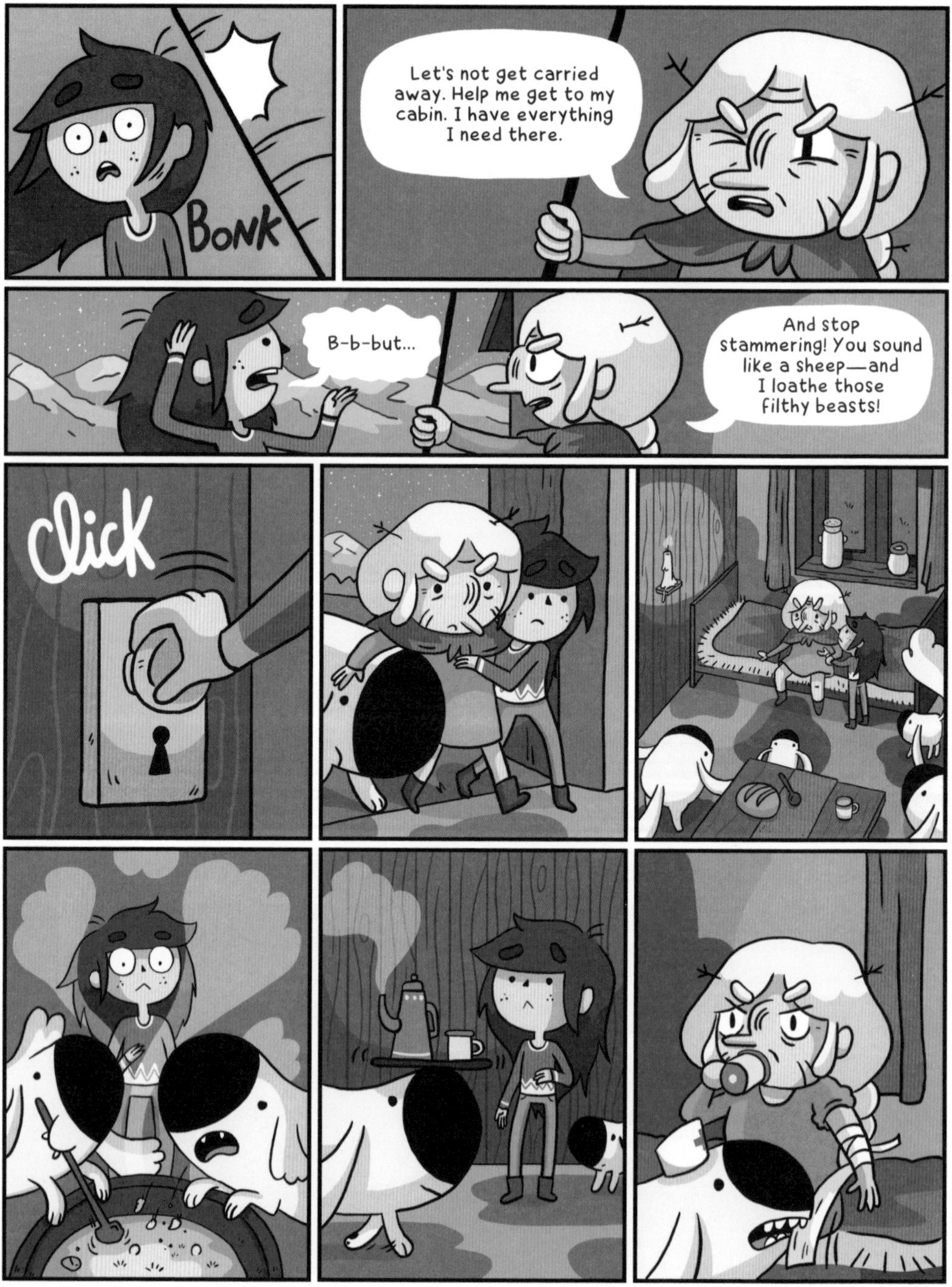
BONK
Let's not get carried away. Help me get to my cabin. I have everything I need there.
B-b-but...
And stop stammering! You sound like a sheep—and I loathe those filthy beasts!
Click

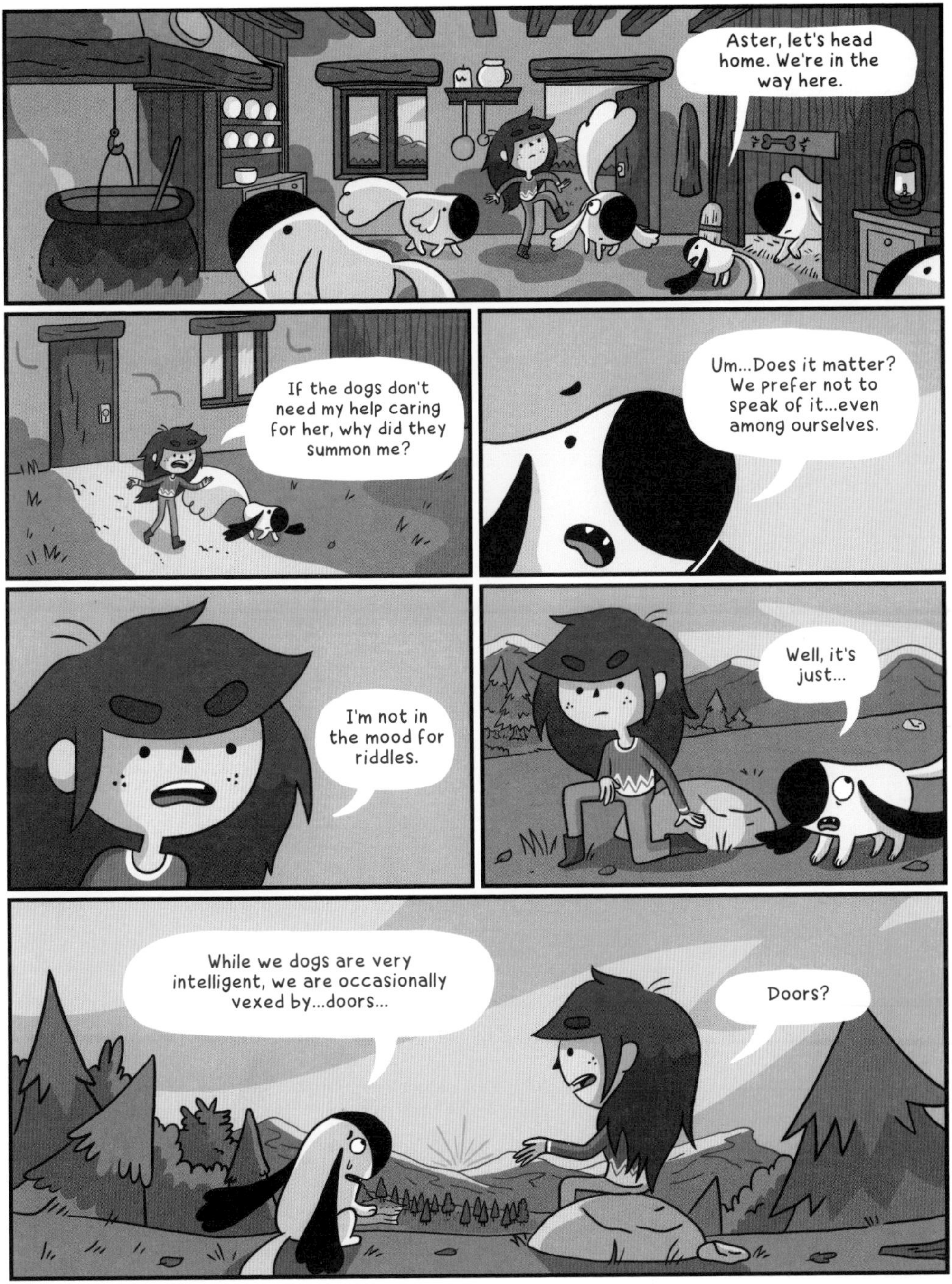
Aster, let's head home. We're in the way here.
If the dogs don't need my help caring for her, why did they summon me?
Um...Does it matter? We prefer not to speak of it...even among ourselves.
I'm not in the mood for riddles.
Well, it's just...
While we dogs are very intelligent, we are occasionally vexed by...doors...
Doors?

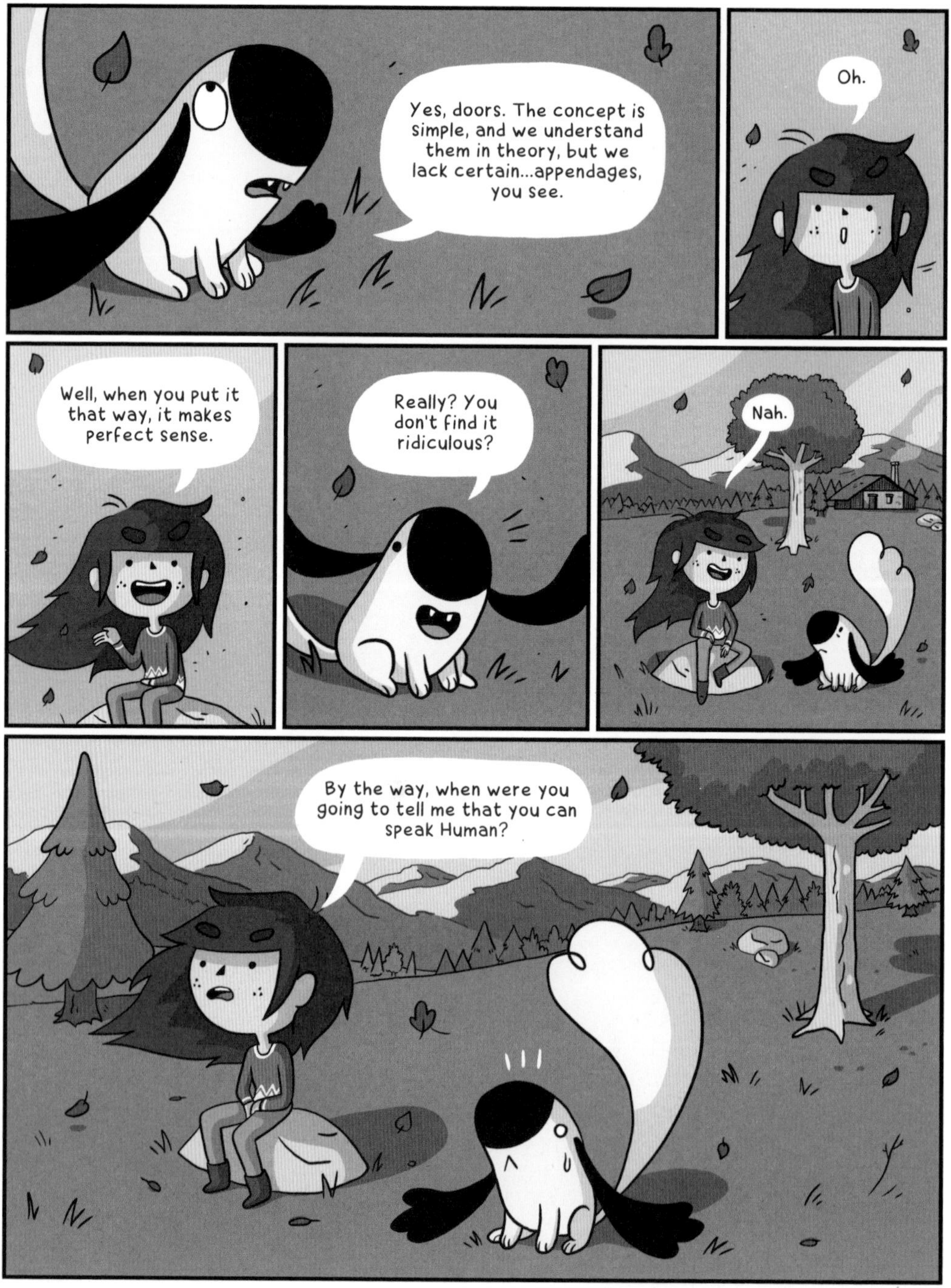
Yes, doors. The concept is simple, and we understand them in theory, but we lack certain...appendages, you see.
Oh.
Well, when you put it that way, it makes perfect sense.
Really? You don't find it ridiculous?
Nah.
By the way, when were you going to tell me that you can speak Human?

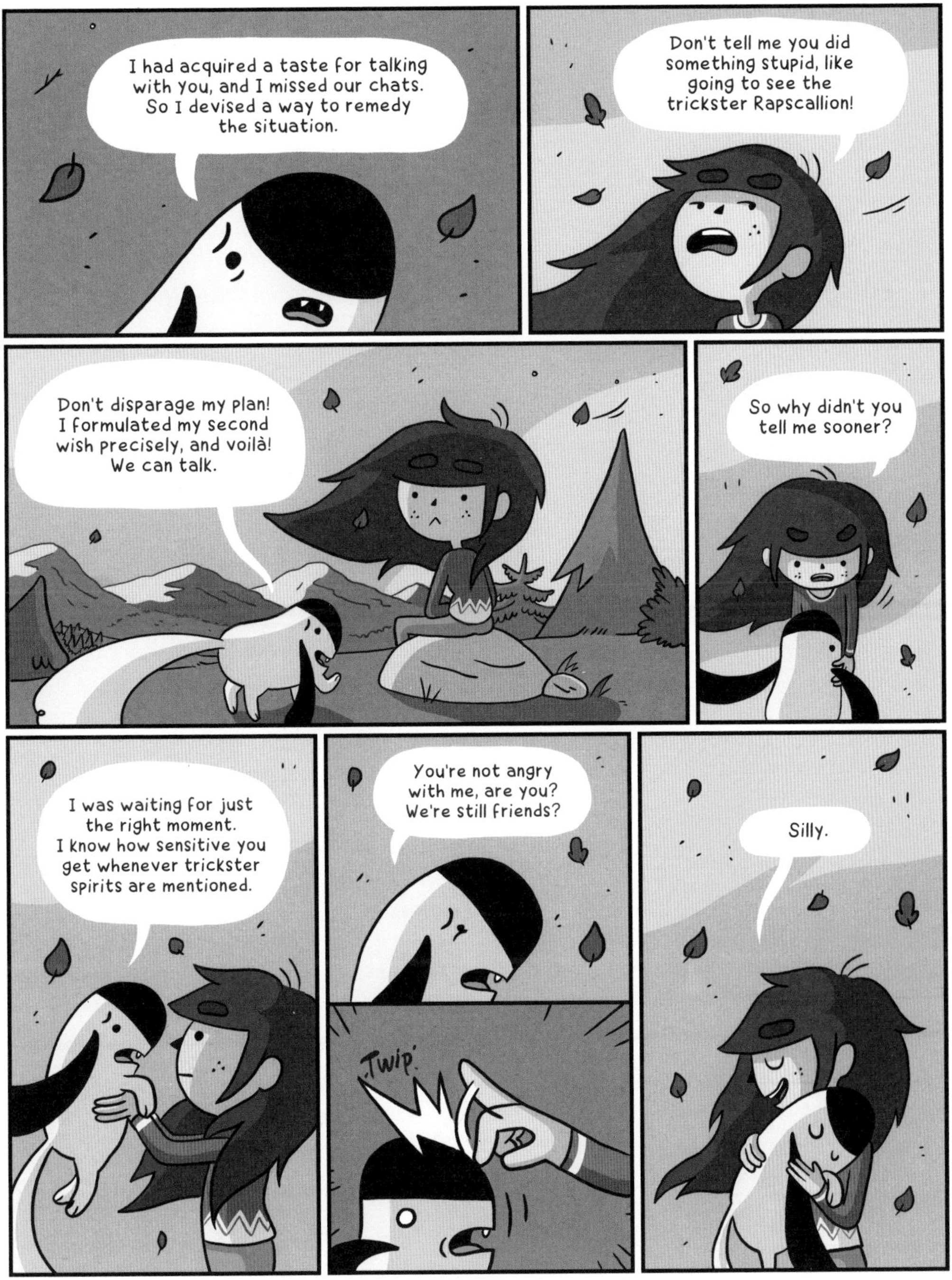
I had acquired a taste for talking with you, and I missed our chats. So I devised a way to remedy the situation.
Don't tell me you did something stupid, like going to see the trickster Rapscallion!
Don't disparage my plan! I formulated my second wish precisely, and voilà! We can talk.
So why didn't you tell me sooner?
I was waiting for just the right moment. I know how sensitive you get whenever trickster spirits are mentioned.
You're not angry with me, are you? We're still friends?
TWIP
Silly.

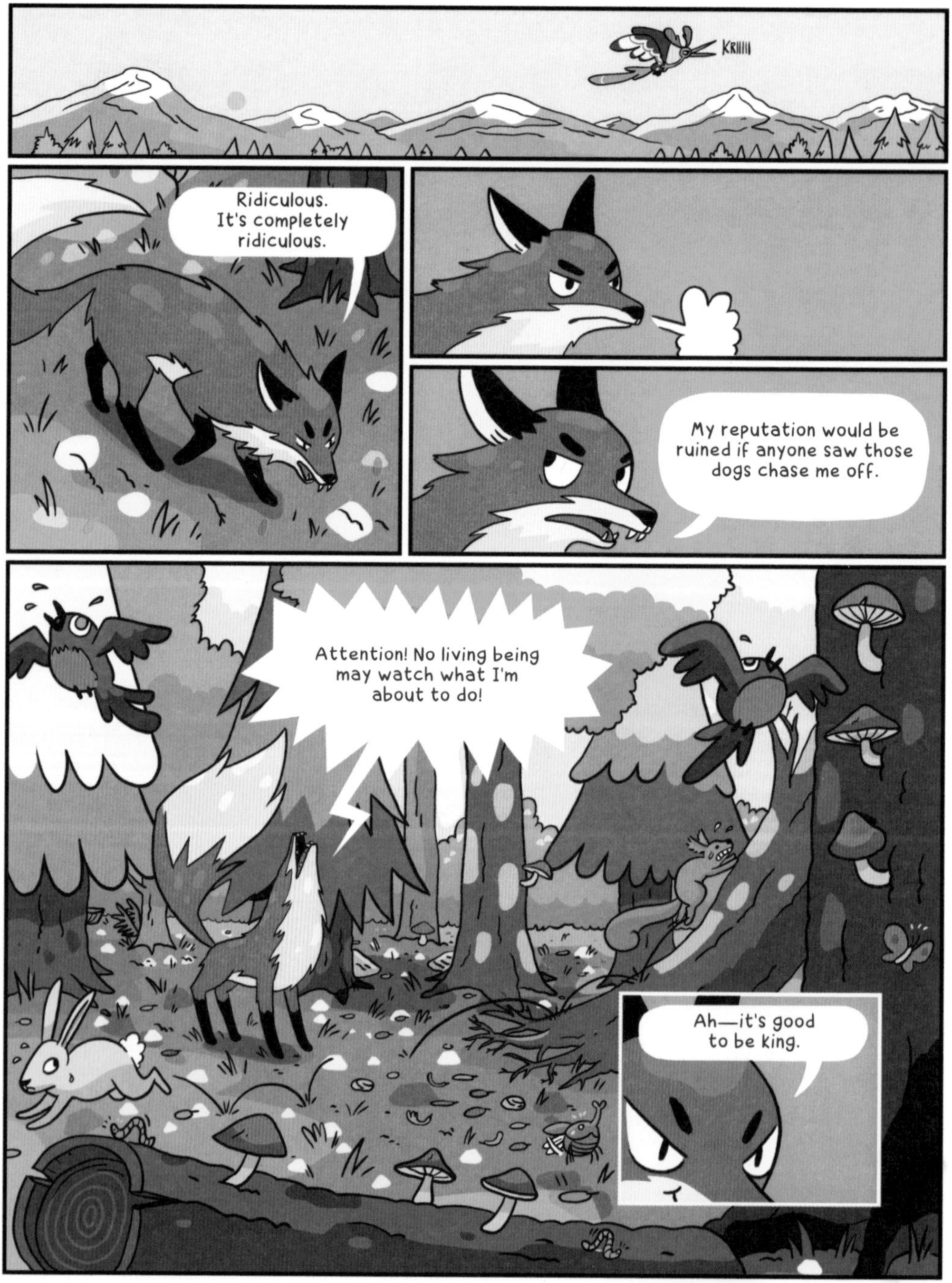
KRIIIII
Ridiculous. It's completely ridiculous.
My reputation would be ruined if anyone saw those dogs chase me off.
Attention! No living being may watch what I'm about to do!
Ah—it's good to be king.

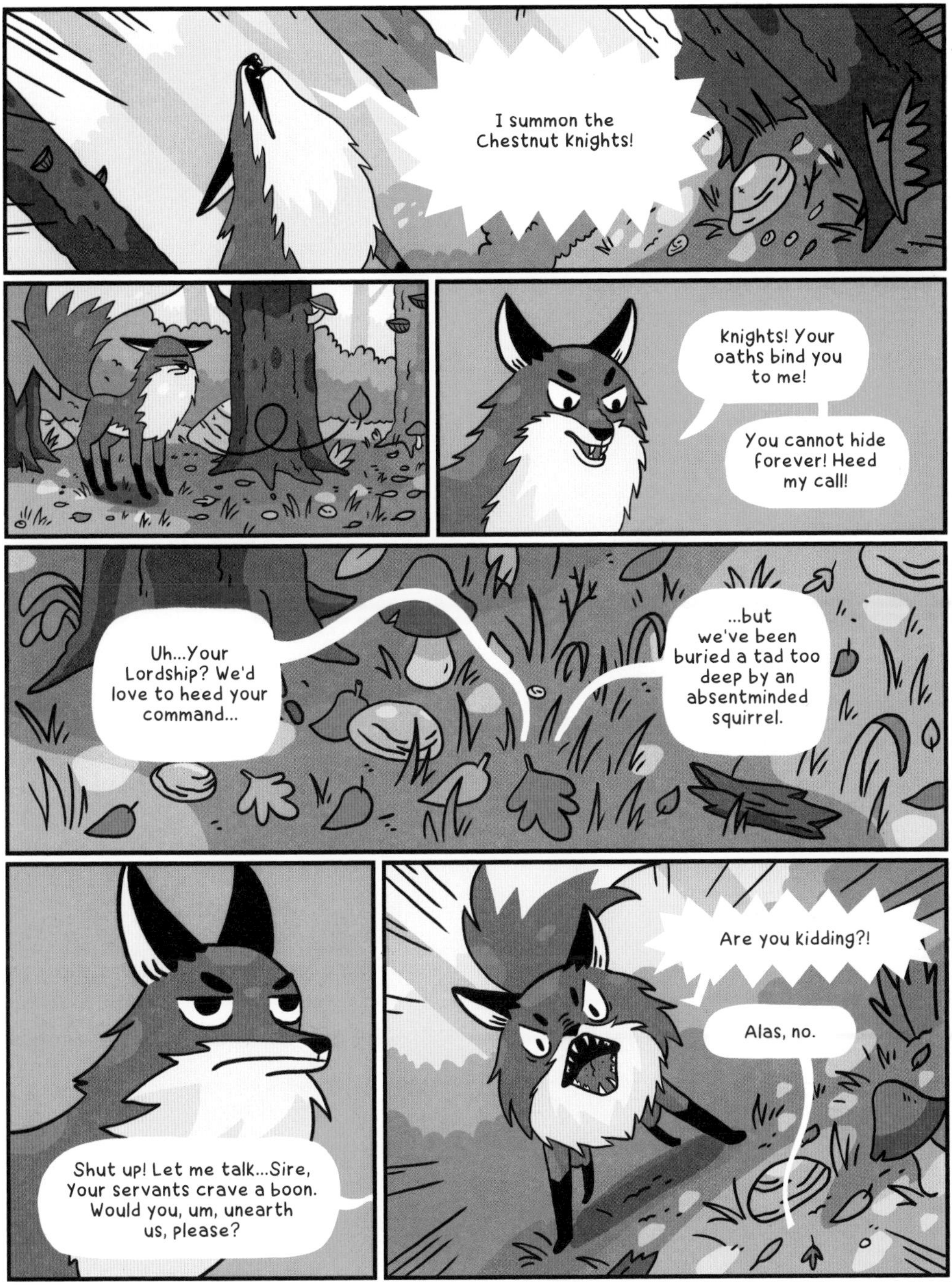

I summon the Chestnut knights!
Knights! Your oaths bind you to me!
You cannot hide forever! Heed my call!
Uh...Your Lordship? We'd love to heed your command...
...but we've been buried a tad too deep by an absentminded squirrel.
Shut up! Let me talk...Sire, Your servants crave a boon. Would you, um, unearth us, please?
Are you kidding?!
Alas, no.

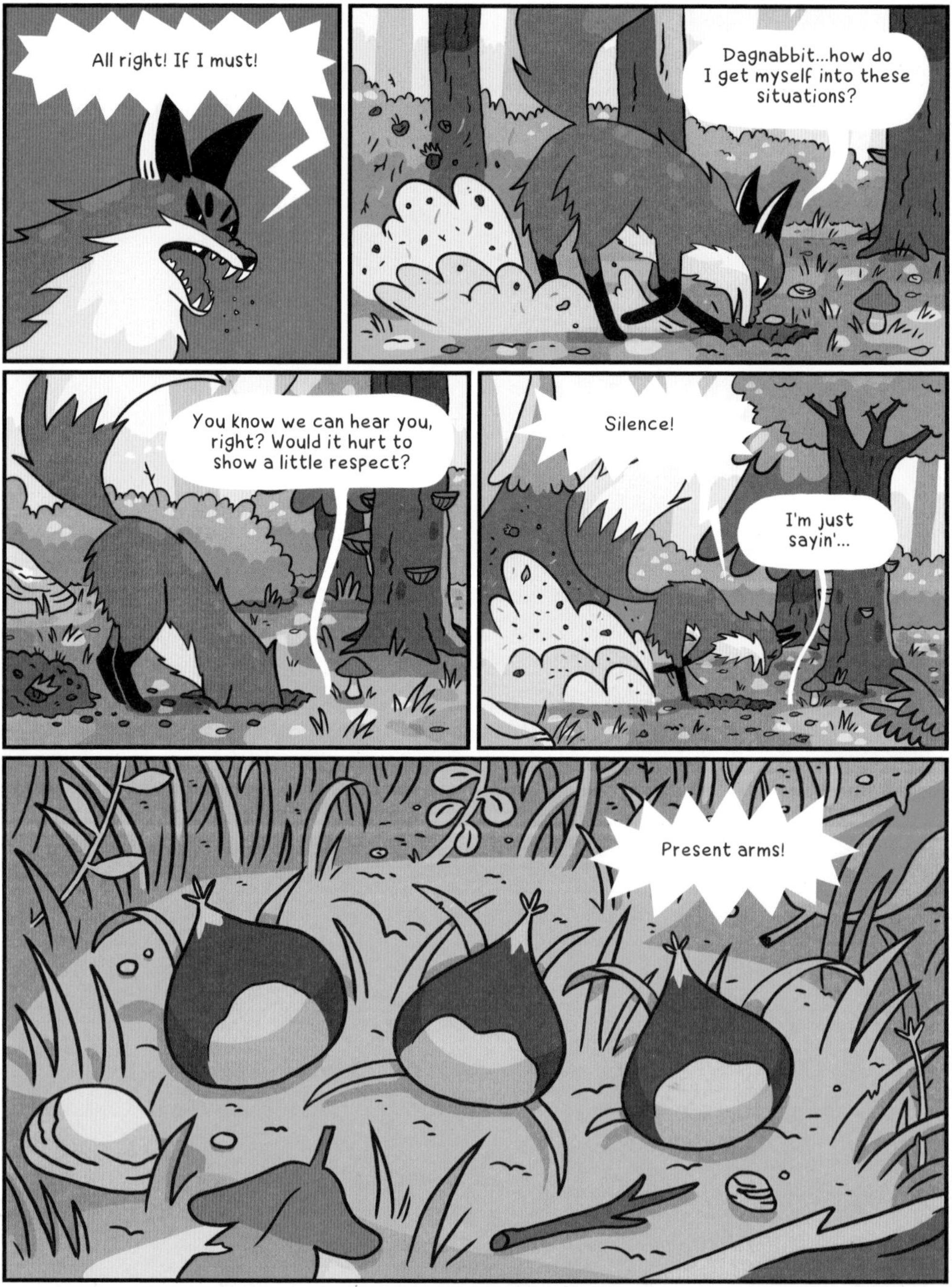

All right! If I must!
Dagnabbit...how do I get myself into these situations?
You know we can hear you, right? Would it hurt to show a little respect?
Silence!
I'm just sayin'...
Present arms!

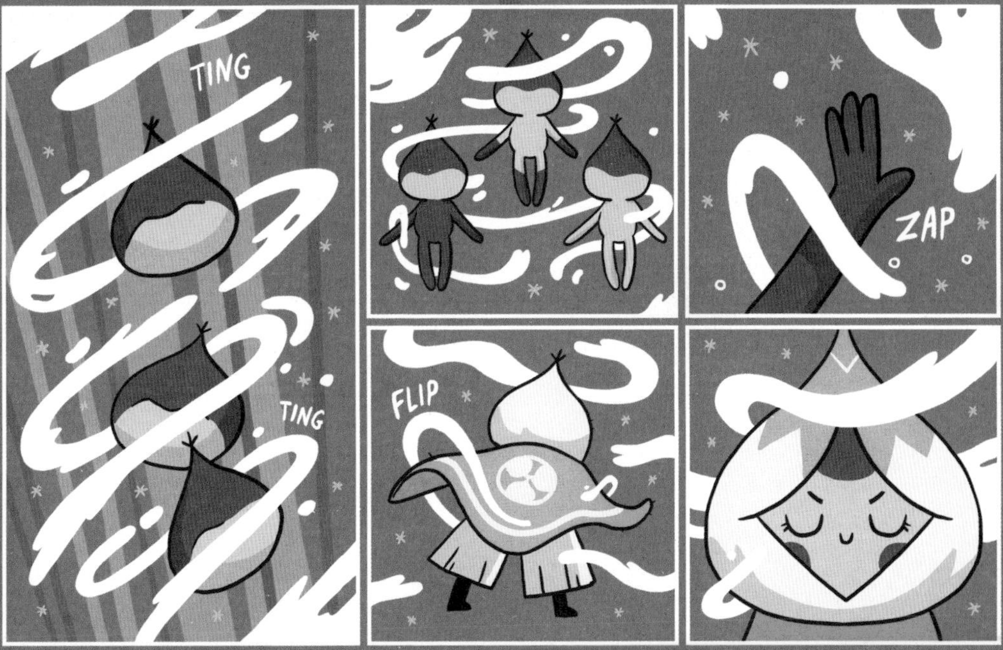
TING
TING
ZAP
FLIP

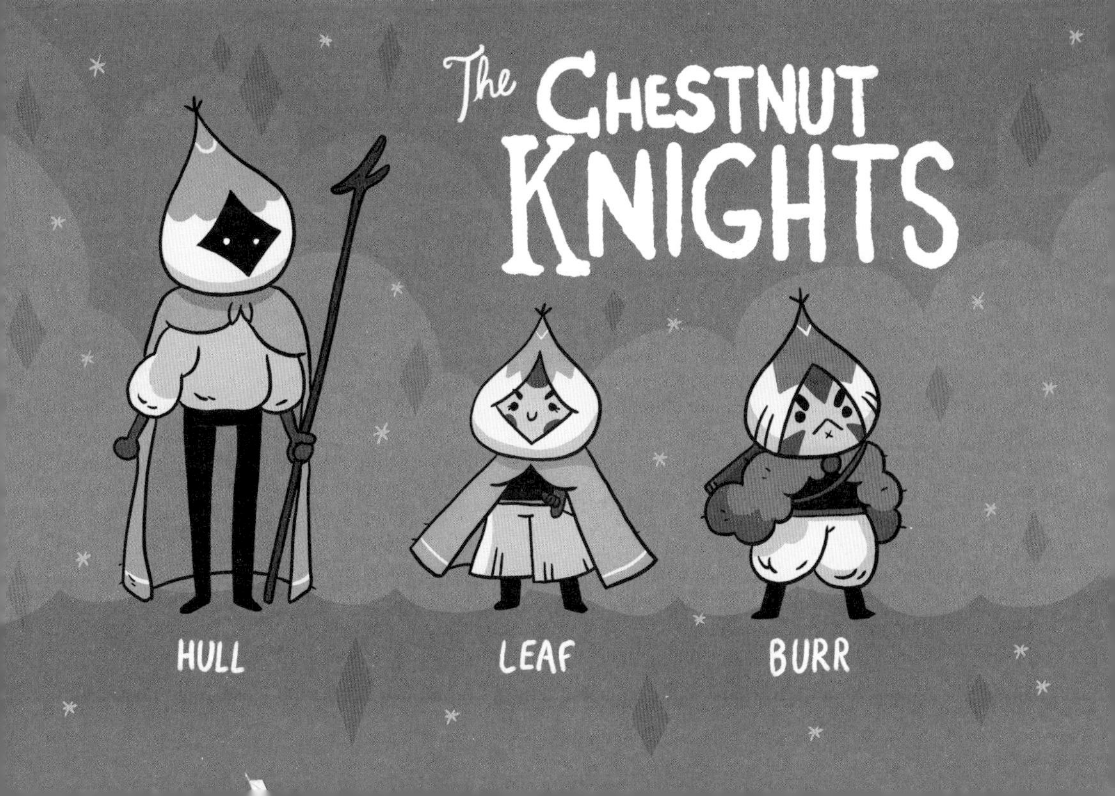
The CHESTNUT KNIGHTS
HULL
LEAF
BURR

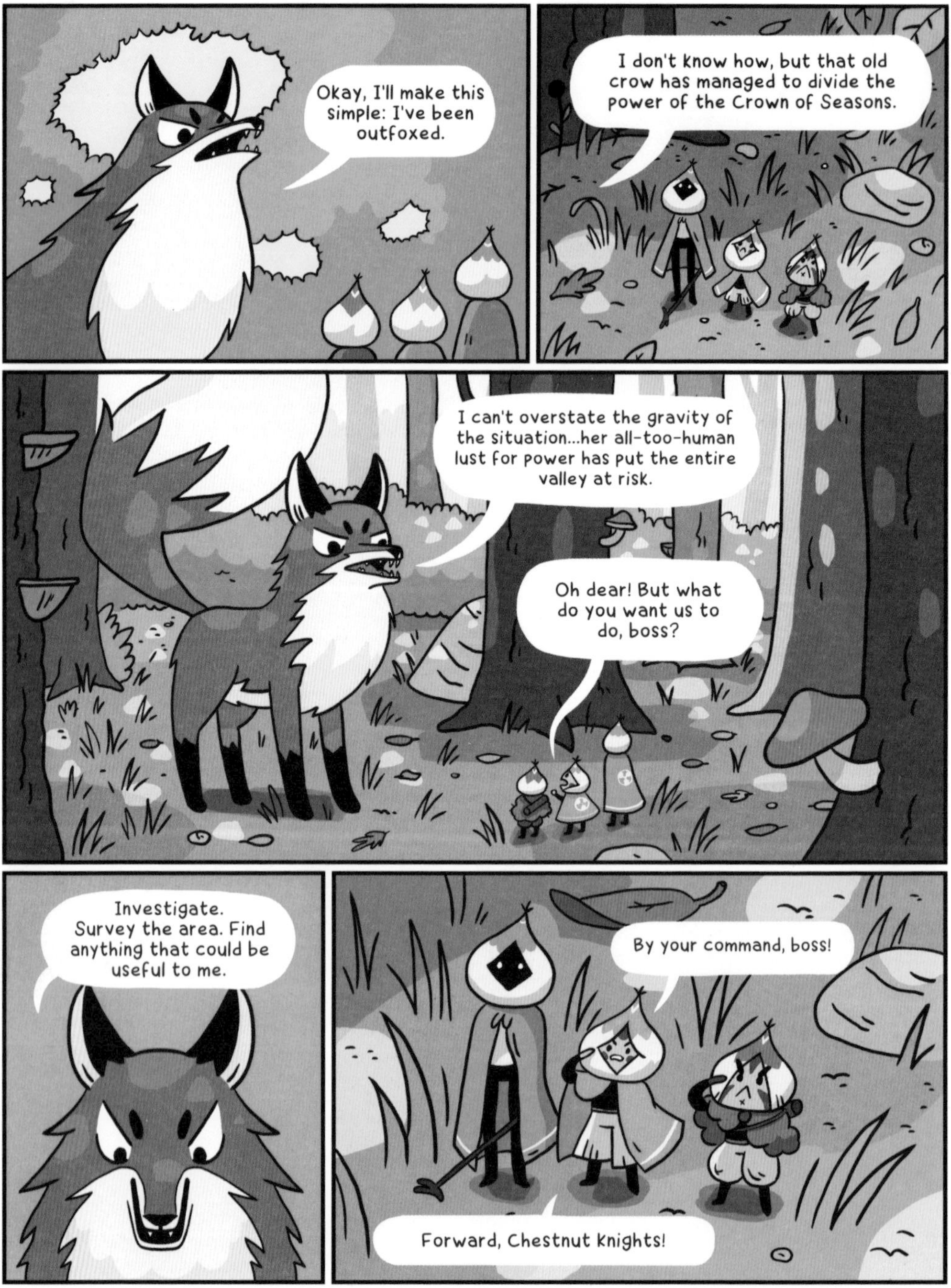
Okay, I'll make this simple: I've been outfoxed.
I don't know how, but that old crow has managed to divide the power of the Crown of Seasons.
I can't overstate the gravity of the situation...her all-too-human lust for power has put the entire valley at risk.
Oh dear! But what do you want us to do, boss?
Investigate. Survey the area. Find anything that could be useful to me.
By your command, boss!
Forward, Chestnut knights!

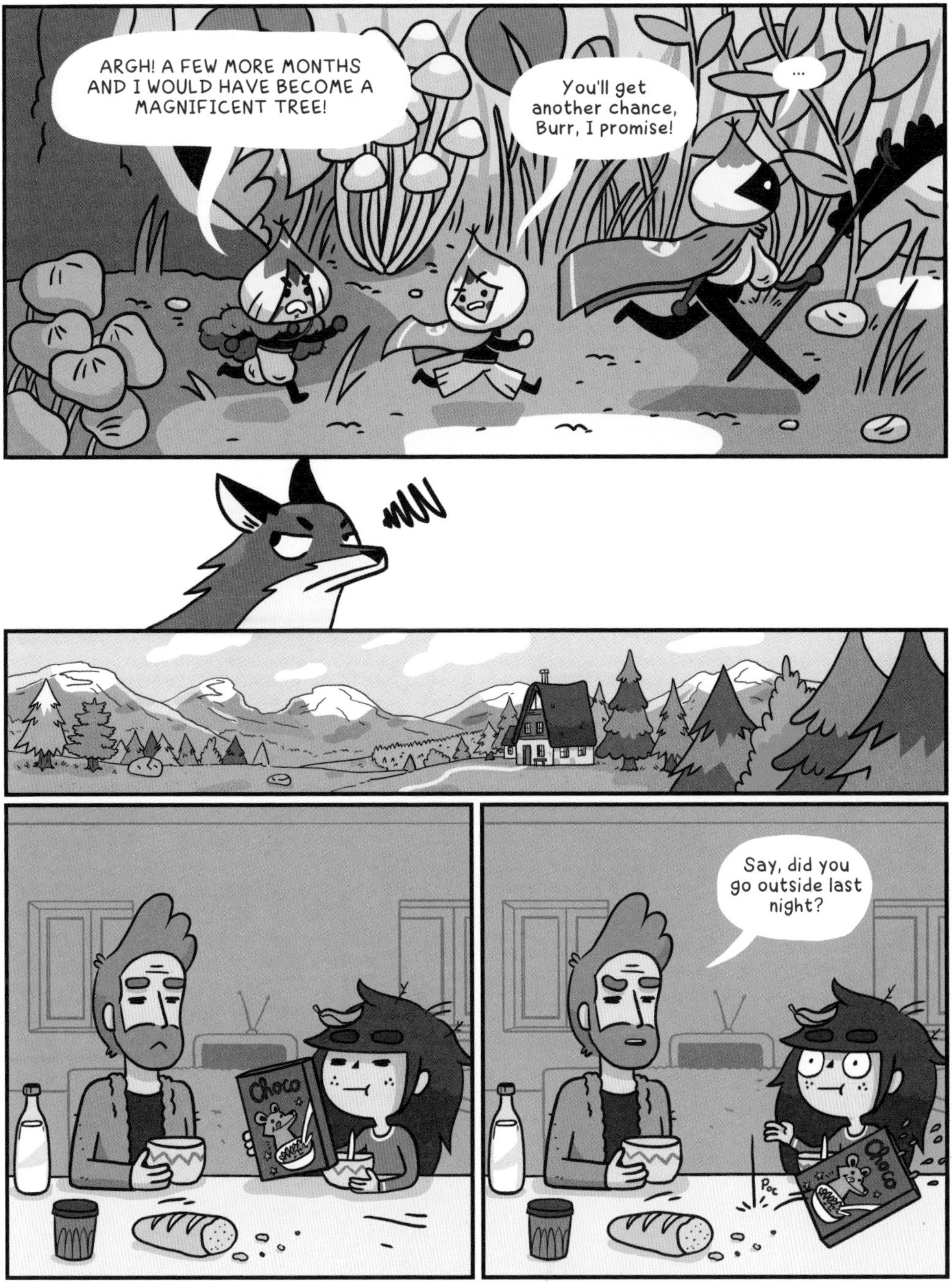

ARGH! A FEW MORE MONTHS AND I WOULD HAVE BECOME A MAGNIFICENT TREE!
You'll get another chance, Burr, I promise!
...
Choco
Say, did you go outside last night?
Poc
Choco

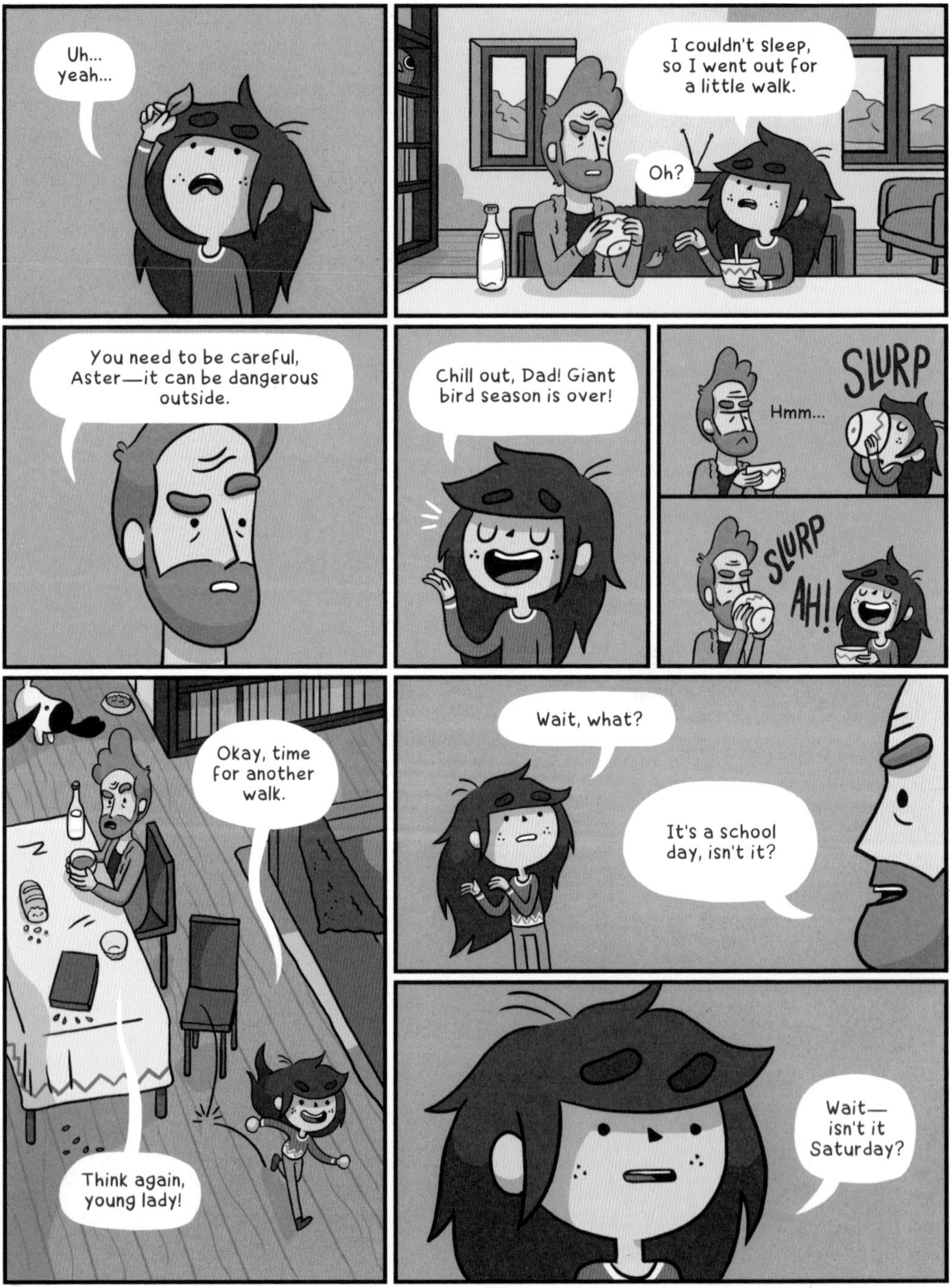
Uh... yeah...
I couldn't sleep, so I went out for a little walk.
Oh?
You need to be careful, Aster—it can be dangerous outside.
Chill out, Dad! Giant bird season is over!
SLURP
Hmm...
SLURP
AH!
Okay, time for another walk.
Think again, young lady!
Wait, what?
It's a school day, isn't it?
Wait—isn't it Saturday?

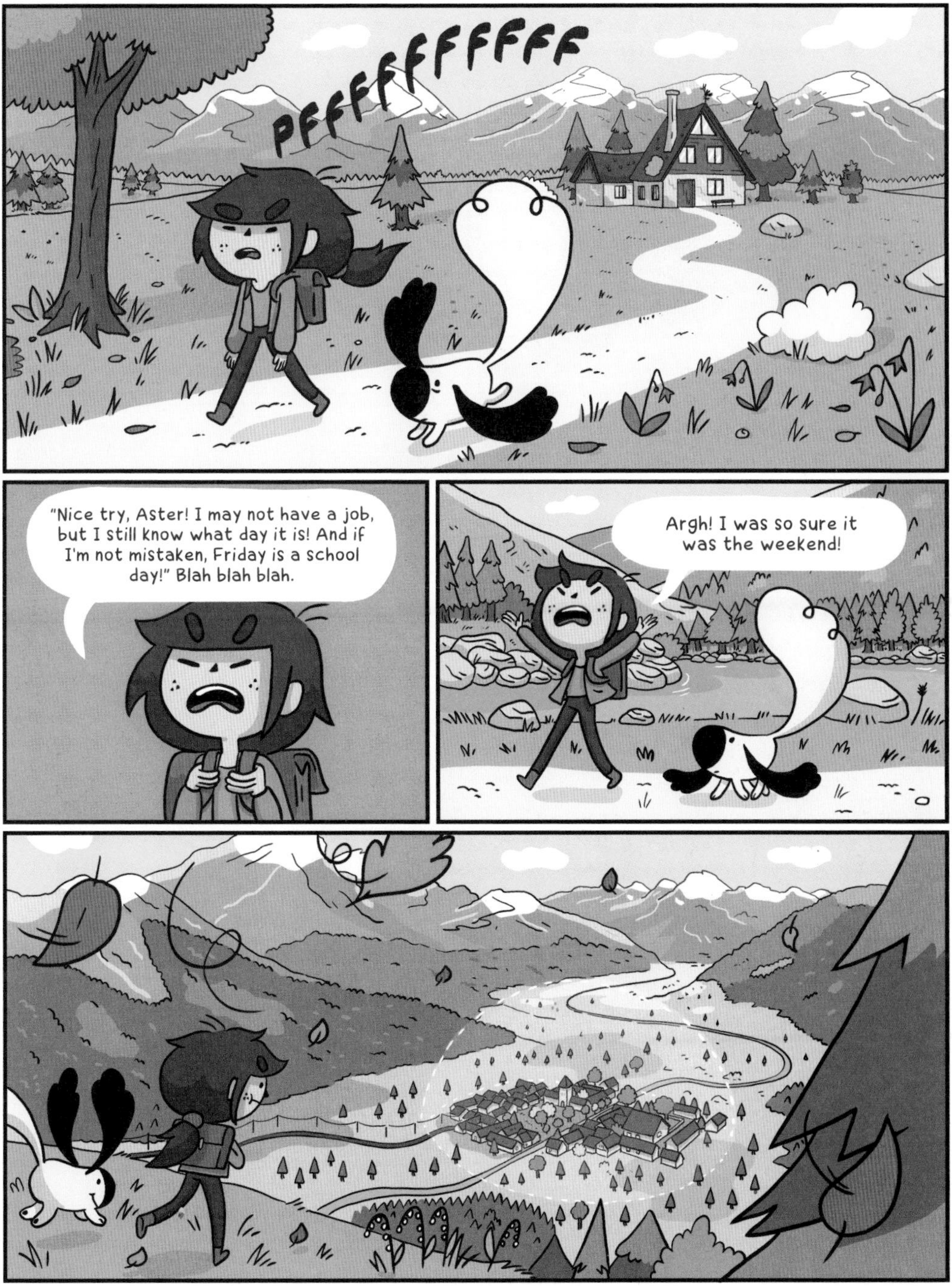
PFFFFFFFFFFF
"Nice try, Aster! I may not have a job, but I still know what day it is! And if I'm not mistaken, Friday is a school day!" Blah blah blah.
Argh! I was so sure it was the weekend!

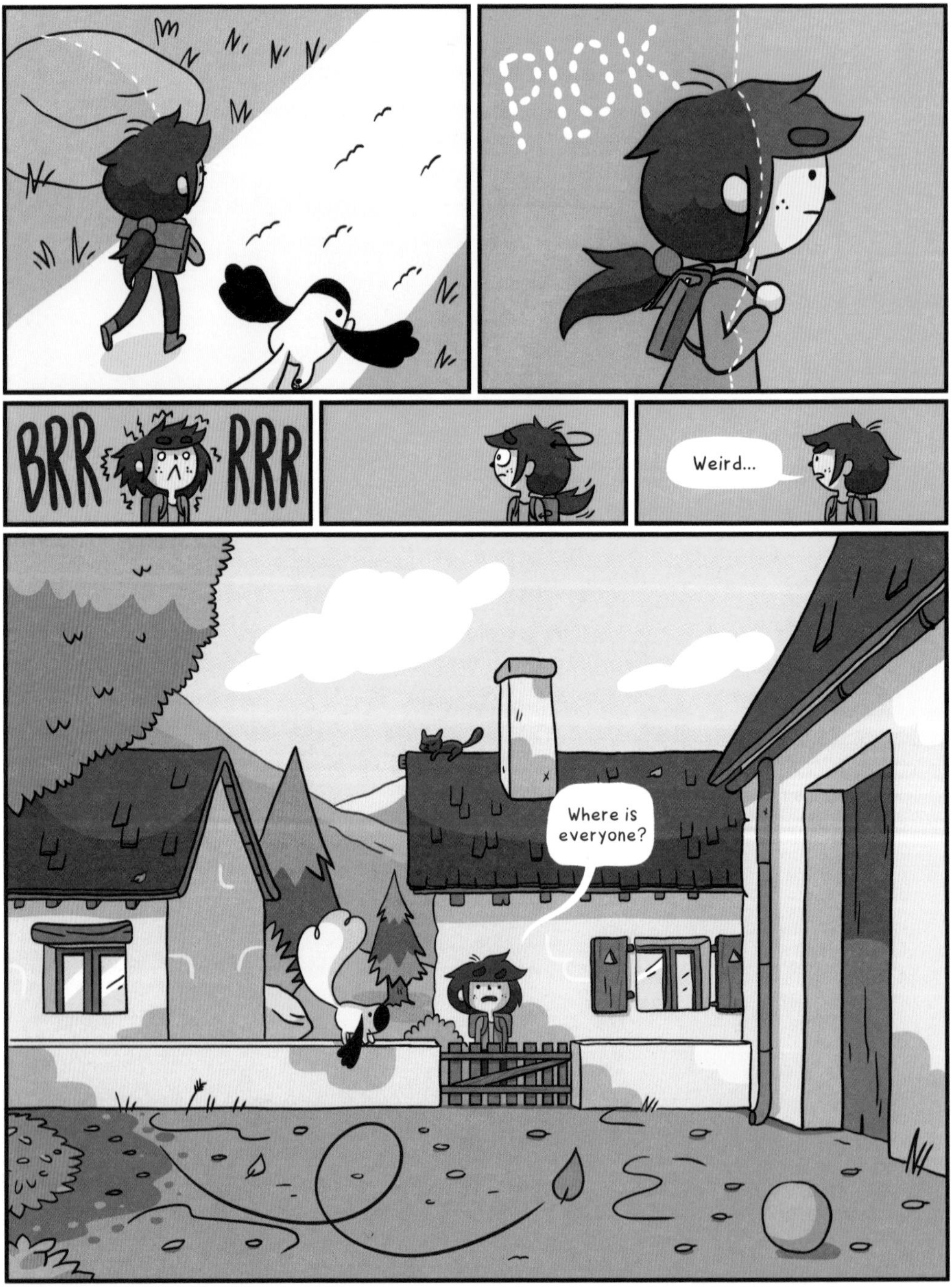
PIOK
BRR RRR
Weird...
Where is everyone?

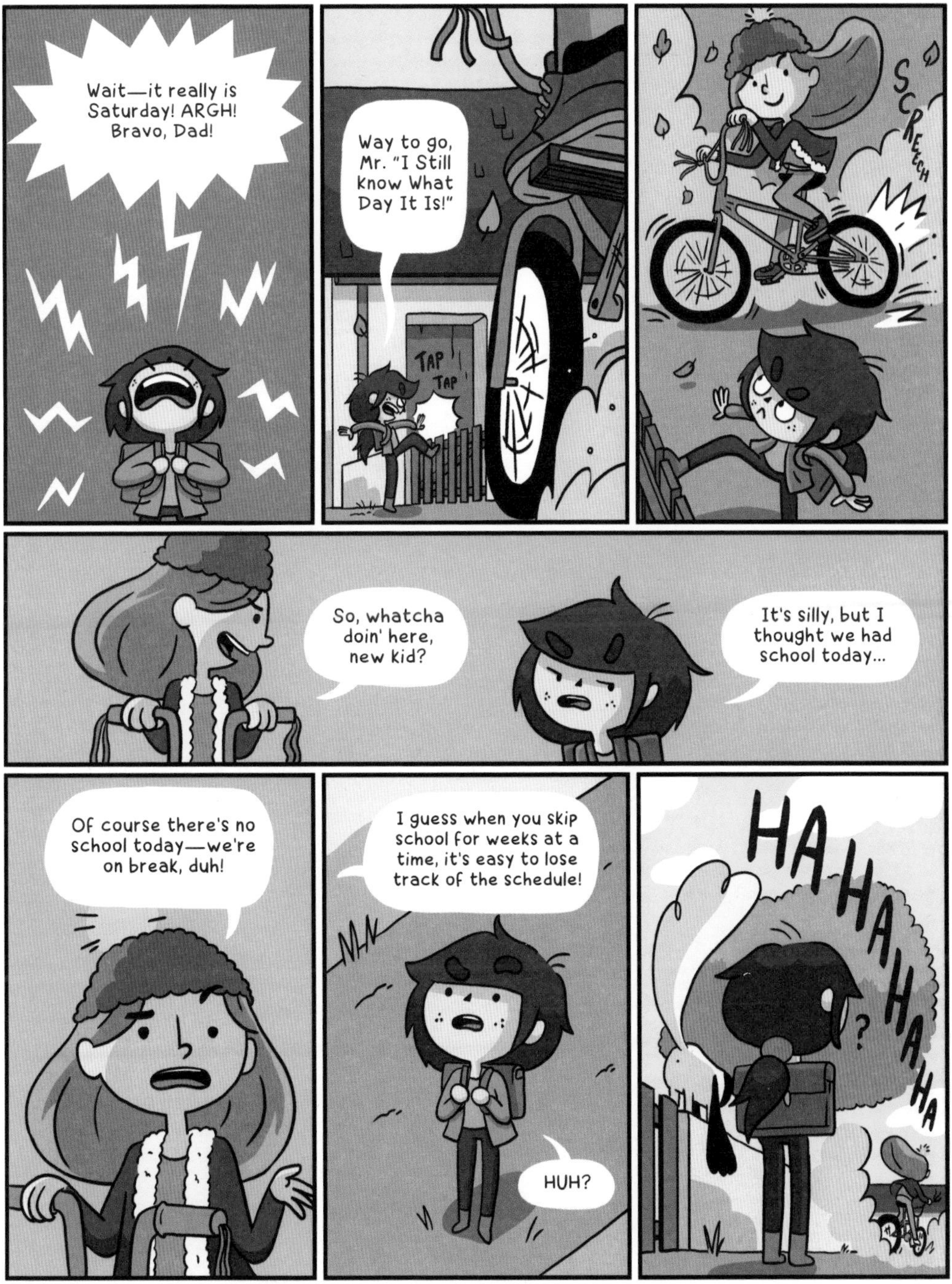
Wait—it really is Saturday! ARGH! Bravo, Dad!
Way to go, Mr. "I Still Know What Day It Is!"
TAP TAP
SCREECH
So, whatcha doin' here, new kid?
It's silly, but I thought we had school today...
Of course there's no school today—we're on break, duh!
I guess when you skip school for weeks at a time, it's easy to lose track of the schedule!
HUH?
HA HAHAHAHAHA
?

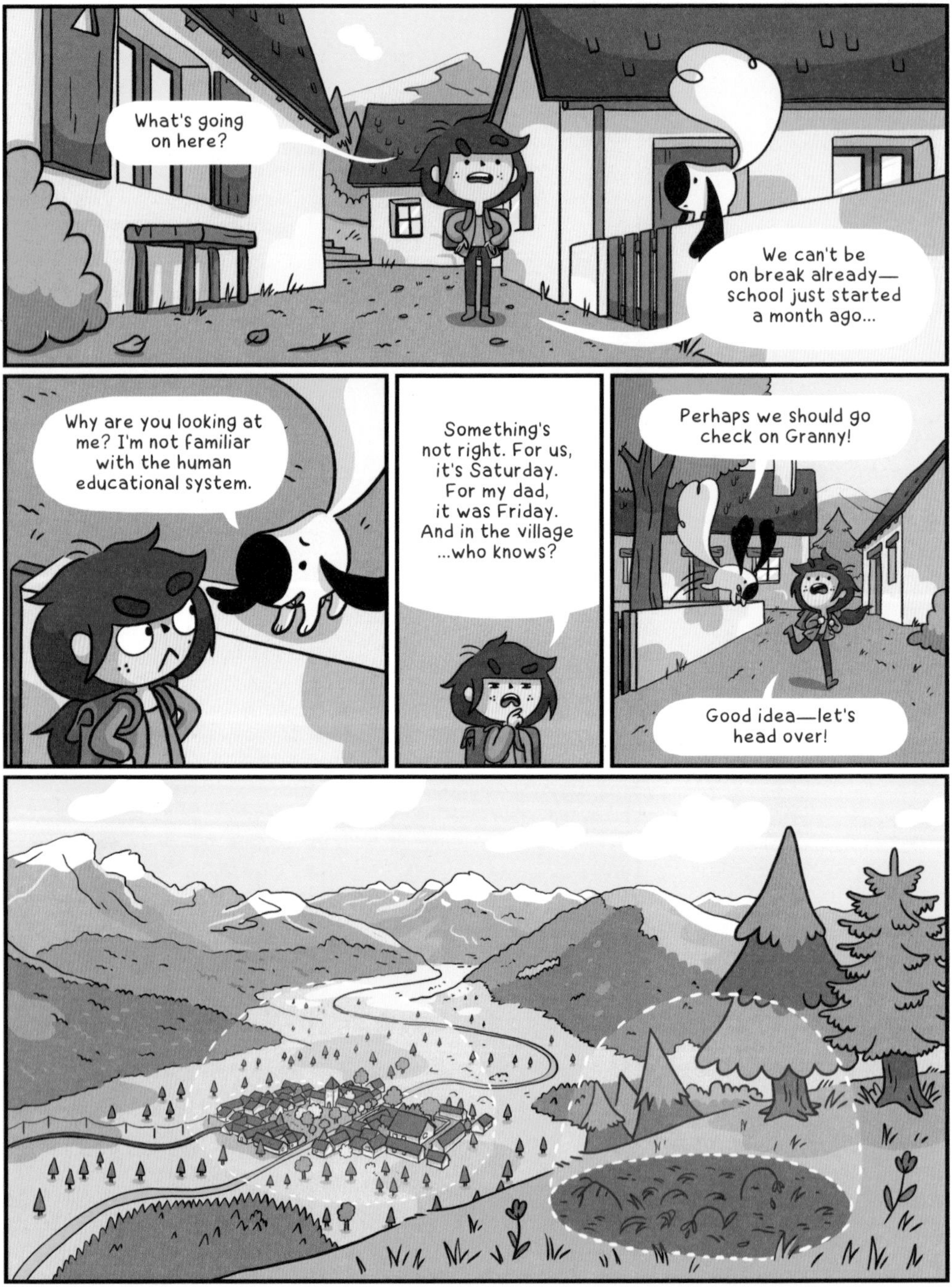
What's going on here?
We can't be on break already—school just started a month ago...
Why are you looking at me? I'm not familiar with the human educational system.
Something's not right. For us, it's Saturday. For my dad, it was Friday. And in the village ...who knows?
Perhaps we should go check on Granny!
Good idea—let's head over!

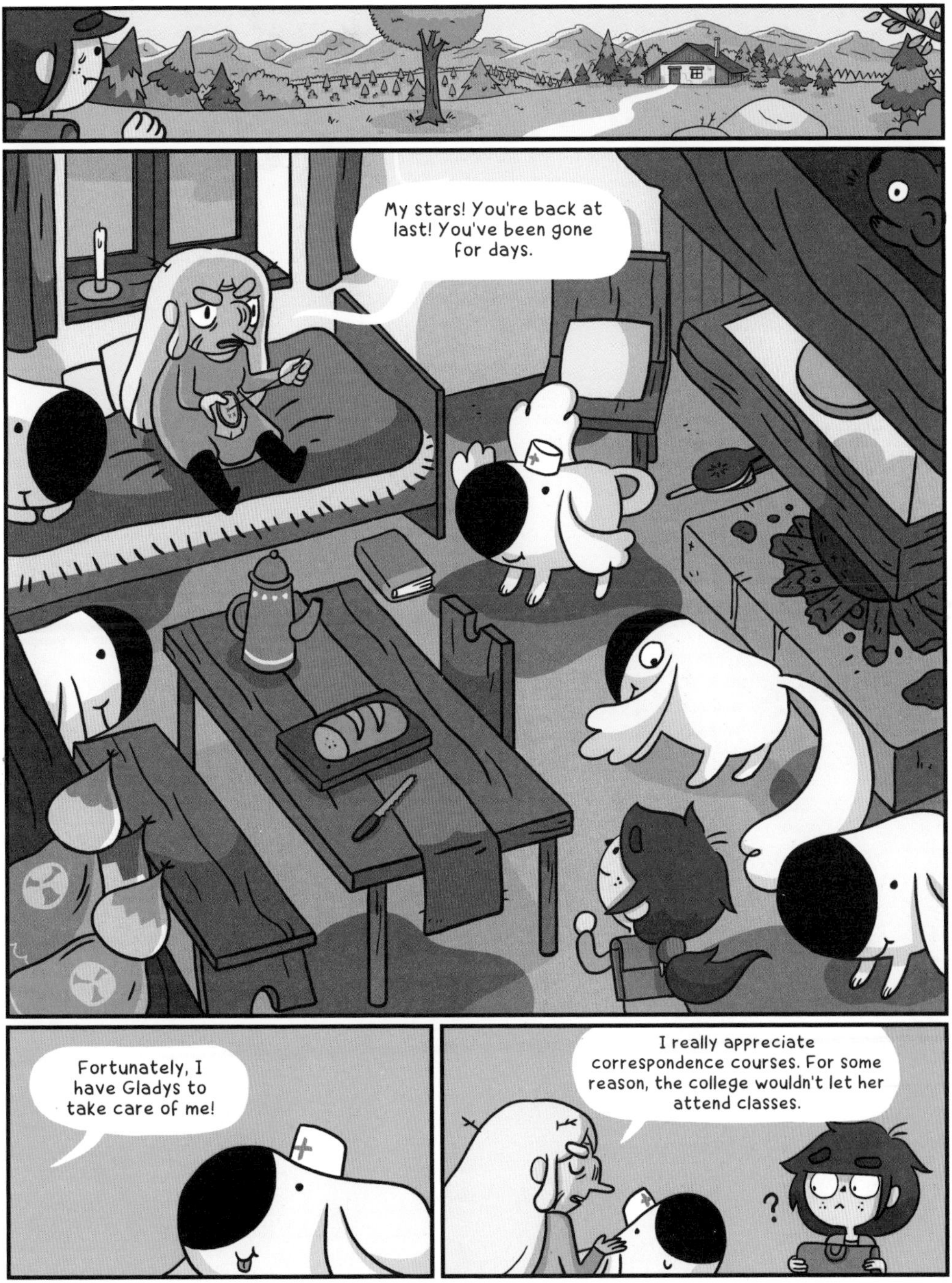
My stars! You're back at last! You've been gone for days.
Fortunately, I have Gladys to take care of me!
I really appreciate correspondence courses. For some reason, the college wouldn't let her attend classes.
?

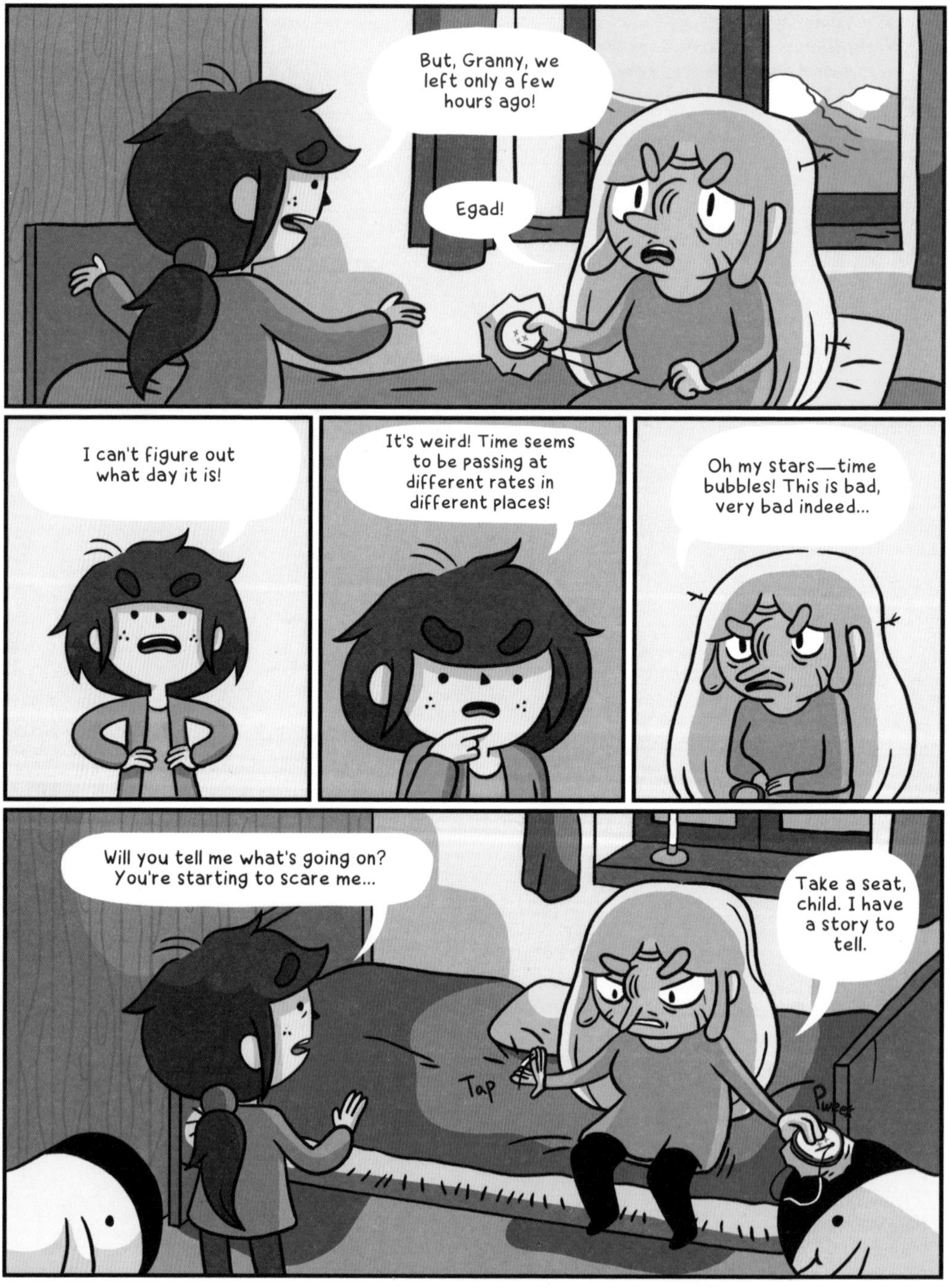

But, Granny, we left only a few hours ago!
Egad!
I can't figure out what day it is!
It's weird! Time seems to be passing at different rates in different places!
Oh my stars—time bubbles! This is bad, very bad indeed...
Will you tell me what's going on? You're starting to scare me...
Take a seat, child. I have a story to tell.
Tap
Pweet

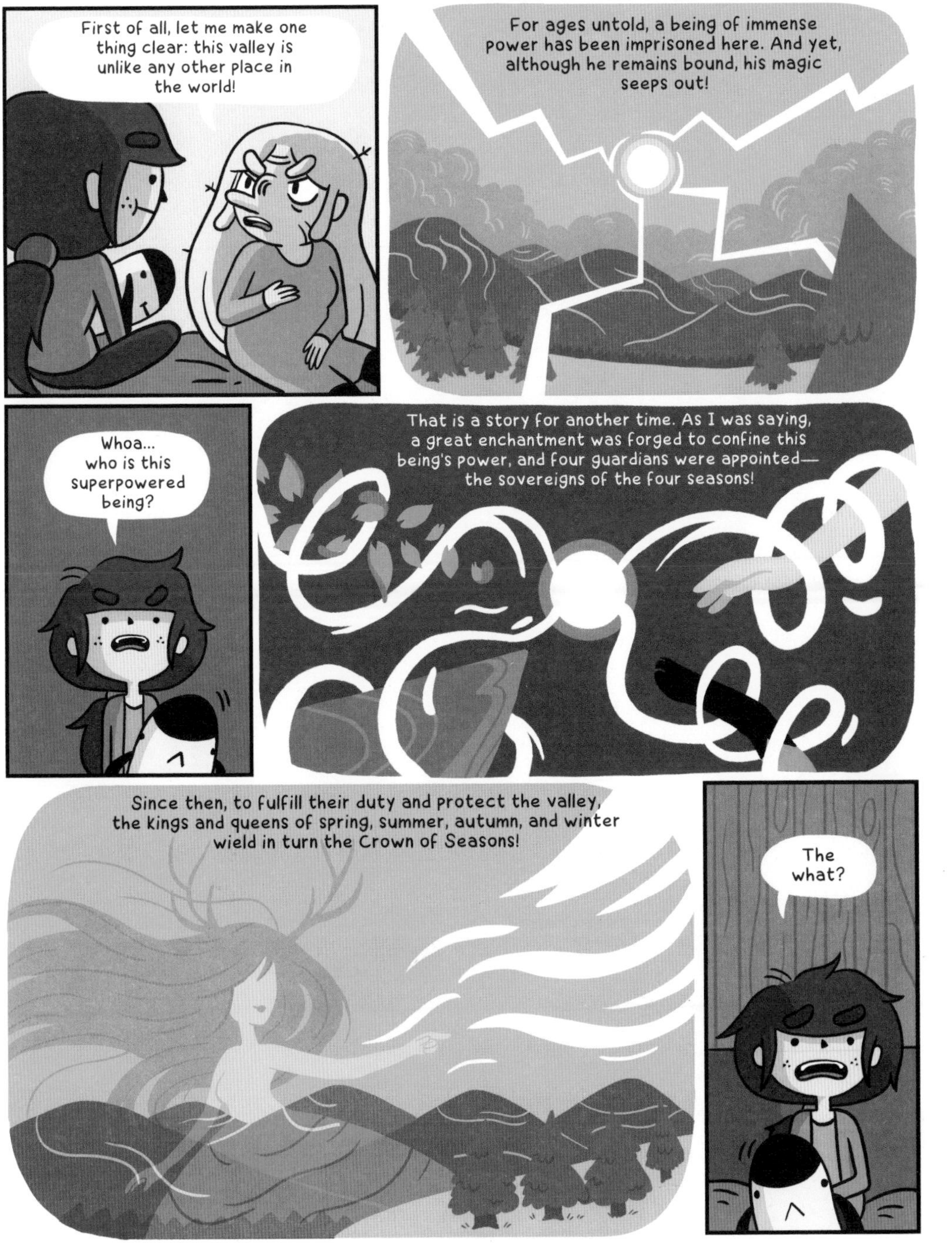
First of all, let me make one thing clear: this valley is unlike any other place in the world!
For ages untold, a being of immense power has been imprisoned here. And yet, although he remains bound, his magic seeps out!
Whoa... who is this superpowered being?
That is a story for another time. As I was saying, a great enchantment was forged to confine this being's power, and four guardians were appointed— the sovereigns of the four seasons!
Since then, to fulfill their duty and protect the valley, the kings and queens of spring, summer, autumn, and winter wield in turn the Crown of Seasons!
The what?

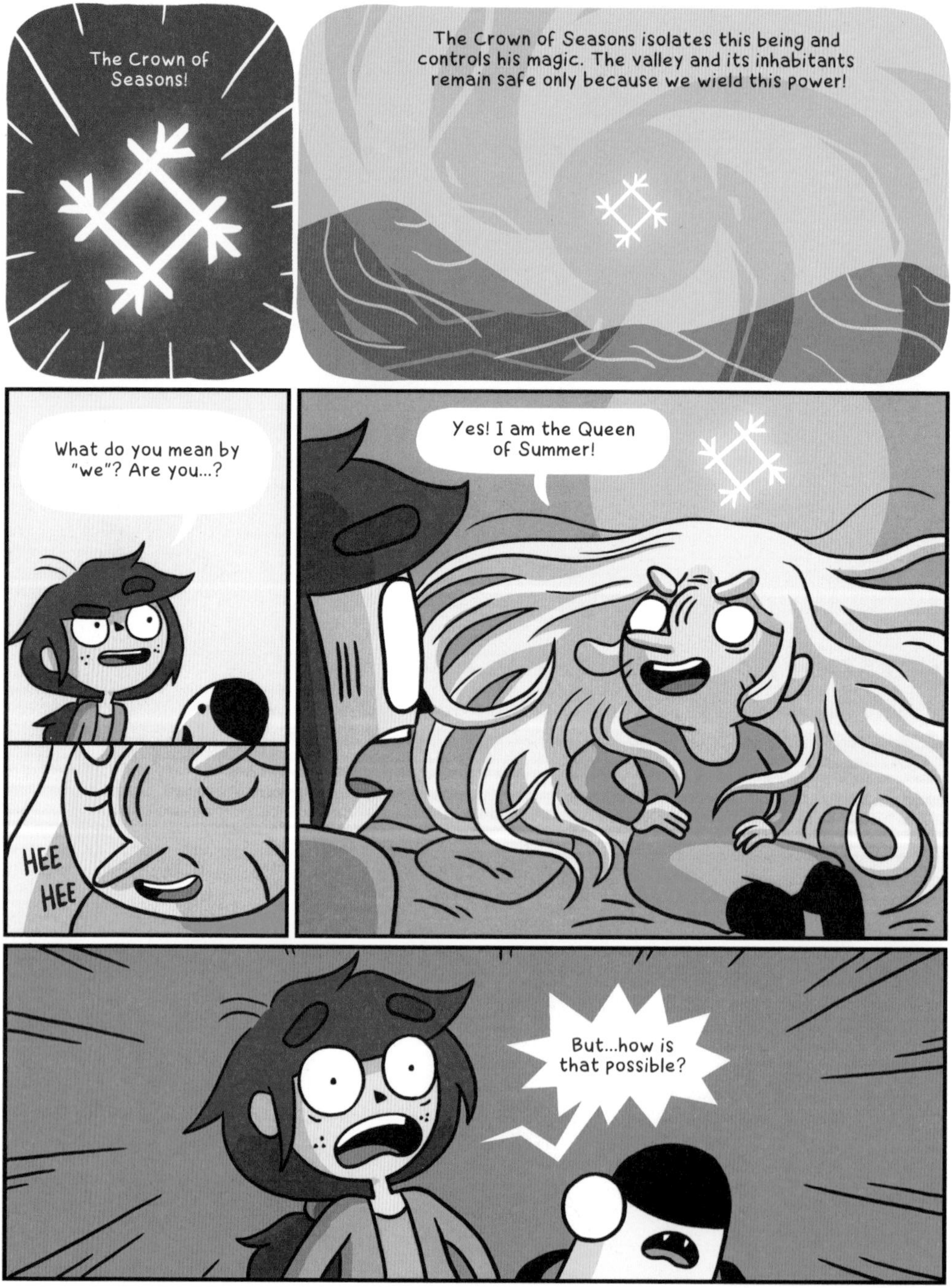

The Crown of Seasons!
The Crown of Seasons isolates this being and controls his magic. The valley and its inhabitants remain safe only because we wield this power!
What do you mean by "we"? Are you...?
HEE HEE
Yes! I am the Queen of Summer!
But...how is that possible?

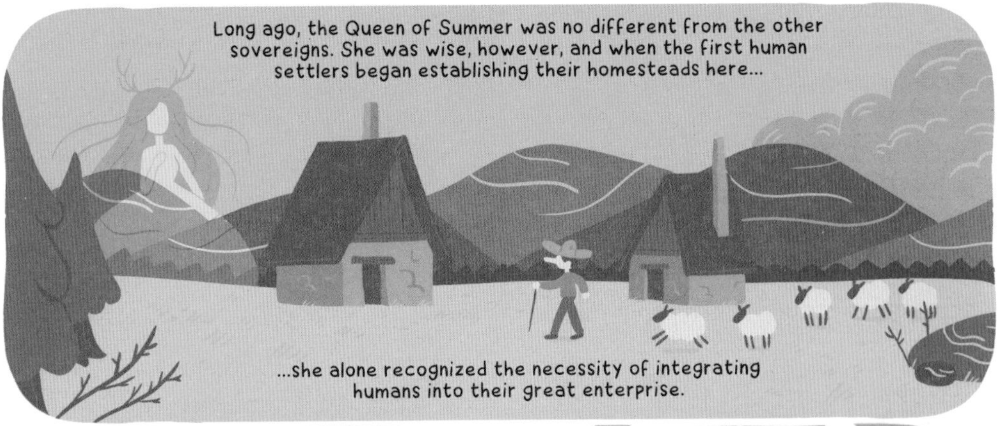
Long ago, the Queen of Summer was no different from the other sovereigns. She was wise, however, and when the first human settlers began establishing their homesteads here...
...she alone recognized the necessity of integrating humans into their great enterprise.

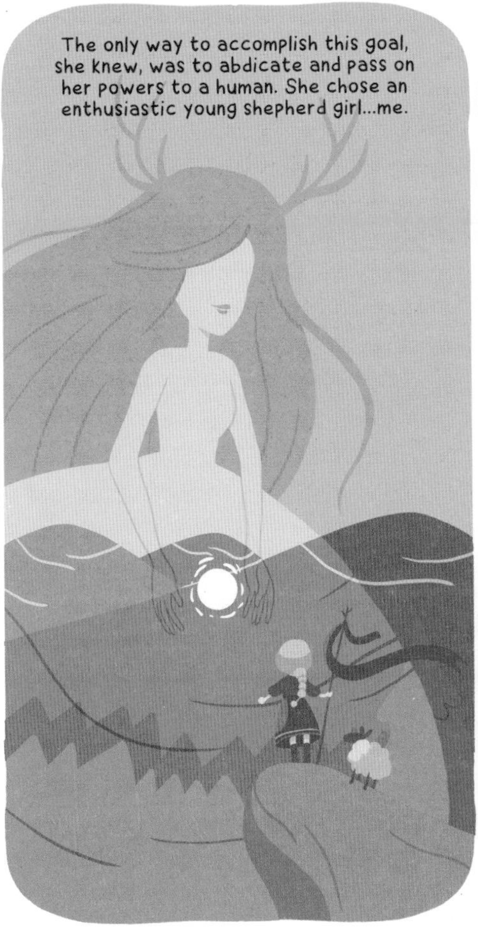
The only way to accomplish this goal, she knew, was to abdicate and pass on her powers to a human. She chose an enthusiastic young shepherd girl...me.

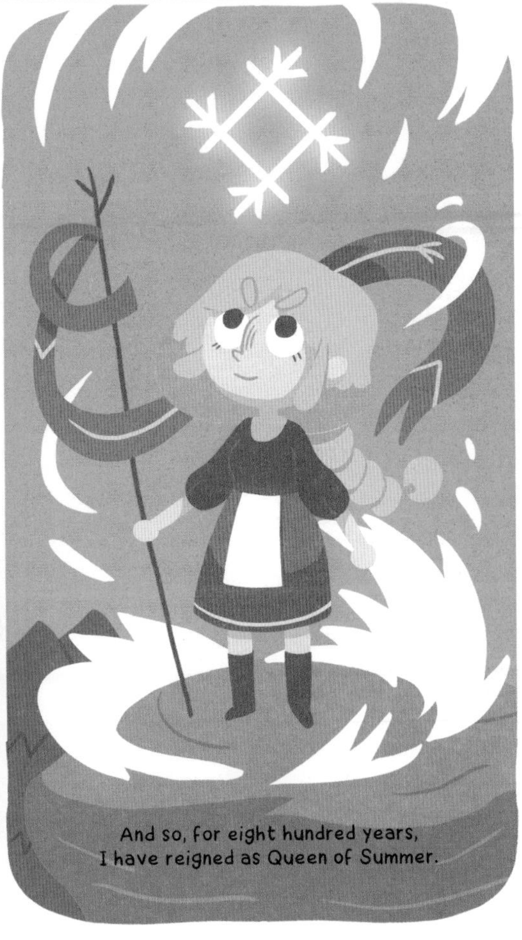
And so, for eight hundred years, I have reigned as Queen of Summer.

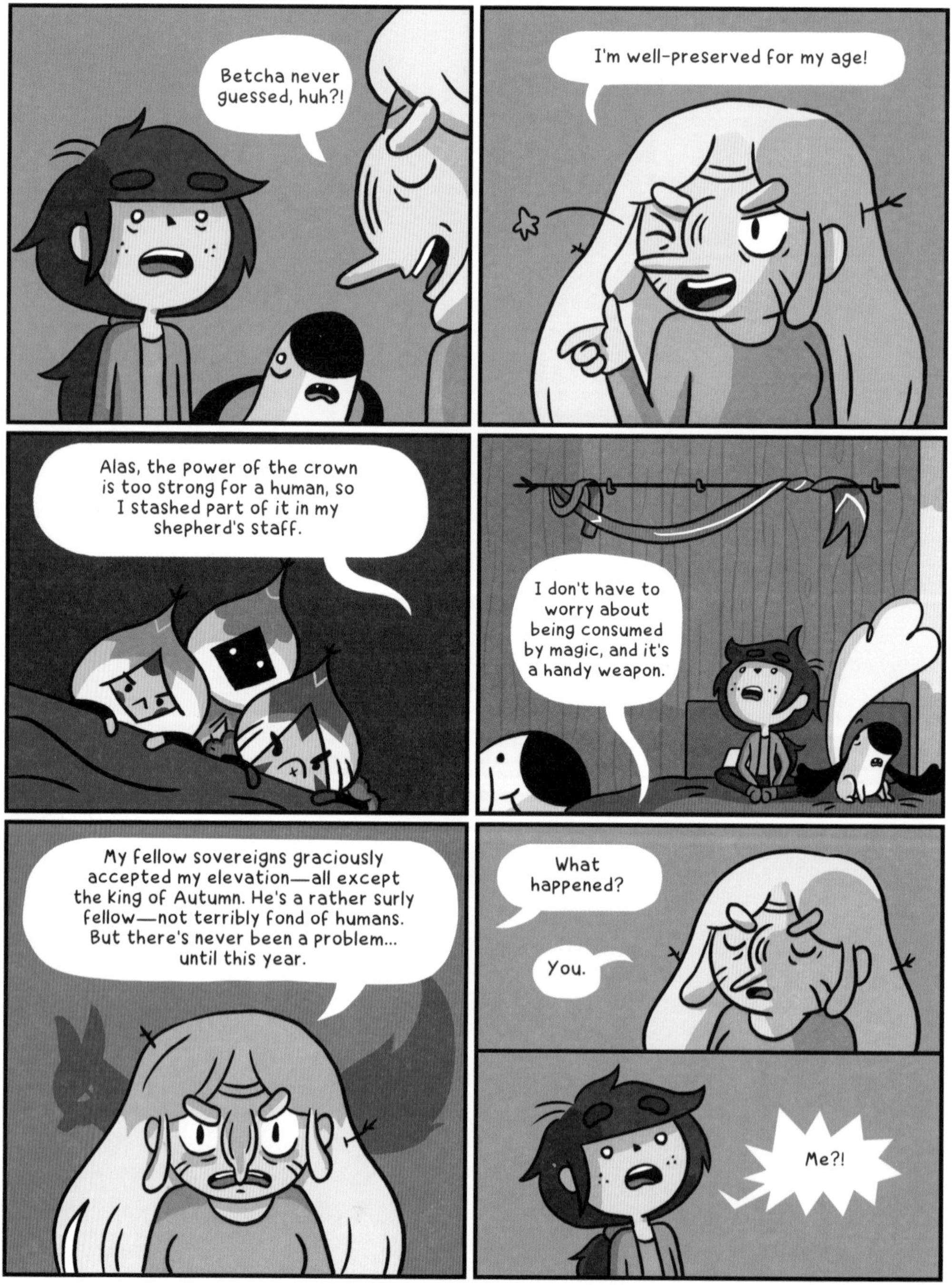
Betcha never guessed, huh?!
I'm well-preserved for my age!
Alas, the power of the crown is too strong for a human, so I stashed part of it in my shepherd's staff.
I don't have to worry about being consumed by magic, and it's a handy weapon.
My fellow sovereigns graciously accepted my elevation—all except the king of Autumn. He's a rather surly fellow—not terribly fond of humans. But there's never been a problem... until this year.
What happened?
You.
Me?!

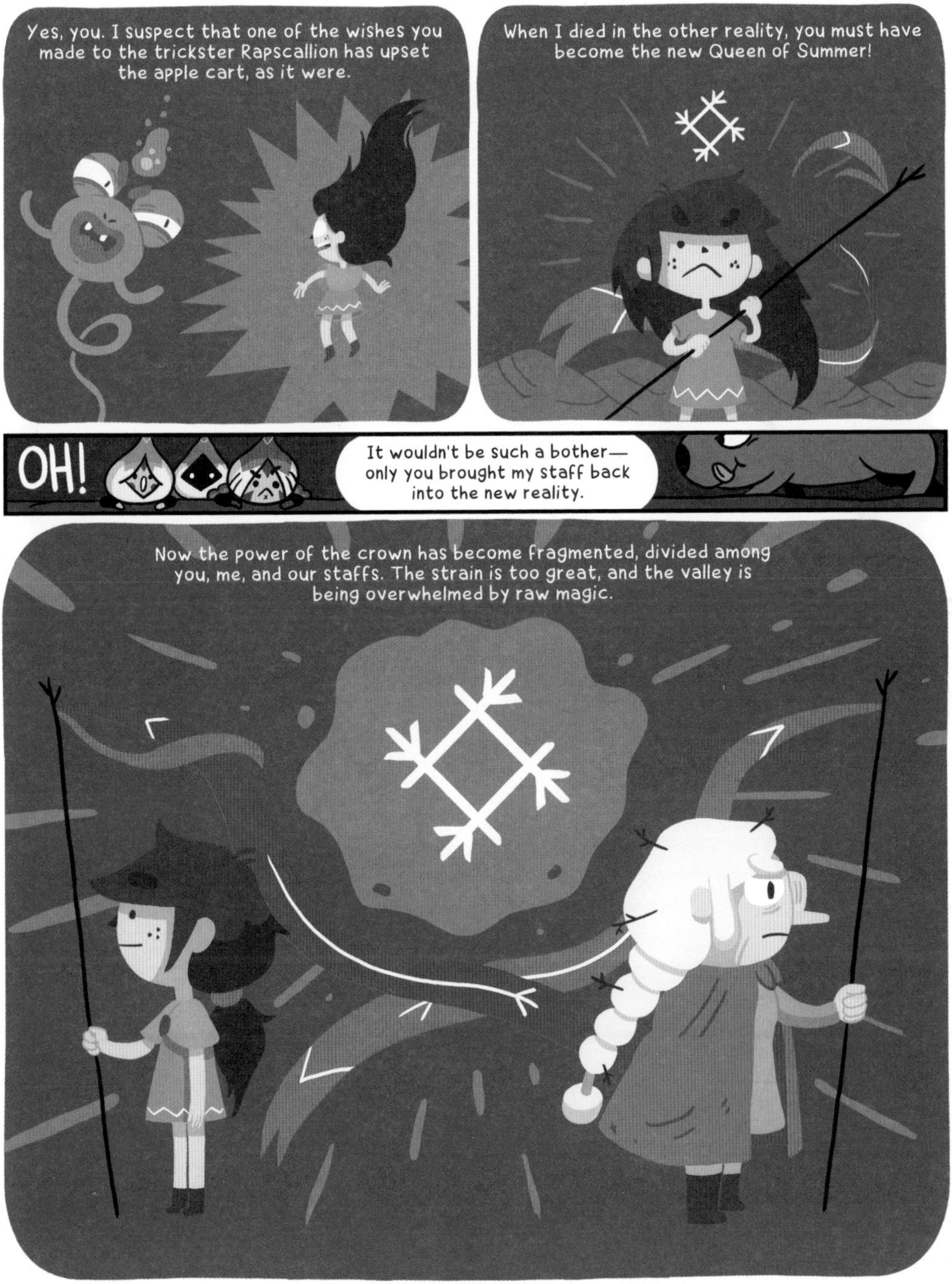
Yes, you. I suspect that one of the wishes you made to the trickster Rapscallion has upset the apple cart, as it were.
When I died in the other reality, you must have become the new Queen of Summer!
OH!
It wouldn't be such a bother—only you brought my staff back into the new reality.
Now the power of the crown has become fragmented, divided among you, me, and our staffs. The strain is too great, and the valley is being overwhelmed by raw magic.

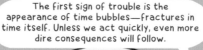

The first sign of trouble is the appearance of time bubbles—fractures in time itself. Unless we act quickly, even more dire consequences will follow.

Okay...so what's the plan?

The first step is to reunify the power of the crown. I need you to scurry back to your house as quickly as possible and retrieve your staff.

We have uncovered vital information! If the staff thingy has magic power, the boss will want it right away! It's our job to get it before the snot-nosed kid does!

...

YES, CHIEF!

CLAK

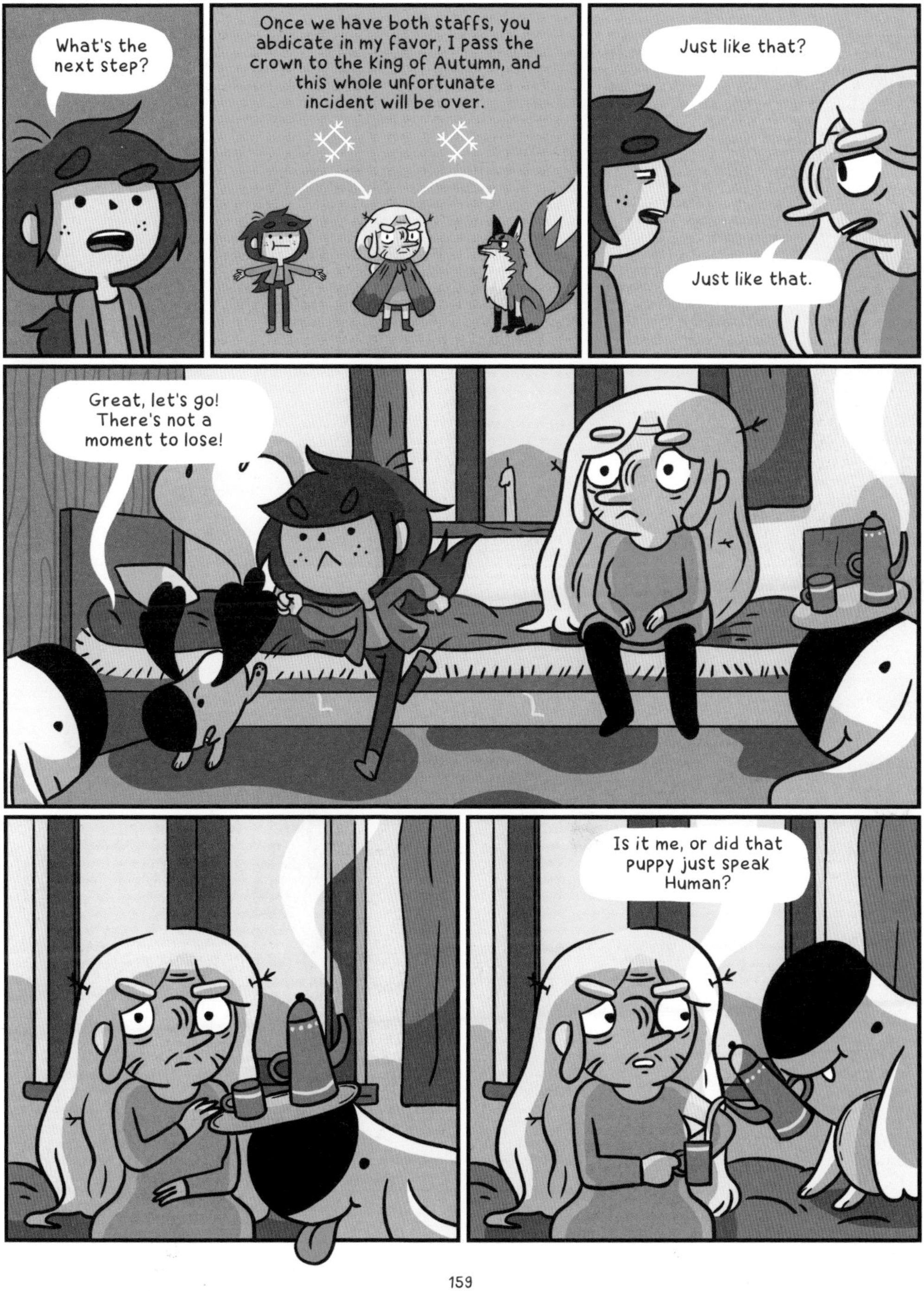
What's the next step?
Once we have both staffs, you abdicate in my favor, I pass the crown to the King of Autumn, and this whole unfortunate incident will be over.
Just like that?
Just like that.
Great, let's go! There's not a moment to lose!
Is it me, or did that puppy just speak Human?

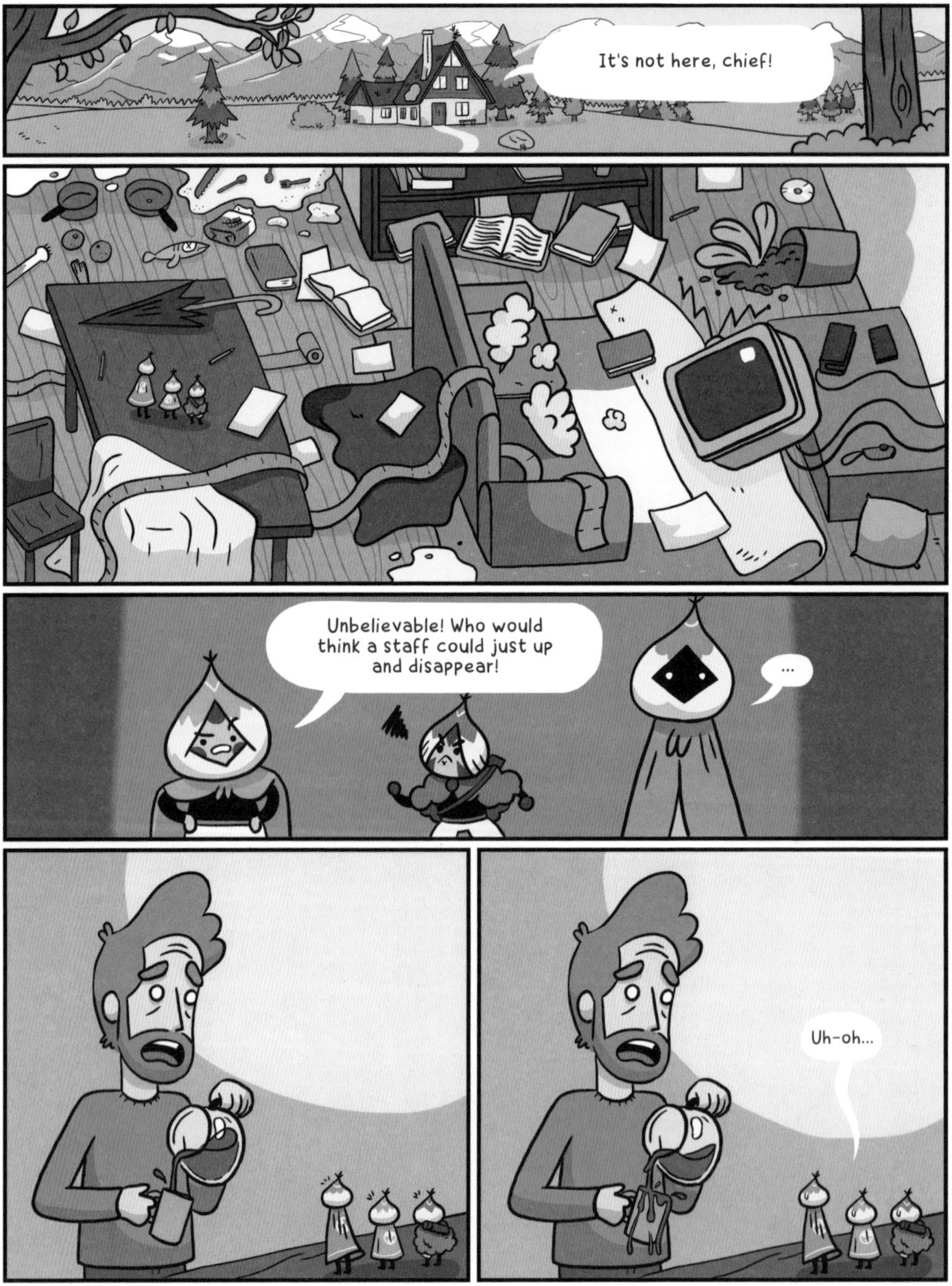
It's not here, chief!
Unbelievable! Who would think a staff could just up and disappear!
...
Uh-oh...

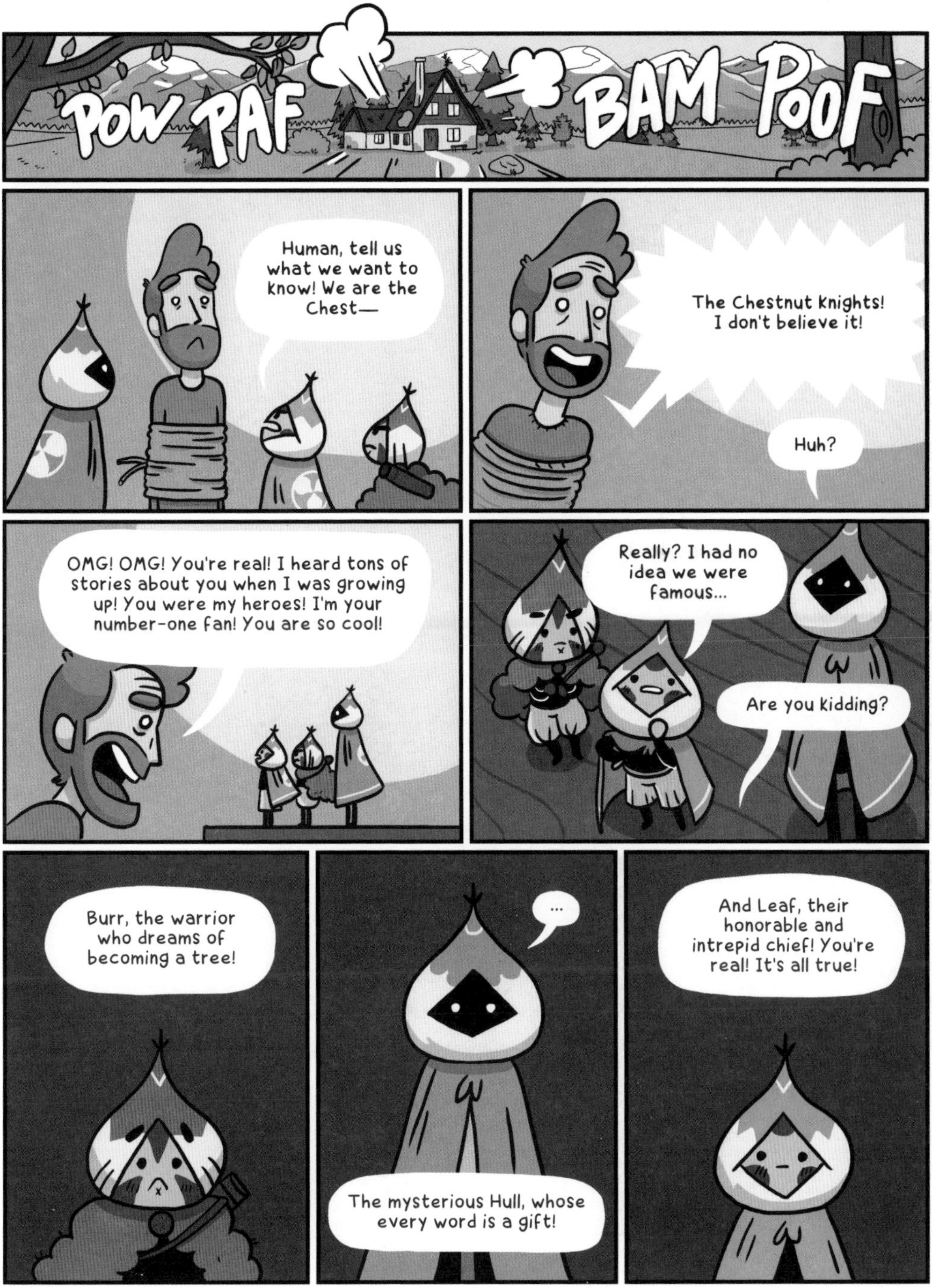
POW PAF
BAM POOF
Human, tell us what we want to know! We are the Chest—
The Chestnut knights! I don't believe it!
Huh?
OMG! OMG! You're real! I heard tons of stories about you when I was growing up! You were my heroes! I'm your number-one fan! You are so cool!
Really? I had no idea we were famous...
Are you kidding?
Burr, the warrior who dreams of becoming a tree!
...
The mysterious Hull, whose every word is a gift!
And Leaf, their honorable and intrepid chief! You're real! It's all true!

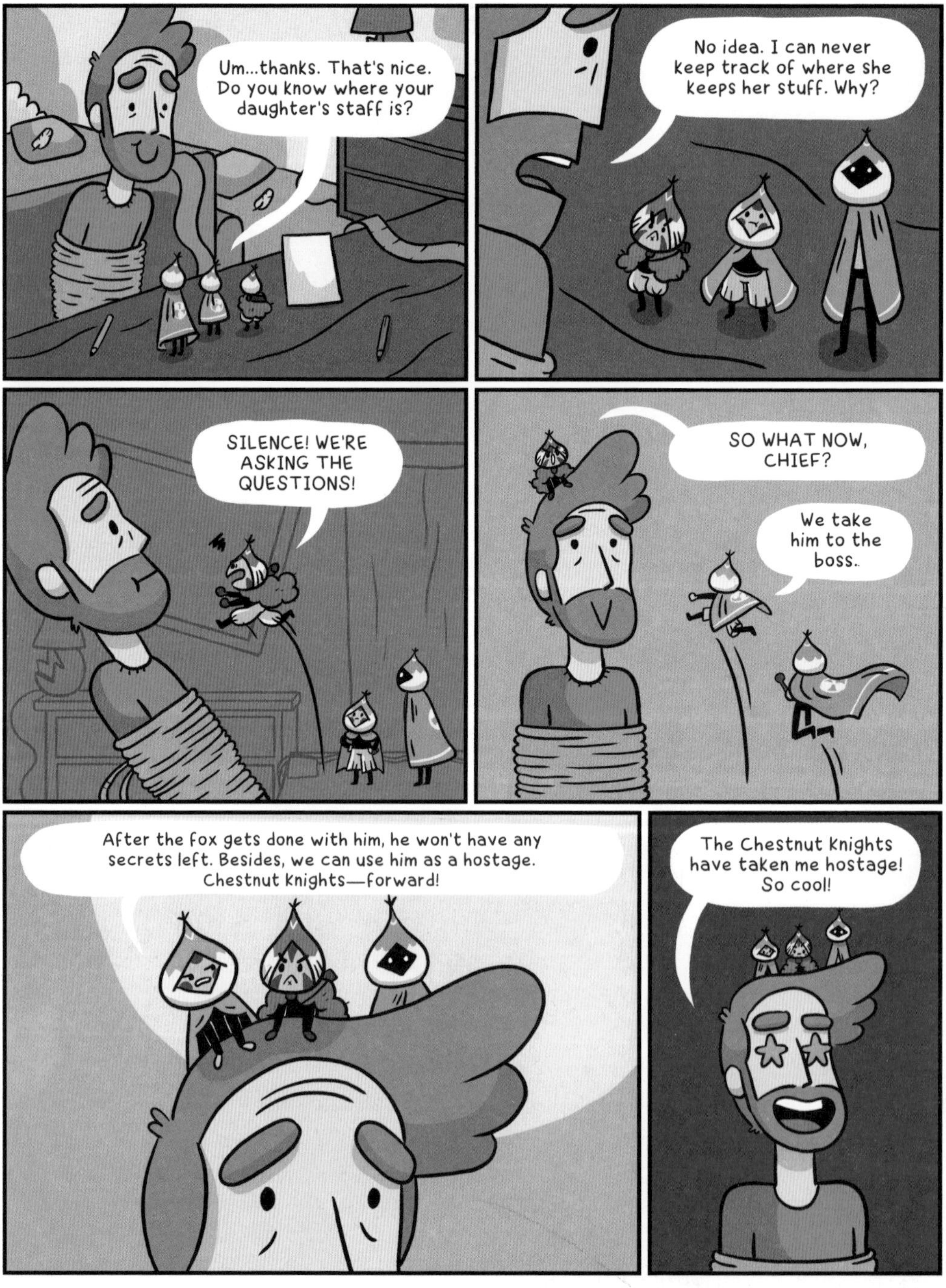
Um...thanks. That's nice. Do you know where your daughter's staff is?
No idea. I can never keep track of where she keeps her stuff. Why?
SILENCE! WE'RE ASKING THE QUESTIONS!
SO WHAT NOW, CHIEF?
We take him to the boss.
After the fox gets done with him, he won't have any secrets left. Besides, we can use him as a hostage. Chestnut Knights—forward!
The Chestnut Knights have taken me hostage! So cool!

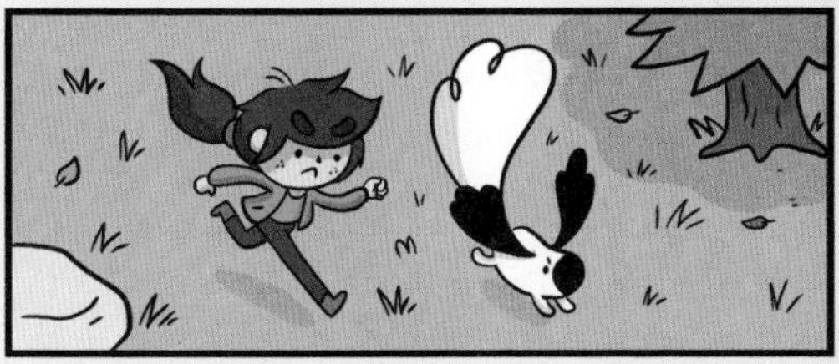

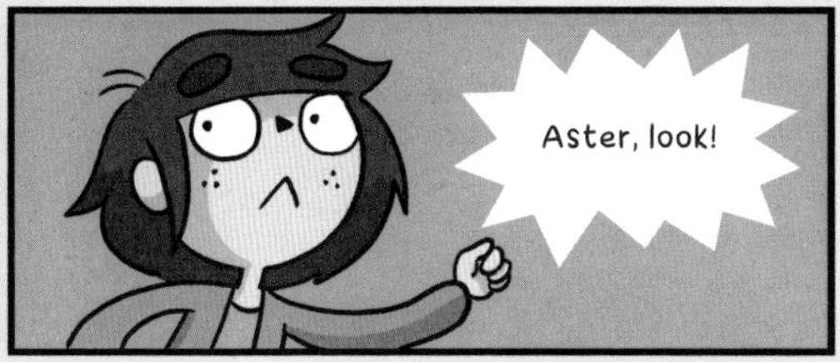
Aster, look!

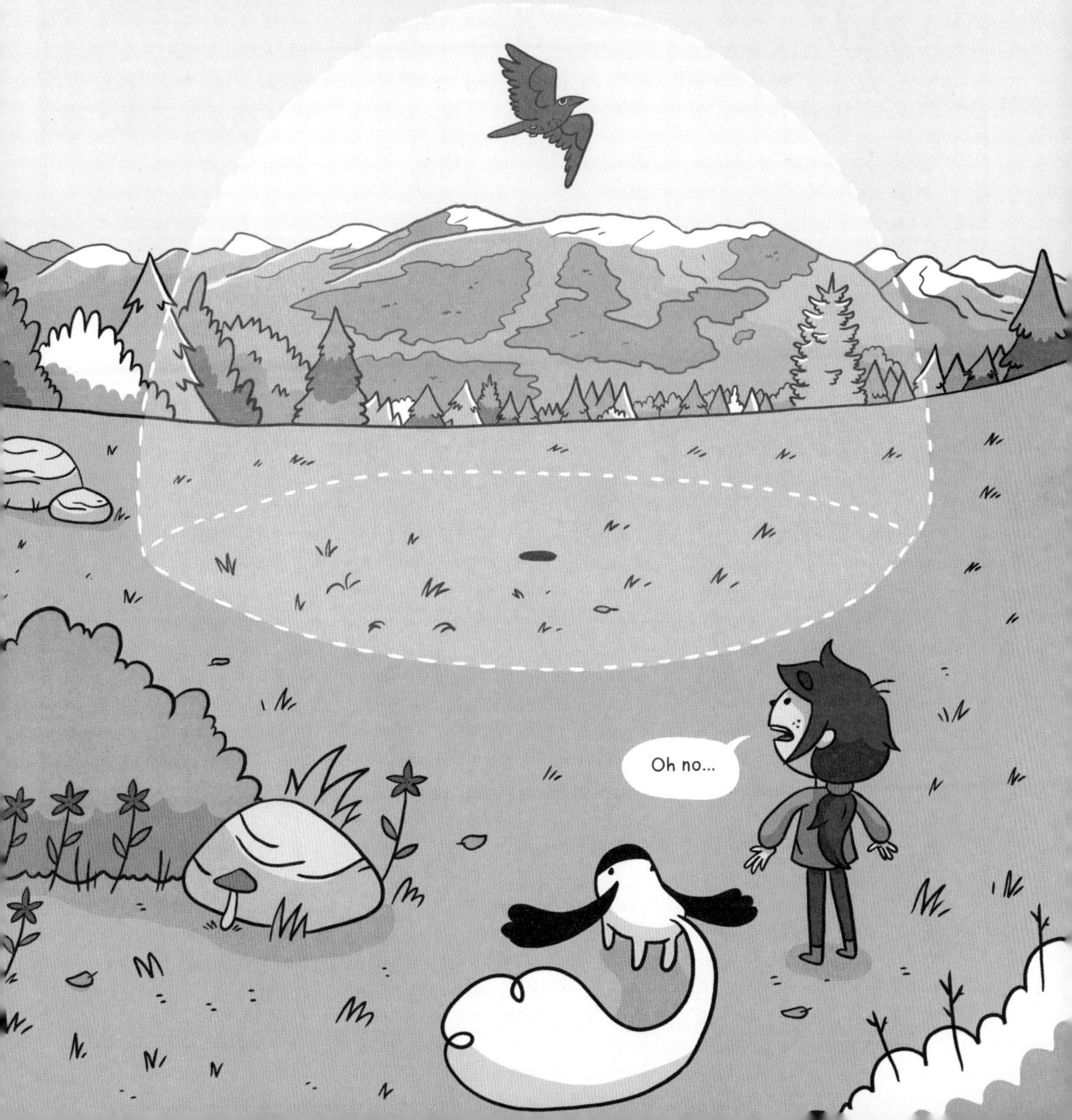
Oh no...

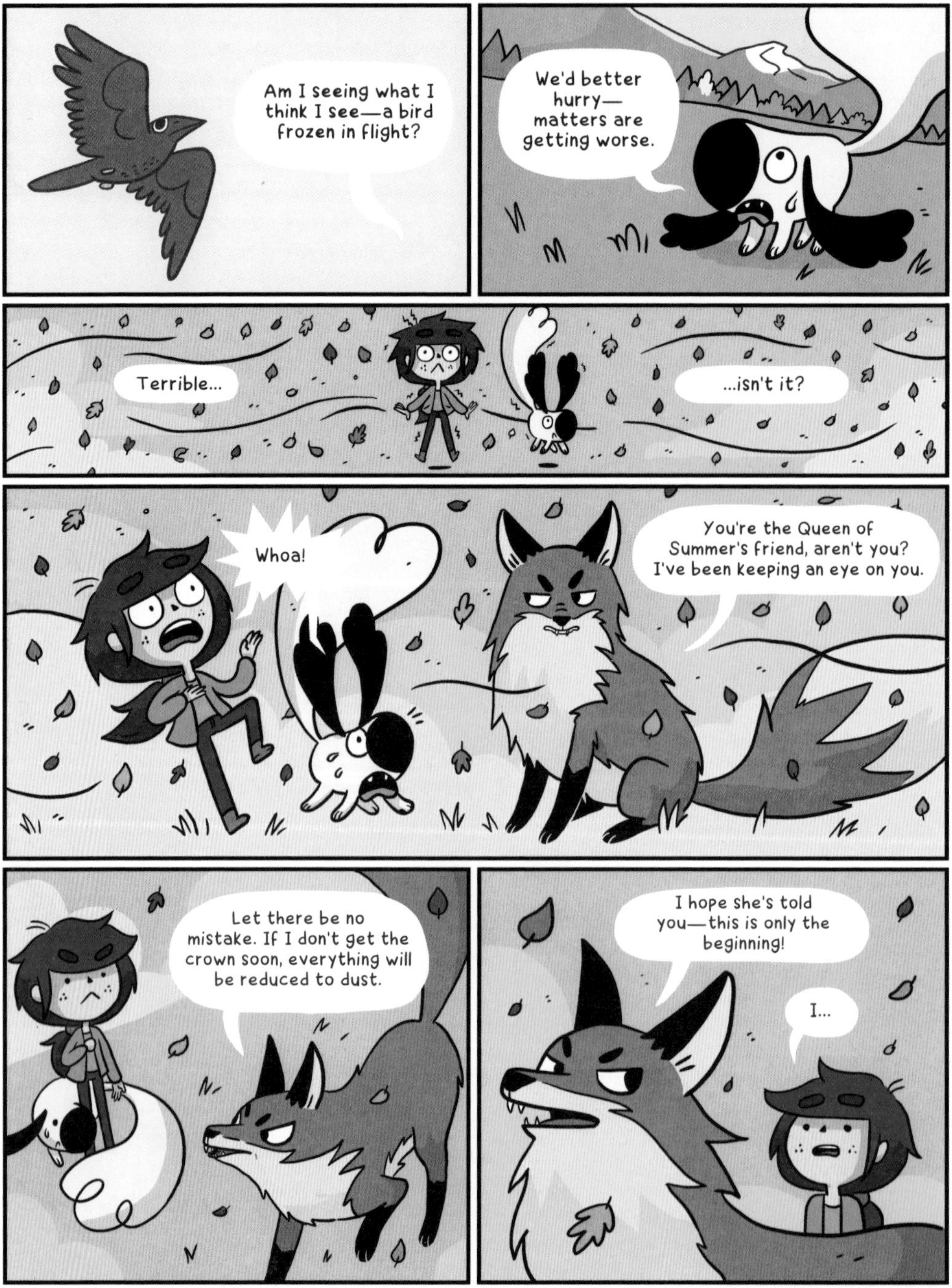

Am I seeing what I think I see—a bird frozen in flight?
We'd better hurry— matters are getting worse.
Terrible...
...isn't it?
Whoa!
You're the Queen of Summer's friend, aren't you? I've been keeping an eye on you.
Let there be no mistake. If I don't get the crown soon, everything will be reduced to dust.
I hope she's told you—this is only the beginning!
I...

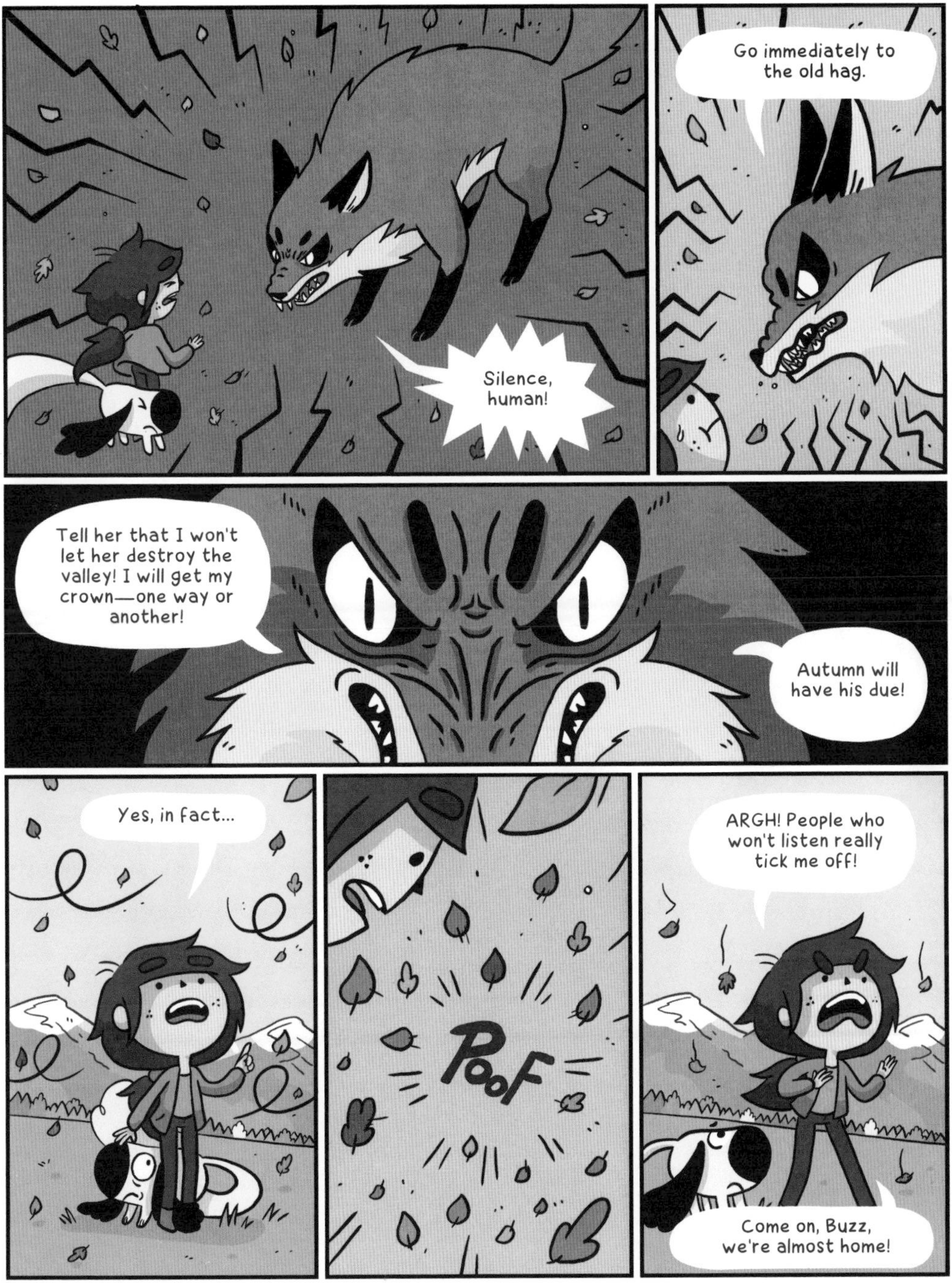
Silence, human!
Go immediately to the old hag.
Tell her that I won't let her destroy the valley! I will get my crown—one way or another!
Autumn will have his due!
Yes, in fact...
POOF
ARGH! People who won't listen really tick me off!
Come on, Buzz, we're almost home!

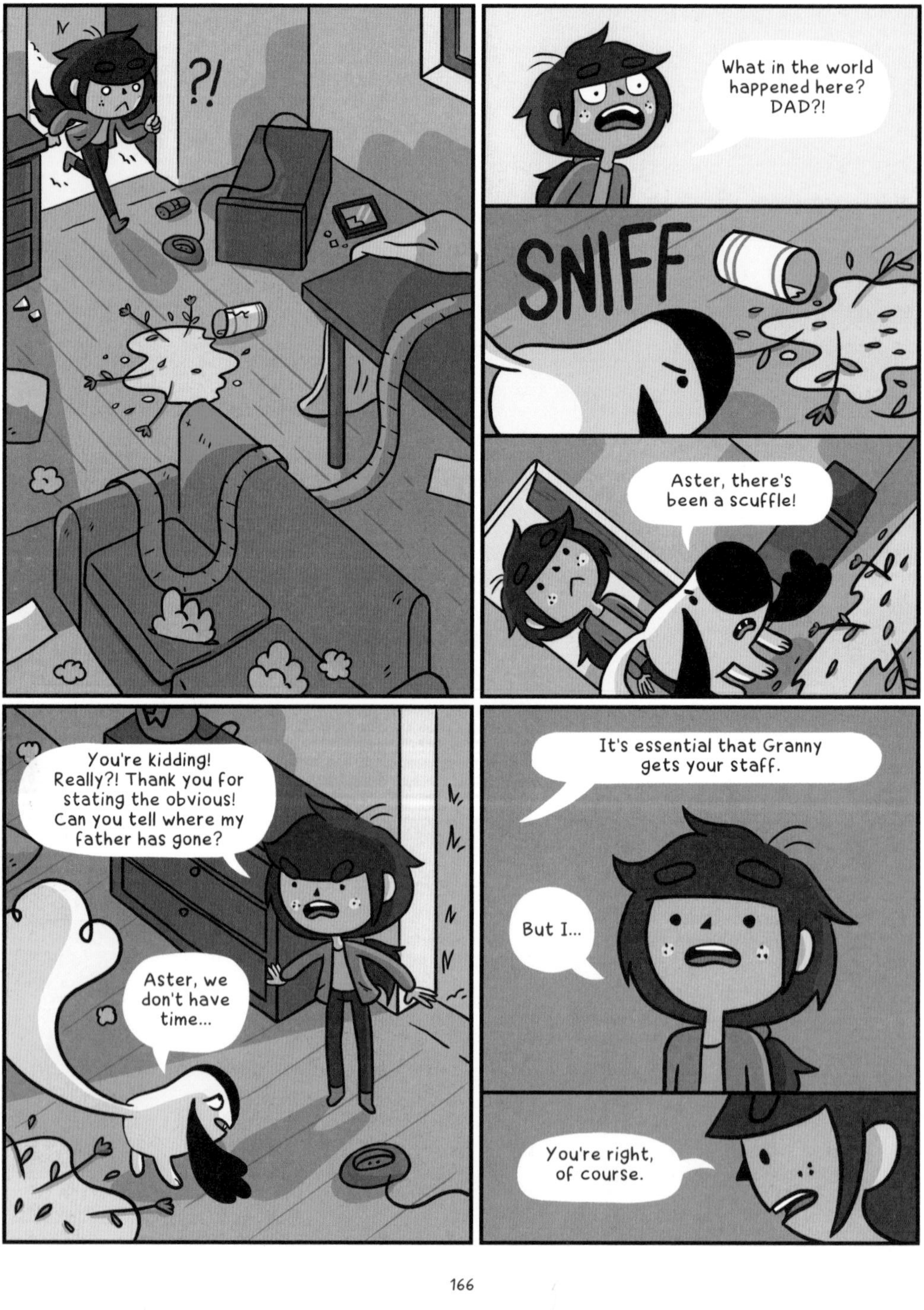

?!
What in the world happened here? DAD?!
SNIFF
Aster, there's been a scuffle!
You're kidding! Really?! Thank you for stating the obvious! Can you tell where my father has gone?
Aster, we don't have time...
It's essential that Granny gets your staff.
But I...
You're right, of course.

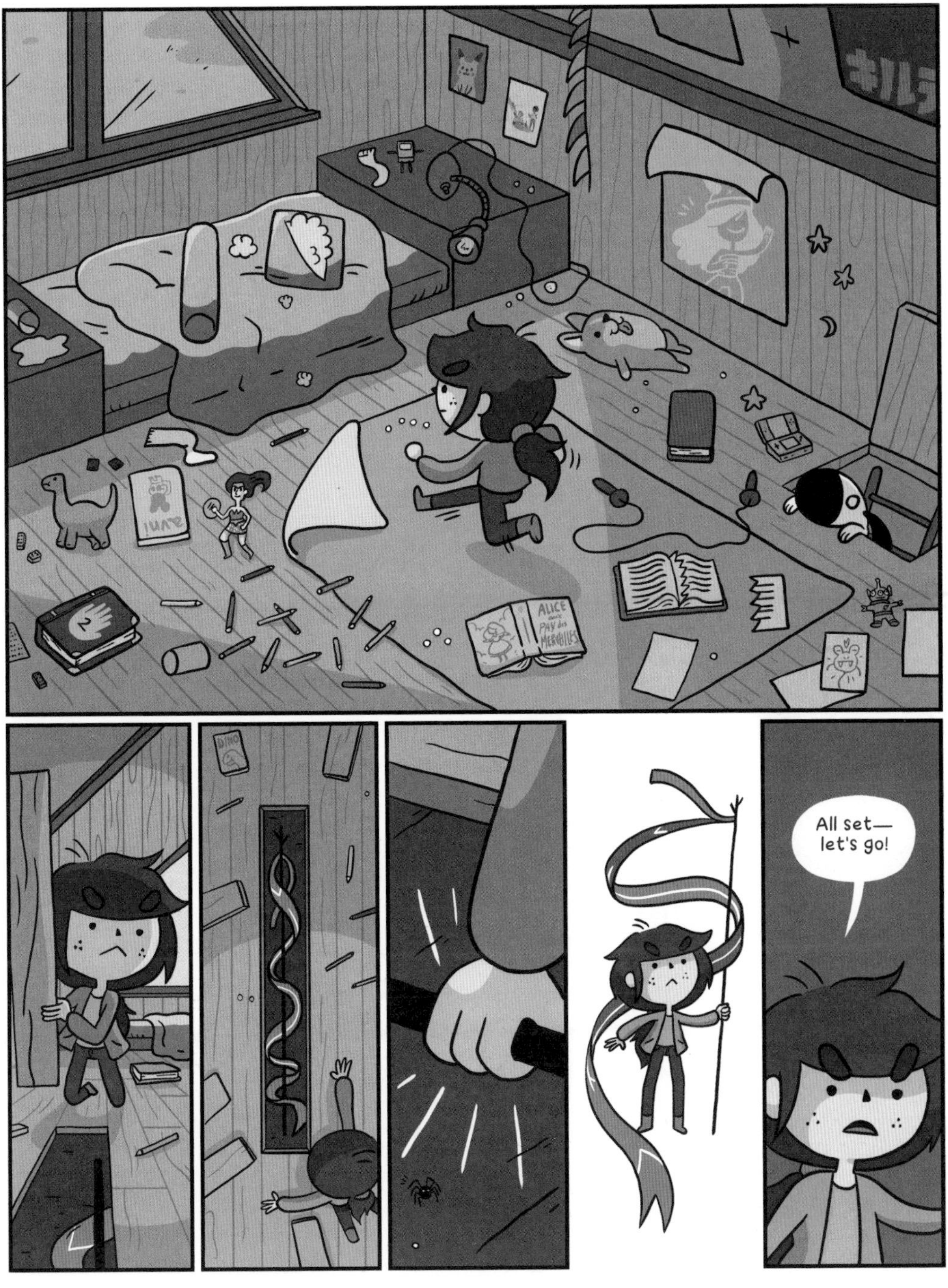
All set—
let's go!

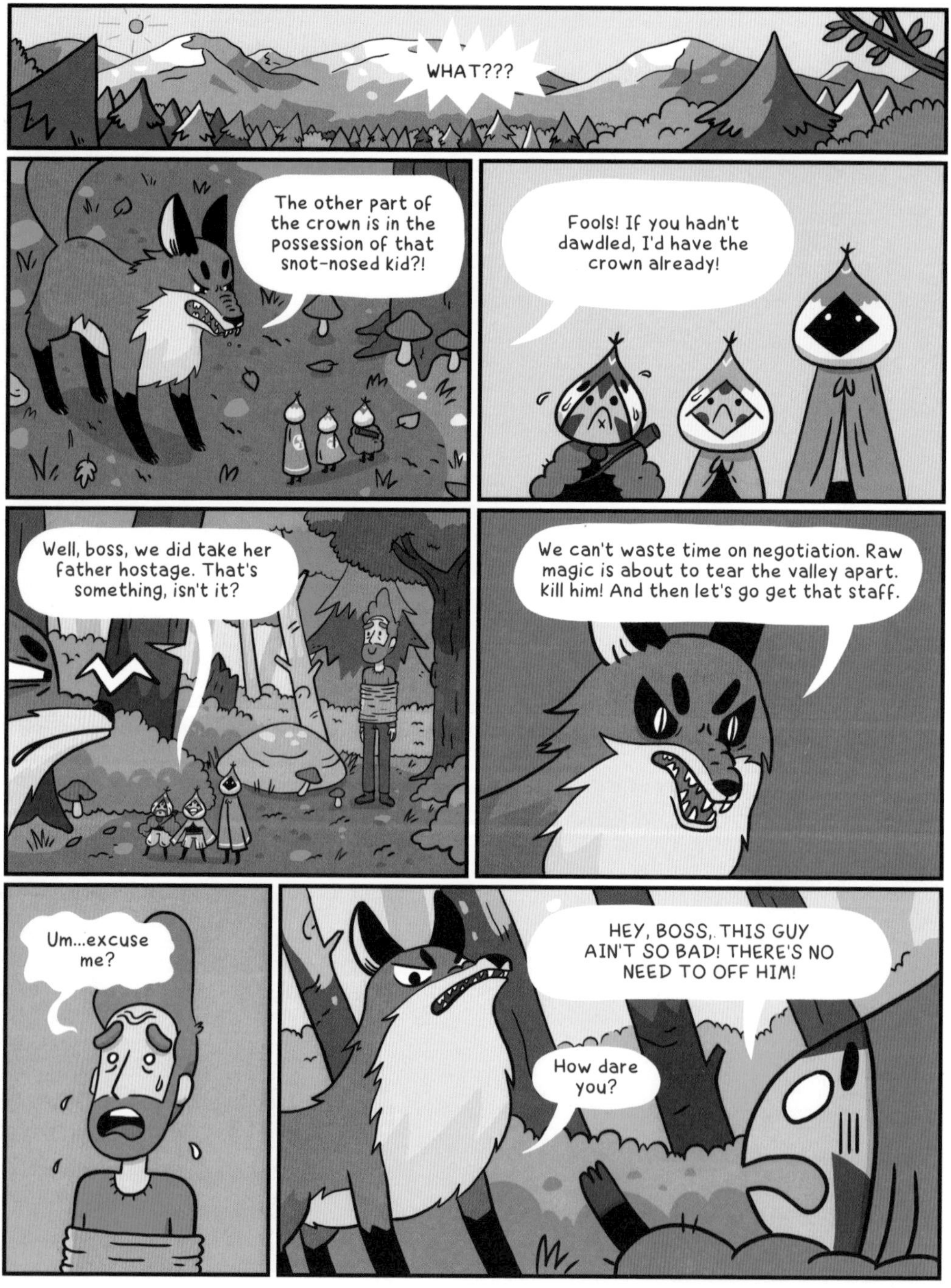
WHAT???
The other part of the crown is in the possession of that snot-nosed kid?!
Fools! If you hadn't dawdled, I'd have the crown already!
Well, boss, we did take her father hostage. That's something, isn't it?
We can't waste time on negotiation. Raw magic is about to tear the valley apart. Kill him! And then let's go get that staff.
Um...excuse me?
HEY, BOSS, THIS GUY AIN'T SO BAD! THERE'S NO NEED TO OFF HIM!
How dare you?

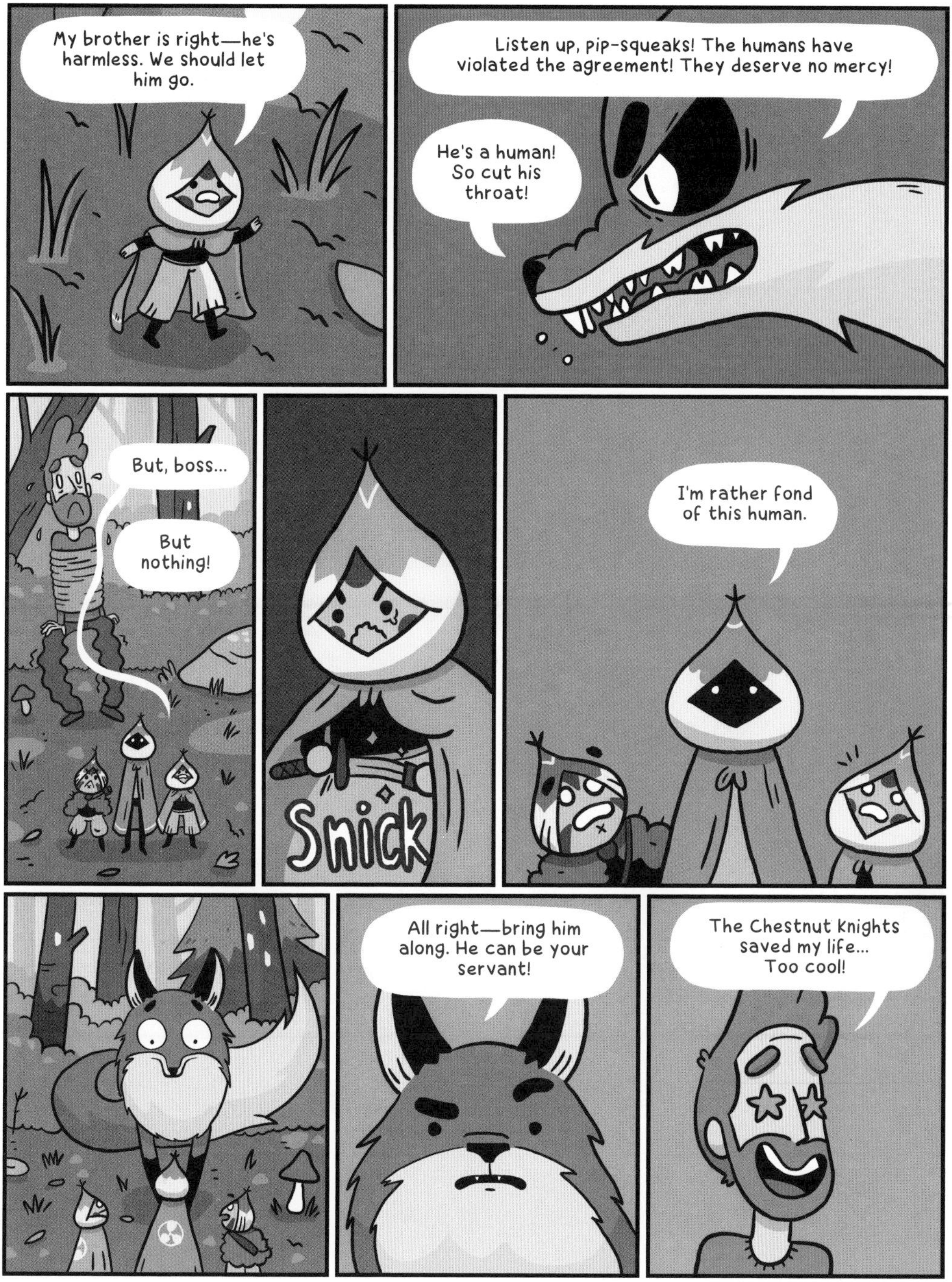
My brother is right—he's harmless. We should let him go.
Listen up, pip-squeaks! The humans have violated the agreement! They deserve no mercy!
He's a human! So cut his throat!
But, boss...
But nothing!
Snick
I'm rather fond of this human.
All right—bring him along. He can be your servant!
The Chestnut knights saved my life... Too cool!

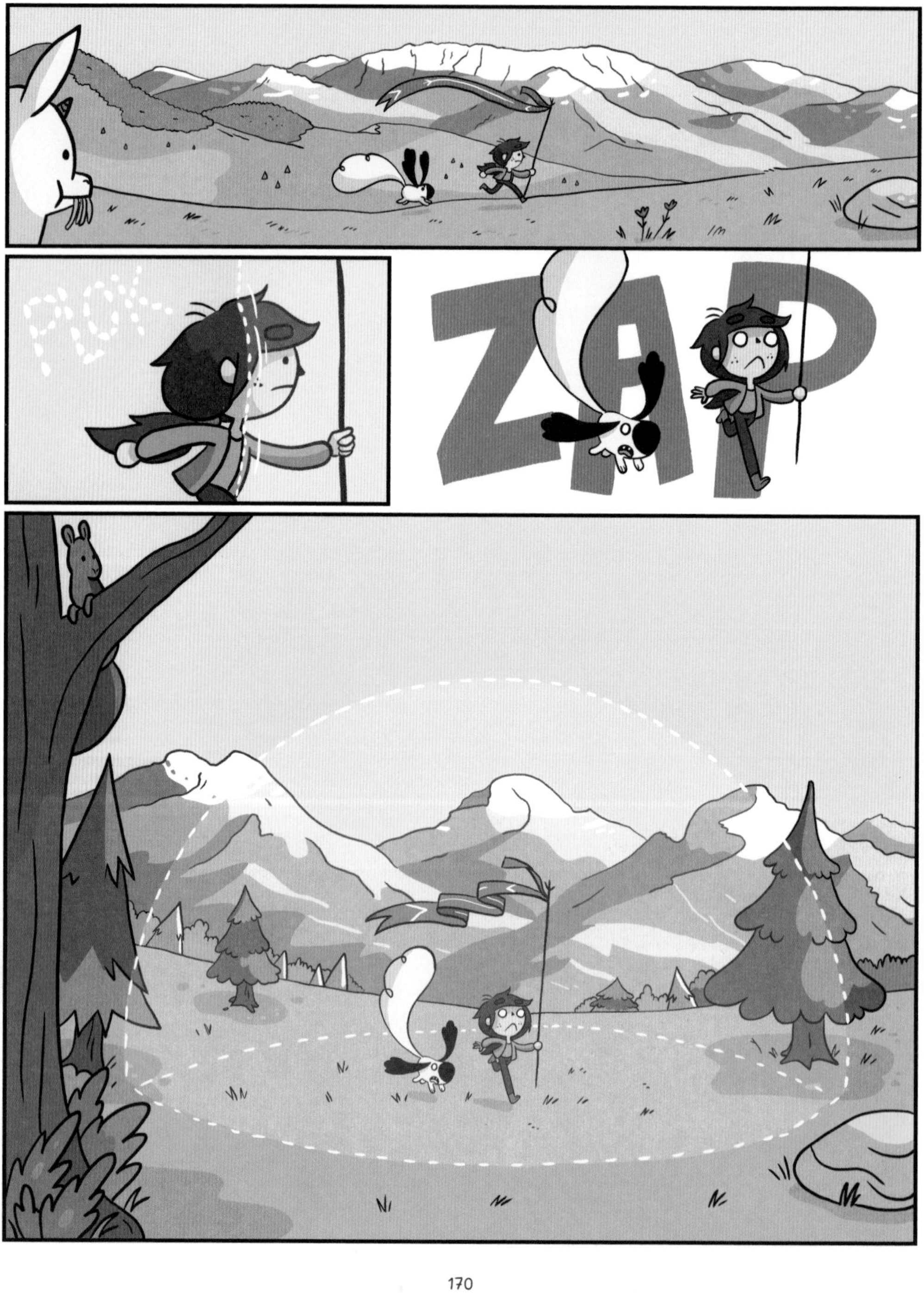
POK
ZAP

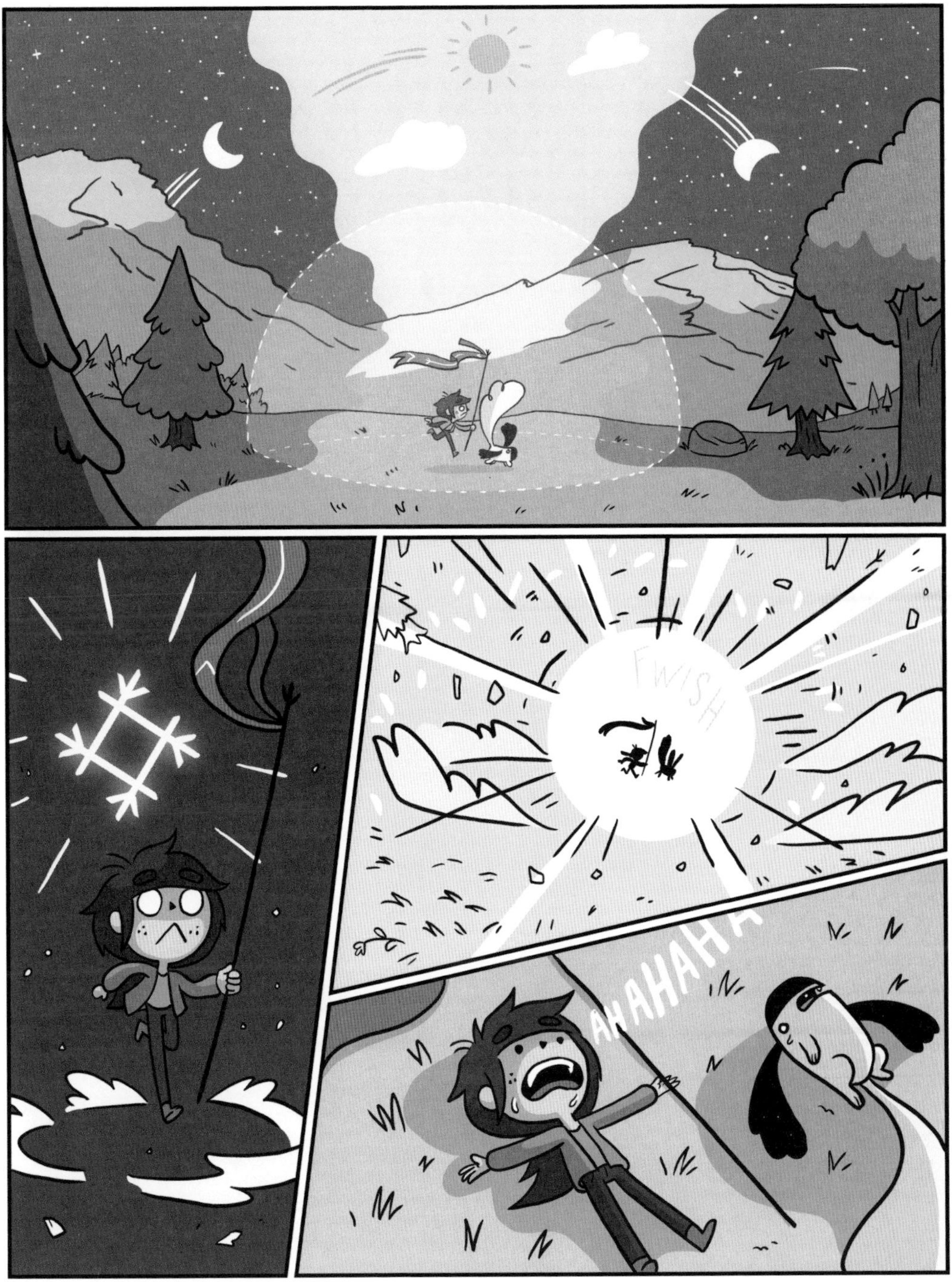
FWISH
AHAHAHAHA

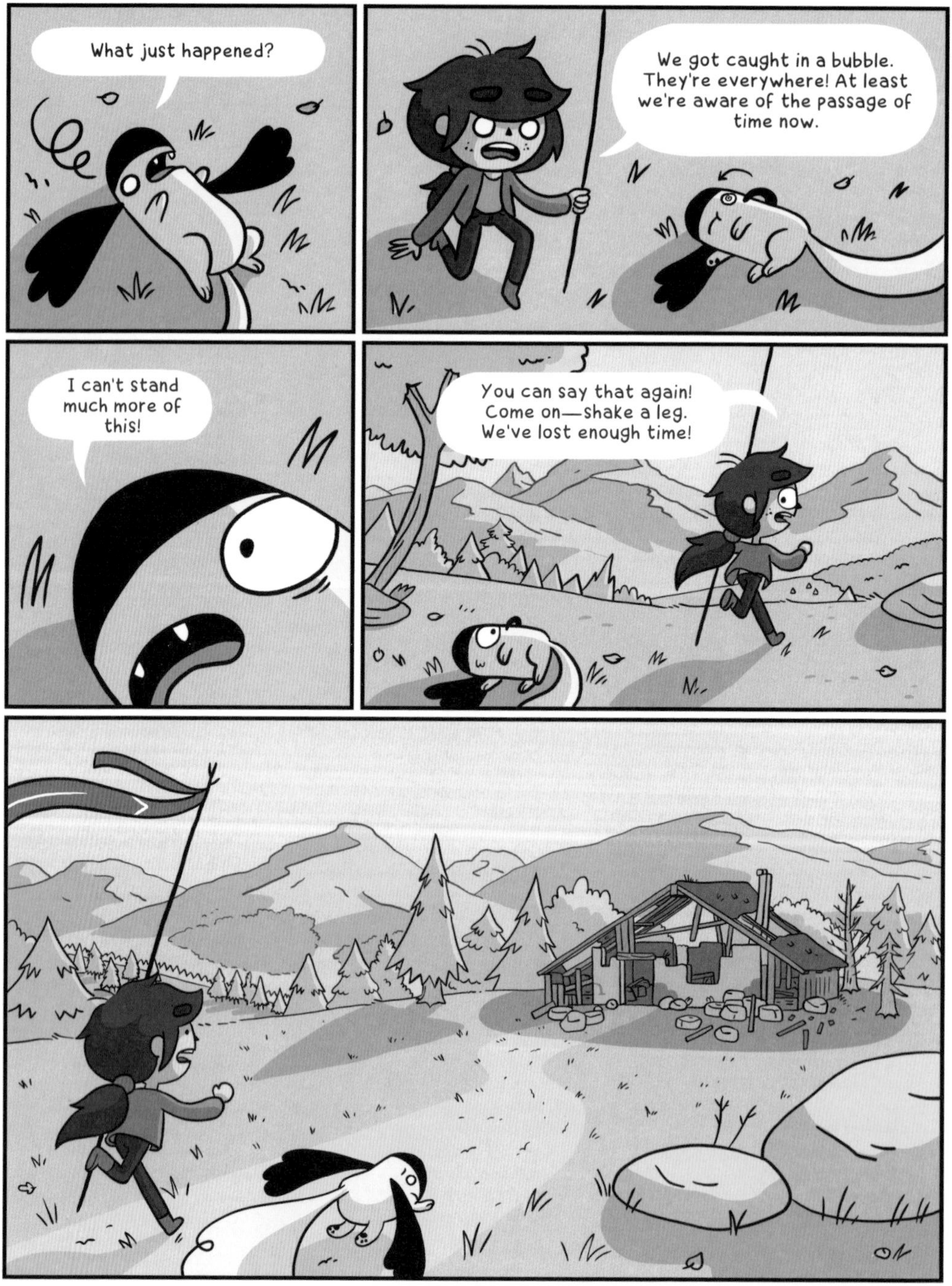
What just happened?
We got caught in a bubble. They're everywhere! At least we're aware of the passage of time now.
I can't stand much more of this!
You can say that again! Come on—shake a leg. We've lost enough time!

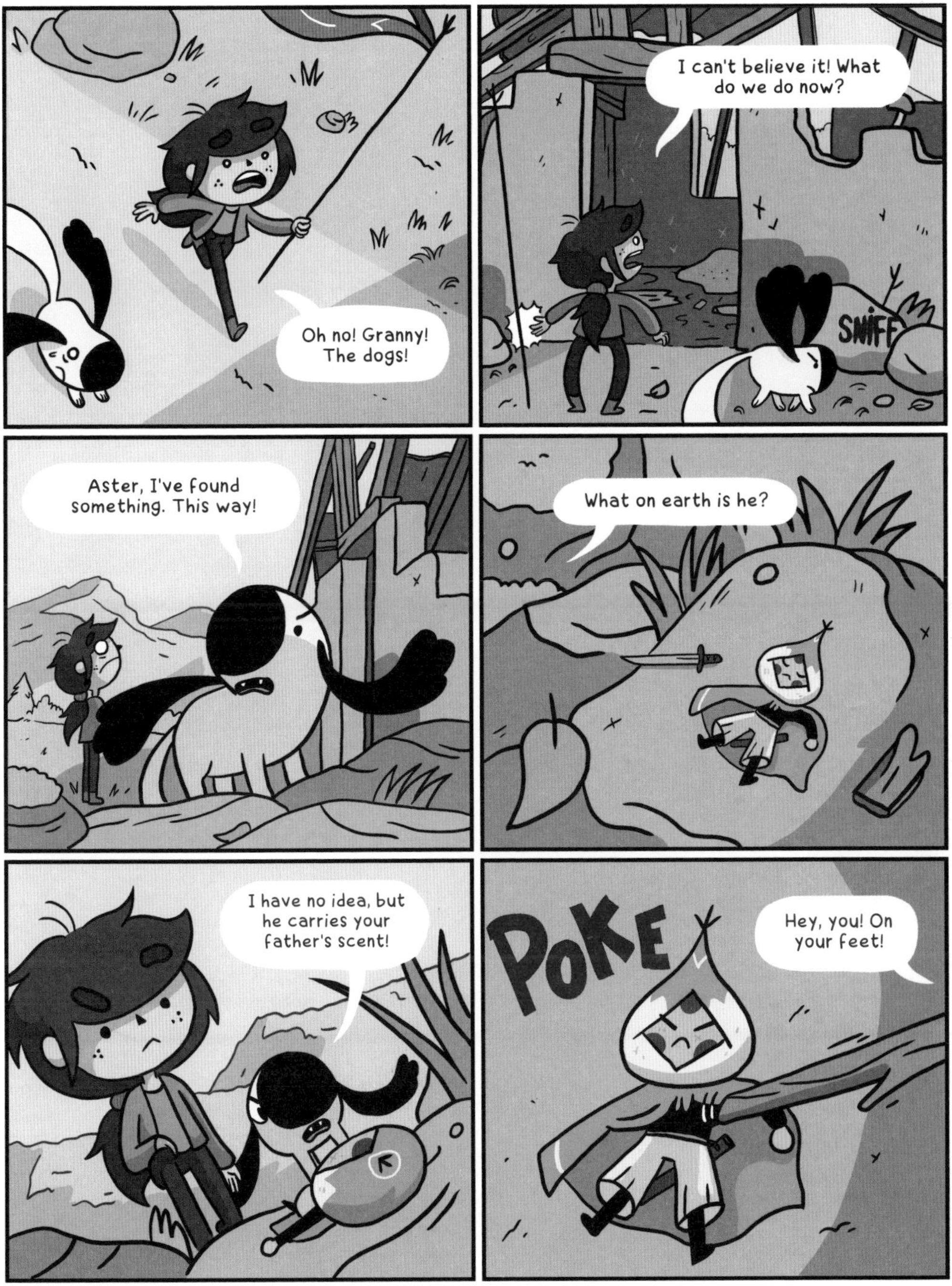
Oh no! Granny! The dogs!
I can't believe it! What do we do now?
SNIFF
Aster, I've found something. This way!
What on earth is he?
I have no idea, but he carries your father's scent!
POKE
Hey, you! On your feet!

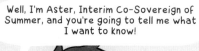
What exactly are you doing here?

I am Leaf, Captain of the Chestnut knights, in the service of the fox, king of Autumn.

Well, I'm Aster, Interim Co-Sovereign of Summer, and you're going to tell me what I want to know!

Where's my father? And Granny?

Lady Aster, we had planned to exchange your father for your staff and thus force the other Queen of Summer to give us her power.

But nothing went according to plan.

CLING

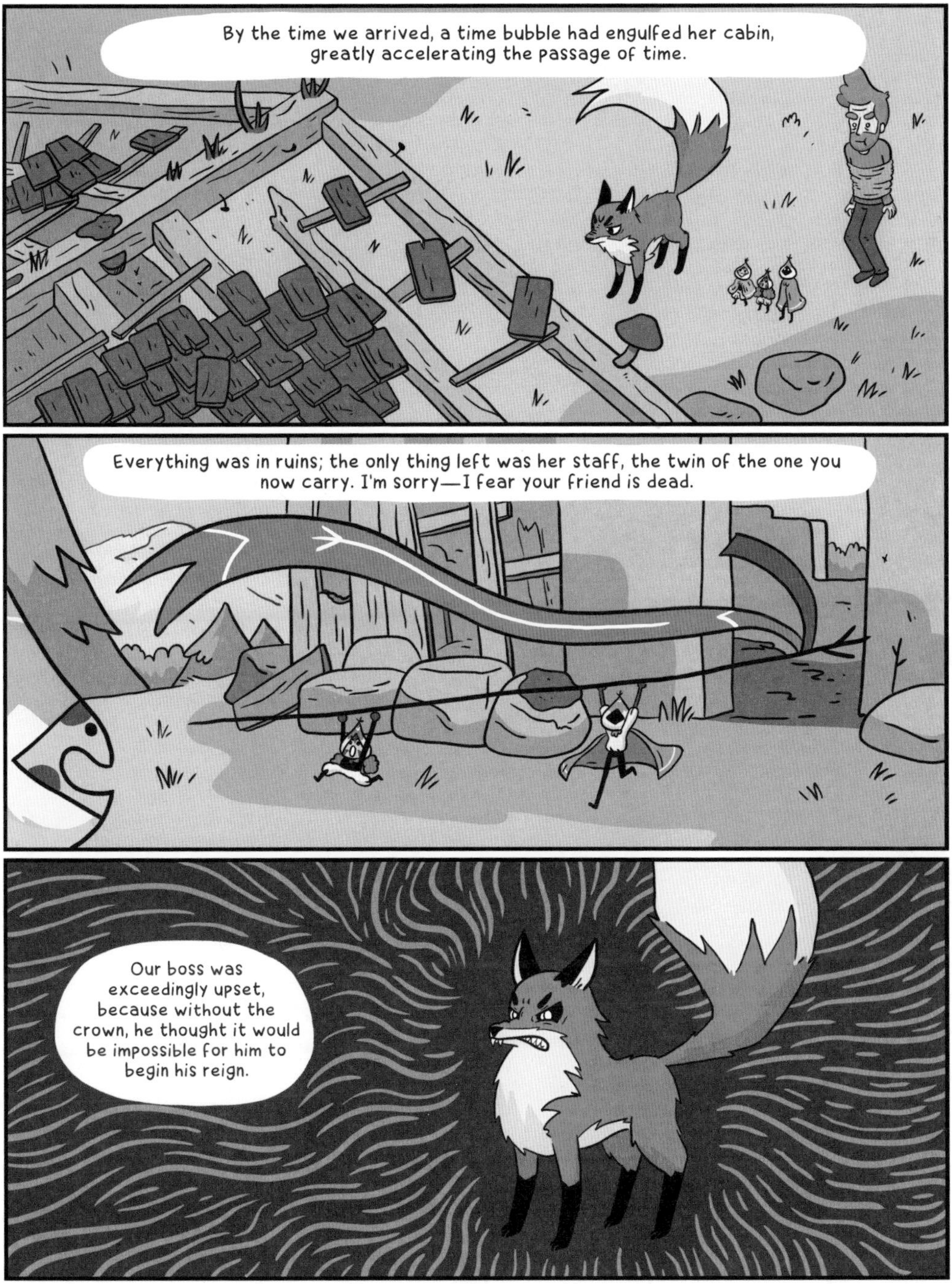
By the time we arrived, a time bubble had engulfed her cabin, greatly accelerating the passage of time.
Everything was in ruins; the only thing left was her staff, the twin of the one you now carry. I'm sorry—I fear your friend is dead.
Our boss was exceedingly upset, because without the crown, he thought it would be impossible for him to begin his reign.

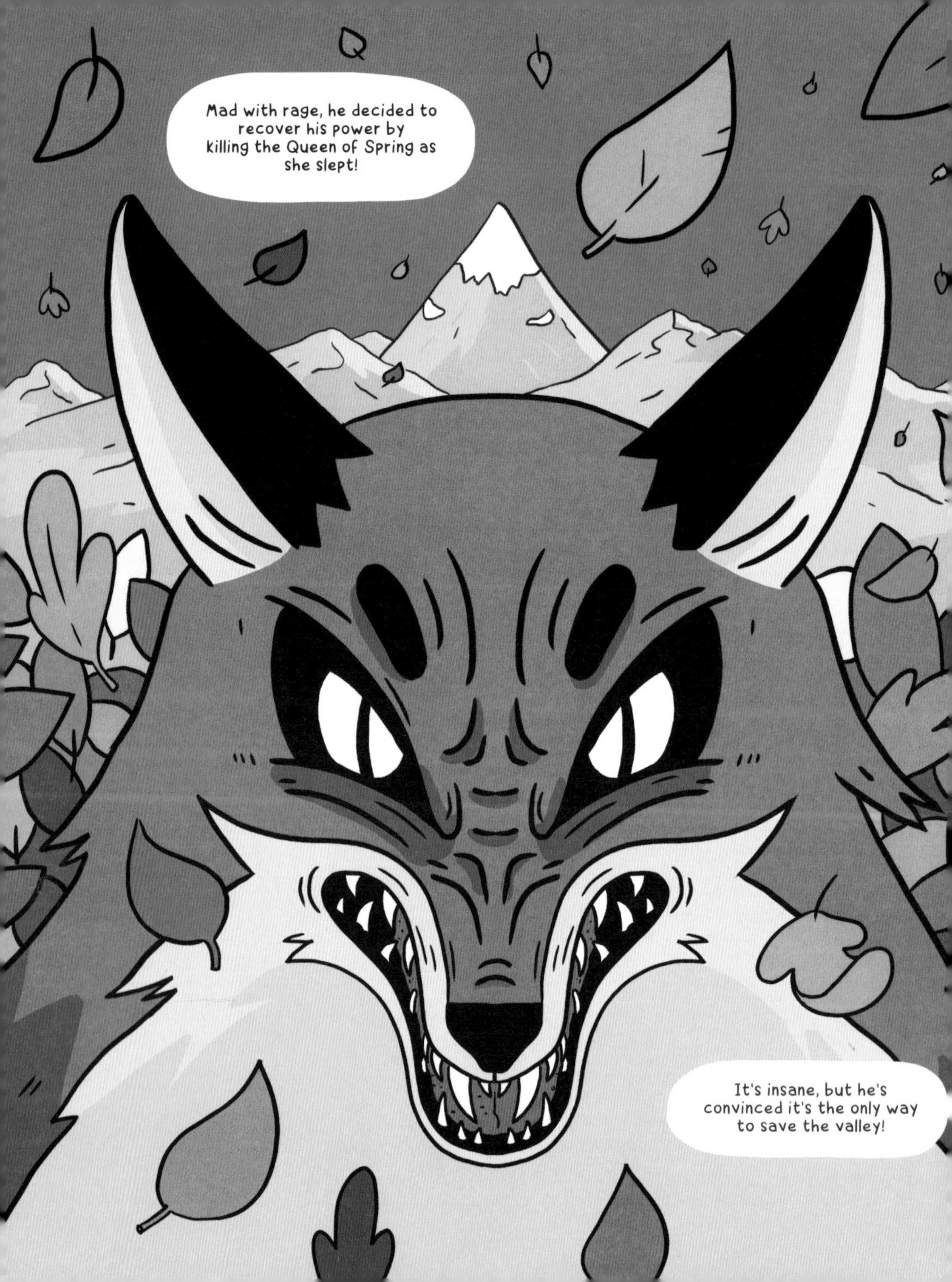
Mad with rage, he decided to recover his power by killing the Queen of Spring as she slept!
It's insane, but he's convinced it's the only way to save the valley!

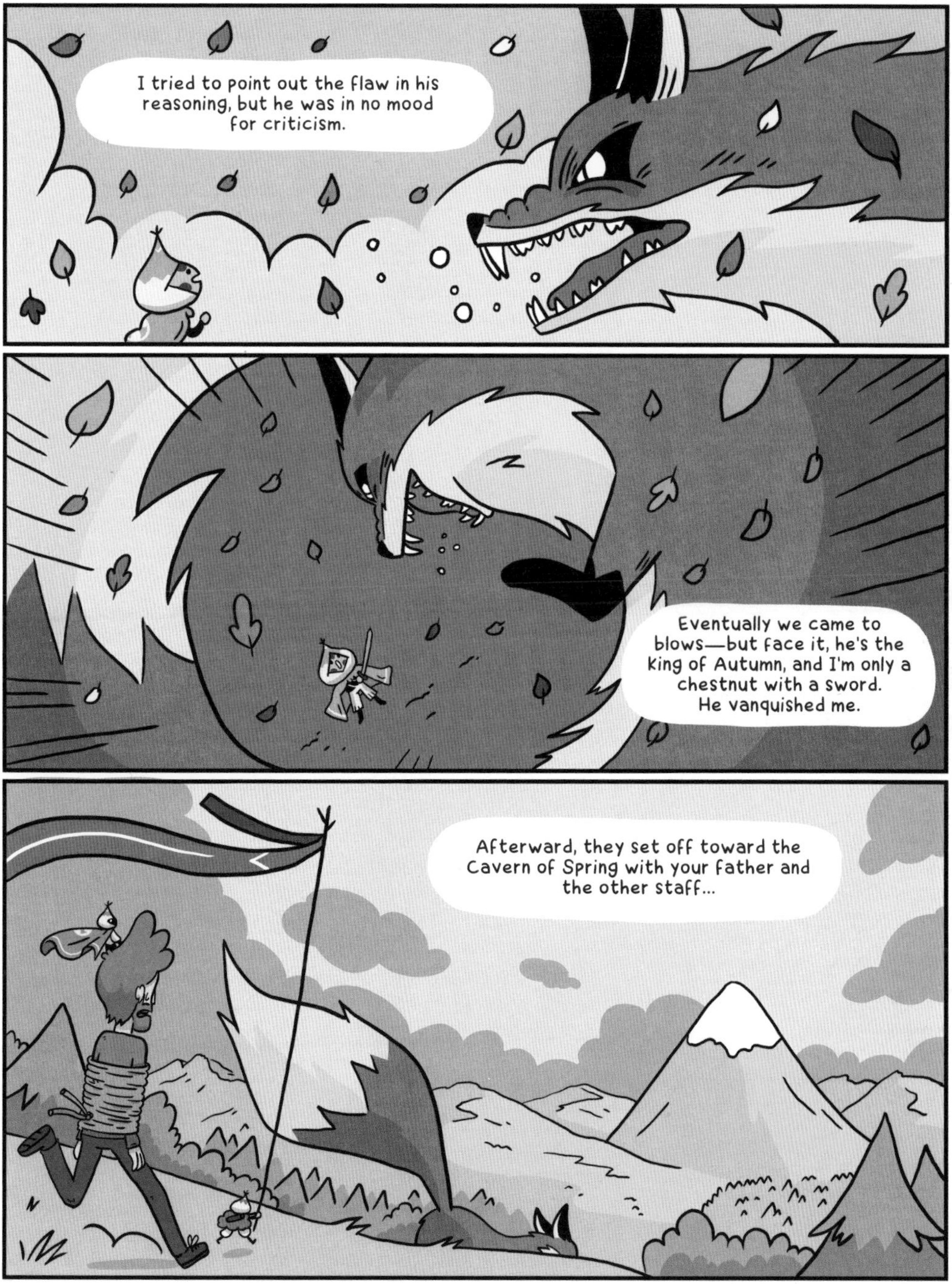
I tried to point out the flaw in his reasoning, but he was in no mood for criticism.
Eventually we came to blows—but face it, he's the King of Autumn, and I'm only a chestnut with a sword. He vanquished me.
Afterward, they set off toward the Cavern of Spring with your father and the other staff...

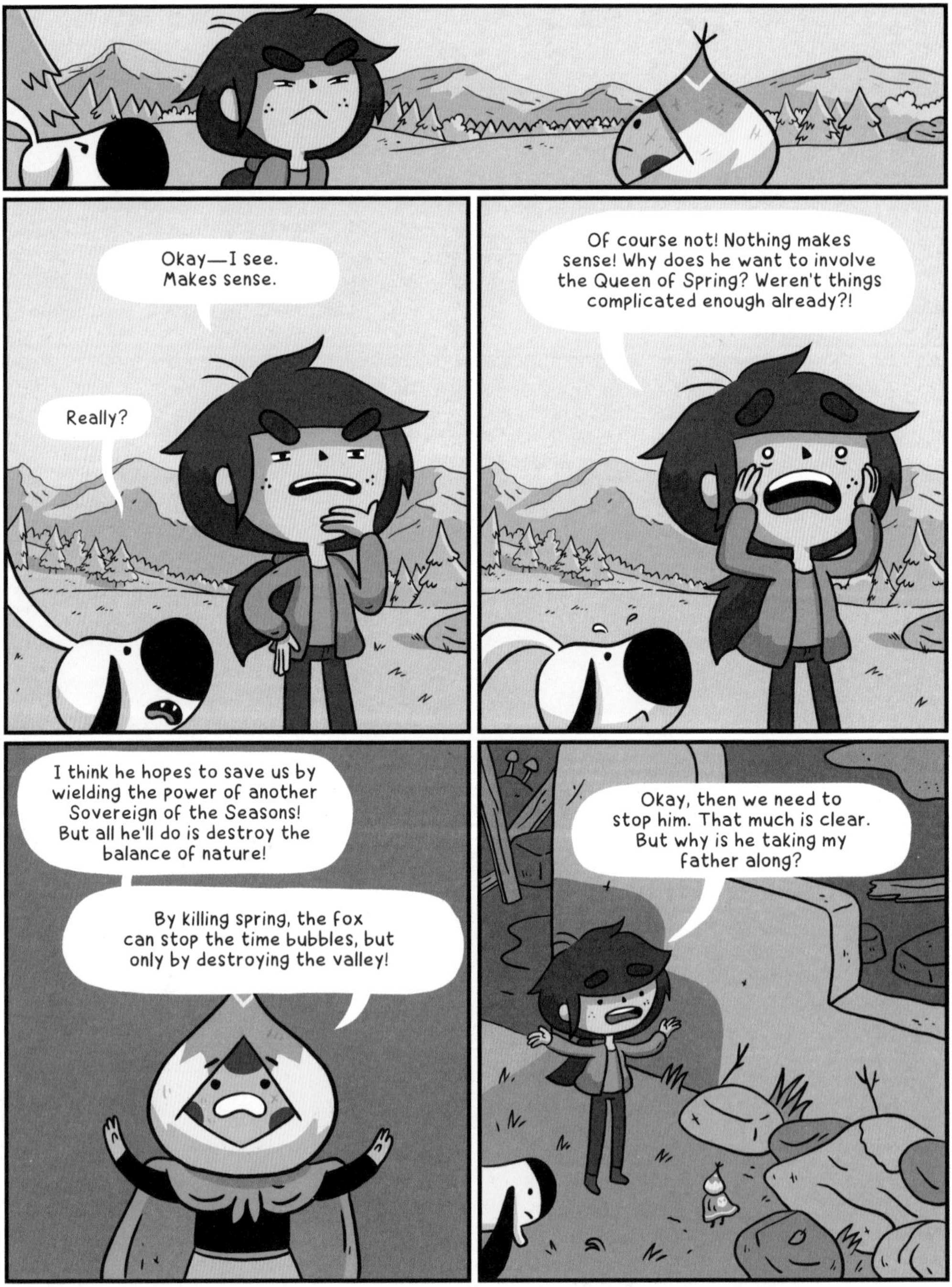
Okay—I see.
Makes sense.
Really?
Of course not! Nothing makes sense! Why does he want to involve the Queen of Spring? Weren't things complicated enough already?!
I think he hopes to save us by wielding the power of another Sovereign of the Seasons! But all he'll do is destroy the balance of nature!
By killing spring, the fox can stop the time bubbles, but only by destroying the valley!
Okay, then we need to stop him. That much is clear. But why is he taking my father along?

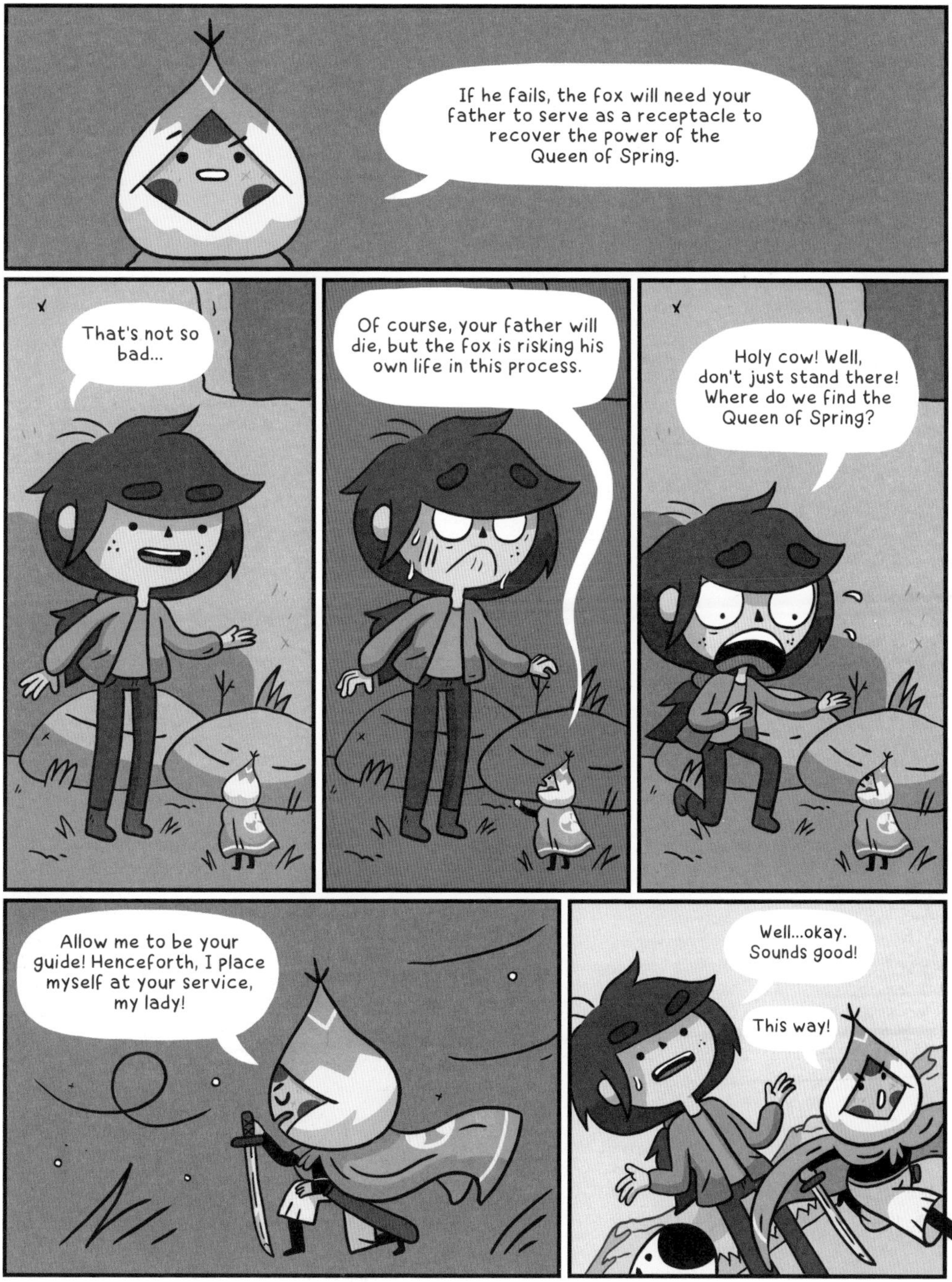
If he fails, the fox will need your father to serve as a receptacle to recover the power of the Queen of Spring.
That's not so bad...
Of course, your father will die, but the fox is risking his own life in this process.
Holy cow! Well, don't just stand there! Where do we find the Queen of Spring?
Allow me to be your guide! Henceforth, I place myself at your service, my lady!
Well...okay. Sounds good!
This way!

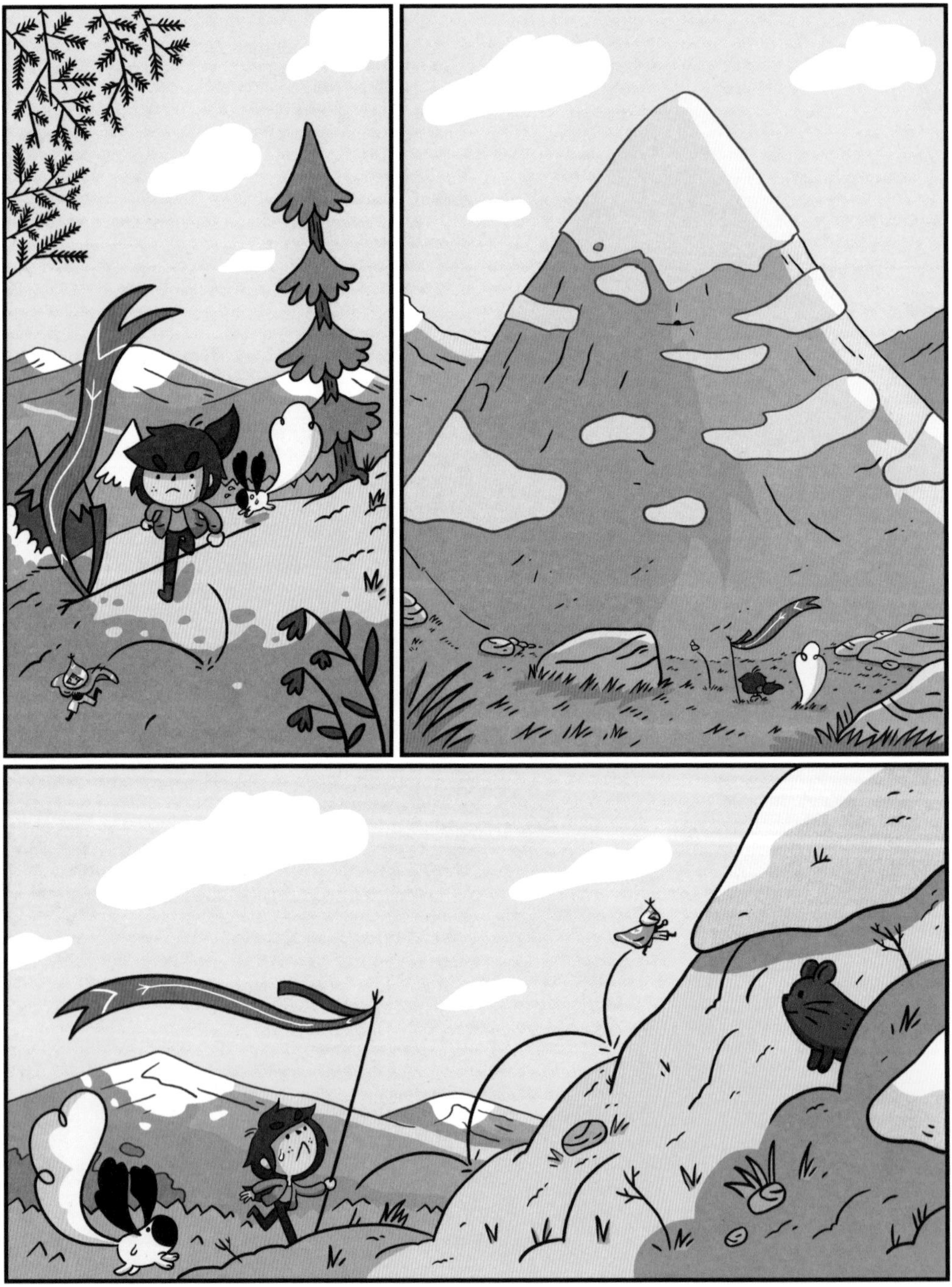

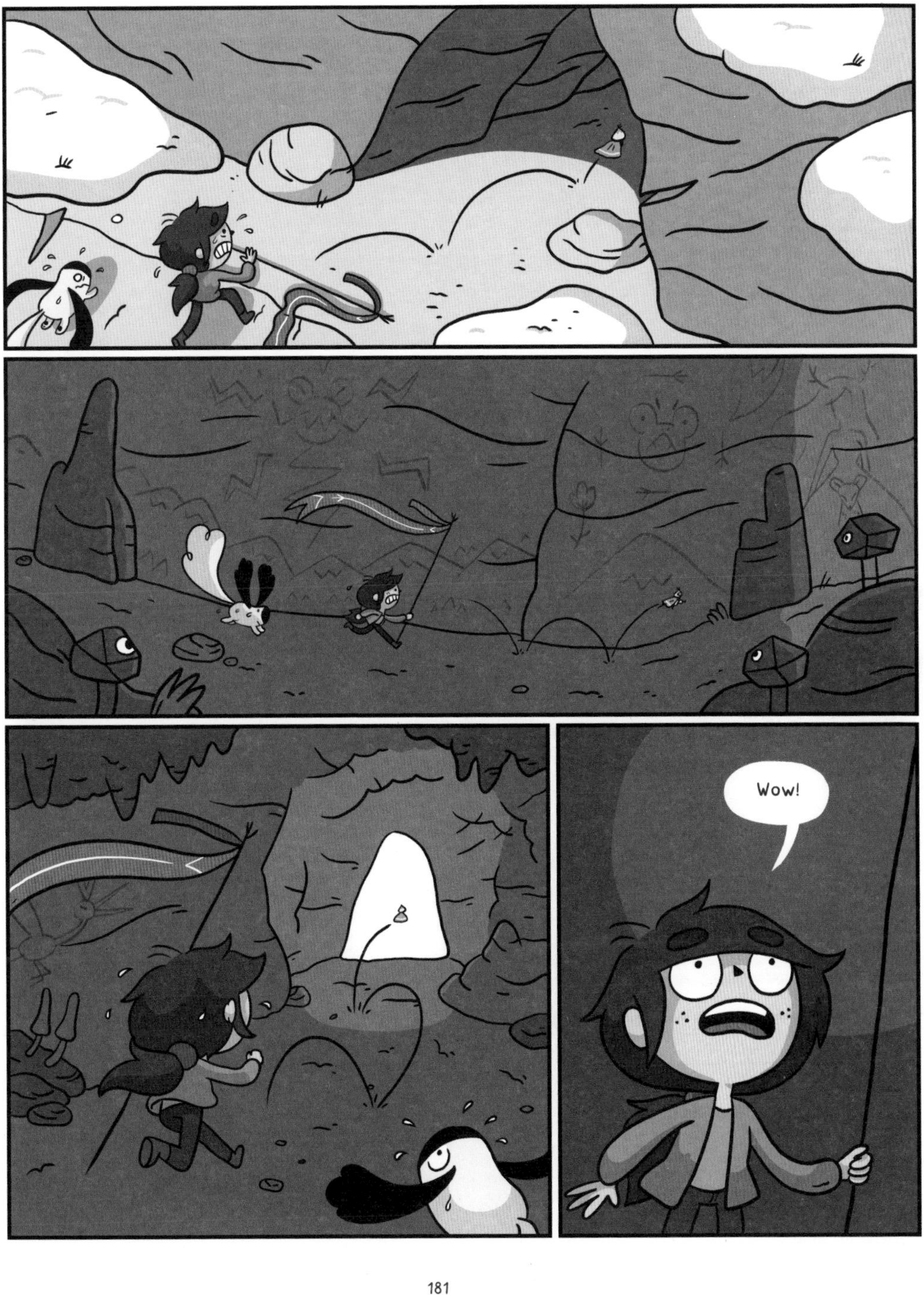
Wow!

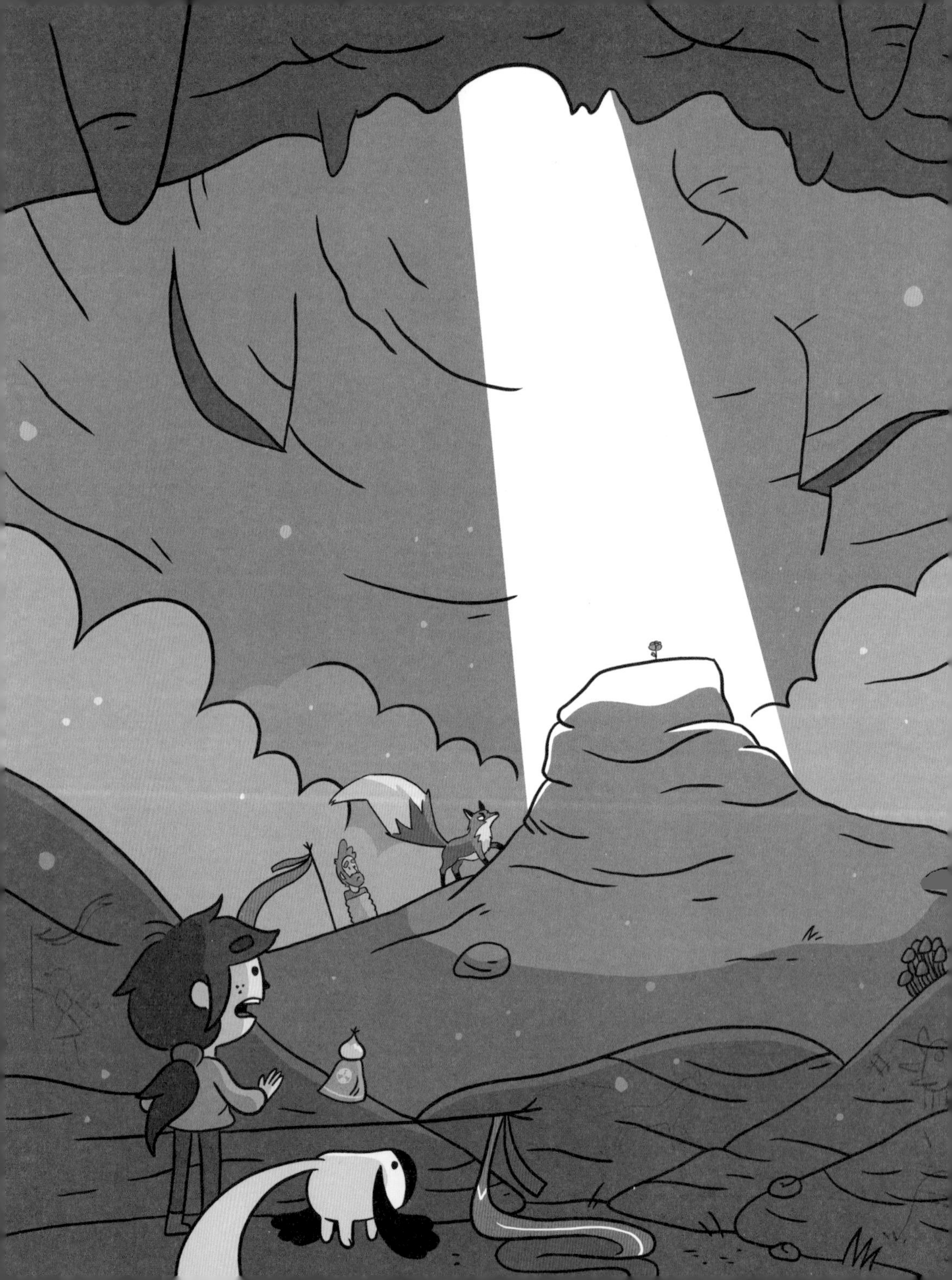

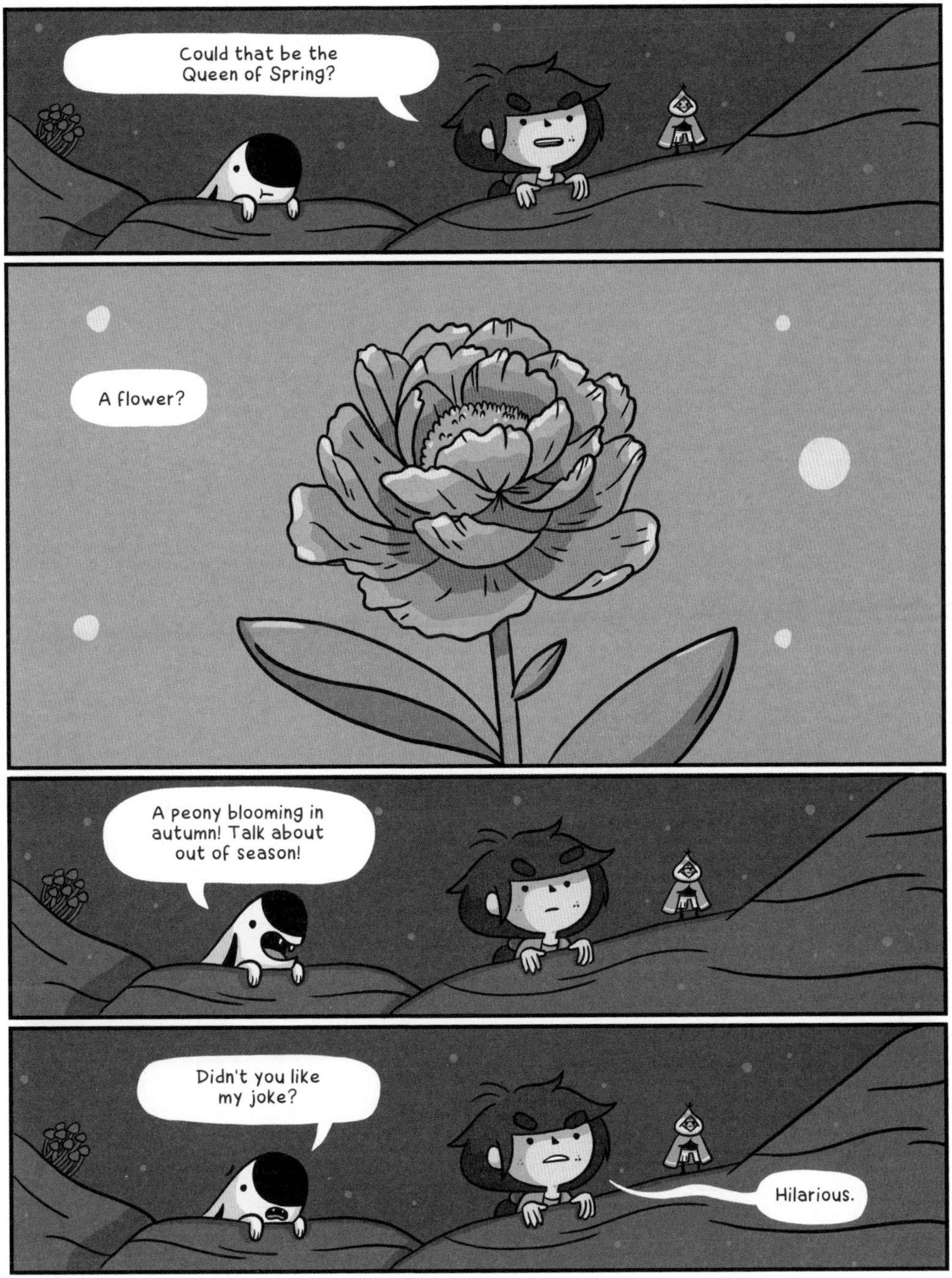

Could that be the Queen of Spring?
A flower?
A peony blooming in autumn! Talk about out of season!
Didn't you like my joke?
Hilarious.

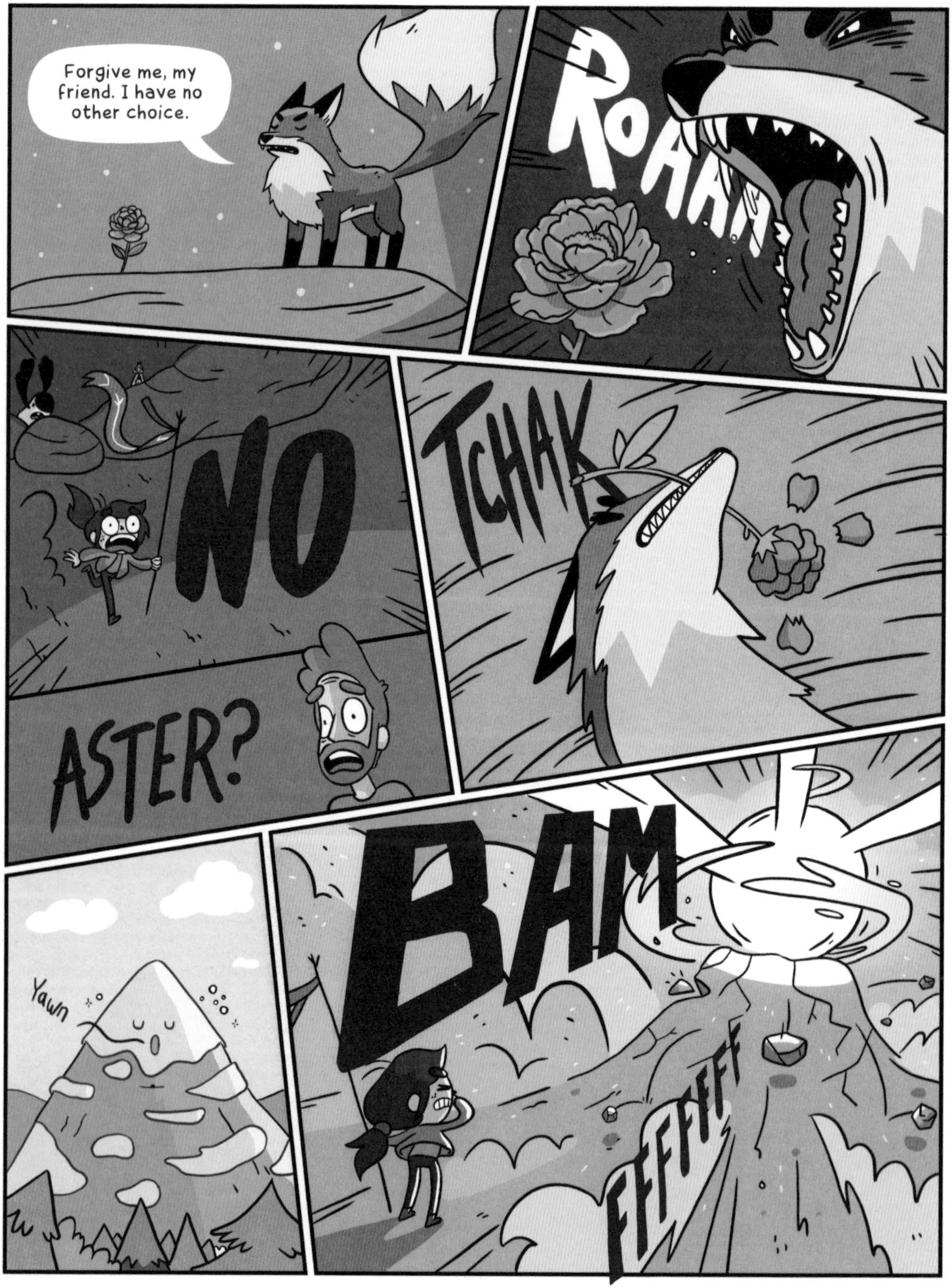
Forgive me, my friend. I have no other choice.
ROAAAR
NO
ASTER?
TCHAK
Yawn
BAM
FFFFFF

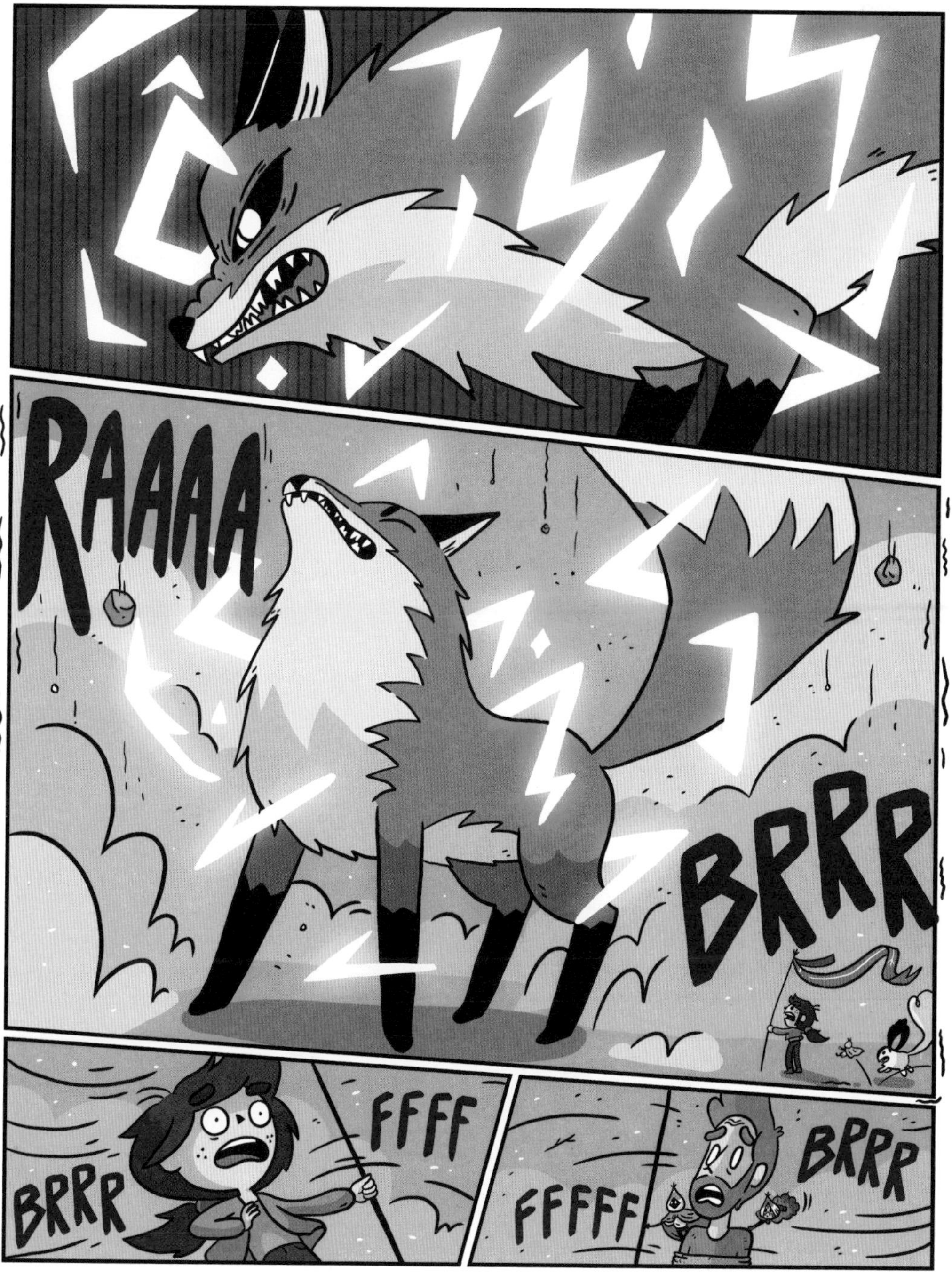
RAAAA
BRRR
FFFF
BRRR
BRRR
FFFFF

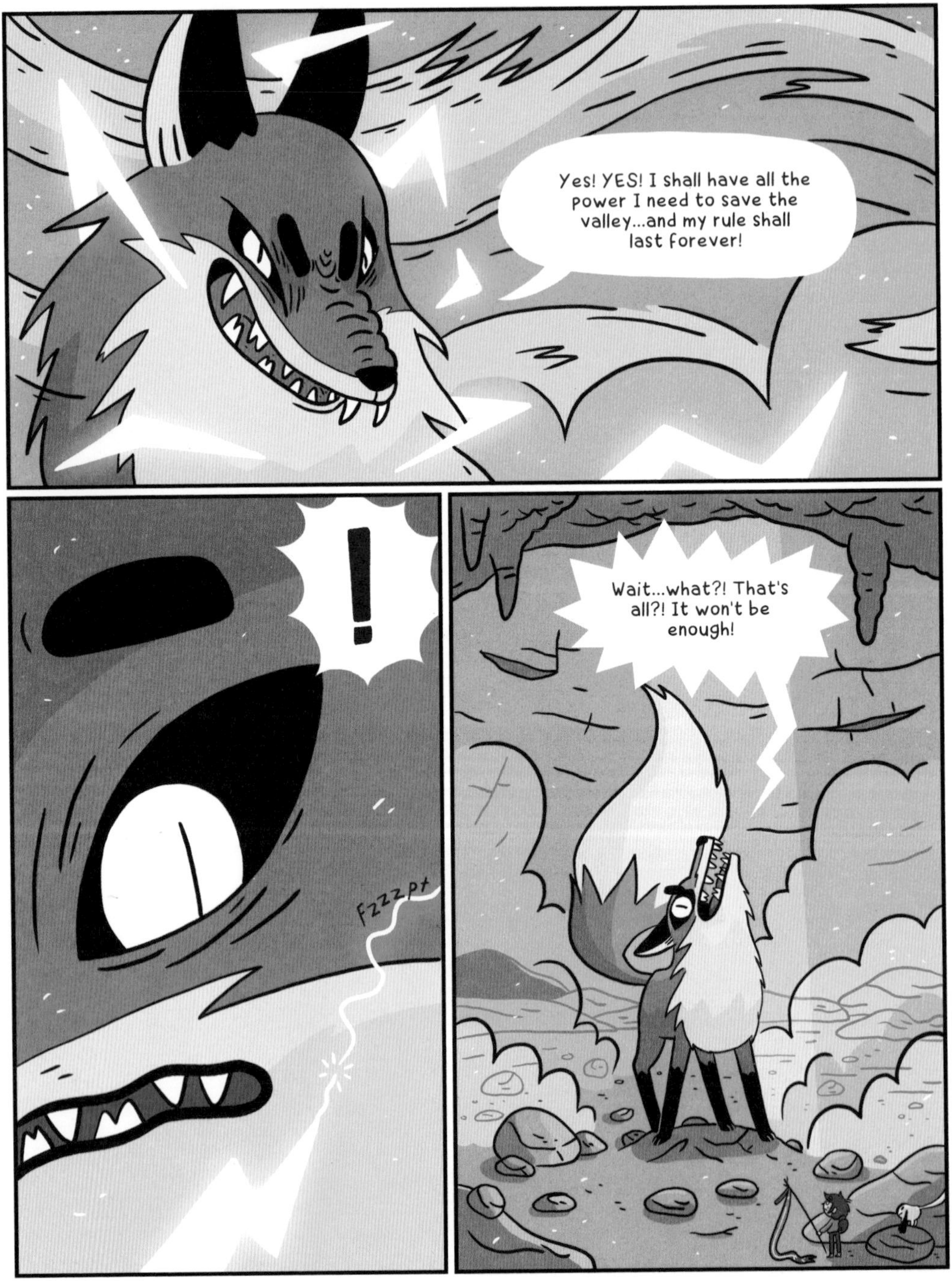
Yes! YES! I shall have all the power I need to save the valley...and my rule shall last forever!
!
Fzzzpt
Wait...what?! That's all?! It won't be enough!

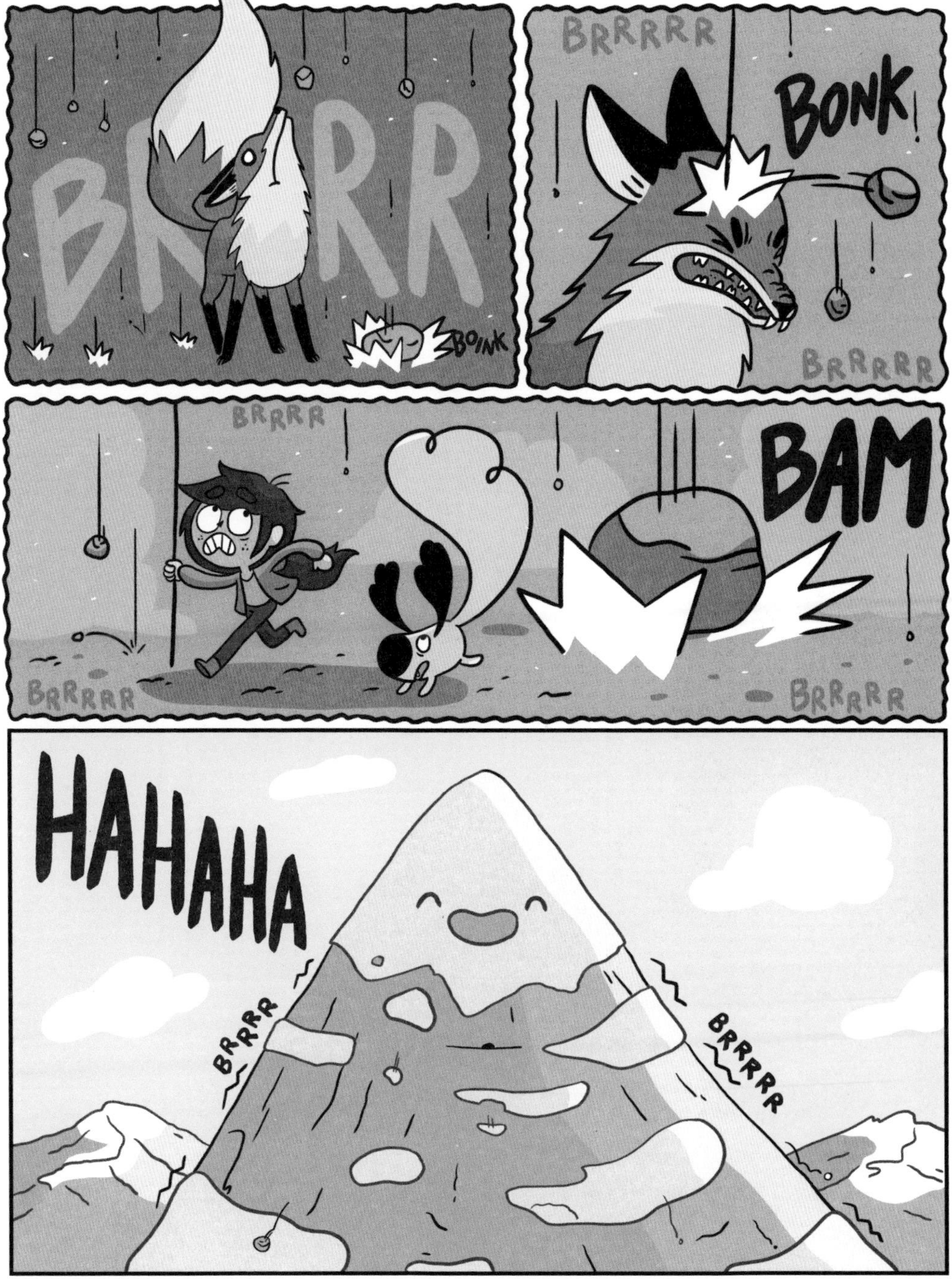
BRRR
BOINK
BRRRRR
BONK
BRRRRR
BRRRR
BAM
BRRRRR
BRRRRR
HAHAHA
BRRRR
BRRRRR

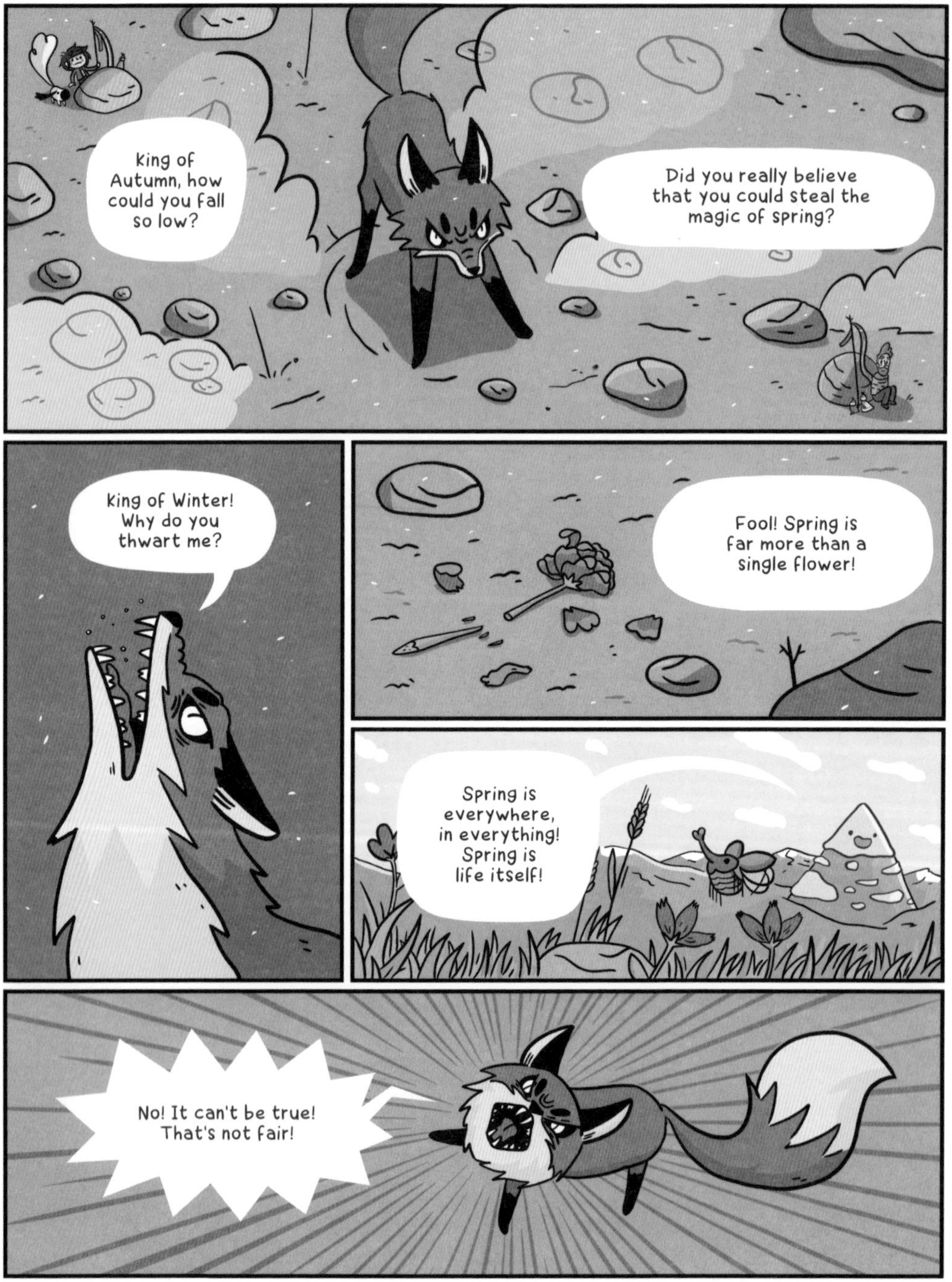
King of Autumn, how could you fall so low?
Did you really believe that you could steal the magic of spring?
King of Winter! Why do you thwart me?
Fool! Spring is far more than a single flower!
Spring is everywhere, in everything! Spring is life itself!
No! It can't be true! That's not fair!

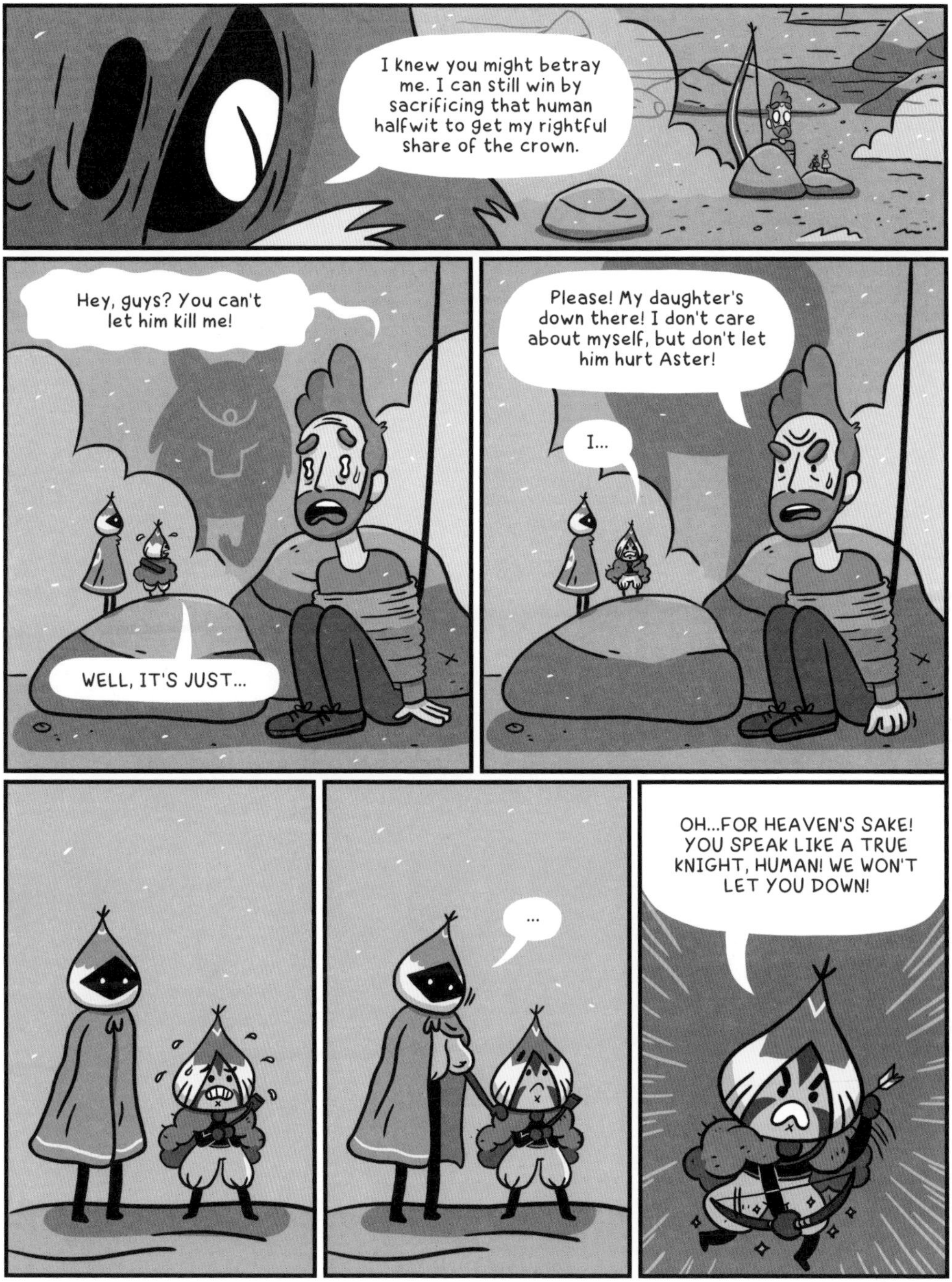
I knew you might betray me. I can still win by sacrificing that human halfwit to get my rightful share of the crown.
Hey, guys? You can't let him kill me!
WELL, IT'S JUST...
Please! My daughter's down there! I don't care about myself, but don't let him hurt Aster!
I...
...
OH...FOR HEAVEN'S SAKE! YOU SPEAK LIKE A TRUE KNIGHT, HUMAN! WE WON'T LET YOU DOWN!

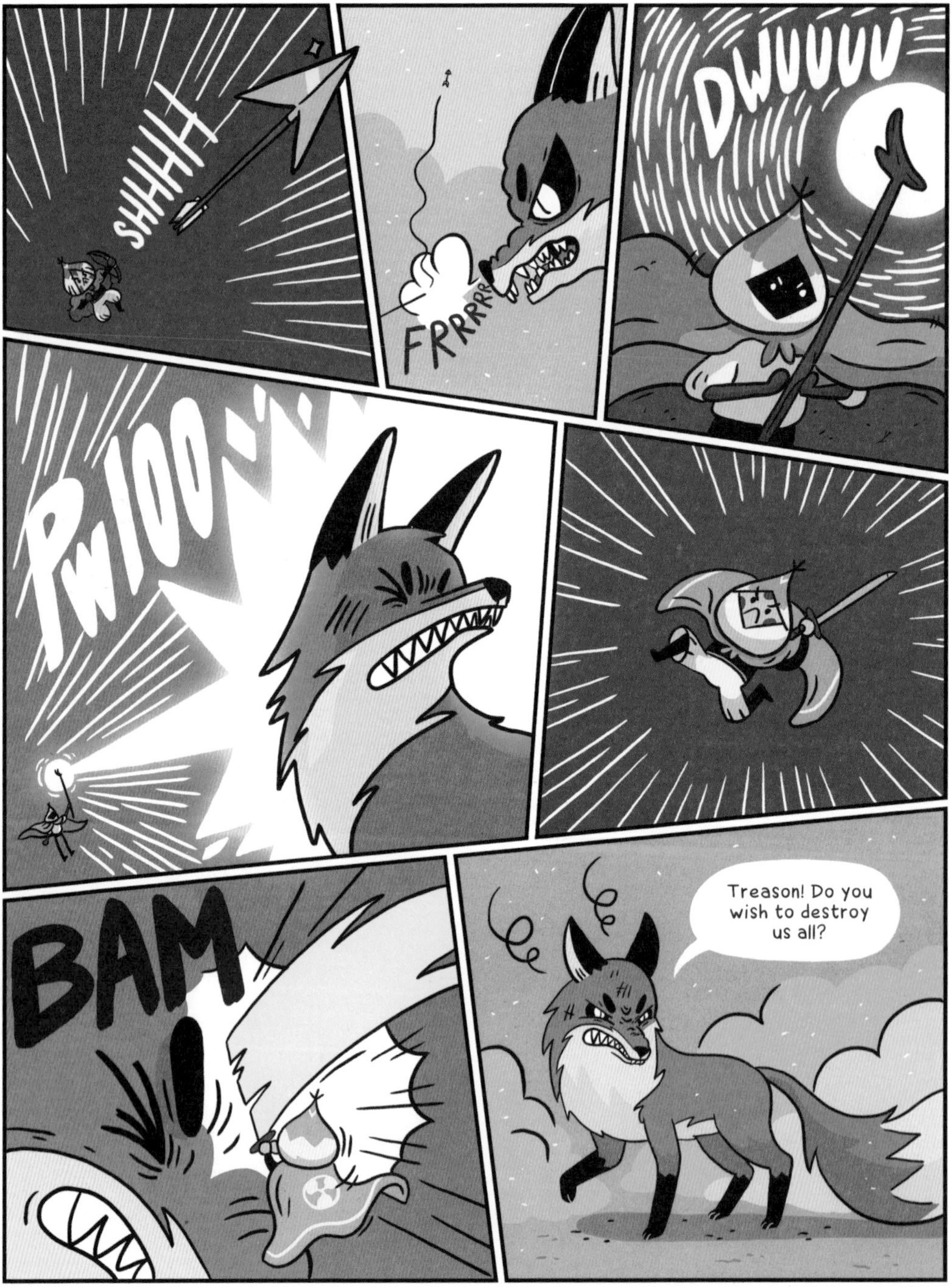
SHHHH
FRRRRR
DWUUUU
PWIOO
BAM
Treason! Do you wish to destroy us all?

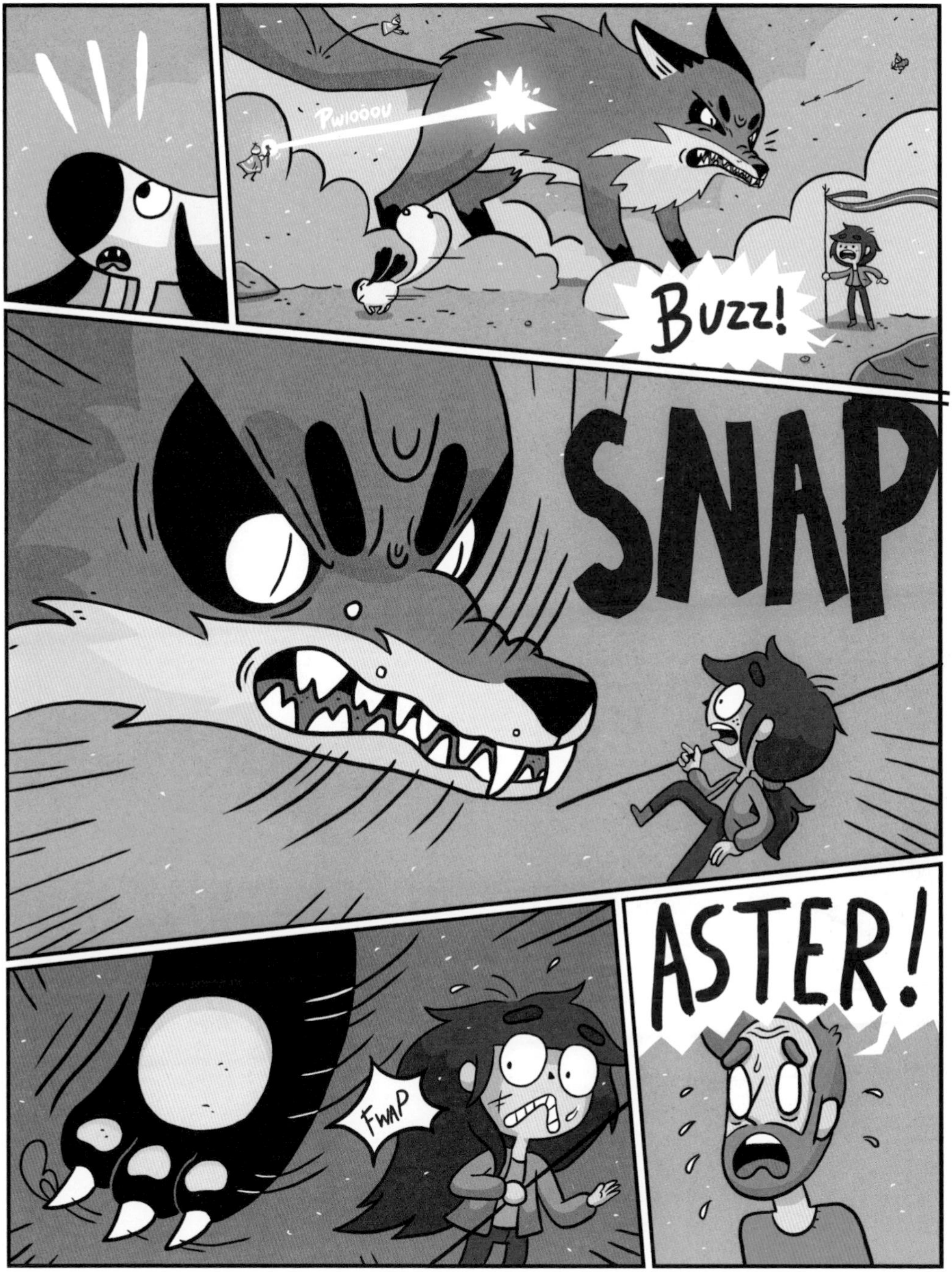
PWIOOOU
BUZZ!
SNAP
ASTER!
FWAP

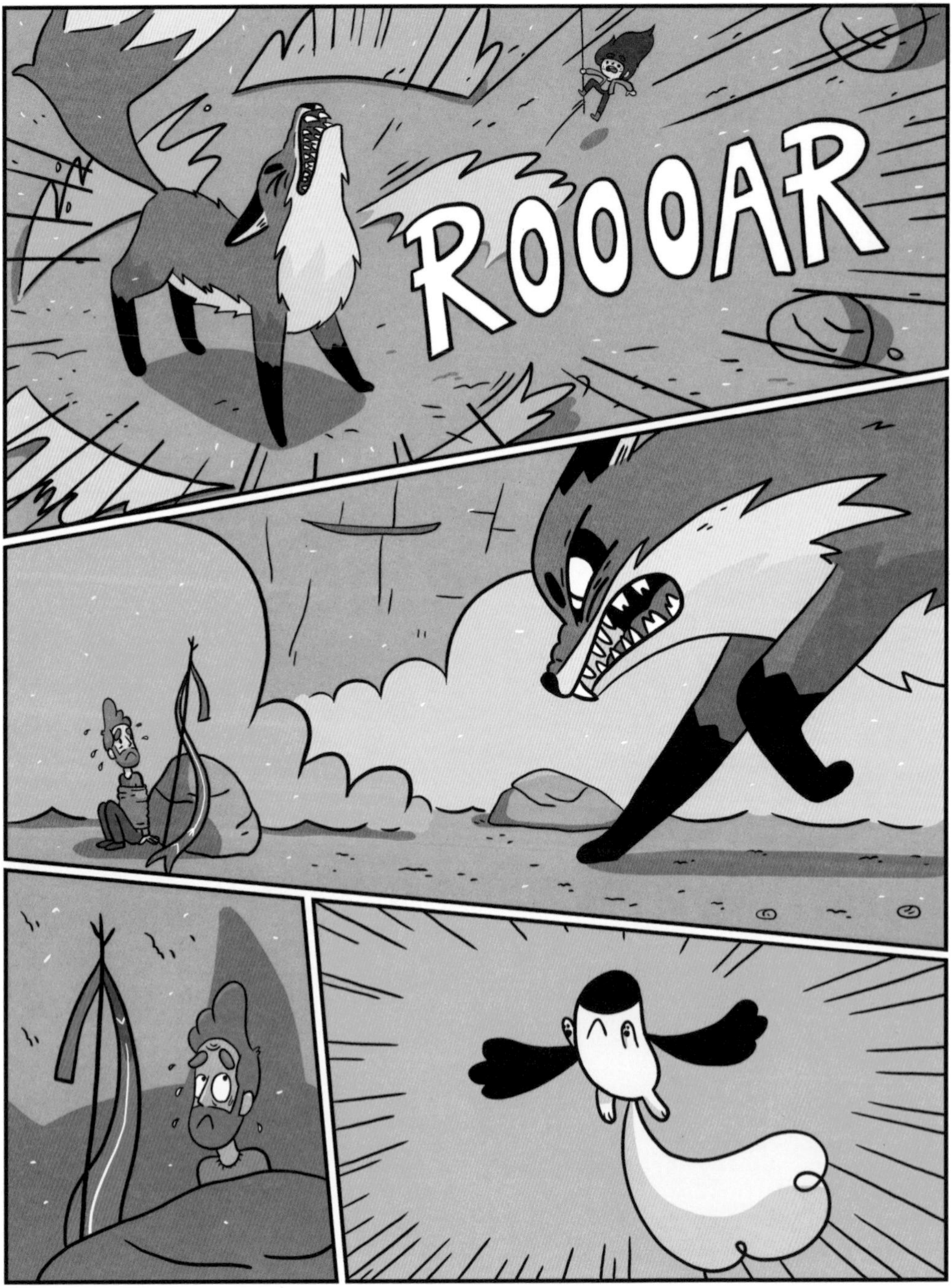
ROOOAR

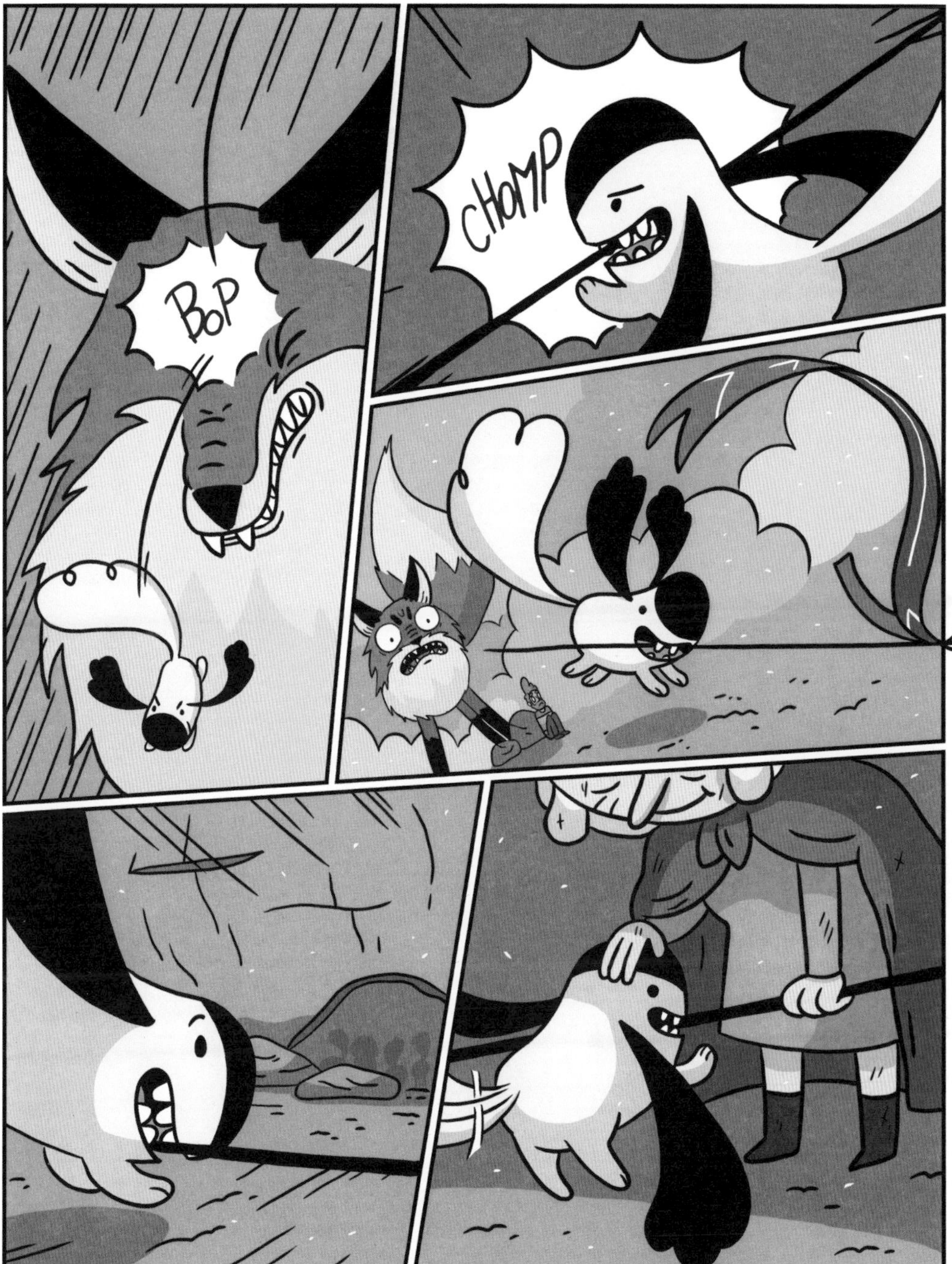
BOP
CHOMP

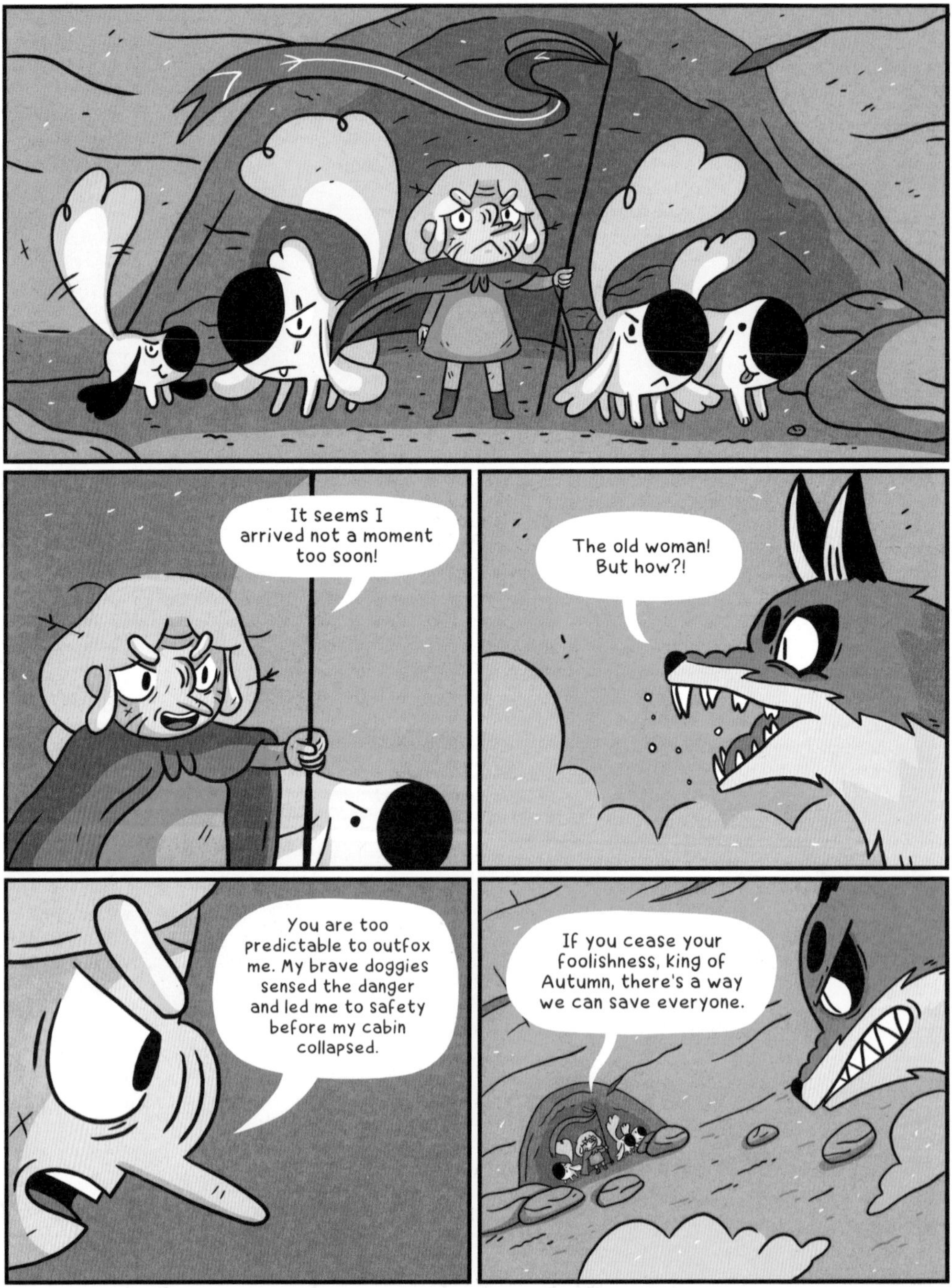
It seems I arrived not a moment too soon!
The old woman! But how?!
You are too predictable to outfox me. My brave doggies sensed the danger and led me to safety before my cabin collapsed.
If you cease your foolishness, King of Autumn, there's a way we can save everyone.

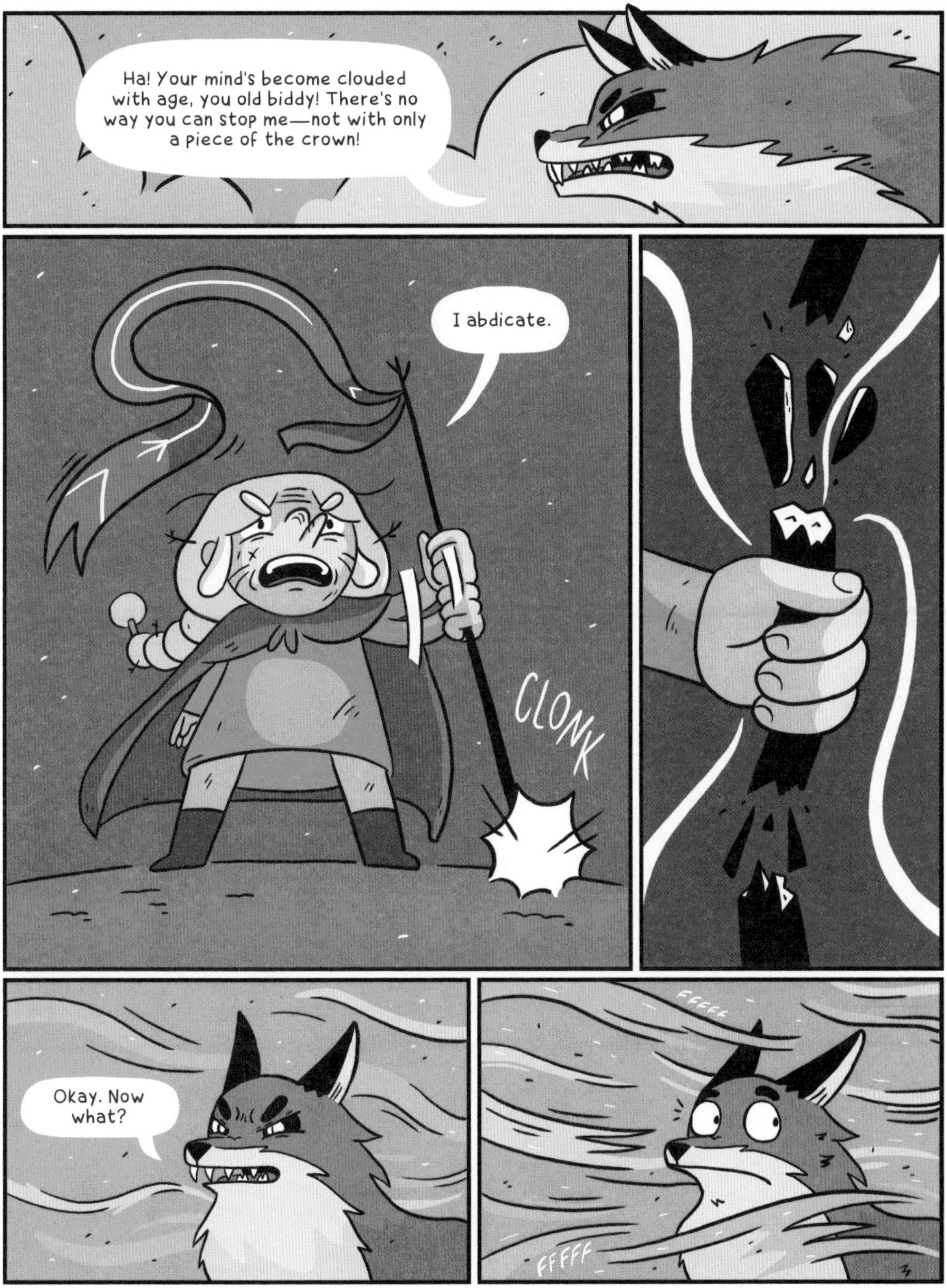
Ha! Your mind's become clouded with age, you old biddy! There's no way you can stop me—not with only a piece of the crown!
I abdicate.
CLONK
Okay. Now what?
FFFFF
FFFFF

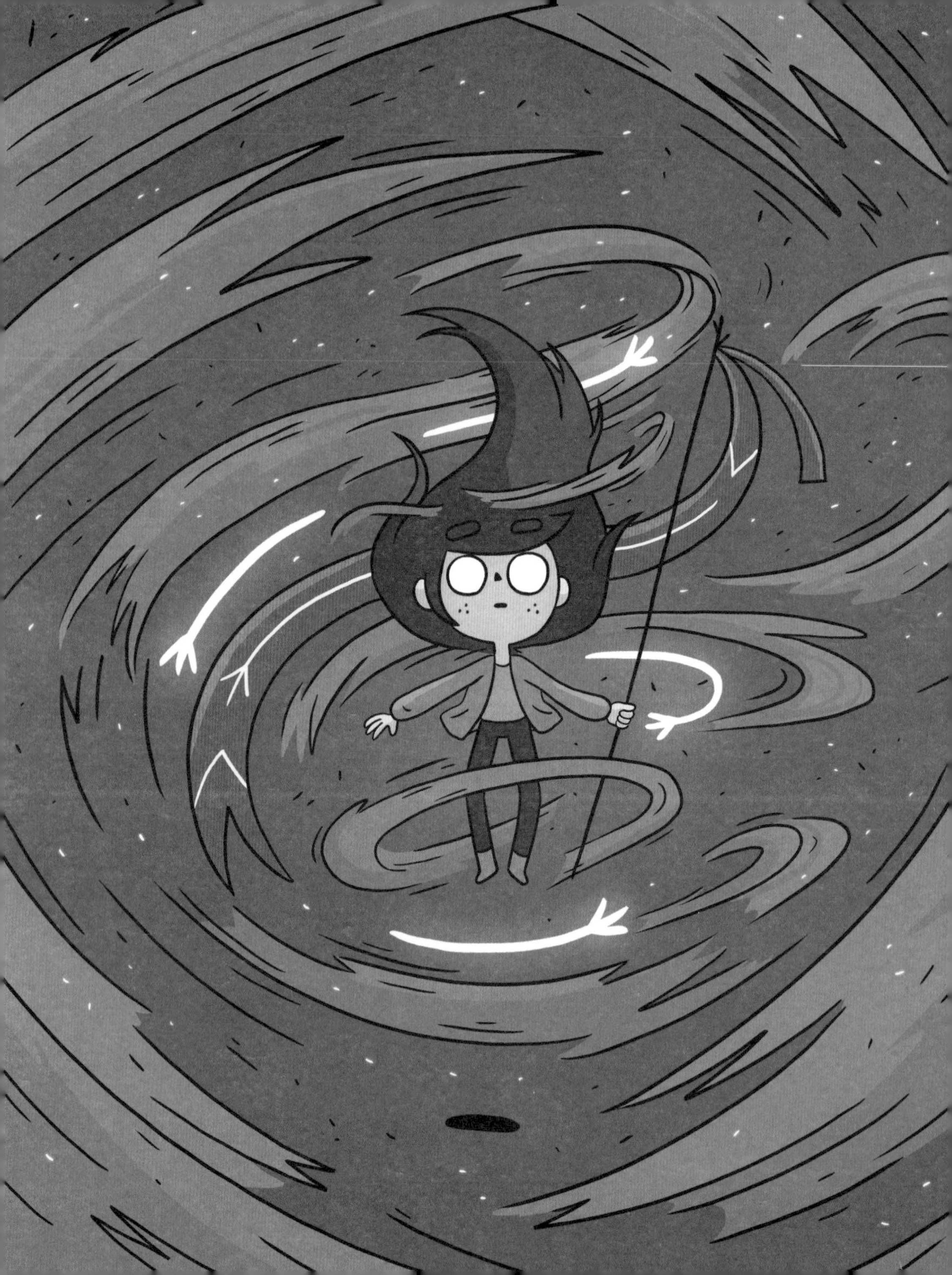

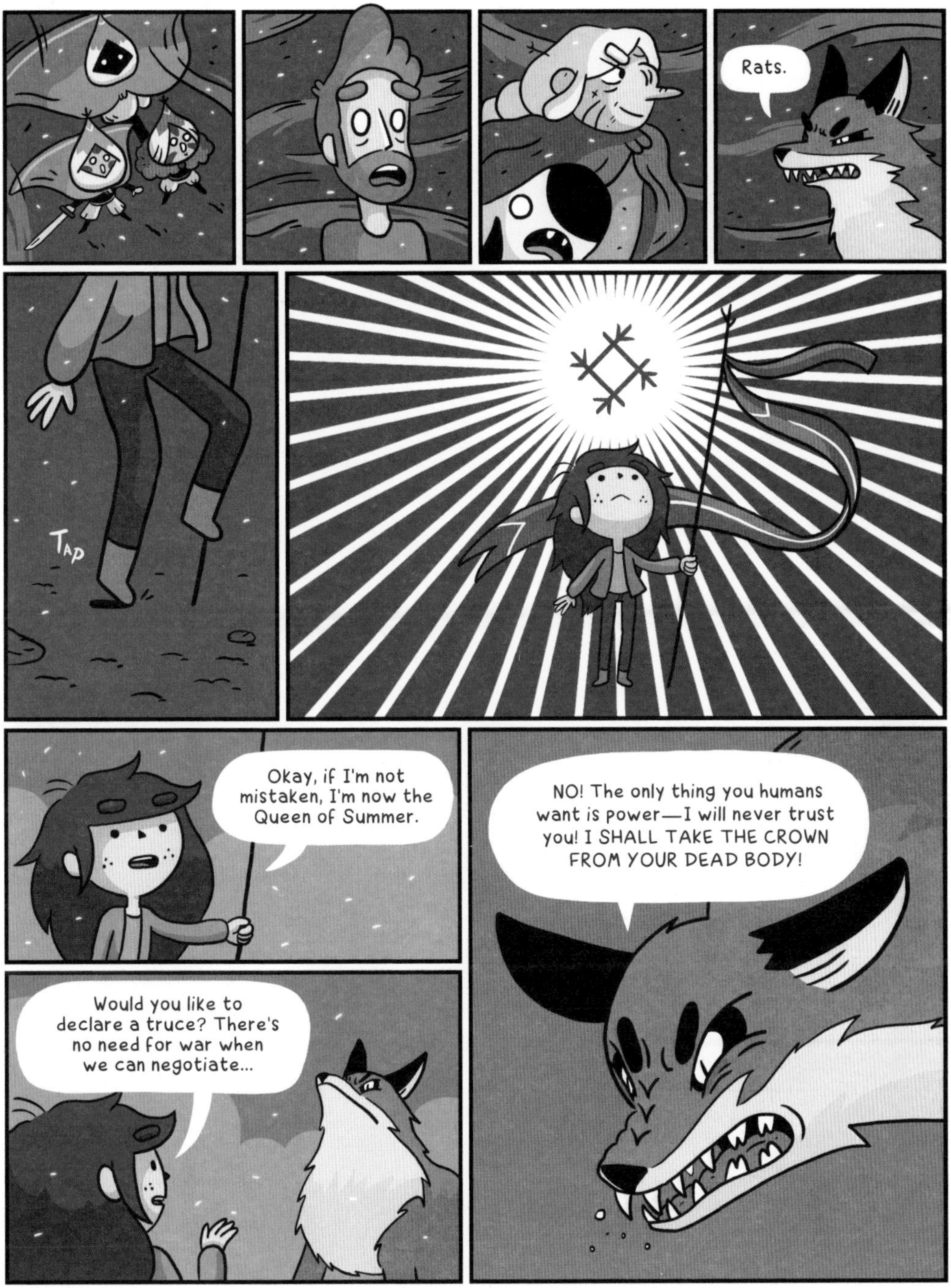
Rats.
TAP
Okay, if I'm not mistaken, I'm now the Queen of Summer.
Would you like to declare a truce? There's no need for war when we can negotiate...
NO! The only thing you humans want is power—I will never trust you! I SHALL TAKE THE CROWN FROM YOUR DEAD BODY!

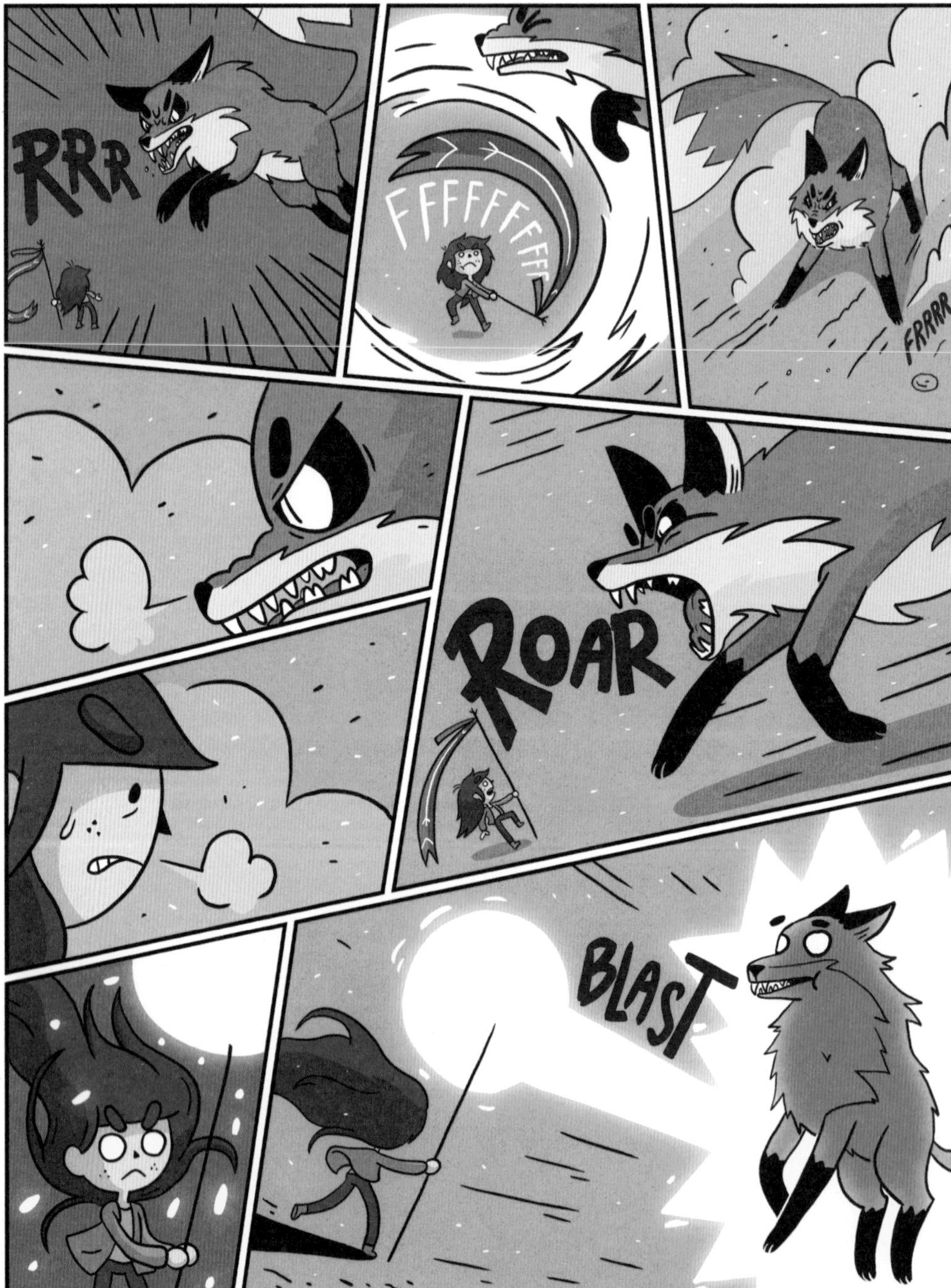
RRR
FFFFFFFFFFF
FRRRR
ROAR
BLAST

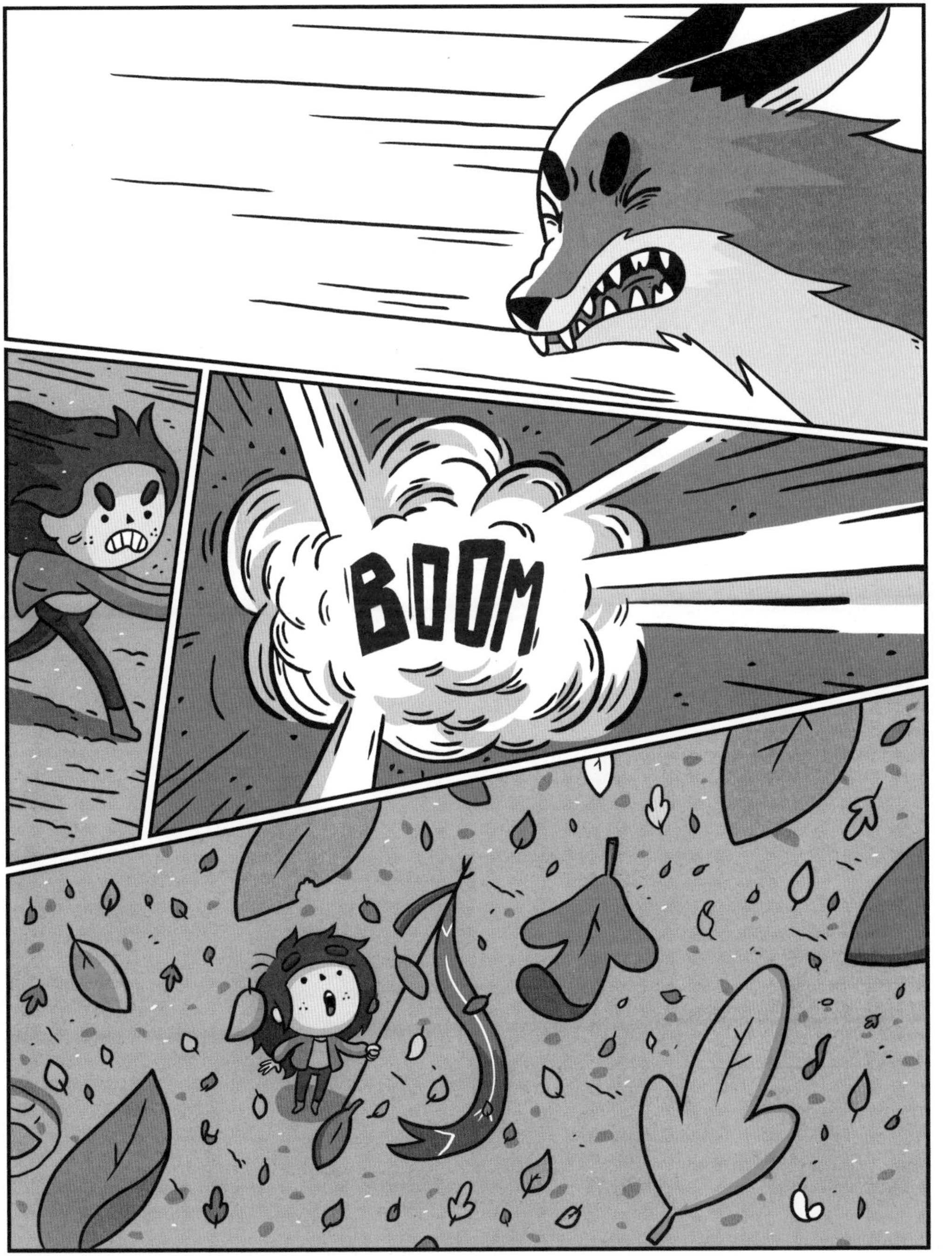
BOOM

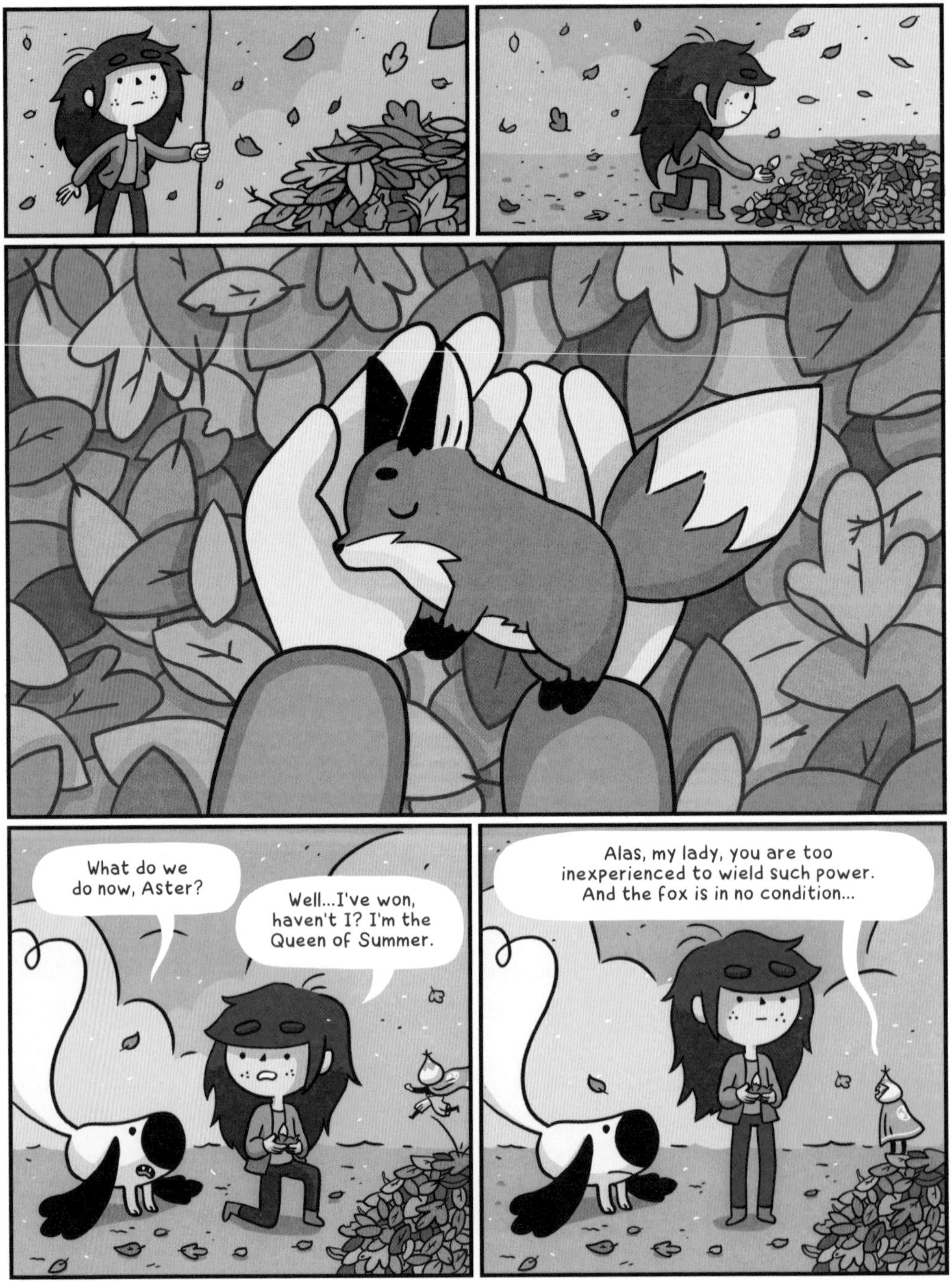
What do we do now, Aster?
Well...I've won, haven't I? I'm the Queen of Summer.
Alas, my lady, you are too inexperienced to wield such power. And the fox is in no condition...

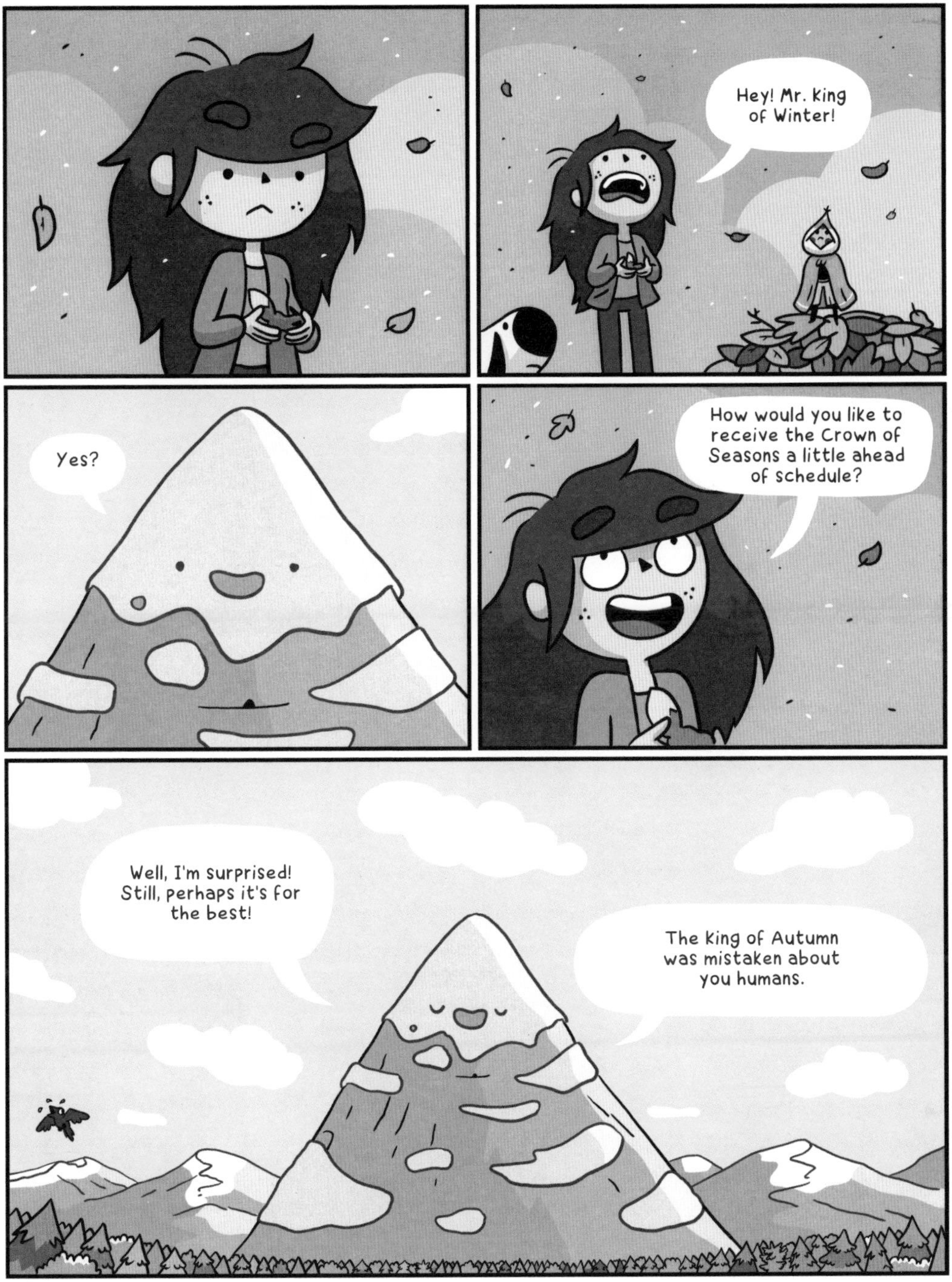
Hey! Mr. King of Winter!
Yes?
How would you like to receive the Crown of Seasons a little ahead of schedule?
Well, I'm surprised! Still, perhaps it's for the best!
The King of Autumn was mistaken about you humans.

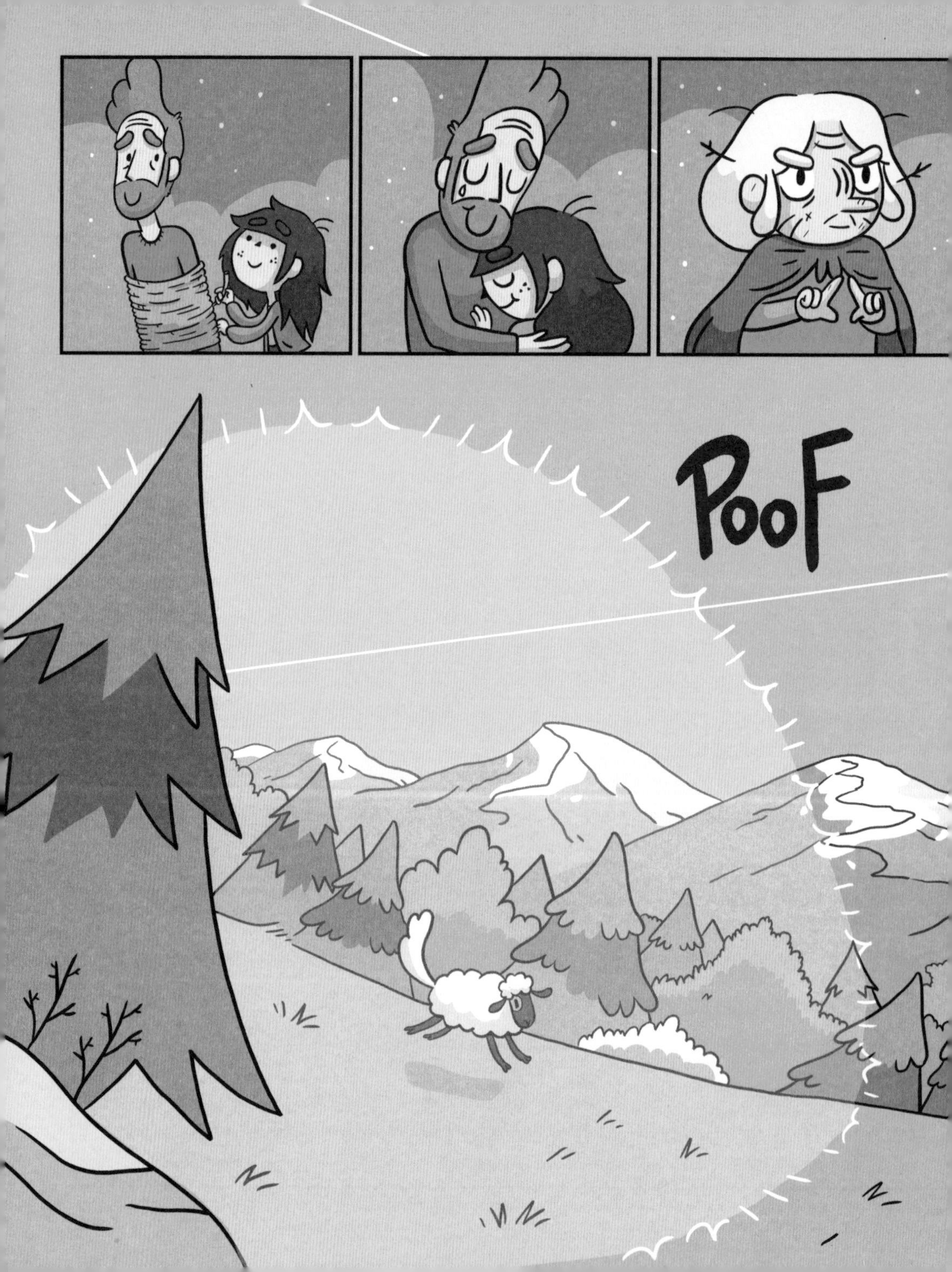
POOF

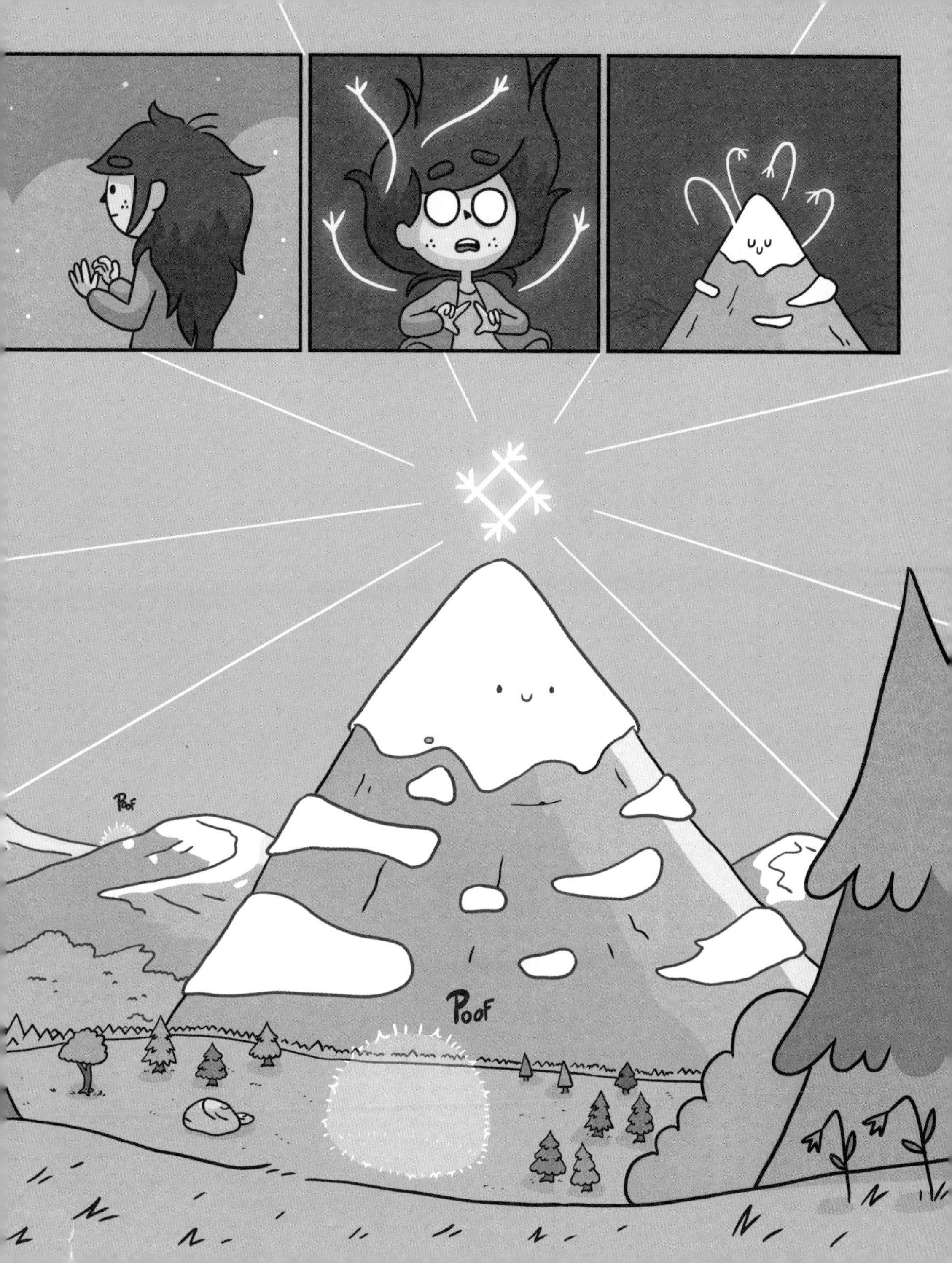
POOF
POOF

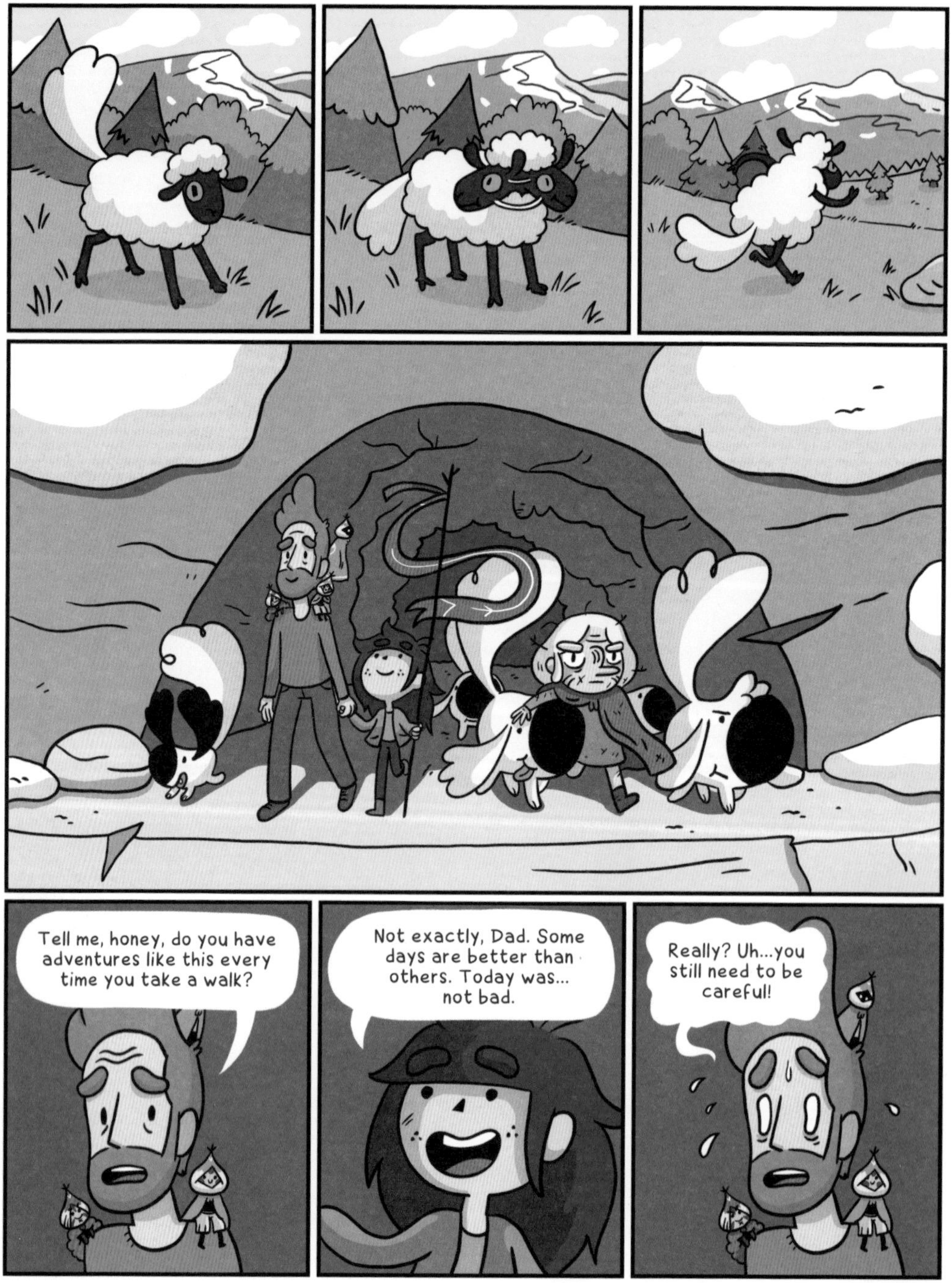
Tell me, honey, do you have adventures like this every time you take a walk?
Not exactly, Dad. Some days are better than others. Today was... not bad.
Really? Uh...you still need to be careful!

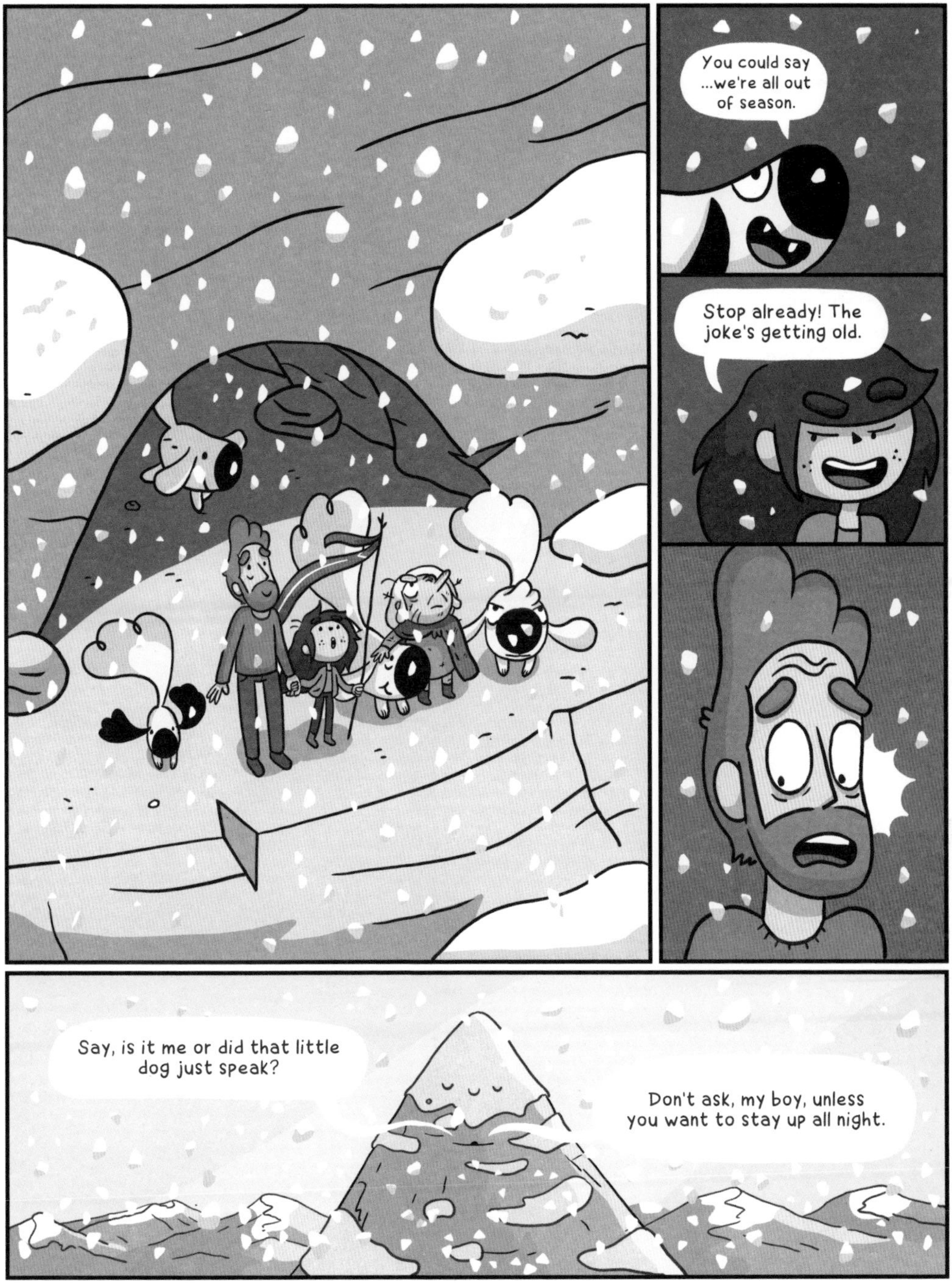
You could say ...we're all out of season.
Stop already! The joke's getting old.
Say, is it me or did that little dog just speak?
Don't ask, my boy, unless you want to stay up all night.

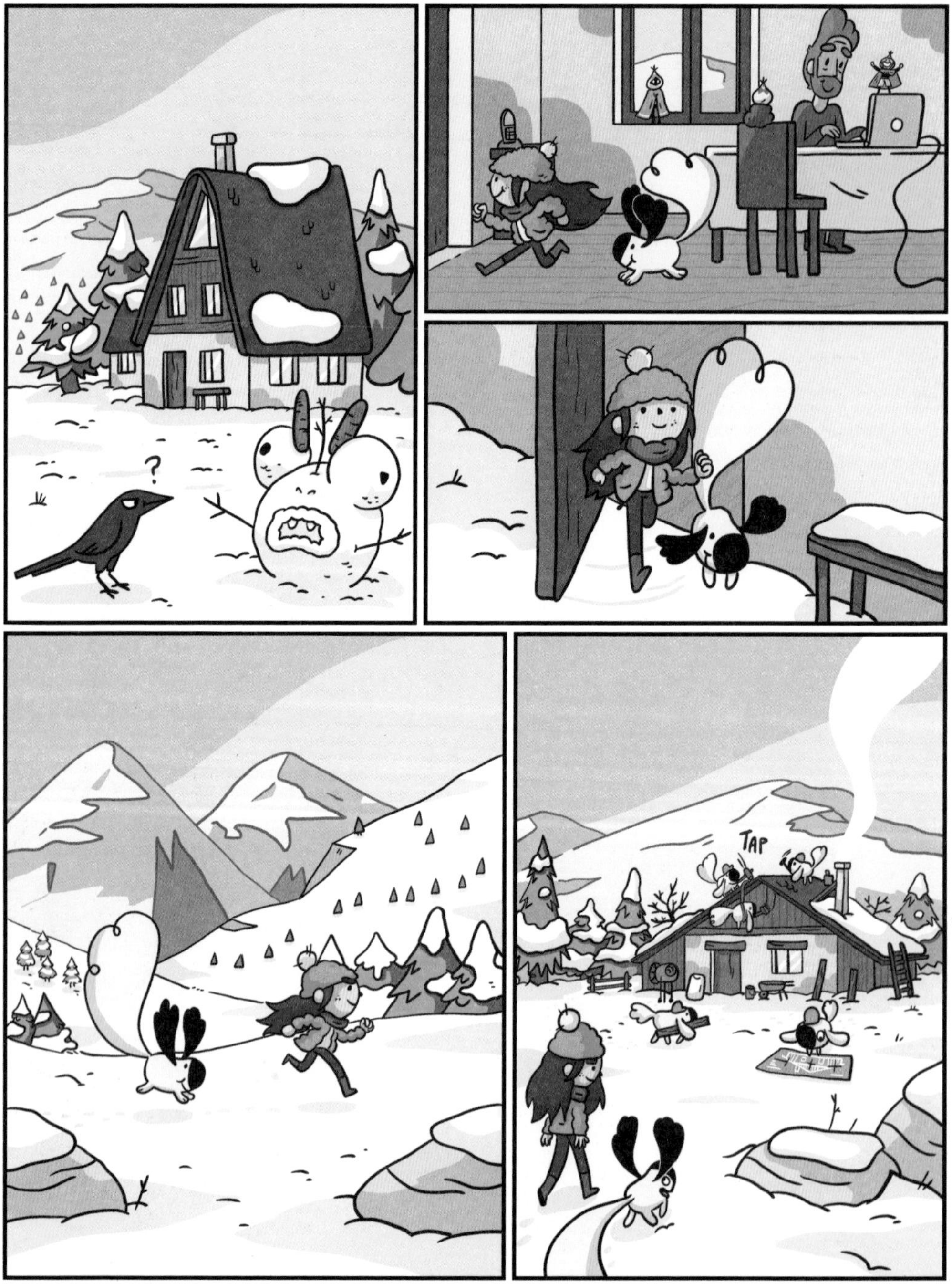
?
TAP

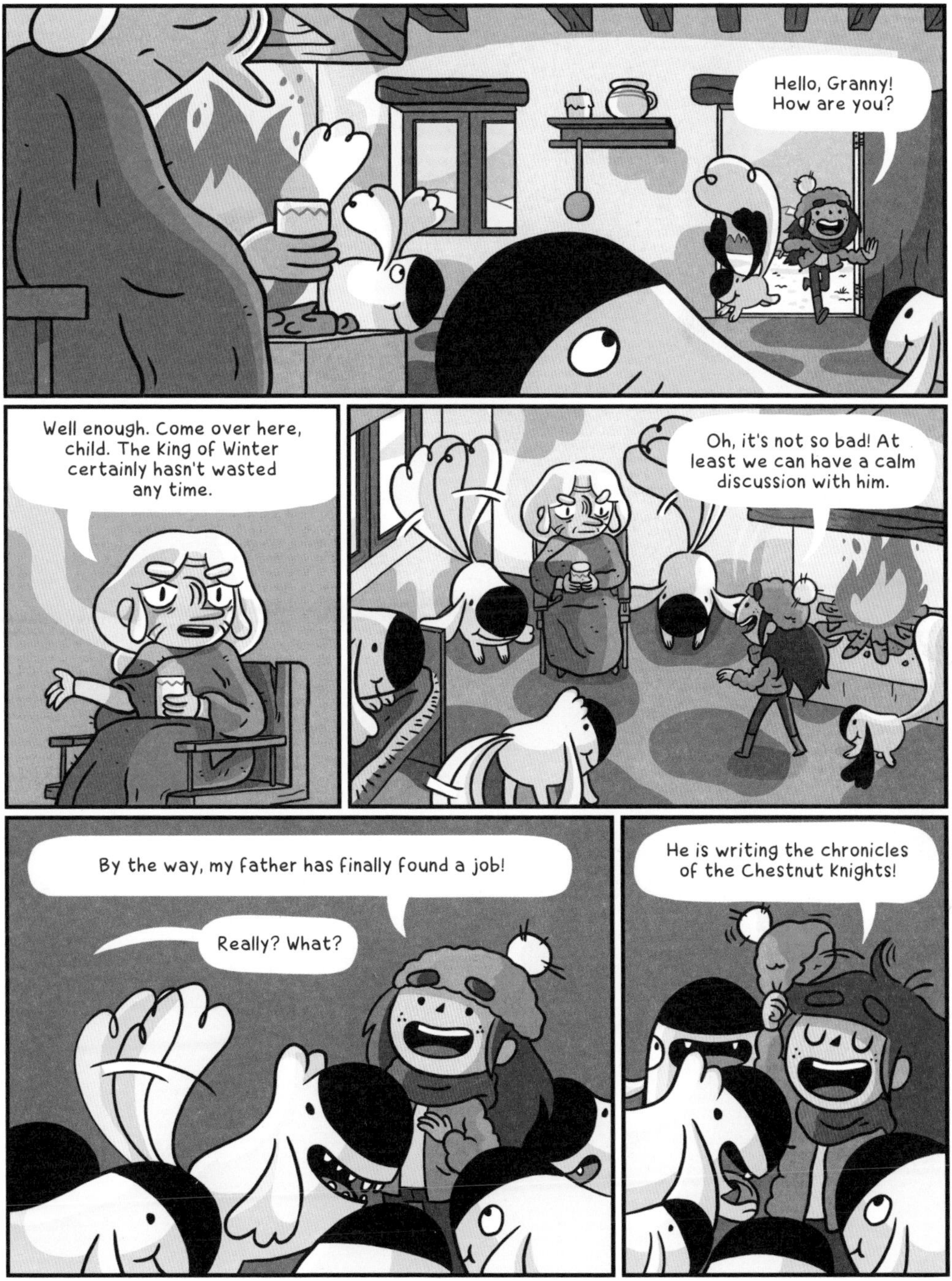
Hello, Granny! How are you?
Well enough. Come over here, child. The king of Winter certainly hasn't wasted any time.
Oh, it's not so bad! At least we can have a calm discussion with him.
By the way, my father has finally found a job!
Really? What?
He is writing the chronicles of the Chestnut Knights!

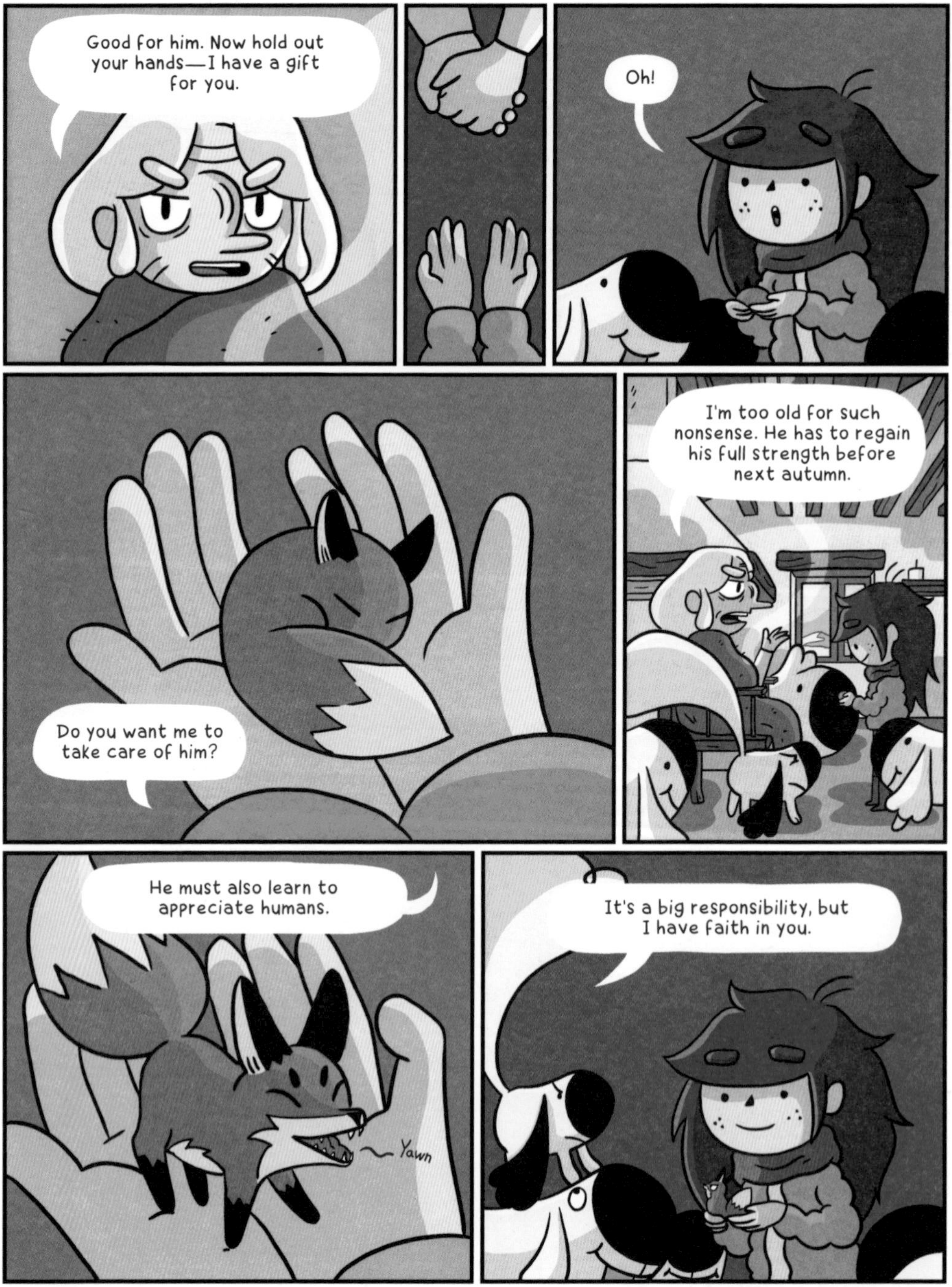
Good for him. Now hold out your hands—I have a gift for you.
Oh!
Do you want me to take care of him?
I'm too old for such nonsense. He has to regain his full strength before next autumn.
He must also learn to appreciate humans.
Yawn
It's a big responsibility, but I have faith in you.

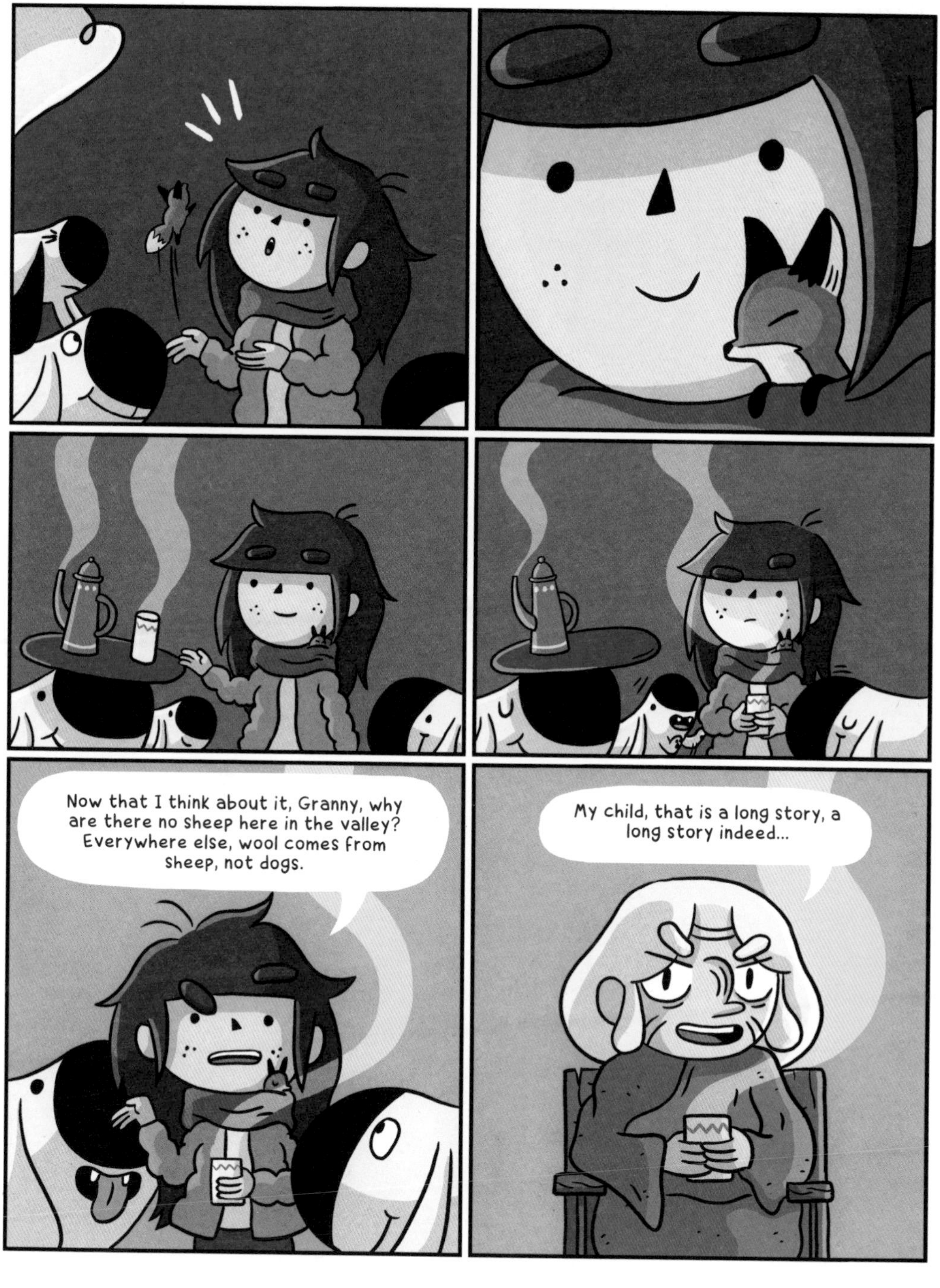
Now that I think about it, Granny, why are there no sheep here in the valley? Everywhere else, wool comes from sheep, not dogs.
My child, that is a long story, a long story indeed...

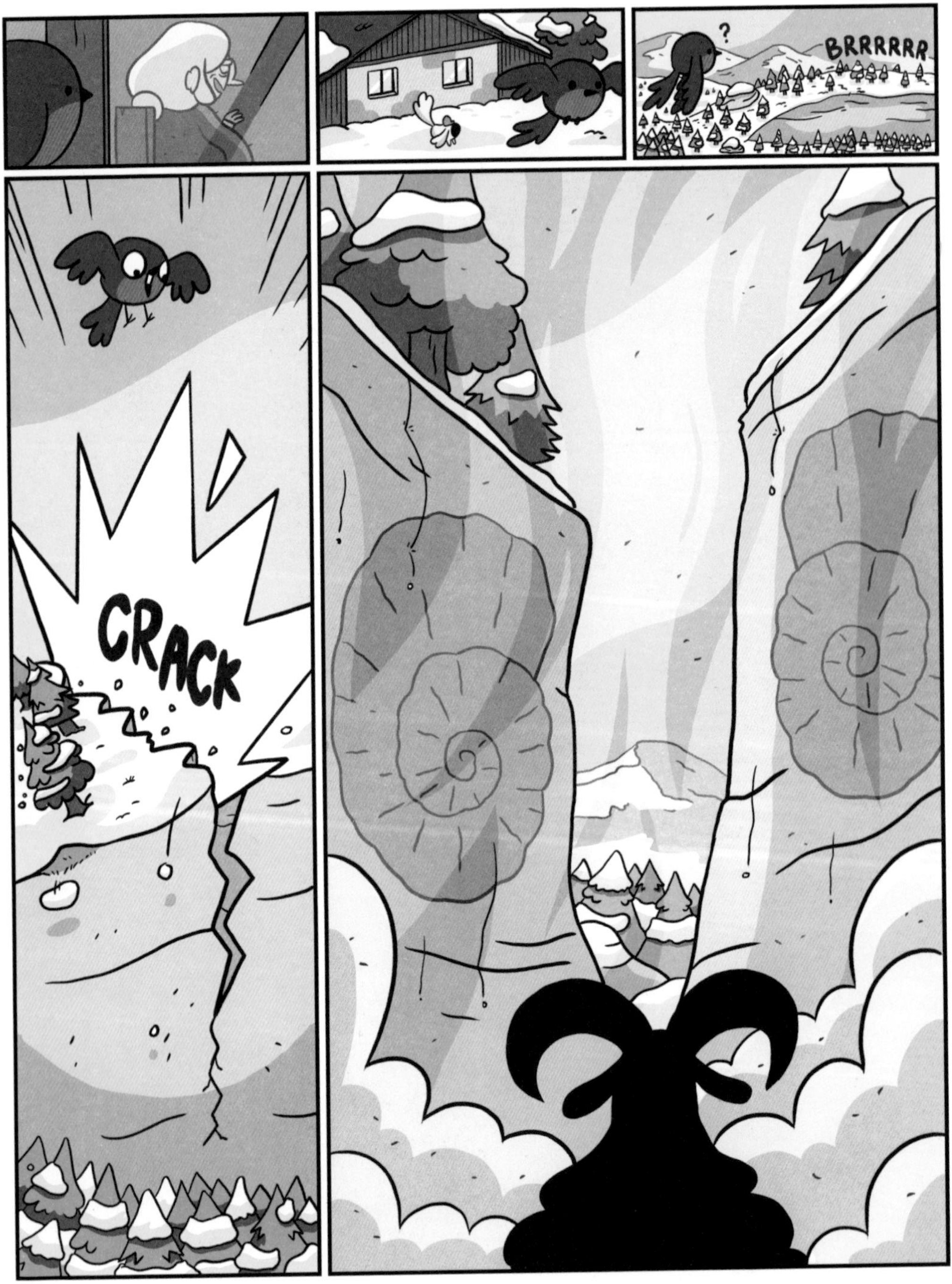
?
BRRRRRRR
CRACK

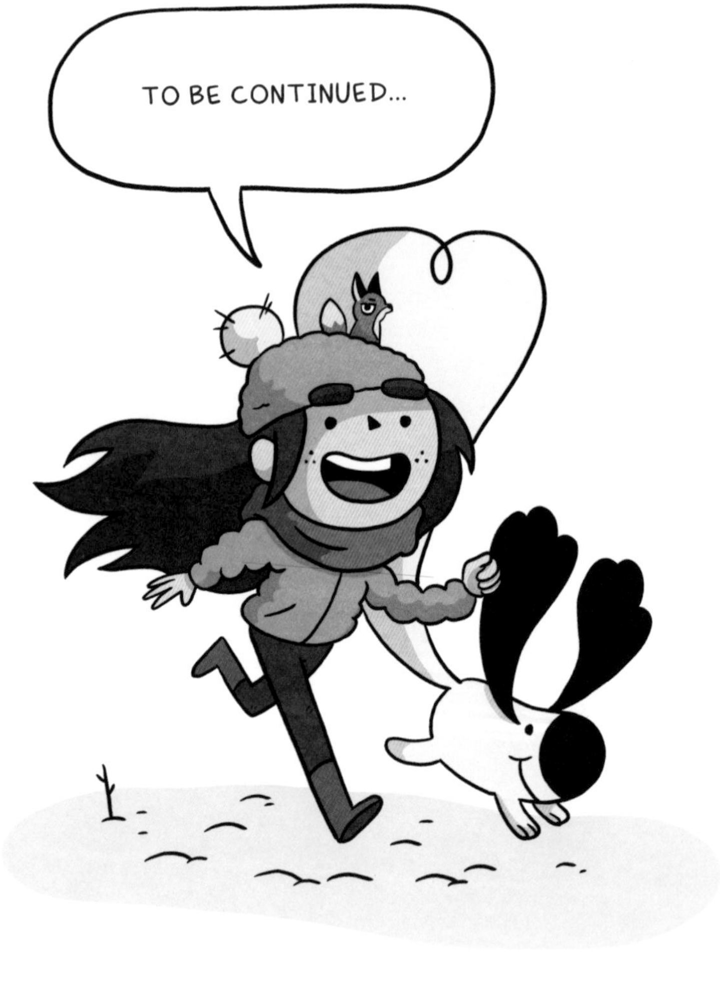
TO BE CONTINUED...

Aster and the Accidental Magic was thumbnailed with
pen on paper, then inked and colored in Photoshop.
The book is lettered in Hawthorn.

ASTER + BUZZ'S
Map of the Valley
Forest
The Chestnut Knights
ALWAYS CRASHING THE PARTY?
Our house
LAME! (NO CHANGE)

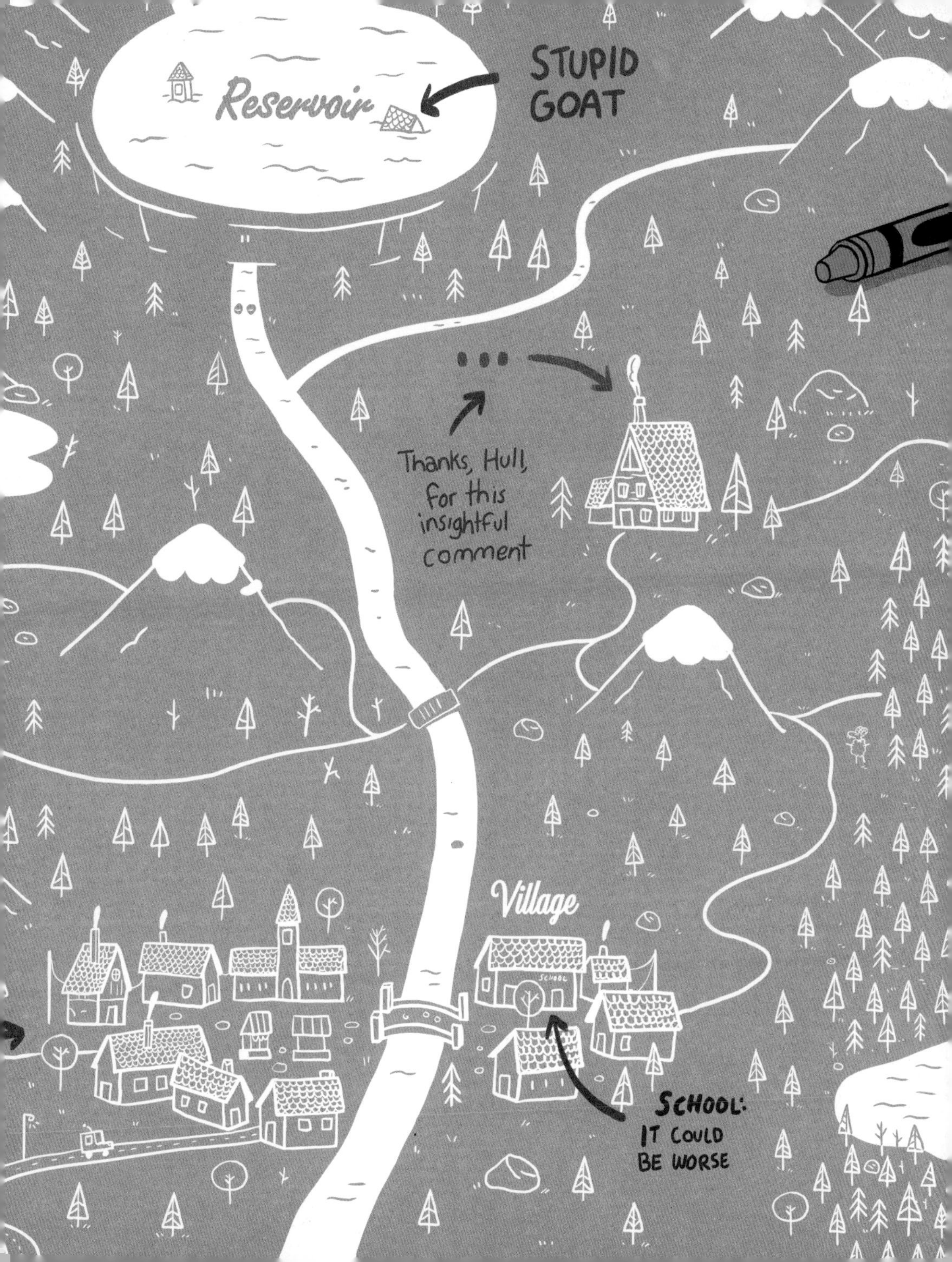

Reservoir
STUPID GOAT
Thanks, Hull, for this insightful comment
Village
SCHOOL
SCHOOL: IT COULD BE WORSE

THE CHARACTERS OF ASTER

ASTER

BUZZ

Aster has a strong personality for a ten-year-old. As a city dweller, she is NOT enthusiastic about the idea of moving to the mountains. But she can't resist the call of adventure, and it looks like this nowhere town might have more than enough excitement for Aster and her new friends.

Buzz is a small woolly dog who doesn't have wool. He's Aster's closest and most loyal friend, and was given to her by Granny. It turns out that he's really chatty, as Aster quickly finds out once he gains the ability to talk.

MOM

DAD

Aster's mother is a well-known ornithologist (person who knows a lot about birds) who moved her family to the mountains so she could continue her studies and stop the invasion of giant destructive crows. She tends to analyze every situation with a scientific approach.

Aster's father has quit his job to follow his family to the middle of nowhere. Since he grew up in the mountains, he knows a little about the environment...and some of the characters Aster might come across. Too bad he can't help being bored to death anyway.

GRANNY

THE TRICKSTER RAPSCALLION

Who is that mysterious old shepherdess who keeps giving Aster weird advice? And why does she have woolly dogs instead of sheep?

One of the oldest and most powerful spirits of the universe...beware of the wishes he grants! He is good at twisting other people's words for his own amusement.

THE KING OF AUTUMN

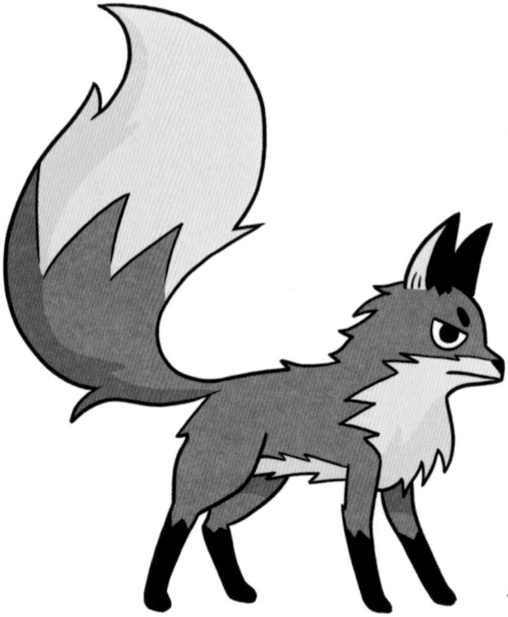

The King of Autumn is a fox who means business. Despite his good intentions for the countryside, his hatred of humans stops him from finding a peaceful solution.

THE KING OF WINTER

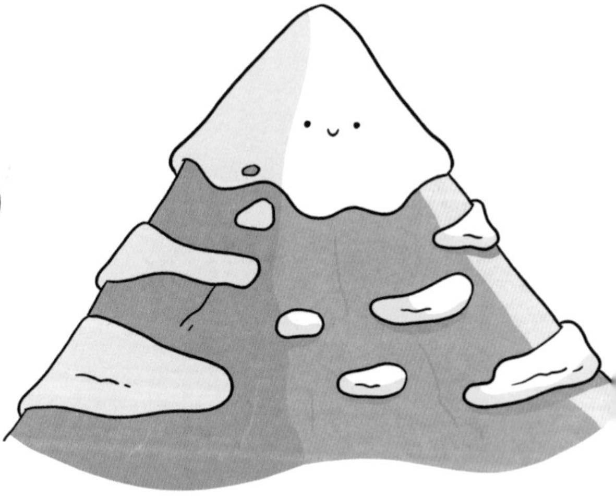

The King of Winter is a mountain. He takes up a lot of space, but he is good-natured and has a great sense of humor. Nobody knows where he comes from, but it's clear that he's been around for a very long time.

THE CHESTNUT KNIGHTS

HULL   **LEAF**   **BURR**

The Chestnut knights are legendary mountain warriors who follow their hearts. They might be in service to the king of Autumn, but that doesn't mean they can't make up their own minds about the situations they find themselves in.

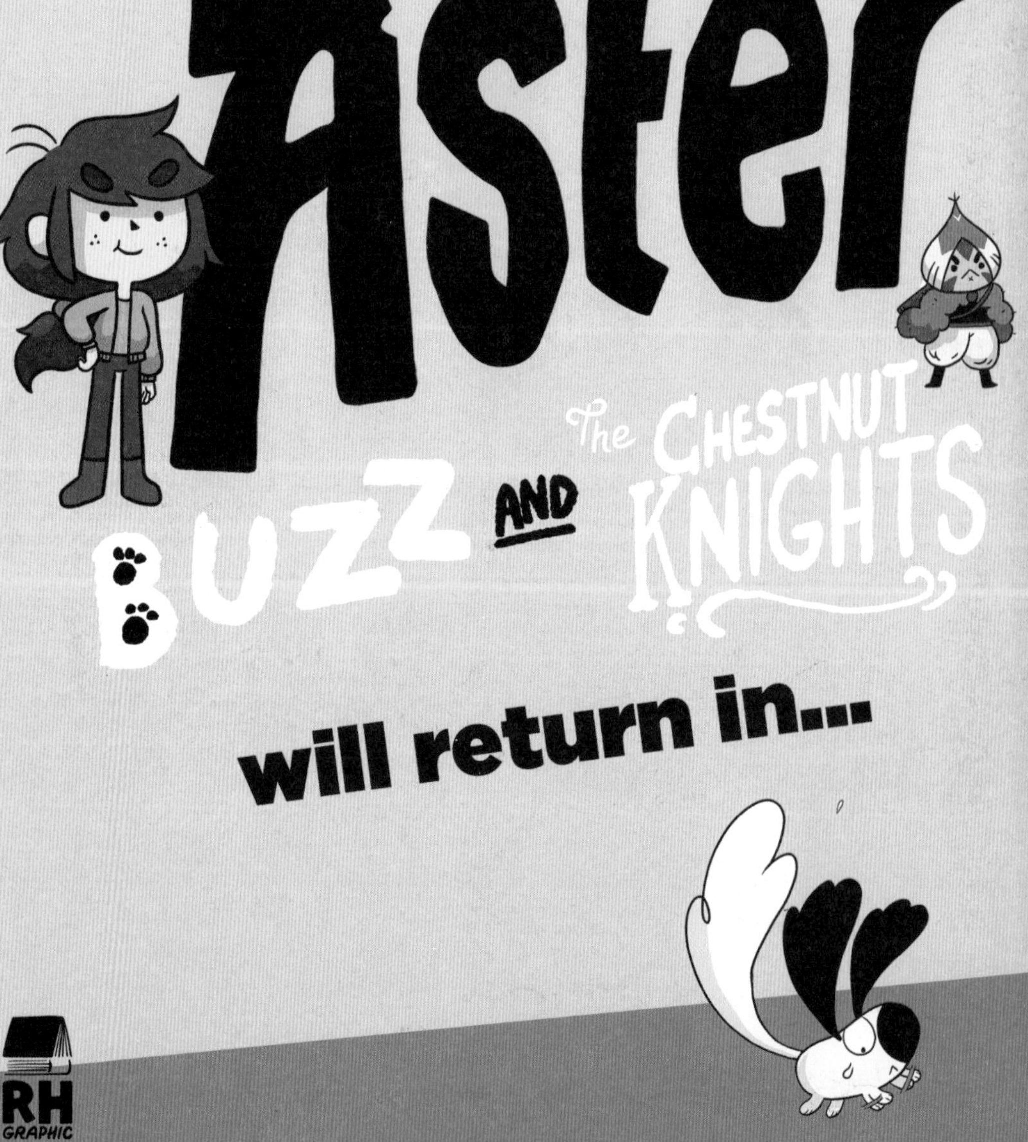
Aster
The Chestnut Knights
Buzz and
will return in...

RH GRAPHIC

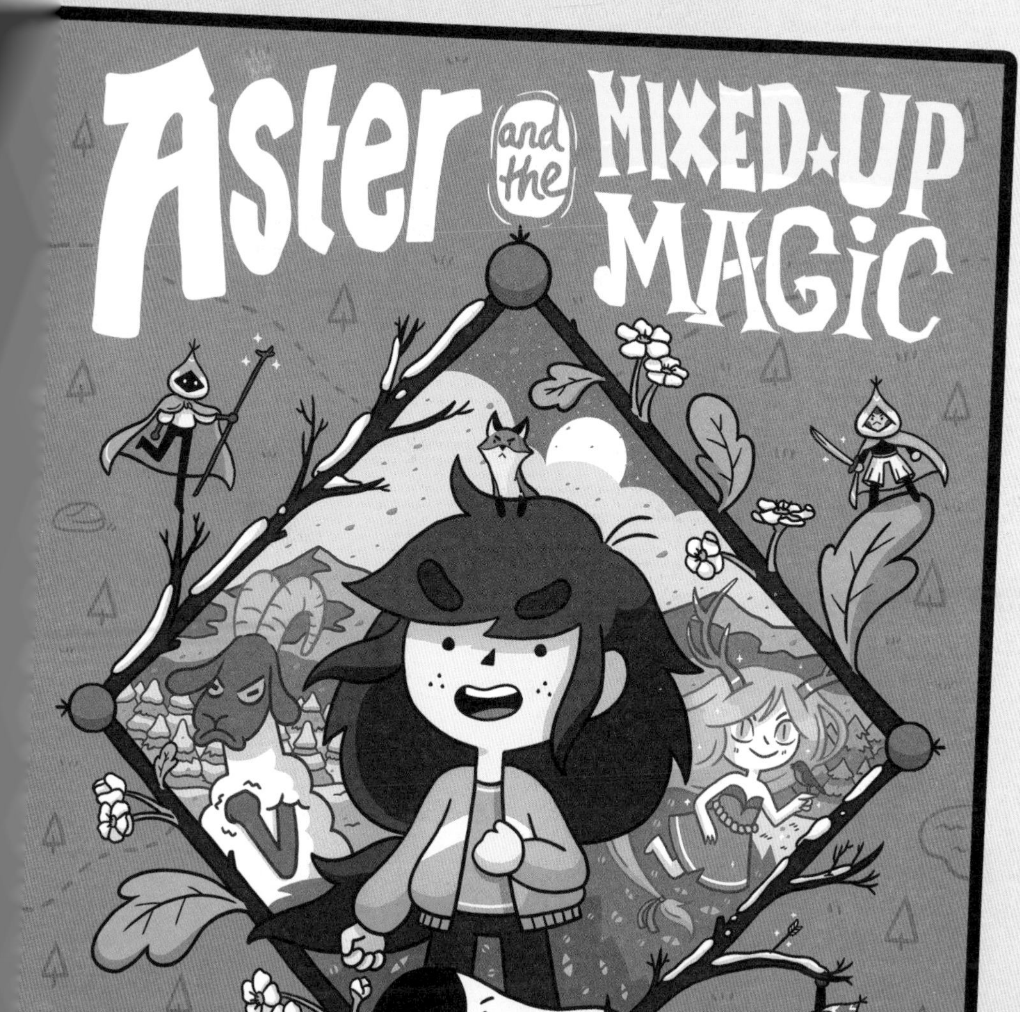
Aster and the Mixed-Up Magic
THOM PICO
KARENSAC

RH GRAPHIC
THE DEBUT LIST

BUG BOYS
By Laura Knetzger

Bugs, friends, the world around us—this book has everything!
Come explore *Bug Boys* for the fun, thoughtful adventure of growing up and being yourself.

Chapter Book

THE RUNAWAY PRINCESS
By Johan Troïanowski

The castle is quiet.
And dull.
And boring.
Escape on a quest for excitement with our runaway princess, Robin!

Middle-Grade

ASTER AND THE ACCIDENTAL MAGIC
By Thom Pico & Karensac

Nothing fun ever happens in the middle of the country . . . except maybe . . . magic?
That's just the beginning of absolutely everything going wrong for Aster.

Middle-Grade

WITCHLIGHT
By Jessi Zabarsky

Lelek doesn't have any friends or family in the world. And then she meets Sanja. Swords, magic, falling in love . . . these characters come together in a journey to heal the wounds of the past.

Young Adult

FIND US ONLINE AT @RHKIDSGRAPHIC AND RHKIDSGRAPHIC.COM